Bayou Nights
by
Nicola Trwst

NgH Press
San Francisco, CA

Bayou Nights
Copyright ©2012 by Nicola Trwst
All rights reserved

Discover more of Nicola Trwst's work at
www.nicolatrwst.com

Published January 2013 by NgH Press

978-0-9855208-3-0

Publisher's Note:
This is a work of fiction. Names, characters, businesses,
places, events and incidents are either the products of the
author's imagination or used in a fictitious manner. Any
resemblance to actual persons, living or dead, or actual
events is purely coincidental.

Many people are to thank for helping me bring *Bayou Nights* to press. It really *does* take a village.

For sharing their professional knowledge:
Dr. Charles Palmigiano
Carlos Rafael Batista in Punta Cana
Haitian sugar cane cutters in Punta Cana
Stan Klueh of Klueh's Nursery
Pat Williams Esq.
Mark Baradat and Clifton J. Rakic at Bullseye Shooting Range

For sharing their critiques, ideas, and patience:
Margaret Lucke, Bette and J.J. Lamb, Shelley Singer, Judith Yamamoto, Diana Orgain,
Cynthia Greenberg, Vicki Dobbs Beck, Stanton Close, Jill Cagan, & Frances Palmigiano

And my editors:
Jay Schaefer
Marie Roughan
Debbie Blasco

Prologue

He'd pinned her to the soft earth. Caught her unawares. She squirmed, turning her head inch by inch. Her hair, wedged beneath his hand, pulled at the roots. She bit into his fat wrist like a snapping turtle, tearing and holding until he rolled off.

"Filthy whore."

She sat up and sucked in a breath. Ah, sweet summer air. "You two bricks shy or what? That ain't no way to treat a lady. Now, get me up."

Baring his teeth, he turned away. "I'm sorry."

"You should be."

The blow came fast, knocking the breath from her lungs. Something deep inside cracked. She gasped. Gulped. Searing pain shot across her chest. Tears bubbled up. His other fist caught her upside the head. A flash of white lightning behind her eyelids and then everything went dark.

Her eyes burned. That was the first thing she noticed. They wouldn't open. For a second or two, she struggled to figure out where she was. Then, she remembered.

Panic squirmed like mud worms in her chest, but she lay still, listening, and taking in every noise. She must have passed out. Now, she felt like she was floating on a lily pad.

The moon was gone or maybe it wasn't. With her eyes stuck shut, she couldn't much tell.

The night's cooling breeze raked her raw skin. The air was thick with the scent of night-blooming flowers.

The Cadillac's door slammed, its heavy sound carrying across the empty field. She stiffened. Bit her lip to keep from crying. The motor roared to life. She listened as it faded with the distance. She listened until the hum sounded as if it was coming from inside her head.

She'd liked the car. Flashy. She liked flashy. Before tonight, she'd liked him, too. Hell, everyone did. Was high in the cotton, but could hold his own. Always left decent tips.

Damn, she knew how to pick 'em.

Weeping sounds pulsed up from her throat, but she couldn't feel the tears. Her face was wet, sticky wet. But where were the tears? Why weren't there tears?

She caught her breath. No time to panic. She had to hightail it out of there. But her chest really, really hurt. He had fists like cinderblocks. Just lifting her arm felt like someone shoving a knife down between her ribs.

She lay still again, smelling the night gladiolus. Drifting.

"What was that?" Her twitch sent a ripple of hurt through her chest. A bullfrog croaked. Not close, but close enough. She must have fallen asleep again.

He was gone. He'd driven away. Hadn't he? Her thoughts were jumbled tighter than a ball of yarn.

She was cold. Too cold for this time of year. And her stomach felt queasy. She just wanted to lie a spell, but she'd best get over to the road. Her eyelids felt swollen to the touch, the left worse than the right.

"Ouch!" She couldn't find her left cheekbone. Was like it wasn't there. Weird. Maybe her face was just too swollen.

That jerk. Wait till she told Clyde what he'd done. He'd go after Mr. Fancy Pants with a stick.

Was that another car? She listened, her limbs tensing.

Her dress was bunched up around her breasts. Thank God she wasn't naked. Probably couldn't make it all the way home, but if she wanted to get help, she'd have to get over to the road. No one would find her back here.

Let's go back in the field, away from the road. It's more romantic.

And she'd followed like a giggling school girl. When would she learn? Why the hell did men always have to hit! Was she wearing a sign that said *"punch here"*?

And this guy was the champ. Hit harder than her ex on a good day.

More tears that had no place to go welled beneath the lids. Was that footsteps? Was it her imagination? She was breathing too fast. She needed to calm down and get out of here. Fast. She pushed up with her hands, but lightning bolts of pain shot through her chest. Oh, hell.

That wasn't going to work. Hurt too bad. She'd have to roll over and crawl. It was the only way.

"God, I'm done with men. Done, I said." Her voice sounded strange, garbled. She rolled over and pushed up to her hands and knees. "I know I said that just a few weeks ago, but this time I mean it. Lord, if you can see fit to get me home, I will never so much as look at another man."

"I can help you with that," said a familiar voice.

She swung her head toward the sound, her eyelids still glued shut. Her trembling arms risked giving out. She hunched back, rested on her knees.

"Thought you could help me relax, but you let me down, Sweetheart."

Her lower body still throbbed. He'd torn her up down there. "I done what I could. Please, don't hit me again."

"No, you didn't. You kept passing out. And I'm still in need."

"Okay, okay, well…" It'd hurt worse, but she couldn't take another fist. "I can do it better. Let's try again. Just don't hit me."

"Heard you're through with men."

"Not you." She gulped in a breath, the words frozen on her lips.

"That's good, Sugar, but I can't have you telling tales, can I?"

"I won't tell nobody. Promise, please Mr.—"

The kick caught her between her ribs and her stomach. She was flying, weightless. And for an instant, pain free. Then, thunk. She crashed.

Facedown. Arms splayed.

She spit away the grass. Coughed. She coughed again, but couldn't clear her throat. Couldn't catch a breath. She struggled to her knees, fighting for air.

There was none.

Chapter 1

Wednesday June 15, 2005
Baton Rouge, LA

Claire Rivet sat straight-backed, eyes downcast, and hands clasped on the mahogany table before her. Anyone who didn't know her might think she was praying. She never prayed.

The judge, his robe open against the heat, flipped through his notes. Shoes scraped the tongue-and-groove flooring, newspapers rippled open and shut, voices passed in guarded whispers. It looked to Claire as if all of Baton Rouge had turned out to hear the verdict.

When the rear door flew open, a hush fell over the courtroom and heads turned to watch the jurors file in behind the bailiff. Claire watched too. Each face, each tense muscle held a clue and a good prosecutor's job was to decipher those clues into victory or defeat. She saw what she was looking for on the face of juror number four, a fifty-year-old school teacher from the East side of town.

The jury foreman read the verdict: guilty, on all four charges. A collective sigh rose and faded into the mechanical clank of an air-conditioner built for an earlier era.

The courtroom began to empty. Claire watched as Leroy Milson was cuffed and led out the back. She stood and gathered her notes into three separate file folders already thinking about her next case: a burglary, one latent fingerprint, one eyewitness.

Erwin Tyson, the investigator who'd worked the Milson case with her, reached over the rail and patted her back with his rough hand. She felt other congratulatory taps as she loaded her briefcase. She smiled and nodded as another "Congratulations" flew her way. Why were they congratulating her? It always made her wonder. She'd been hired to prosecute criminals, to get the likes of Leroy Milson off the streets. There was no right way, wrong way, good way, or bad way of doing this. She was doing her job.

LaVerne reached a hand out. "Thank you, Mz Rivay."

Claire shook the dark hand with a sure grip. The bruise under LaVerne's left eye had faded to a shadow. "Thank you, LaVerne. Your testimony put him away. Take care of yourself."

"Yeah, you, too."

Claire glanced at her other client, Wendy, seated in the third row. Wendy's husband nodded and forced his lips into an unsure smile, but kept his arm locked around his wife's shoulders. Wendy, head bowed, was focused on a secret world, a world where she was in control, a world that no longer existed outside her mind. If she didn't slit her wrist within a year, she might have a chance, but Claire had seen women like Wendy before and she recognized destruction when she saw it. Leroy had made a mess there.

LaVerne would make it. Claire knew that much. LaVerne was a fighter. She'd grown up fighting and she'd keep on fighting until she had her life back, or whatever could pass for a normal life after Leroy's violation.

Claire shoved open the heavy oak door. Hot humidity as thick as coal dust gagged her as she stepped onto the granite courthouse steps. Before she could move, cameras and microphones surrounded her, dwarfing her beneath the taller reporters vying for her attention.

"Back up, I can't breathe."

She knocked a long microphone away from her mouth. She hated this part of the job. She would just as soon leave these vultures to her colleagues, but she'd been warned to be nicer. Her boss, the DA, had told her to make the press her friend. Felt like befriending an alligator; never knew when you'd be eaten alive.

"How do you feel about today's verdict?" someone asked.

Sweat beaded on her upper lip and brow, under the sparse bangs, and the long dark strands cascading past her shoulders. "It's correct."

She tucked her head and pushed forward, the crowd of reporters parting and regrouping around her.

A man shoved a fat black microphone toward her nose. "You have a one-hundred-percent conviction record on rape cases, what's your secret?"

Was that true about her conviction rate? "Let me through, please."

She flashed through her last few cases, most of which were plea bargained down to a lesser offense in order to find and charge accomplices, or to collect evidence on someone higher up the food chain. A necessary tactic, and one she deplored. But a rapist? Never. She refused to bargain. If he was caught, she wanted him off the streets, forever. A stand that almost saw her fired last winter when a rapist she was trying was tied in with drug smuggling down in the Gulf. His lawyer wanted to deal, said the man had the goods on two South American players.

"Do you expect an appeal?" a reporter asked.

"What do you think about the rape in Raceland?" asked another.

"Are you handling the Clifford case?" asked another.

She focused on the blonde with the high voice and urgency pasted on her face. An icon. The sort favored by the networks. "What rape?"

The blond who'd asked about the Raceland case stepped forward. "The young woman found beaten to death. Will you prosecute?"

Claire's step faltered. A wave of vertigo overwhelmed her. What a stupid question. Always stupid questions. "Raceland's out of my jurisdiction. Please, let me through."

She broke out of the crowd and headed for Erwin's gray Taurus, waiting at the curb. Another one, she thought, sliding into the passenger seat. "What woman in Raceland?" she asked Erwin as she slammed the door.

Erwin removed his glasses and wiped the lenses with the bottom of his shirt. "Oh, that's a bad one. A twenty-two-year-old, raped and beaten to death. Young waitress, poor thing. Actually, she was found in a field between Raceland Junction and Bowie. I heard the body was taken to New Orleans for the autopsy."

"Why not here?"

"Orleans's closer."

Claire closed her eyes and massaged her throbbing temples. Sweat glued her dark strands to her face and neck. "Drop me at home. I'm finished for the day."

Erwin pulled into traffic. "That's one for the books."

"Can't I take an afternoon once in awhile?"

"Sure you can, but you never do."

She glanced out the window. Dark bulbous storm clouds marred the horizon. A bad one blowing in. She pictured the young woman, lying in the field. A field. Another image popped into her mind, but after years of practice, she was able to shove it away before it could take hold.

She imagined the waitress. Had she died quickly, or had her life ebbed away as she fought off the pain?

Again the image tried to force its way in.

A field.

She reached for the air-conditioning vent and focused the stream of cool air on her face. Jurisdiction or no, she had to learn more about the rape. For too long, she'd put off what must be done.

Chapter 2

Wednesday June 15, 2005
Baton Rouge, LA

Claire's apartment complex could be seen through the trees. Four three-story buildings surrounded by a landscaped park of green grass, dogwoods, and a row of pine benches, which remained empty despite the inviting scenery. This time of the year, the residents preferred air-conditioning and a mosquito-free environment to the spray of white flowers.

Erwin stopped at the curb. "Door to door."

Claire turned to face him. They'd worked together for a few years now and, although he was a bit of a flirt, she liked him. He was good at finding secrets—dark, sinister secrets. "Twenty-two, you said?"

"Do I know what you're talking about?"

She reached for her briefcase. "The waitress in Raceland, her age?"

"Twenty-two, yeah, I believe so." He pulled the handbrake. "Why so interested?"

"Reminds me of an old case."

"How old?"

She exhaled and rubbed her temple. "Gee, a long time. I'm not sure." Twenty-five years, she thought, and each day that passed made it that much longer.

"What about statute of limitations?"

She reached for the handle. "It was a kid. There's no statute of limitations."

"Probably not the same perp then. I hear they're thinking about changing that law, too. Sorry day that'll be."

She opened the door. Thick, hot air rushed the cool interior. "Thanks for the lift. Listen, if you hear anything more about the Raceland woman, would you let me know?"

"Will do. It'll be all over the evening news."

* * *

The incoming storm weighed on her as she climbed the darkening stairwell. She reached to unlock the deadbolt on her apartment door, but as she touched the lock with her key, the door pushed open and a sliver of light escaped into the dank hallway. Odd. She knew—without hesitation—that she'd locked it before leaving for court. Her memory echoed the turn of the key and the click of the bolt as it fell into place.

She looked at the lock, the handle, the doorframe's edge. No signs of forced entry.

Rumors of stalking, of death threats, often circulated after difficult trials, but mostly after an acquittal when the accused felt superior to his accuser. Still, after five years as assistant DA, she wasn't about to take chances. Her thoughts returned to this morning's courtroom, and Leroy Milson's conviction.

Sloppy Leroy, an easy convict—one eyewitness, two sperm samples, pubic hairs, and even fingerprints—too proud or too stupid to be careful. But what struck her now, alone in the corridor, was his defiance, his angry stare directed at her words, her evidence, at her. As the foreman read the verdict, she'd watched Leroy hang his head, his anger spent. Such sweet validation came in those moments, when the guilty gave in to their guilt, when they understood they could not escape.

She glanced back at the deadbolt. No, Leroy's reign of terror was over. Whoever was inside had used a key.

With fingertips extended, she pushed the door farther open and called, "Vincent?"

The spicy smell of Vincent washed, spritzed, and on his way to the office, embraced her as she stepped through the doorway. Though diluted by time and too much humidity, the odor's constancy comforted her. She drew in a breath, pulling the sweetness into her lungs.

"Vincent?" she called again, her palm pressed to her forehead to sooth the building pressure.

Movement at the end of the entrance hall. A shadow cast from a distant overhead lamp. She tensed, half turned to escape as a patch of dark hair appeared, trailed by the squelch of tennis shoes over oak flooring. Ah! She hated that sound.

A second later, Vincent backed around the corner into the entrance hall holding a large brown carton between his hands, his strained shoulders stretching his LSU tee shirt. A rush of desire surprised her. He lowered the carton onto two other boxes, then aligned the weight and adjusted the corners. She smiled despite the pounding between her temples, despite the tiring humidity, despite the stacked boxes, which most likely signaled one of Vincent's mini-dramas.

She bent and placed her briefcase beside the entry table. "Don't tell me—you're quitting law again." Her voice was harsher than intended.

"What gives you that idea?"

"Jeans, a tee shirt, the boxes, and…you aren't at the office?"

Lines creased his forehead. His expression looked as if he were working her words into a plausible context, as if deciphering a foreign language.

But she remembered every detail: his outrage after being asked to defend a child molester; his suffering when the partners questioned the value of his religious convictions.

How could he forget the nights of agonizing, the angry discussions, her repetition of the Sixth Amendment like a mantra?

"So, why are you home in the middle of the day?" she asked. Why now? An Excedrin and a soft pillow were the only conversations she desired. They were her words of love, words of encouragement, words to "cease and desist."

"I could ask you the same… Aren't there other victims in need of your services?"

"Ooh, you are in a nasty mood." Drama, he wants drama. "There's a storm moving in. I have one hell of a migraine. This one's so bad, my closing arguments sounded more like a dying wolf on Demerol." Stop now. Her fingers massaged the bridge of her nose. "Days like this I think I should have become a meteorologist. But we won, since you asked."

"Yeah, Claire, like *you* would lose."

"Whoa, who pissed in your corn flakes? I hardly win all my cases."

"Oh, that's right. But this wasn't a car thief or drug dealer, was it? It was a rapist. Show no mercy, right?"

She hung her head. Why was he so angry? "You still haven't told me why you're home so early." She turned to close the door behind her.

"Isn't it obvious? I'm moving out."

Her hand clamped the doorknob. Her focus blurred, then popped back. So like Vincent. She took a deep breath, wondered if she'd heard correctly—had he said…? Of course, he had. What was it her brother Philippe said about relationships? Sometimes they're like peanuts, sometimes like hulls. Well, Vincent sure was a hull and a half when he got all tied in knots.

She checked her watch—11:52—as if it were important to know what time he'd walked out on her, 11:52, 11:52,

11:5—. Had she done something? Not done something? She locked the deadbolt, then realized her error, and unlocked it.

"We've been engaged for a year." His voice softened. "You still refuse to set a date for the wedding."

"Not again!" She regretted her tone the moment she heard it, but she needed to lie down.

As she turned, he reached for her, a show of tenderness. She shrugged him off, pulled her arm away. Fine, if he wants to leave, let him. She always knew this day would come.

"I don't need a restraining order to know when it's time to go." He slapped the side of a box. The violence startled her.

"Vincent." She paused, wondering if she should speak, if she should try yet again to make him understand. "I don't want you to leave."

"You don't want to marry me either."

"Can we talk about this after the storm?"

"After the storm, after dinner, after next week. Typical. No, we need to finish this once and for all. Here—now."

"Yes, counselor." She summoned the energy for what lay ahead, her discourse, his doubts, her cajoling, his submission. Sure, she could convince him to stay. He wanted her to—that was the game, played out before in other ways—but she couldn't hold him forever. Yes, she loved him, his kindness, his intelligence, and yes, even his insecurity. She loved that he was way too moralistic and religiously closed-minded, even when it infuriated her. But she trusted him, well, not with everything, a flaw in her character, not his. And…he deserved happiness. He wanted the white picket fence, whereas a badly lit apartment was fine with her. He wanted the dog and the kids. She hated animals.

"Don't you have anything to say?" His voice wavered. She heard the fear. He was begging her to find the right words, begging her not to let go.

But she didn't have the right words. She had secrets. Some so violent they would crush his spirit, suck the gentleness from his bones. He was better off leaving. He deserved better. He deserved more.

"Tell me again why you aren't ready, or is it simply that you don't love me?" he asked.

Her glance drifted to the boxes.

He stepped closer. "Tell me again how you want to concentrate on your career, although—"

"Where will you stay?" she asked.

The question hung in the air between them. Solid. Biased. It changed forms—surprise, anger, doubt, and finally pain. She hadn't meant to hurt him. How easily it happened. A simple question now separated them like strangers. Gone was the trust, the faith, that they would endure no matter what.

He straightened, stood erect, looking more like an adolescent trying to make a point. So emotional.

"Sherman's lending me his sofa until I find my own place."

Hadn't she warned him of her need for logical order and her discomfort with emotion? But he hadn't listened; he'd laughed.

"Leave your keys on the entry table."

She brushed past, heading for the kitchen and a six-pack of Excedrin. The decision was made. She wouldn't weaken this time. Safely behind the closed kitchen door, she stopped and pressed her back against the wood. The cabinets melted in front of her eyes, their golden color and pine texture blending in kaleidoscopic patterns. She tried to breathe, but the air was too thick.

He had a right to leave. He had a right to the life he wanted. She filled the teakettle with water. Through the kitchen window, the Baton Rouge skyline darkened with

dense gray clouds. A wall of rain climbed the slope toward
the apartments, soaking roads, rooftops, and cars as it
crawled closer.

The front door slammed. The sound vibrated through the
thin walls. She walked back to the entrance, now empty of
boxes. On the entry table by the door, two silver keys lay on
the polished surface.

"Vincent?"

She listened for sounds of his presence, sounds that drove
her crazy when she was studying a case, or preparing a brief:
humming, the click and whine of his exercise bike, light jazz
from his stereo, but in the resounding stillness, she heard
only the echo of the last three years.

Her hand flew to the gold cross on a chain at her neck, a
gift from Vincent, a piece of him she could hold on to.

What had she done?

Then, the storm struck. Rain beat down on the roof and
slapped at the windows. Raindrops bounced across the
balcony and spilled over the gutters.

Chapter 3

Thursday June 16, 2005
Raceland, LA

Blistering sunlight reflected off the fluorescent road sign pointing the direction to Raceland Junction. Claire parked her Sunfire next to it. She jumped the drainage ditch and stood poised at the edge of the field. Although the overhead sun blinded her, she made no move to shade her eyes. Bees buzzed nearby as if to warn her off. She stood her ground.

The girl's name had been Tanya Bonaventure. Twenty-two years old. Cajun. Had she been pretty? Homely? Average? The newsprint photo was from high school and too grainy to tell.

Sweat pooled at the small of Claire's back beneath her tee shirt and shorts. A grasshopper leaped onto her bare leg, startling her. She flicked it off and glanced at her watch. 10:30.

Grasses, tall and still green from spring, filled her view along with the yellow dandelions, or pissenlit as Ma called them. So similar, she thought, focusing on the yellow flowerets.

Claire was ten years old again, standing in the field where the snapdragons and black-eyed Susans grew. Ma would be mad; she'd warned her not to go so far from home, but what was the danger in picking a few flowers? Ma liked her bouquets, always displaying them in a jar on the dining table, calling them her bowl of sunshine. The yellow Susans with their long, narrow petals were Claire's favorites. They mixed well with white petunias and cattails from the bayou.

When they'd found her that day, legs spread, arms broken, and blood pouring from her insides, the yellow bouquet lay crushed in her tiny hand, held so tight that the stems had lost their life, gone to heaven along with her future children.

"Ma'am, this is a crime scene."

She jerked her head toward the voice. A male deputy in a dark uniform reached out to steady her. He was young with a freckled faced and big teeth. Too young to be in uniform. His crew cut was fresh, leaving an arch of pale skin over his wide ears.

"You okay?" he asked.

How old was he? she wondered. "Sorry, I didn't hear you approach." He couldn't be out of high school, maybe some type of training program. The shoulders of his uniform hung as loose as they would on a kid playing dress up. She held her hand out. "Claire Rivet. I'm with the DA's office in Baton Rouge."

The deputy took her hand; even his grip was childish, too eager, too tight. Yes, too young and just the type to be stuck out here on surveillance detail. Where had he been when she'd arrived?

She nodded toward the field. "I would like to take a look at the crime scene."

"Ah, don't know. I'm not supposed to let anyone near it. You're a DA?"

"Assistant. I wanted to…" No, she didn't, did she? What had she hoped to accomplish? "I wanted to see the area. Get an idea of what happened here."

"Something pretty bad if you want my opinion. Ain't seen nothing like that girl's face, all… You say you're out of Baton Rouge?"

"Is there someone you could call, perhaps the investigating detective?"

The deputy looked uncomfortable. Oh yes, he'd screwed up. He'd left the scene and now he didn't want anyone to know.

Not her problem. "I have a cell phone," she said, reaching into her handbag. "I'll call if you just give me a name and number."

"Ah, no, that's not necessary. Stay here. Rivay, you said."

"Yes, but written with a T."

"I'll call it in, see if anyone minds."

The deputy ambled toward his car a few yards down the road. Claire remained at the edge of the field, turning her gaze back to the four stakes planted into the earth some forty feet ahead. Red police tape was strung stake to stake, bowing above the grasses, marking off a rectangular area.

How had Tanya ended up there? Had someone given her a lift after work? It had been late, dark. Had she walked? Or had someone parked along this road and waited? Had she tried to escape? Run? The memory of a fist. The crack of a bone.

Claire squeezed her eyelids shut against the images. But above her, the animal sneered. Sun glinted off a gold canine tooth.

"Ma'am. Ma'am."

Claire opened her eyes. She was on the ground, the deputy beside her, holding her head like a worried parent.

"Ms. Rivet?"

"I'm fine, I'm good." She lifted up on her elbows. "It's the heat. I'm not used to...so humid." She wiped her forehead with the back of her hand.

"You aren't pregnant, are you? My wife faints all the time when she's expecting."

"That's the last thing I am. Please, could you help me up?"

"Here you go. Hold it now, not so fast. Don't get your head to spinning."

"I'm sorry. I'm just not used... Please. Stop fussing. I'm fine."

Looking as if he'd been insulted, the deputy backed away.

"What's your name?"

"Padgett. Deputy Padgett, ma'am. I called in your request and the Major said it would be all right as long as you don't go past the tape. The Major wants to keep the crime scene clean until all the evidence has been processed."

Claire glanced across the field to the red tape. "I'm not feeling all that well. I'll come back. Who's handling the case?"

"That would be the Major his self."

Claire waited, but the deputy didn't offer the major's name. "His name?"

"Oh, Major Argrais. We just call him the Major." Padgett fiddled with his belt buckle. "He's head of criminal operations for the parish."

"Thanks for your help. Sorry if I frightened you." Claire walked toward her car.

"Hey, you okay to drive?" he called after her.

Chapter 4

Thursday June 16, 2005
Green Acres, LA

Philippe Rivet hung up the telephone, but held on to the receiver. He bowed his head against the questions plowing through his mind, questions he didn't want answered.

"Who was it, chéri?" Suzanne, his wife, asked over the sizzling and popping of sausage and eggs in the frying pan.

"Claire's coming." His hand dropped to his side. He pressed his back against the cupboard and crossed his arms. He was a large man, big boned like his daddy, but as his right leg crossed his left, he felt himself growing smaller, tightening, curling, as if trying to disappear.

"Good." Suzanne shuffled the scrambled eggs, the metal spatula scraping the iron pan. She reached for a plate. "I'll fix up Chet's room. Chet can sleep in the den. He'll like that. Be like a sleepover."

"She's not staying here. She wants to stay out at the house."

"That shack, you're kidding." Suzanne set the plate of eggs on the table. "You all right? You're looking whiter than a priest's smock on Sunday."

Philippe stepped over to the table. He pulled up a wooden chair, not one of the four he'd made, but one he'd found at a construction site and stripped to match the others. His finger caressed the seat as he lowered himself. He liked working with wood. He liked its strength, its texture, its changeability, but mostly he liked that it didn't give him any trouble. He could cut it, glue it, hammer it, and the wood ceded to his hands.

Aware of Suzanne's stare bearing down on him, he picked up a fork and scraped a lump of eggs onto his plate. Eat, just eat. He lifted a forkful to his mouth. What could he say? He'd no idea why his sister wanted to stay in the old place. Lord knew it held bad memories for her. Hell, the place held bad memories for all of 'em. Now, she was some fancy lawyer up in Baton Rouge—she could afford the best hotel in New Orleans. Certainly, she could afford the Roadway Inn if she didn't want to stay here.

"Can I get some coffee?" he asked. Anything to get her eyes off him. Woman could make a priest cuss.

The plate of sausage clinked his as she dropped it down. "You look odd. Did Claire say something to upset you?" She reached across the table for the coffee pot and sat beside him, her leg rubbing up against his as she poured the steaming liquid into his mug.

Woman couldn't get any closer without sitting in his lap. "I think it's strange, that's all. No electricity, no running water—why don't she go to a hotel, or come here?"

"She grew up there, she's got her own memories," Suzanne said. "Maybe she misses her ma. Listen, I'll go over and air out the place before work. You need to check and see if the well's still producing."

"It is. I checked about a month ago."

Oh, shit. He shoveled another load of eggs into his mouth. He'd put his foot right in it and no way was Suzanne fixing to let that slide. Naw, she was looking at him again with that look of hers, that look of superiority. He swallowed hard. "Yeah, I still go over and check the place from time to time. Is that such a crime?"

She patted his arm. "If you still care about the place, why's it so difficult to believe Claire does?"

He shrugged. He remembered better than anyone what had happened to his little sister. Hell, he'd found her. Lying unconscious, face down, and all that…red. He sucked in air.

"Philippe?"

"Just remembering."

"Well, I gotta go if I'm going by the house first," she said. "See you at five. You'll be here, right?"

He nodded, but half heard what she'd said, his thoughts locked on the scene of twenty-some-years earlier. He'd been seventeen, his first sexual experience still fresh on his skin. What was her name—Hilly, Dilly—hell, he should remember his first lay. Jilly! short for…Julienne. Julienne Lacombe. That was it. Jilly suited her better. She'd been in his math class. He remembered that all right. Took him forever to ask her out. Then they'd gotten serious just after Easter break, and they'd gone all the way one Friday night after a school dance. Afterwards, he'd had to pick the leaves off her fancy dress while she giggled. They'd both been more than a little nervous. A second time, they'd met in her father's tool shed. Whew…that night was something.

Then he found Claire. Her little body broken. And violated. Arms and legs bent to odd angles. Blood. He'd never seen so much blood in his life. When he'd picked her up, he'd thought she was dead. Couldn't believe the little gurgle of liquid that pushed up through her throat. The doctors performed a miracle that day.

One afternoon and everything changed. His world became unbearable. Jilly had tried to comfort him in her special way, but he found her moves more repulsive than exciting. After two more weeks and three more attempts, he knew for sure he'd never get a boner again. At seventeen, his roger had dried up like grapes left too long on the vine. The pleasure he'd once felt, the total release, had been replaced with the image of his little sister's blood-soaked body.

Boy, he was glad when Claire left for college. Her absence helped weed the horrific image from his soul. And later, he'd met Suzanne on a contracting job. Cajun women knew how to take charge and a good thing, too. She'd been diligent, even insistent, in helping him overcome his "problem." It took two more years and only by God's grace and his love for Suzanne had he been able to be normal again.

So why in heaven was Claire coming back here—back to the scene? What demons would be served?

She'd said something about taking a leave of absence. Sounded like an extended stay. She mentioned a project long overdue. What did that mean? Oh, he had an idea, but with any luck, he was overreacting. Claire had gone on to have normal relationships. Hell, she and that guy, Vincent, seemed real happy, maybe even marriage happy. Might be just a coincidence that she'd become sort of famous prosecuting rape cases. Yeah, right. And maybe he was Wyatt Earp and this here was the OK Corral.

Chapter 5

Thursday June 16, 2005
Villette, LA

Claire passed the overturned cane truck for the third time. She slapped the steering wheel with the ball of her palm and swallowed back a curse.

"She-it." She said it anyway, hearing the southern drawl as she did. Earlier too, when she'd called her brother, she'd heard the drawl wiggle into her voice. Funny, how going home did that. She wasn't ashamed of her roots, but in a courtroom, she needed a voice that rang of authority, of intelligence.

Okay, a little ashamed. But just thinking so felt like betrayal.

"Sorry, Ma."

Slowing the car, she scanned the foliage and trees around the overturned truck. She didn't mind that she was lost. After all, she hadn't been back to the house in years, not since Ma's death. And she didn't mind that the nearest gas station was ten miles away because she had no intention of asking for directions. But what wrenched her gut every time she laid eyes on it was that rotted cane truck abandoned at the side of the road, its ribs half-buried in the earth like a dinosaur from another age. The rusted skeleton had lost everything to the scavengers of the night—picked over to furnish the poor.

People didn't abandon trucks by the side of the road in Baton Rouge or New Orleans, but this was Villette, the poorest section of Lafourche Parish. Not listed on any map, only the locals knew its boundaries. Ma used to say,

"Villette's a one-horse town except no one can afford the horse."

White trash. Those two hated words hissed through her head. Ma'd preached that rich folks, poor folks were all the same in God's eyes, but the kids at school had a different point of view. Those nasty little kids. Where were they today—fishing out in the Gulf, working in a chemical plant, abandoning cane trucks by the side of the road?

Shameful thoughts. "Forgive me, Ma."

Had she always been so spiteful? And it was spite, not jealousy. She'd never coveted. Sure, they hadn't had much growing up and they'd had neighbors that most people couldn't look in the eyes, but the land was theirs, passed down through three generations of Ma's family. How many of those snooty classmates could say they lived on land that once bore the Villette plantation, Ma's grandfather's plantation? Course that was before the bayou changed direction and turned most of the forty acres into a new waterway.

No, she'd never coveted. Ma had taught her that much.

Ma would've liked Vincent with his high religious morality. Vincent would've liked her, too. Everyone liked Ma. Why was she thinking about Vincent? That fish was fried.

In the middle of the two-lane road, she whipped her car around and headed south again. "House, I know you're out here somewhere, and I *will* find you."

She pulled off the road, braking too hard and skidding across loose gravel at the shoulder. She flung open the driver's door and coughed as hot air burned her lungs. Baton Rouge was hot, humid even, but nothing compared to the mugginess set off by the bayous. Here, the air was massive like a living entity, clinging to her skin.

From the expanse of asphalt stretching before her, rippling heat waves wafted upward, blurring the edges of the black and green horizon. She slinked along, like in the old days, figuring the path would be more visible on foot.

She brushed her face with the topside of her arm. "Shewwwww."

Rather than rolling her sleeves, she pushed them up and hooked them over her shoulders. Air-conditioning, how had she lived without it? Again, she felt ashamed. Had she moved so far away from the little girl who rode to school in a motorboat, who played with flowers and butterflies instead of dolls and plastic toys?

Kudzu climbed, coiled, and choked the nearby pines and low-growing bushes. The lush growth betrayed her memory. Sulfur that blew off the bayous fouled the air with the stench of rotten eggs.

She smelled something sweet too: magnolia…honeysuckle? No, something else, something she couldn't name—a memory. Ma's place had to be close.

Images flickered through her mind like fireflies at dusk. Oh, it would come to her, she couldn't force it. Her gait slowed, easing into a sense of comfort, into a sense of home.

Several yards ahead, a plastic orange strip was tied to a pine branch and hanging limp. The strip was high enough in the tree that she must have missed it in the car, driven right under it, but so foreign in nature that it must mean something.

Sure enough, behind the pine, a rough path reached into the woods. Peppergrass and dropseed camouflaged the opening, but when she bent to look, the plants were ragged and abused, smaller leaves clumped by tire imprints.

She hiked back to her car and drove to the path, following the tire grooves through a grove of Spanish Oaks. Small bushes and large weeds clawed at the undercarriage as she bounced over the rough terrain. Farther, through a sparse growth of young hickory trees, the wooden roof shingles on Ma's house rose into view. And then the house, looking so tiny to her adult eyes.

A green Ford pickup was parked in front. Her eldest brother lay sunning on the hood. Philippe sat up as she pulled into the clearing.

When had he gone gray? His wiry ponytail and beard still needed trimming—that hadn't changed—but instead of the chestnut brown he'd always sported, his hair was dusted with age. What was he? Forty-two? Three? He looked a decade older. And he looked shorter, too. The roll of his shoulders didn't help the illusion. Funny—she'd never noticed that he slumped. She remembered him as a towering omniscient figure, her mythical hero.

She stepped from the car. "Weren't you taller the last time I saw you?"

"Yeah, and weren't you smarter?" He reached to hug her, then paused.

She, too, leaned forward, understanding his dilemma. After her attack, she'd hated physical contact. But after the annihilation of her college boyfriend's ego, she'd conquered that particular fear. "It's okay, I'm touchable, remember?" His last visit to see her felt like more than just two years ago.

They embraced.

"And what was that 'smarter' remark about?" she asked. She hefted her black bulky suitcase from the rear seat, banging it against the door.

She stepped aside to allow Philippe room to grab the box of groceries she'd picked up in Luling.

"With that fancy education, why you wasting time 'round here?" He shoved the car door shut with his hip and led her up the front steps. "Or does a certain rape case have something to do with it?"

She stopped mid-stride.

He must have sensed her hesitation because he turned and added, "Been thinking about it all day—it's why you come back, ain't it? Come on inside. It's hotter'n a pancake griddle out here."

The screen door smacked shut behind them. She set her suitcase by the front door and joined Philippe at the plank dining table their father had built before she was born. So familiar. The smell of lemon polish, the way the sunlight sprayed through the screen, Philippe unloading the groceries. For an instant, she felt as if she'd never left, as if the last ten years had been a dream that she was now awaking from.

But Ma wouldn't be calling from out in the garden; Brian wouldn't burst into the house all excited about some stupid bug. Never again.

Claire picked up a box of spaghetti and carried it to the pantry. "The girl was beaten to a pulp, left in a field to die. Ring any bells?"

Philippe yanked out a cereal box. "Let the past go, it's in God's hands now."

"You know, I love it when people talk about God and rape in the same sentence. If this 'God' of yours is as *just* as everyone keeps telling me, how can he allow such a horrible thing to happen to a child?" Here was where their philosophies parted. "The Law is my bible. Justice my God." The Law. At least it kept her sane when all else failed.

"God's ways aren't always clear. You have to trust."

"Oh, please. I suppose you also believe in the tooth fairy."

"What happened to you was awful. I admit it, but—"

"*What* happened to me?" She took a step toward him, got up in his face the way she did to a defense attorney she didn't like. "Say it. I just want to hear it from one person in this family."

He kept stacking the cans, then turned away. "What good will that do?"

"It happened." She spoke to his back. "It's not some piece of gossip you heard over a beer. It happened to me. You, Ma, Joe, even Brian never spoke about it. How do you think that made me feel? My dirty little secret."

"Brian was a kid, a year older than you, I don't think he knew."

"It happened. I was ten years old. Do you know what that monster did to me?"

With the gentleness of a caress, he lifted a loaf of bread and placed it on the table. "I found you." He paused, whispered, "Course I know."

She backed off, walked to the sofa, and leaned against the arm. "I've been hiding this all my life, same as I was taught. Now, I have a chance to put Billy Ray Cobb away. I can't let that go."

Philippe shook his head and kept shaking it, but what struck her was that he didn't react in the least to her revelation. Not so much as a raised eyebrow.

"You knew it was Cobb?" She heard her voice break.

"Ma told me, a few days before she died."

"Ma? Ma knew?" Suddenly the room was too warm. Her thoughts spiraled. "But it wasn't... How? I didn't even... I was fifteen when I figured it out. When did Ma find out?"

She sank down on the sofa arm. Both Ma and Philippe had known. They'd left her screaming with nightmares and crying over imagined fears and never, ever said a word. Why hadn't someone done something? Why hadn't they had Billy Ray arrested? Claire went rigid, fighting her growing anger.

"I got to say, I never really believed Ma," Philippe said. "'Cause one thing I know about Cobb, he's the kind to have someone else do his dirty work. Keeps his own hands clean."

What she was hearing? Such a strange thing to say about a rapist. She looked at her brother, but he was staring down at his feet, toeing an imaginary object. Was he ashamed? He should be.

His head swung up. "Can you really tell me that this vendetta doesn't have something to do with the elections?"

In two steps she was at the table. "Vendetta! Is that what you think it is?" She snatched up the loaf of bread and two cans of chopped tomatoes and stomped toward the panty, trying to find the words that would calm her down. Okay, she was a little shaken to learn that Ma had known, but that was no reason to beat Philippe up. He'd said he didn't know until Ma died. She took a deep breath and focused her words. "I'm talking about a rapist. This has nothing to do with any elections."

"Right. You've suspected Cobb for years, but you're just coming out with this now that he's running for sheriff?"

The two cans thumped as they hit floorboards. Her fist tightened right through the loaf of bread. She braced her back against the pantry doorway. What year was it? Which election? Oh, no.

"Billy Ray's running for Criminal Sheriff?" Her knees weakened. She dropped the bread and grabbed the countertop as the room shifted. "The man who raped me—the word is *rape*—wants to wear a badge." Her voice trembled. "People trust a sheriff. They feel protected by that badge."

Philippe didn't move. He didn't speak for the longest time. "You were ten. You didn't know then what happened, what makes you know now? And a Cobb at that. Does Vincent know about this?"

"No. He doesn't." What did this have to do with Vincent? Was Philippe so thick he couldn't understand the power Billy Ray would wield as sheriff?

"You can't tell Vincent," Philippe said. "It'll kill him. You can't dredge this all up again. It'll ruin us all. Joe and I, we got a business. Ma was a respected woman around here. She did work up at the hospital."

Her legs wobbled like new spring twigs as she made her way back to the table. "This doesn't have to do with you, or Ma, or Vincent." Her voice was unsteady. Too much to process at once, but she had to convince him of the danger. "There's a serial rapist out there. He has to be stopped before another woman ends up like Tanya Bonaventure." She pointed at Philippe's chest, a gesture that reminded her of Ma.

"No, Claire," Philippe shoved her finger away. "This is about you and what you want. Ma spoiled you after what happened. You don't care about anyone else long as you get what you want." He slammed a bar of soap down on the table and tossed the empty grocery box toward the front door.

Anger pulsed through her energizing every cell, but she vowed not to use it against her brother. "Philippe," she said slowly, deliberately, "you don't know me very well. I know because I don't know you very well. We're family, but the difference in our ages practically makes us strangers."

She drew in a slow breath to steady her voice. "I've always felt that what happened was my fault. Ma told me not to go to that field. I knew it was dangerous."

She looked him in the eye and saw he was listening. "I've never told anyone. Never. For a long time, I thought I'd been attacked by a wild animal, a bear, or a wolf. Silly huh, but that's what the mind does—tries to make sense. Please, try to understand that I need to resolve this. For myself, yes, but I won't let him hurt another woman. How many have already suffered, maybe died to satisfy his hatred?"

"You seem awfully sure of yourself. You got to have something. What is it? What evidence you got against Cobb?"

She hesitated. Her gaze fell across the plank table as she thought back to the first time she'd recognized Billy Ray Cobb. She didn't remember where she'd been or what she'd been doing. But she remembered the part of the nightmare that made it real. "His tooth. He has a gold tooth." That sounded lame even to her, but it was more than just the tooth.

It was the way his jaw tensed, the way he pursed his lips, the way his hair slung to one side. And those eyes, crystal cold and so full of... What? After all these years she still couldn't give it a name.

Philippe laughed, a sad, soulful laugh. "A gold tooth? Half the parish has a gold tooth. Gold's cheaper than those real colored ones. Looky here, I got one myself." He pulled his cheek out with his index finger so she could see inside. When she didn't look, he released the cheek. "Folks 'round here can't afford more."

"Cobb could afford more."

"That ain't the point. You're accusing a man because of a tooth everybody and their neighbor has. That what they teach you in law school?"

"Look. I know what I know. I just have to find a way of proving it." And she knew more. Something else nagged at her, but she couldn't put her finger on it, not yet.

Philippe's lips pressed into a thin line, his eyes looked past her.

She didn't want to fight. She needed time to absorb this new information, time to figure out her next move. She searched the room for a peace offering and noticed the log walls had been swept free of cobwebs, the wooden furniture had been polished. A fresh percale sheet was tucked around the worn sofa. Suzanne had done a nice job. "The place still smells like Ma's gumbo," she said.

Philippe slapped the tabletop with his palm. "Ma's gumbo, hell." His fists clenched and he shook them as he spoke. "See, that's what I'm telling you. You're living in that fantasy world Ma created. She wouldn't let the real world touch you after what happened."

She held her hand up to stop him. "Philippe."

"Naw, you stop. You blame us for not talking about it, well, what good does talking do? We were dirt poor thanks to that spineless father of ours—who knows, reckon he did us a favor blowing his brains out—but fact is, William Cobb has a name behind him and family money. Now, I know you're some hotshot lawyer up in Baton Rouge, but you're going to need some strong evidence to convict a Cobb in this part of the state, something more than a gold tooth. What kind of evidence you got after twenty-five years? You got some DNA stashed away somewhere?"

She knew he was right. She'd thought the same thing a million times in the last twelve hours, but there was a way; working trials all these years had taught her that much. She just had to find it.

Before she could speak, he said, "All you'll do is ruin your reputation. You'll wreck your career. Why? And for what?"

"Let's not fight."

"Was a long time ago. Move on." He walked over to the front door and picked up the empty box. He hung his head. "Propane tank's hooked up and ready to go." He pushed open the screen and turned back to look at her. "Give us a ring if you need anything. There's a phone booth in Lockport, or you got one of those cell phones?"

The door slammed shut.

She was alone.

And afraid.

For the first time in years, she felt vulnerable to forces she couldn't name, let alone control. The house. It brought back a past confused by good and evil.

Chapter 6

Thursday June 16, 2005
Bayou, LA

A wood fire crackled, its ghostly halo filling the darkened glade. Mamma Anna limped to the center of the crowd. No longer young, she held herself tall and as regal as the bad hip would allow. A wine-colored turban, rimmed with rows of dangling wooden beads, crowned her head and defined her as the Priestess of Ceremonies. Chiffon veils—red, orange, yellow, and violet—hung from her belt, bouncing and twirling with each labored step.

Around her, twelve women and four men danced to the drums, arms flying, bodies shimmying, knees bouncing. Her congregation, loyal believers all. In song, their voices carried out over the bayou, echoing off the still water and descending into the moonlit night.

Bernadette, her assistant, swayed to the beat, yet stayed ready to hand out any props the spirits might demand: a black bowler for Baron Samedi, red lipstick for Ezili Freda, a staff for Papa Legba, perfume for Mademoiselle Charlotte. Bernadette deserved the status that came with the position. She'd served loyally these last years. Angering a spirit—a loa—with the wrong prop could prove dangerous or even fatal. But Mamma Anna needn't worry, Bernadette knew her business.

Mamma Anna glanced at the paper in her hand, a photocopy of a newspaper photograph. The woman who looked back from the grainy image was much too stern, young yet aged by anger. The poor thing had seen evil. They'd both seen evil.

She ripped the photograph into tiny squares, careful as always to tear top to bottom, then right to left. She danced toward the fire, the lame leg slowing her. The crowd opened, giving her a wide path.

The fire's heat scorched her skin as she scattered the newsprint above the blaze. The pieces floated for an instant as if on an unseen cloud, and then one by one tumbled toward the hungry flames.

One last ingredient—tonight it would be red milkweed—to turn thoughts homeward. She drew a handful of the red-orange blossoms from a pouch on her belt and tossed her last offering into the fire. In silence, her request was made. Spinning, pirouetting. The dull ache disappeared as she danced back to the center and the group closed around her.

The rada drums commanded: the dull pop of the short one, the rolling rhythm of the medium one, and the deep and alluring tones from the large bass. They called to her, spoke the language of her soul, and told her the time was right.

Mamma Anna sprinkled cumin in a circle, protecting her sacred aura from undesirable spirits. From a makeshift altar of chicken crates and wire, she grabbed a rum bottle and splashed the distilled sugarcane over the herbs. She threw her head back and brought the bottle to her lips. Liquid heat rolled down her throat, spilled over her lips, and flowed down her chin.

She set the bottle back on the altar and spun in three circles. The beads on her turban clicked with their own rhythm as she moved.

"Awee-wee," she chanted with the others. "Awee-wee."

Papa Legba, the guardian, threw open the gates. The chill of the spirit world drew near. The power of the spirits infused her broken body. She, the mighty Priestess, felt no pain. Tremors started in the center of her body, then crawled, vertebra by vertebra, up her spine toward her heart. She lost control of her arms. Her legs began to twitch. Her head rolled side to side, picking up speed with each drumbeat, and flickering pinpricks of light glowed beneath her eyelids.

The ground below tugged, yanking her feeble frame, and her legs gave. She collapsed against the moist earth.

"Awee-wee, Ahhh…," the others chanted.

The drumbeat switched to *aux champs*, a more military rhythm signaling the presence of a grand loa's spirit. A bright light exploded behind her eyes. An acrid taste filled her mouth. She clutched her face and rolled back and forth, sweeping away the circle of herbs with her clothing.

"Awee-wee, Awee." The words frozen on her lips. Silence carried her far from the drums, the chanting, and singing.

Her thoughts scrambled, filling her with an empty, hollow sensation. He was near. She prayed for his mercy as his spirit took control of her body. He filled her small frame, every organ, every muscle, stretching the skin, smoothing the wrinkles until she felt twenty years younger and as strong as an ancient oak.

His deep male voice sprang from her lips. "That woman there with the red hat doesn't need my help. She's too lost inside herself to listen."

Mamma Anna's eyelids fluttered, her lips moved, a conduit for the male spirit. "I don't want you to waste your time with her," he commanded.

She nodded her agreement because she had no voice of her own, and she knew that later, once the spirit had left her, she would have no memory of his instructions. For that, she depended on her *hunsi*, Bernadette.

"I require two chickens and a rabbit during the feast of Saint Jean's Eve."

The rabbit. She tried to focus. It was important. What about the rabb—

Her thoughts crumbled. She couldn't concentrate.

"The girl will come." His voice was deeper as he tried to raise her hand.

The girl? What girl? she wanted to ask, but a violent spasm ripped through her body, rocked by a vacuum that sucked her down, down into the earth.

Her eyes popped open. Cypress trees bowed over her, their branches bent to caress. She tried to sit, her head heavy, laden with ancestral truths. Her eyes fixed on a dark object hidden within the cypress's fingerlike leaves. A bird— gigantic—took flight, bearing the god off to a distant land.

"He'll be back," she said, batting at the air with her weak hands as if to push him farther away. "He could've fixed this leg of mine," she mumbled in French. She folded her legs under her and tried to stand, but the left one went slack, sending her back to the earth.

Bernadette appeared at her side, wrapping massive brown arms around her weakened frame. "Here, Mamma Anna, let me help you."

Weakness—she hated it; not a trait for an all-powerful mambo. But Baron Samedi was digging her grave and most of her followers knew it. With any luck, her business would be done before it was too late.

Bernadette lifted her to her feet. "He says the girl's coming. Is she the one you've been telling me about?"

"The girl…" Mamma Anna said, the words difficult to form. The girl would come. Oh, praise God. "She's hardly a girl anymore but a powerful woman in the world of men. But her naïveté, the things she does not see, makes me think of her as a girl."

The ceremony had been worth it, even if her bad leg didn't agree. Now, she needed to save her strength. The feast of Saint Jean's Eve was less than forty-eight hours away, and the fire in her leg was growing, burning her hip. Two days earlier the pain had crawled into her arm, but the black water had washed it out, and for now, kept it out.

Mamma Anna released Bernadette's strong arms. Her glance fell on the woman wearing the red hat and a memory stirred deep inside her. "Praise us all, the spirits will sleep tonight." She faced Bernadette. "We don't need anything else until the feast. Nothing else, now that the girl's coming."

Alone, she made her way along the water's edge back to her cabin. All was quiet except for the uneven rhythm of her footfalls. Darkness didn't bother her. Her eyesight was perfect, but the pain in her leg was another matter. Seven days of festivities wouldn't be easy, but if the girl did her bidding, the pain would be a small sacrifice. Baron Samedi could carry her spirit away, if only she could convince the girl.

Chapter 7

Friday June 17, 2005
Villette, LA

Claire was flying, soaring over endless fields of red milkweed, orange oceans, and green seas. Poplars appeared like raindrops, few and spread apart, then a storm of laurel oaks spread beneath her.

The wind blew fresh against her face as she sailed over lakes and farmhouses. Then darkness swallowed her, a haven where she could rest. But there was no peace here. She wasn't alone. Nearby, a shadow hovered, blending in and out of a gray mist rising from the earth.

The shadow took on a female form and out of the vaporous haze emerged a black woman, her skin rich with color and lined with wisdom. She floated, half-blocked by the mist, her caftan billowing in the breeze. Her face appeared and disappeared behind the haze, but Claire sensed she wanted to speak. The gray clouds parted again. The figure floated forward, her mouth opened into a perfect "O."

A bloodcurdling scream.

Claire's hands flew to cover her ears, but she was knocked off balance. She fell, twisting, turning, and falling faster and faster into the dark void below.

She bolted upright in the bed, her sweat-soaked nightshirt glued to her skin. The room was quiet but for the beating of her heart. Outside, the cicadas were silent. She listened for screaming nutria out near the bayou, for croaking bullfrogs. Not a sound. Even the house, with its old floors and weak walls, were still—not a creak, not a crack.

She longed for her third floor apartment with its single entrance and heavy deadbolt. A high-powered drill might get past that lock, but that would make some noise. And she missed Vincent, the gentle roll of his chest as he slept. She reached across the bed as if to touch him, but her fingers landed on the empty mattress. She pulled the cotton sheet up and around her where she lay.

Here, in this house, she'd never felt safe. As a child she'd half-expected that animal, the bear or wolf that had attacked her, to come back and finish her off along with her mother and brothers. Silly childhood fears. But now the quiet...

Something was wrong. She felt the animal near.

She lifted her cell phone from the side table and pressed the glow button—1:55—half the night to go. What if someone were outside? What could she use as a weapon?

If someone were inside, surely, she'd hear, but she didn't hear anything except her own panicked breathing. Weren't there mythic beasts that frightened all other animals into silence?

Could Philippe have fixed the house so well that it no longer popped with the day's cooling? Or maybe it had been vacant long enough that...that what?

Pale moonlight leaked through a small window over the bed. Flat on her back, she stared into the semi-darkness, identifying every shape, every shadow. Her ears ached from straining to hear something, anything.

Something raced across the sheet, its legs pressing into her as it ran. She grabbed the cell phone and flashed its glow in time to see a fat wood spider leap from the mattress and scuttle across the flooring. She shivered. When she was younger, they used to wake her up, running across her face. They'd frightened her then, too, but now she took comfort knowing there was still other life on the planet.

She lay back. When she was too frightened to sleep as a child, Ma would sprinkle oak leaves around her bed.

"Oak leaves are for bravery," Ma'd said. "You've no need for fear when bravery is protecting you."

Had it helped? She couldn't remember, but it sure hadn't hurt. Tomorrow she'd gather some oak leaves and scatter them around the bed, if for no other reason than to feel closer to Ma.

* * *

The kitchen door was closer to the well than the front, but was stuck, swollen with humidity, and wouldn't open. Claire put her left foot on the frame and gripped the brass knob with both hands. She pulled with her arms and pushed with her bent leg. The door squeaked and moaned, but held tight. She stopped, took a breath, and tried again.

"Ieeeee."

A sound like a rifle shot and the door broke free, throwing her to the floor. She rolled over, laughing. It felt good to laugh. It helped wash away the stupidity, the complete idiocy of lying awake half the night waiting for the bogeyman. She had to get a grip. How could she bring a monster like Cobb to justice if she was afraid? And she was afraid. In the past, she had stalled herself with excuses—needing to learn more about the law, not wanting to hurt Vincent, not ready for her colleagues to know her shame—all the reasons why she'd put off coming after Billy Ray before, boiled down to nothing more than fear.

She stood, tugging her tee shirt down. She remembered when the door had stuck one miserable January after five days of constant rain. They'd each taken a try at opening it, even Philippe, the stronger of the boys, but Brian was the bright one who thought to go outside and try from the other side. He'd burst through the doorway, soaked to the bone, and had landed almost where she had.

Sweet Brian. What demons had driven him to the grave?

She pushed open the screened door, the hinges creaking with age.

Billowing live oaks shaded her on the wooden stoop and the sweetness of fresh blooms filled her lungs. The morning was alive with song—June bugs and honeybees buzzing, robins chirping, and blue jays the loudest of all.

A light mist, left over from the cool dawn, spread like fingers through the treetops, but the day already promised heat.

The two new buckets left by Philippe had collected bugs and a few fallen leaves. These buckets were twice the size of the old ones, cutting down the number of trips she would need to make to fill a bath.

"Thanks, Philippe."

Her brother. Man, he riled her like no other and she didn't know why. Maybe because she remembered him more as a father figure than a brother. And what did she know about him? The obvious. He was a good husband, a good father. He had his own business, which had survived several economical hits so he must be good at it. But who was he under his wiry beard? And what did he do or say that got her dander up so quickly? She knew defense lawyers who made it their job to piss her off, but no one did it faster than Philippe.

Philippe and Billy Ray Cobb.

Was that it? Was her anger her fear turned upside down? Her fear that Philippe was right? She had no proof against Billy Ray and after twenty-five years she wasn't likely to find any. What would the mighty Randolph Cobb do when she accused his son of serial rape? Or perhaps murder? The man had connections all the way up to the governor, maybe higher. With the oil deals he'd brokered over the years, he'd have to. Philippe was right about one thing: accusing a Cobb was no easy task. She'd need strong evidence.

But he must be stopped. Before November. One way or another she had to stop him.

She flipped the first bucket over, banged the bottom to break the insects free. As she picked up the second bucket, she spotted something, a tiny sack, stuffed under the doorframe. She let the buckets fall at her feet and reached for it. About the size of her palm, the sack was made from stiff, gray cloth and tied shut with red yarn.

A gris-gris. Sold in every curiosity shop in New Orleans to ward off illness, to bring riches, or to enhance love relationships. None of which interested her.

How long it had it been there? The cloth looked clean enough. The yarn fibers were strong and hadn't been touched by rain. She turned the gris-gris over and loosened the knot. She poured the contents into her hand, knowing to do so was said to bring bad luck. *Yeah, sure.*

The largest object was a silver coin, a piece of foreign currency. A scrap of green cotton cloth held a few hair strands, which looked blond as she held them to the sun. Herbs, dried and bundled, smelled exotic yet unfamiliar to her nose.

Then a chill pricked her flesh.

She flicked the last object over with her fingernail. A canine tooth. Worn from use. From its size and level of wear, she judged it to be a dog's, or maybe a wolf's. But the tooth carried memories of another animal—a human one.

Someone wanted to frighten her. Who? Philippe? No way. Philippe and Suzanne had grown up in these parts. They'd laugh at such tricks. But who else knew? And who thought superstition would stop her? The vermin she'd sent to prison were a lot scarier than a little bag stuffed with charms.

She dumped the contents back into the sack and retied the yarn. A strange sensation—as if she wasn't alone—tickled the back of her neck. She glanced up and around.

The grass was overgrown and gone to seed. Dandelions bloomed in the vegetable garden where Ma had once grown tomatoes, squash, spinach, and enough beans to feed a family of five. A few hearty vines like watermelon remained tangled in with weeds. A squash and two thick-stemmed tomato plants looked to be flowering.

Philippe had cleared a foot-wide path to the well and another one to the outhouse, or "other house" as Ma called it. The sweet scent of magnolia blossoms, warmed by the sun, thickened the air.

A blue jay perched on the pump handle and watched as if knowing her destination. A picture of serenity. So why didn't she feel serene? She felt a presence. The blue jay? No. Something else.

"Who's there?"

She listened, her gaze darting across the familiar landscape.

"I'm not afraid of you or your silly gris-gris."

She waited. Could be a cat foraging for food, or a mink burrowing against the day.

She flung the gray sack to the ground, but stopped short of stomping it. She snatched up the water buckets and headed for the well, chin high, but scanning the tall grass with each step. Whoever thought they could frighten her…good luck. She wasn't trembling. She was cold. But, it was seven a.m. and already eighty-two degrees.

At the pump, with a good view of the outhouse, she stopped and listened again. Was someone inside?

Something? Priming the pump, she listened. She opened the faucet. Water splashed the plastic, its pressure slapping the bottom and drowning out nearby sounds. She looked around, prepared.

With the first bucket full, she shut off the water and listened. A single drop fell from the pump, splashing against the bottom of the second bucket. She looked back at the outhouse, imagined herself walking toward it and throwing open the door. What would she find? A few herbs tied together and a dog's tooth. Enough. If she was going to be frightened, let it be over something real, something lethal like a knife or gun.

Or a rapist.

She opened the water again, watching the bucket fill. A black crow screeched as it swooped down over the path, its wings floating, rising close to her. She screamed and threw her arms up to protect her face. She inched her arms down. The bird was gone.

Home. Would she ever get used to it?

Chapter 8

Friday June 17, 2005
Lockport, LA

The Criminal Operations Center was ten miles west in Lockport. A white box of a building with a concrete parking lot. Government efficiency. The air-conditioning was running strong enough to freeze meat. Claire rubbed her bare arms, waiting her turn in line.

The receptionist behind the waist-high counter wore a sundress cut low enough to reveal a pair of flabby, sundried breasts. Over the dress, she wore a simple cotton sweater, the sleeves shoved up to her elbows. She pushed a paper at the man in front of Claire and leaned around him to make eye contact.

"Next."

"Claire Rivet," she said in her most professional voice. "I'd like to see Major Argrais."

She'd dressed in a narrow navy skirt and a sleeveless white blouse. She carried the leather bag she used as a briefcase, although today it contained only a blank legal pad and a sharpened pencil. This wasn't her jurisdiction so she had to tap every advantage to be taken seriously. She didn't mind. She knew the game and she was good at it. And unless Major Argrais was a total ass, he'd welcome her input into the case. Unfortunately, she'd met her fair share of total asses. In her experience, law enforcement was made up of three types: those who wanted to help, those who just needed a job, and the most dangerous, those who had something to prove.

Argrais would reveal himself soon enough.

The receptionist bent over a colorful pamphlet, a ballpoint pen poised between her fingers. "He's a busy man. What's this regarding?"

"I'm with the Baton Rouge District Attorney's Office." In truth, she'd taken a leave of absence, but who was going to check? Certainly not this woman.

The receptionist picked up the telephone receiver and spoke in a sweeter tone. "Major, a Ms. Rivet here to see you from the Baton Rouge DA's Office."

Her head bobbed as if she were listening to music on the other end. Her attention remained on the pamphlet. She giggled before putting down the receiver.

"He'll be right up," she said dryly.

A row of plastic chairs lined the painted cinderblock wall. Claire meandered back to them, but as she thought about sitting, an athletic-looking man called to her.

"Ms. Rivet." He held out a hand, his starched shirtsleeves rolled halfway up his arm. "How pleased to meet you. I'm Major Argrais." Although older, early fifties at least, something in his stance reminded her of Vincent. "I've followed some of your cases. Please, come on back."

He led her down an ivory painted corridor lined with mustard-colored doors. Even his energetic step was reminiscent of Vincent's. Was this a preview of Vincent in fifteen years? She imagined his dark hair streaked with gray much like the Major's. *Not bad.*

The office was at the end of the corridor. A room with a view, if she counted the one-by-four-foot double-glassed indentation near the ceiling as a window.

The Major walked around a wooden desk that looked like the ones her grade school teachers had used. "Have a seat."

She picked up a framed photo of the Major, two boys of equal height, a younger girl with tight curls, and a determined-looking woman with short dark hair. "Your family?"

"It's a few years old. My boys are up at LSU now."

"Nice school, I went there." She set the frame down.

"Didn't I read you were from around here?"

"Villette."

"Villette?" He said with a rise in tone. "How did you get to LSU from Villette?"

At least he didn't try to hide his surprise. He knew well that all fifty-eight citizens of Villette lived so far beneath the poverty level they only surfaced during hurricane season. And as much as she disliked talking about her personal life, if she wanted information, she needed to create a bond with this man. She depended solely on what he wanted to share.

"My mother was well educated; she made sure her children were also. My younger brother and I received full scholarships to LSU."

"Is your brother a lawyer, too?"

"No. He died. But I have two older brothers living in the area. They run their own development company."

"I'm sorry for your loss." He paused, leaned forward placing his arms on the desk in front of him. "Knowing your reputation, I'm assuming you're here because of the rape and murder in Raceland. Does the M.O. match something you're working on?"

Right to business. Suited her, but because he was a decent sort, it made formulating a lie that much more difficult. "From what I've read in the newspaper, it does. I was wondering if you could tell me anything that wasn't printed?"

Information kept from the press helped weed out the crazies who randomly confessed to everything from running a stoplight to robbing a grocery store to committing murder in the first degree.

He wagged a tanned finger at her. "Why don't you tell me what you have that fits?"

Here was where things might get tricky. How to tell the truth without telling too much? "It's an old case, twenty-five years ago a ten-year-old girl was brutally raped and beaten and left to die in a field not far from where Ms. Bonaventure was found."

"How come I didn't come across it in the database?"

"Did you have a database back then?" She waited for the question to sink in. "Who knows how the records were kept."

"Sounds like a pedophile case. You say the girl was ten."

"Except my suspect was young also, eighteen at the time. Not everyone who has sex with a minor is a pedophile. I've spoken with several psychologists who work in the violent crimes domain and rather than a pedophile, I believe, from the information I've gained, that he was and is an opportunist, preying on the weaker."

In fact, she'd spent hours with psychologists, profiling the case and had learned that at ten, she'd most likely been Billy Ray's first victim or at the very most, his second. Violent tendencies may start early in life, but brutal rape was a symptom that usually manifested around the late teens, early twenties and after some type of inciting incident. She'd spent hours wondering what type of inciting event had caused Billy Ray to ruin her life.

"Who's your suspect?"

Now, her turn to withhold. The power-pitch. If she dropped the ball, he'd never respect her enough to tell her anything. "I'd rather not say until I have more evidence. I don't want to cloud your investigation with unnecessary information."

He reared in his chair and crossed his arms over his chest. The playfulness of his expression gave way to suspicion. He'd read about her. What did he think he knew?

And what did she know about him?

Not long ago, several of the southern parishes, Lafourche included, were riddled with corruption. The governor had used secret police, informants, and a lot of the taxpayers' money to clean house, but corruption was like a rusty car. You could sand and polish it shiny, but the rust always returned.

"My suspect's an important man in the region," she added. "Before I spread his name all over town, I need some concrete evidence. That's where I'm hoping you can help."

He tipped his head. "Understood. But now, you got my curiosity spinning."

He waited, his stare boring into her. She felt its pressure pushing in on her, egging her to comply. He was good. But she was a master at this maneuver. It worked on witnesses, too.

Enough.

"Was there any forensic evidence in the Bonaventure case?"

Argrais leaned forward again, placing his elbows on the desk. "The body's being autopsied today. Her attacker was strong. I can tell you that. Her face was smashed in and it looks like he used his fist to do it. Takes a pretty strong fist to break an orbital bone. Also the rape was violent. Anal tearing. Vaginal bruising. Some damage looks postmortem, but we won't know for sure until after the autopsy."

"Sick man beats a woman after she's dead?"

He nodded. "The only forensic evidence that looks promising was a couple of hairs, looks to be dog hairs. Ms. Bonaventure didn't own a dog."

"DNA?"

"No. Latex. He wore a condom."

"Calculated. Any leads?" As if Argrais would tell her after she'd refused to tell her suspect.

"There's a work/release facility not far from the site. I have a detective over there. We're also looking at people she knew. She worked in a diner over in Raceland. Just broke up with her boyfriend a few weeks back. Boyfriend was in a bar. Lots of witnesses. So anytime you want to tell me your suspect's name, I'm ready and willing to listen."

Would he be? In her experience, lawmen tended to stick together. DAs were treated better than the general public, but most officers still considered DAs on the outside of law enforcement. The one thing in her favor was that William Cobb wasn't yet a lawman. Five months to the November elections. And if that wasn't enough, Cobb's father could buy just about anybody. Even police.

"There's no DNA on the old case either." There, tit for tat. "My hope is to link some newer cases. When I've done that, I'll tell you his name and we'll try to match this case, see if he had an alibi for Tuesday night. You didn't come across any other similar M.O.s in that database of yours, did you?"

She knew his answer before she'd asked because she'd checked the database several times. But people talked, rumors circulated, and that was the real information she was after.

Argrais shook his head.

Was he holding back? Of course, he was.

Chapter 9

Friday June 17, 2005
New Orleans, LA

Claire stepped inside the New Orleans Library, her best bet for Internet access.

Three floors and ultra modern, light filled the building and she might have taken it for a business center but for the dry smoky scent of print. During her years as a law student, she'd fallen in love with that smell.

Signs pointed the way to a bay of computers. All but two were PCs. She first tried to read her office email, but she wasn't able to connect. Next, she tried the Internet icon to see if the problem was the computer or her lack of skill. The Internet opened with surprising speed.

Now what?

She spotted an information sign on a desk near the magazines. A woman with a pinched face, a straight back, and a striking resemblance to her third grade teacher sat behind the desk, her chin jutted forward.

"Excuse me. I've been trying to log on to my email account, but it's not working. Is there someone who could help me?"

The woman looked back to the terminal. She touched something on the screen that Claire couldn't see.

Claire waited. She glanced again at the silver aluminum plaque that read "Information Desk."

Should she ask again? Was she interrupting? Patience, she reminded herself. But she had work to do, a violent rapist, a murderer to catch. The clerk, with the speed of a slug, typed one-handedly still pointing to the screen.

As Claire started to speak, the clerk said something.

Claire feigned a smile. "I'm sorry, what did you say?"

"Over there." The clerk pitched her head. "In the brown shirt, Marshall. He can help you."

Marshall, tall with milk chocolate skin, drooped. His eyes drooped, his shoulders drooped, his polo shirt drooped, even his lips hung down at the corners, creating a droopy jowl. But as Claire approached him, another word came to her mind. Mulatto. A label people used with the same hatred they used for "white trash."

White trash. Those words again. They'd shadowed her from the moment she'd returned to Villette. She couldn't shake them loose. Reminders were everywhere—Ma's house with the few worn pieces of furniture, the garden overrun with pokeweed, the nearest grocery twenty miles away, the nearest phone, ten.

"Excuse me, the woman at the desk said you could help me with the computers."

Without looking at her Marshall nodded and placed his magazine back on the rack. He slogged over to the computer bay.

"I've tried accessing my office email, but I kept getting an error message. I seem to remember I need a code or something."

He pointed to the keyboard without a word. She sat and retyped the address. When the error message appeared, he leaned over her shoulder to read the screen.

"Server IP address. Yep. Looks like there's a firewall. You won't be able to read it remotely."

"But others from my office access theirs remotely."

"Their accounts have a different setup that allows them access. Call your IT guy and have your account parameters changed."

Right. With resources stretched thin, all the government offices shared the same IT facilities. Changing anything, even a password, was a harrowing, time consuming experience. "Is there something else I can do? I need to receive communications while I'm in the area. I don't have phone reception where I'm staying so I can't get messages."

"Best thing, set up a temporary account on one of the free servers. When you leave, delete it."

"How does a temporary account work?"

"You get a bunch of advertisements, but if that doesn't bother you..." He flicked his hand at the screen. "Many of them have good filter systems now anyhow."

"Can you show me how to set one up?"

He dragged a chair across the rug and sat next to her. He started typing. She liked the idea—temporary email. It would make a great response network for her inquiries. She could go to online message boards and direct all communications back to an email site that she could delete once she had the information she wanted. The best part—no one at her office would have access to it.

Marshall showed her how to set up a Hotmail account. After he left, she first searched the Internet for the "Cobb" name plus the word "Louisiana." Way too many entries popped up: Cobb county, Cobb.com, Cobb Bar Web page, Cobb Institute of Archaeology and Cobb International.

Cobb senior ran a conglomerate for several oil refineries, she selected Cobb International. William's name wasn't listed anywhere in the website. She did another search for William Cobb.

Blue Belt Contracting's website.

She clicked it open and the homepage filled the screen, a picture of William Cobb in the upper left hand corner. His lips curved, but rather than smiling it almost looked like he was sneering. *Fitting.* His colorless eyes were small and deep-set, overshadowed by thick blond eyebrows. He didn't look particularly smart, but he didn't look like you could pull the wool over him either.

She sent the photo to the library's printer.

A highlighted tab under a list of Blue Belt's recent construction projects read, "About our CEO." She clicked open the tab.

William Cobb. Born in Thibodaux, Louisiana in 1963. Grew up in Raceland. Attended Tulane University, but graduated in 1985 from Nicholls University. *Interesting.*

Tulane was an expensive private school, Nicholls, a state school. Why had he downgraded? She scribbled a note.

He married Marlene Rutherford and moved to Houma, Louisiana to start a family. *Quaint.* Two boys, Marc and Mathieu.

She thought about what kind of father he'd make. What good could he possibly instill in those boys? What bad? She didn't want to go there. Instead, she looked back to the website.

Last bit. Current address: New Orleans where he was running for Criminal Sheriff of Orleans Parish.

Not much. She needed to hire a private detective, someone who could do the grunt work while she looked for other victims of Cobb's rage.

She logged onto Tulane's homepage and found an online magazine. An op-ed page offered a format for entering short submissions. She typed up a piece about an ex-Tulane student now running for sheriff and sent it. Would the magazine print it? And if they did, what was she hoping it might generate? The piece was too general. She needed to touch that one person who had information she could use, yet she must not slander. She wanted Billy Ray in court, but not because he was suing her.

Another search turned up message boards on different subjects. She selected a political board and posted just enough information about Cobb to start a discussion. If the discussion bore fruit, she'd add more information or direct inquiries. A long shot because there wouldn't be any students who remembered Billy Ray, but maybe a professor, or an administration clerk.

She checked the alumni page. He wasn't listed. She checked for Marlene Rutherford and found that she used the name of Marla and had graduated in 1985.

His wife was a Tulane alumni, but not Cobb. How did that sit with the big man? She found the white pages website and did a search for Marla Cobb in Orleans Parish. The search came up empty. The phone number could be listed under William's name. Even so, she did a second search in Lafourche Parish. Marla Cobb in Houma popped up. Either an old address or Cobb was living in New Orleans and his wife was living in Houma. She jotted down the number.

She closed her notebook. The online message boards gave her another idea, a way to reach the computer illiterates who comprised most of the people she knew. Southern Louisiana where change came as slowly as a caterpillar crossing a six-lane highway.

* * *

Around the corner from the library, she found a print shop. The clerk had his head in a comic book.

"I'd like to have a flyer made. Can you do that here?"

The boy leaped up as if she'd called him to attention. He was well over six feet and way too skinny. "Yeah, we do that. How big and what you want on it?"

Good question. She dropped her briefcase on a desk and popped it open. She took out the copy of Billy Ray's photo from Blue Belt's webpage. "I want normal paper size. She pointed to a stack of multicolored paper. "Like those." She handed him the copy. "How about this photo and some text?"

"Looks good. You want me to print it up on the computer?"

Printed would look better than handwritten. "Will it take long?"

"No. I just scan this picture and type out what you want on the side."

"Okay. Put the photo in the upper half and I'll write out some lines for you to type underneath." She took out the legal pad.

The scanner's electronic starts and stops acted as a metronome as she wrote line after line, scratching out two and adding one more. "Okay, I'm done." But she read over the text one more time.

What she'd written, requesting any information on the nominated sheriff, read more like a political smear campaign than a query for information. Who was William Cobb? Why should he earn our vote? The questions would generate political replies, but if only one of his victims responded, she could build a case, two would guarantee her a victory.

She stood next to the clerk as he typed her words into the computer. Billy Ray's frightening grin looked back at her from the screen.

"A hundred copies. Multi-colored paper. Black ink. That right?" The boy asked, his finger poised over a key on the keypad.

"Sounds good."

"Here goes." The clerk hit the key, then rolled his chair back from the computer almost hitting her.

Since Ma's house didn't have a telephone, she directed all inquiries either to her new email address, or to Ma's post office box in Larose.

Another long shot and patience wasn't one of her virtues. Come to think of it, did she even have any virtues?

* * *

Claire spent the next hour posting flyers on lamp poles around New Orleans. When she reached her car, she plugged her cell phone into the lighter socket. Without electricity at the house, the car was the only place to recharge the battery and she wanted to call Marla Cobb.

The hour drive from New Orleans to Larose was peaceful compared to the Larose post office. Friday was payday. It looked as if half the parish was crammed into the long but narrow office. The folks in line were cranky and smelled like a week's worth of hard labor. Several complained about the lack of air-conditioning and the two postal clerks looked ready to throw everyone out.

To reach the bulletin board, Claire squeezed between a fisherman who hadn't showered in a long, long time and a squat gray-haired woman missing her front teeth.

A clipboard of America's Most Wanted was nailed to the upper left corner. Any other time, Claire would have read the posters for every detail, but not today.

Next to a "Pickup for Sale" flyer and another for a missing twelve-year-old, she tacked her own notice—an eight-and-a-half-by-eleven yellow paper with William Cobb's feral smile. Who could look at that face and want to give the man a badge?

"Isn't that the guy running for sheriff?"

Driving in the pushpin, Claire glanced over her shoulder. "That's him." Was it possible she'd already come across someone who knew Cobb?

The woman was older and African-American. Her face was round; her skin darker than most. She was dressed in a long, pastel skirt and a bright blue peasant blouse. A beaded turban wrapped her head.

"Do you know him?" Claire asked.

The woman laughed with a voice surprisingly deep for her thin frame. The sound sent a tremor through Claire, then a memory, a vague impression like a dream washed over her and quickly disappeared.

"I've heard he's a very, very bad man, but I don't know him. I don't know any bad men." The woman laughed again, not so deeply the second time.

Claire found the woman's behavior strange. Maybe she was looking for attention. The loneliness of bayou country plagued those who weren't used to it, and the woman had an accent, familiar yet neither the local Creole nor Cajun.

"Where are you from?" Claire asked, noticing the woman's exotic perfume, a scent of musk and mangoes and a touch of sweet jasmine.

An amulet, gold like the chain that held it in place, bobbed between the woman's ample breasts. A delicate clasp hinted at interior contents, but what held Claire's gaze were the two female images carved into the metal: one resembled the Virgin Mary, delicate in form with hands held in prayer, the other looked to be a monster with sharp teeth and claws curled to attack.

The woman noticed her fixation and raised a hand to the amulet.

"I was born in Haiti. Ma mère gave me this the day I left." She massaged the amulet between long, thin fingers.

French, yes, of course, Ma's accent, although a more musical variation of it.

Claire glanced back at the flyer. "Who told you the man was bad?"

"I hear things. Here and there."

The woman's reply became garbled among a deluge of images in Claire's mind. Forgotten words, hanging on the edge of thought. She touched her forehead as if to wrestle the faint images into a memory. A dream? Déjà vu?

A wave of nausea washed over her. She shoved through the human mass for the door, her balance unsteady the first few steps.

"I knew your mamma," the strange woman said.

What was going on? Stopping in the doorway, Claire turned to find the woman too close for comfort. "What did you say?"

"I knew her from Notre Dame. We did charity work together."

Notre Dame de Grâce. The family church. Every Sunday, she, Ma, and her brothers would pile into the skiff and meander through the bayous down to Larose for an hour of prayers and forgiveness. "You must have me confused with someone else. My mother's been dead a long time."

"I was at her funeral."

Claire stepped outside, the hot air less refreshing than she'd hoped.

The woman followed her out. "She spoke about you all the time, you know. Told me you're a fancy lawyer up in Baton Rouge."

That strange feeling flared again. Claire's instincts told her to get as far from this woman as her feet would take her. But why? Where was this conflict coming from?

What had spooked her? The singsong Haitian accent?

She took a step back. Ma had died while she was still in school, more than a year before she'd passed the bar exam. How did the woman know she was a lawyer?

Perhaps an error of speech, an assumption. But a more likely scenario, one that wasn't the least bit frightening, was that she'd tried several newsworthy cases and the old woman recognized her from a newspaper article. She probably wanted something like money or free legal advice.

She faced the woman. Despite the strange jewelry and beaded turban, the woman's eyes were clear, intelligent, and blacker than Claire had ever seen. They stayed fixed on her, as if studying her.

The woman smiled in a way that wasn't quite a smile, but a communication.

Claire relaxed. Country people, simple with simple needs. Eccentric, maybe, but simple. No reason to get her back up. Down here she needed to let go of her courtroom mentality, needed to stop doubting and looking for double meanings. She needed to remember the goodness Ma had taught her. Ha, goodness—who had time for goodness? She had a rapist to catch.

"Excuse me, but—"

"Yes, Catherine was a good woman. Everyone loved her."

The use of her mother's Christian name seemed desperate. But, she couldn't just walk away, not from a friend of Ma's.

"It's nice to meet you, Madame…" She knew a little French, what little Ma had taught her. She held her hand out to the woman, who took it in hers, but instead of shaking it, she turned it over and caressed the palm.

"Folks calls me Mamma Anna," she said with a sudden Creole dialect. She looked into the palm.

Claire pulled her hand away, held it against her heart, and started to walk. The woman gave her the creeps. She knew things, but then she didn't. She spoke perfect, though accented, English, but then switched to a Creole dialect.

Yet hadn't Claire done the same thing with Philippe—fallen into a dialect more comfortable? What was so unusual about that? Why did this woman bother her so?

She had approached her using Ma's name. When that hadn't worked, she'd tried the Creole, a more casual laid-back approach as if to seduce her. Oh, the woman wanted something.

Quickly, Claire reviewed their conversation. The woman had known Billy Ray. She'd known Ma. Was this about Billy Ray? Did she have information? *Wishful thinking.* What then? Ma? Law school?

"Will I see you in church Sunday? We'll light a candle for your mamma." Mamma Anna had dropped the Creole and spoke as before.

Claire stopped walking and glanced at the amulet again. Her discomfort was centered there in the contrasting images. With her friendliness and kind words, Mamma Anna radiated the goodness of the Virgin, but with her vagueness and multi-accents, she exuded the malevolence of the demon.

And then there were the other images, the ones trying to break through Claire's memories as if she somehow knew this woman, which was not possible. "I'm afraid I'm not much of a believer anymore."

"All the more reason to go to church. Where else can you find the answers to human suffering?"

"Are you implying I'm suffering?"

The woman remained silent, walking along the sidewalk beside her.

"Listen." Claire stopped again. She'd reached her car. "I'm sorry, but I have to go. Perhaps—" She turned.

Mamma Anna was gone.

Claire bent and glanced inside the row of parked cars. She walked back to the post office and peered inside, but the line had dwindled to two men and the clerks waved her out the door. They were closing.

She walked back to her car. No sign of the old woman.

Tricks to create suspense. Oh, the woman wanted something or, maybe, knew something. She was teasing her, manipulating her. Well, it wouldn't work. She refused to be manipulated.

Isn't that the guy who's running for sheriff?

Okay, it would work. She'd do whatever it took to get information on Billy Ray. If the old woman was a lead, she'd follow it, even to church.

Chapter 10

Friday June 17, 2005
New Orleans, LA

Billy Ray stacked the last of the file folders against the empty wall under the window. He hated moving almost as much as he hated his ex-wife, but the new offices sure were nice even if they smelled of wet paint. He ran his sleeve over the top of the dark walnut desk. Spotless. Classical in style, massive in size, and looking the way a sheriff's desk ought to. He 'specially liked the two-tone brown and those finely carved drawers. Made him look so-phis-tee-cated. Oh, yeah.

He brushed off his sleeve. It sure looked nicer than his daddy's desk.

The gruff voice of his assistant announced his first guest over the intercom. Billy Ray snatched his jacket off the high-backed chair and slipped it on.

He straightened, sucked in his stomach, and puffed out his chest. This made him taller than his old football buddy, but the posture wasn't necessary. Charlie had put on fifty pounds since college, had one of those bellies that hung down over his belt. Most of his buddies did these days—all that loose living. Not Billy Ray though. He slapped his stomach. Rock-solid. Big boned, but helluva good stock.

Charlie swaggered through the door, a box tucked under his arm and a briefcase in hand.

Billy Ray reached out his hand to shake, forgetting about the bandage, discolored and unraveling. "Good to see you."

Charlie paused mid-grip. "Whoa boy, you been sniffing around some married lady again?"

Billy Ray pulled back the hand and slapped Charlie on the back. "Had me a foreman too big for his britches. Sit over here. We can catch up a bit before the others get here."

Charlie spun around. "So these are the new digs, huh. Still has that new car smell."

"What do you think? Furniture was supposed to be here two days ago. Got me a sofa going in there." Billy Ray pointed to the empty back wall. "And a couple of real nice chairs for here." He pointed to the front of the desk where five hardwood chairs were in a half-circle. "These here chairs go in the conference room. Got the chairs, but no table yet. Wish I could've postponed this meeting till next week, but the mayor's calendar's booked solid. What you got there?"

Charlie set the briefcase on the floor and opened the box. "Cigars. Want one?"

Billy Ray peered in and picked one, rolling it between his thumb and finger. He held it under his nose and inhaled the strong pungent smell. "You scoundrel, you been making those midnight runs to Cuba again. I thought the Feds sunk your boat."

"Got me a new one." Charlie grinned. "Thought the mayor might like one of these beauties."

"You a simpleton or what? You planning to offer the mayor an illegal cigar in my office? Please, Charlie. I'm running for Criminal Sheriff here. If I got criminals for friends, how am I ever going to get elected?" He shoved the cigar into his top drawer.

"What you worried about? The job's yours, hands down. The mayor's kissing your bootstraps."

"He ain't kissing nothing yet. He wants the old man's Washington contacts for this wetlands project. Without those, he'd back the old sheriff all the way to next year. After all, he helped put the codger in office. Now, get those things out of sight. We'll smoke one after everyone clears out."

Charlie closed the box and slid it into his briefcase. "So you still going out to the construction sites?"

"Sure. Like to keep my hands in it." Billy Ray waved both his bandaged hands in the air. Charlie laughed at the joke.

The office door opened and a tall, slender man wearing wire-rimmed glasses paused there.

"Robert. Hey, there. Come on in, come in." Billy Ray noticed the man's hesitation. "Robert Juneau, this here's Charlie Dill. Robert's the head of the Sierra Club."

"The Delta chapter," Robert corrected and shook Charlie's hand.

"Charlie's an old football buddy of mine. You ever play football?" Taking in Robert's slight build, he realized the impossibility. "Nope, guess not. Charlie's representing the Lake Pontchartrain Basin Foundation so you guys— Hey there, come on in, fellas. Come in and take a seat. Sorry about the lack of proper furniture, new offices and all."

Two other men in summer suits walked through the doorway. Each started to shake hands with Billy Ray, but pulled back rather than clasp the bandages. Billy Ray ignored their hesitation and continued the introductions. "Glen here's with the Environmental Defense Fund and Barry's with the Louisiana Audubon Council. We're just waiting on the big man hisself and I think I heard the outside door."

Billy Ray strutted to his office door as Mayor Moreau stepped in. It always surprised him how tiny the mayor was in person. Looked like a flyswatter could squash the little bug. "Glad you could make it, Mr. Mayor. Come on in." He shook the mayor's hand, ignoring his pain.

As the others made their introductions to the mayor, Billy Ray dragged his high-backed chair around to the side of the desk. "Mr. Mayor, why don't you sit here?"

"Why thank you, Mr. Cobb."

"Call me William." Billy Ray cut his glance to Charlie. He'd forgotten to remind him to use William in front of these fancy pants.

Billy Ray pulled one of the chairs closer to the mayor and sat. He didn't mind giving up his chair to the mayor, but damn if he'd let the man sit behind his shiny, new desk. He'd done enough ass-lickin' for one day. Here he was hosting this shindig, getting all these men behind the mayor's wetlands restoration project. *Restoring the wetlands.* What a stupid idea. One good hurricane passes through and it's all history. But the mayor had made clear what he expected; this project was his ticket to a senate nomination.

If Billy Ray gave the mayor what he wanted, the mayor would give Billy Ray what he wanted. *Politics.* Hell, any idiot could do it.

"Mr. Mayor, you want to start?" Billy Ray asked.

The mayor stood. "First, I want to thank you all for coming. This project's been taking longer to get off the ground than I had anticipated. As you know, the lawsuit fighting the logging around Lake Maurepas cut our funds considerably, but it has drawn national attention from allies like the Sierra Club." The mayor nodded at Robert. "And the EPA, and other environmental groups that can help us raise money and support for the restoration. Mr. Cobb, William, has been instrumental in attracting some Washington brass. I learned earlier this morning that a federal coalition has been formed to study the financial needs of the coastal restoration project. I can't tell you what this means to Louisiana."

70

The mayor put his hand on Billy Ray's shoulder. He didn't squeeze or pat, just left it lying there like a wet bass.

The mayor continued. "The leader of the coalition is a representative from North Carolina. She's called the 'green thumb' because of her support of environmental issues. She'll get us our fourteen million dollars."

"Do you think the Federal government will deliver the whole sum or will we need to raise part of it?" Charlie asked.

"We're hoping the Feds will give us what we need," Mayor Moreau said, removing his hand from Billy Ray. "But in the end it will be the coalition's decision. I'm glad to count you and your organizations as supporters in this monumental effort. Also, we appreciate Mr. Cobb's time and efforts on this matter and his dedication to this great state."

Everyone applauded.

Billy Ray held up a hand, the ragged end of the worn bandage dangling down past his wrist. He brought down the eyesore, tucking the loose piece into his cuff. "Now, now. Restoring the wetlands is important to us all. Like you fellas, I want the best for my community." Actually, he just wanted to be sheriff. Who cared about a bunch of worthless swamps and bothersome birds? Fourteen million, indeed. What a waste of money.

"So that's where the project stands today," Mayor Moreau said. "A lot farther along than last month, and we're real happy to have the Audubon Council and the Sierra Club represented here today. If there aren't any questions, I suggest we meet again next month, after the Washington coalition has studied the project. And by the way, someone from the coalition might be calling your offices for more data."

"Over at the EDF, we're getting a lot of flak about the levees," Glen said. "Many think they need replacing or, at the very least, reinforcing before we deal with the wetlands. There's worry that if a big storm hits the coast, New Orleans would be wiped off the map."

"I've read the US Army Corps of Engineers' report," Barry said. "The levees are sound enough for now. Let me remind you that it takes sixty odd years for a hardwood to mature. If we don't start reseeding the coastline to push back the saltwater intrusion, we'll not only lose the delicate ecosystem of our coast, but several parishes will be looking at a bleak future."

Robert raised his hand as if he were still in grade school. "If Washington appropriates the money, how long will it take to get the restoration project up and running?"

The mayor stood and stepped around Billy Ray's chair. "We foresee a two-month delay if the money arrives within this calendar year. We've already agreed on bids from subcontractors, but some of those bids run out December thirty-first."

"Glen's right, there's a lot of pressure to repair and reinforce the levees," Charlie said. "If this goes to a vote, I'm afraid the levees might win."

"Hell, the levees will last till we're long gone," Billy Ray said. "It won't go to a vote. That's the word coming down directly from Washington."

The room fell silent as they thought about what he'd said. If they didn't know, they must suspect the extent of Randolph Cobb's Washington connections. Billy Ray's ace in the hole. Only Charlie knew how little he actually saw the old man. Couldn't stand the sight of him, really.

Glen broke the stalemate. "Any other glaring problems? Anything to slow us down?"

The mayor returned to his seat. He paused, stroking his chin before answering. "Like I mentioned earlier, that logging lawsuit has turned the nation's eyes toward us. This problem is bigger than Louisiana. With the November elections coming and the national frustration with the EPA, Washington will be falling over itself to save the wetlands and all the natural animal habitats." His gaze traveled from man to man. "Anything else?"

Everyone applauded. The mayor leaned on the massive desk and faced Billy Ray. "Should we meet back here in your office then?"

"Whatever's convenient for you, sir."

The mayor left first. After more handshaking, only Billy Ray and Charlie were left standing.

"The mayor meets at your office," Charlie said, removing a cigar and cutter from his jacket. "How do you rate?"

Billy Ray pulled his chair back around the desk and opened the top drawer. He grabbed his cigar. "The mayor needs to be seen with me. It cements his support of me for sheriff. That's part of the deal."

"How'd you swing it?"

"Fourteen mill's a lot of money, my friend."

Charlie held the lighter across the desk. "That it is. How's the old man, by the way?"

Billy Ray lowered the cigar. "What do you care about the old man? He got your pocket too?"

"Don't tell me you two are still feuding?"

Billy Ray handed the cigar back to Charlie. "Take your damn cigar. I don't want any part of you if you're dealing with the old man." Billy Ray puffed out his chest and put his hands on his hips.

"Don't be like that. Take the cigar. We're both on the hospital board, is all. He rarely shows for the meetings. I swear. Now take this and enjoy it, damn it."

Billy Ray looked his friend over. Everyone wanted Randolph Cobb's ear if they could get it, but Billy Ray doubted the man would give Charlie the time of day. He snatched back the cigar. He leaned forward to let Charlie light it.

When the light took, he removed the cigar and took a whiff of the smoke twirling off the end. "I can't stand the bastard. Man hands out his money like business cards, but he won't give me a dime. Look at this place." Billy Ray gestured with the lit cuban. "Blue Belt was built by me, from the ground up. Not one penny from the old fart. Only thing he gave me was a four-by-six office, which I outgrew in three months. Hell, there wasn't even room for a secretary."

"He probably wanted to build your character. You know how it is with kids. You got boys."

"Yeah, and he's turned them against me, too."

Charlie leaned back and Billy Ray propped an elbow on his desktop. They puffed on their cigars.

In the silence, Billy Ray thought about his father. He couldn't remember a time when he'd liked the man. But his money and his name had to be tolerated. That's the way it was with family.

As if reading his thoughts Charlie asked, "Didn't the old man get you the sheriff's nomination? And what about using his contacts in Washington?"

"He did just about nothing. I'm not stupid, you know. I've spent enough time around him to see how things work. He wants his name on the restoration project so he found some bleeding liberal to head the coalition. I told him I'd stay with the project, make sure he got the credit he deserves. Then, I went to the mayor and negotiated the sheriff nomination. Moreau wants the restoration project bad, thinks it's his senatorial ticket. So yeah, the old man helped with the nomination. He just doesn't know it."

He inhaled the cigar, remembering his discussion with the mayor. Moreau hadn't wanted to give the endorsement, but in the end, had crumpled for a bunch of smelly swamps.

Now, the election was a different rooster. It'd be up to him to bring it home, but he didn't foresee a problem. Another thing the old man had given him was the Cobb name and he was going to work it like it had never been worked before.

Chapter 11

Saturday June 18, 2005
Villette, LA

Marla Cobb sounded like a first class pain-in-the-butt. But
she had agreed to talk. Claire thought about their phone
conversation as she plugged the car charger back into the cell
phone. When she'd said she was with the DA's office had
Marla actually laughed? And the woman had been quick to
correct her—William Cobb was her ex-husband. All the
better. A woman scorned had more to say than one protecting
her family.

Claire started the car.

The drive west to Terrebonne Parish took twenty minutes
from Villette, fifteen to Houma and another five to find the
address among the sprawling family estates. Looked like
Marla must have received the house in the divorce.

A spread-out mix of ancient oaks formed a natural barrier
between the house and road. Claire turned into the alley of
sheltering oaks and followed the drive to an antebellum
plantation house, pastel blue with white trim. Groomed
flower gardens lined a darker blue porch, which stretched the
length of the house.

Roses scented the walk as Claire climbed the porch steps.

A thin woman with frosted hair, piled high on her head,
answered the door. She wore a floral linen dress, which
floated around her boyish figure. "Miss Rivet, I bet. I'm
Marla Cobb."

Claire recognized the affected speech pattern, one she
heard often in the state capital. It belonged to the southern

wives who believed the South had won the Civil War and their politician husbands were now royalty.

Claire offered her hand. Marla barely squeezed her fingertips with a light, cold grip.

"Please, do come inside."

The willowy Marla led her into a beige living room where the only color came from a few antique pieces.

Marla motioned to the shiny beige sofa. "Please."

"Thank you for agreeing to see me."

Marla swatted at the air as if swatting a fly. "I must say, you incited my curiosity. Would you like some ice tea? It's dreadfully hot today."

"That would be nice, thank you."

Marla reached for a palm-sized walkie-talkie and asked for two ice teas. The new South. She placed the walkie-talkie on the coffee table between them. Her movements were delicate, yet deliberate.

"Lovely house you have."

Marla held up a finger to stop conversation as a young black woman dressed in a starched, white cotton dress walked in with two ice teas and a bowl of sugar cubes on a tray. She placed the tray on the coffee table and rushed out.

"Sugar?"

"No thanks." Claire took the tall glass Marla offered and leaned back into the sofa, the satiny fabric cool against her bare arms.

"Now, why would someone out of the state capital be interested in William, pray tell?"

"We're interested in all the candidates." The lie rolled so easily off her lips it surprised her, but she couldn't very well tell Mrs. Cobb that she planned to put her ex-husband behind bars for a very long time.

Marla looked at her forgivingly. Claire sensed the woman might be smarter than her *grande dame* façade. She didn't look as if she would give up anything she didn't want to, but on the other hand, she had agreed to meet. Just how much did she know about her husband's ruthlessness and how much was she willing to share? From experience, Claire knew that the wives of serial sex offenders were often the last to know, although they knew something. The wives were the first to say they sensed something was off, nothing they could pinpoint, but something not just right.

During the drive over, Claire had practiced questions that might fit a general investigation and open Marla to talking. Time to work it. "With Mr. Cobb running for Criminal Sheriff, we must make sure he hasn't previously participated in any criminal activity. I'm sure you understand."

Marla laughed a breathy laugh. "Randolph doesn't make those kinds of mistakes."

"Randolph?"

"William's father. Randolph Cobb, surely you've heard of him."

Claire nodded. Why would she invoke the father? "Are you insinuating there is criminal activity? Is Randolph involved?"

"Absolutely not." Her words said one thing, her expression of distaste and boredom said another. "Who else have you interviewed?"

"I'm just getting started. Is there anyone you think I should talk to?"

Marla shook her head then said "Charlie, maybe. He's a childhood friend, but he won't say a word against William, loyal to the bone."

The problem with lying was that the conversation didn't flow naturally and with the physical cues Marla was giving off, Claire had to be careful to stay in character. Unsure how to proceed, she tried another line of questions. "I saw that you graduated from Tulane in eighty-five."

Marla smiled genteelly. "That was years ago."

"Did you meet William at Tulane?"

"No, dear, I'm a Rutherford, of the South Carolina Rutherfords."

The lineage. She was surprised it hadn't been served up before now. As if she cared. She waited for Marla to say more. She didn't. Instead, Marla sipped her ice tea, watching from the rim of the glass as if to say, *score one for me*.

Now what? The woman appeared amused that the state government was investigating her ex-husband, but on the other hand, she hadn't said anything positive or negative about him. Maybe she just enjoyed holding others in contempt. Claire'd met women like that in the capital, too.

Claire could play the game. She reached for her tea. The afternoon sun sliced a path to the fireplace mantel where a Chinese vase was on display. The blue of the thin-lined figures etched on the porcelain surface stood out against the overwhelming beige. All pretense. The attitude. The...things.

But she took no satisfaction in knowing how this fabricated world was about to crumble at Marla's feet. Where would the woman's pretense be when Billy Ray was exposed? Would her friends gather around in sympathy or avoid her like a rabid dog?

When Marla finally placed her glass on the tray, the belittling downturned lip was gone. "My father knew Randolph Cobb so when I enrolled in Tulane, Randolph introduced me to William."

"But William graduated from Nicholls, not Tulane. How come?"

"William was a big football hero at Tulane. Unfortunately, that didn't leave him much time for studying."

"He flunked out?"

"Oh, big scandal. Not really his fault though. When he was expelled, the football coach went ballistic, Randolph went ballistic, a teacher was fired. What a mess." She folded her hands in her lap.

"He transferred to Nicholls?"

"Randolph paid a small fortune to the school first, a donation, I believe he called it. Hired a tutor and put an end to William's football."

"What attracted you to him?"

"Rather personal, isn't it?"

"Is it? I'm sorry."

Marla snickered at Claire's discomfort, then drew in a deep breath and glanced away as if she were looking into the past.

Claire wondered what the woman was remembering. Billy Ray was a monster. Could anyone really have loved him?

Marla spoke. "Randolph. The man's a dynamo. I figured William would end up just like him once he matured. Like father, like son and all that. When Randolph came to me…he wanted William settled, you see. I think he was afraid William was one of those funny boys." Marla cut her eyes in Claire's direction. "Never came right out and said it, so don't you go spreading any gossip, now." Her voice was tinged with amusement as if that was exactly what she hoped Claire would do.

"Anyway, the old man talked me into marrying." She reached for her tea. "You can't tell it now, but back then, I was a young beauty, had plenty of suitors. Marriage was the last thing I'd planned on."

Claire was getting nothing, but she had to let Marla do the revealing, otherwise the woman might shut down and close her out. "Why, you're still a very beautiful woman," Claire said as duty demanded, although she found the woman too thin and stuck in the "old South" time warp. "I understand you have two boys?"

Marla nodded. "Mathieu and Marc. Both teens now."

"Are they around?"

"Mathieu's out and about. I'm afraid he's like his father, that one. Marc's more serious. He's spending some time at his grandparents."

Like his father? Another rapist? "How is Mathieu like his father?"

"Always busy, lots to do, here, there. Can't keep still."

"Ah. Does William see the boys often?"

"Oh, sure. He's busy with his campaigning these days, though."

"How do you feel about his running for sheriff?"

"A perfect job for him." The words rolled off her tongue without the slightest hesitation. Too easily.

"How do you mean?"

"You don't know William, do you? If you did, you'd understand why it's perfect for him."

"What about Cobb International? Randolph must be getting on in years. Won't William be expected to take over?"

"Ha." Marla caught herself and drew in her emotions, her embarrassment apparent. "William will never run Cobb International. He's…how can I say…interested in other things."

"Like what?"

Marla huffed. "Oh, I don't know. Randolph wouldn't want him to take over anyway. They've never been what you'd call close."

Sweat tickled the base of Claire's spine. She felt Marla wanted to say something more, but protocol was holding her back. If she could steer the woman in the right direction…but what direction?

"I'm a little confused. Who'll run Cobb International? William is an only child, isn't he?"

"There was a sister too, but she died early on." Marla trailed the sweat on her glass with one finger. "Randolph's grooming my boys to take over."

"I don't remember reading anything about a sister. What was her name?"

Marla offered her an exaggerated look of boredom. "I don't remember her proper name. Whenever anyone mentioned her, and that was rarely, they called her Bunny."

"You and Randolph seem very close."

Marla smiled, and something in her expression went unsaid. Claire pushed on. "How does William feel about the boys running his father's company?"

Again the bored look. Or was it exasperation? "You don't understand, do you? William doesn't like business. He's more…physical. He loves running Blue Belt because construction is a rough and tough world. The company finances are handled by someone else entirely."

Where was this attitude coming from? Claire sensed a deeper spring that she was unable to tap. Marla wanted to tell her something, but she wasn't asking the right questions. Even so, she'd been forthcoming so far.

Claire removed a notebook from her handbag and jotted "Bunny" on an empty page and Charlie right below. "What's Charlie's last name?"

"Dill. Has a place outside Thibodaux."

Claire added the information to the notebook. "You said on the telephone that you've been divorced seven years."

"That's right."

"Was this the family home before the divorce?"

"Yes. A wedding present from father."

Some present, Claire thought. Marla came from money, too, so she hadn't married Cobb as a step up. Her father was a friend of Randolph.

"Did Randolph figure into your divorce?"

Marla forced a frown. "Whatever are you talking about?"

Claire waited, hoping to draw the woman out. Marla sounded overly fond of her father-in-law, leaving the unasked question of whether Mathieu and Marc belonged to William or Randolph. Might be a reason for divorce.

"Sounds to me as if you *are* looking for gossip." Marla smiled, her head tilted playfully to one side.

"I assure you, I'm not. Nothing you say will be made public."

Marla put her tea down, but then picked it right back up.

"Nothing?" She sipped, paused, and sipped some more. Her forehead wrinkled for an instant then smoothed back into the veil of civility. "South Carolina's big fishing country. As a child I remember father catching some sort of fish, had those squiggly fins on it." She wiggled her fingers and scrunched her nose. "Well, he asked me to take the stupid thing off the hook for him and I did, but one of those fins jabbed down into my palm. Hurt like the dickens. I dropped the fish right there on the sand. We had a bucket full of water that we were putting the catch into. But that fish flipped and flopped, rolled and hopped all over the place and I couldn't grab it to get it into the bucket. All it wanted was to get into that water, but it did everything to make that impossible."

Was Marla telling her that she was the fish, flipping and flopping, but not asking what she wanted to ask? "I love South Carolina. Such a beautiful state. You must miss it."

"Oh, I do. But my life is here now with my boys and my…friends." She smiled almost genuinely for the first time.

"I can tell you're a smart woman, a graduate of Tulane, South Carolina royalty, so if your *ex*-husband was involved in anything illegal I don't think you'd put up with it." She emphasized *ex* to egg on Marla. "Do you know of any illegal activities that your *ex*-husband may have participated in?"

Marla shook her head, her eyes downcast. "This *is* getting tiresome."

Flunked out. More physical. And the remark about Randolph. What was she not saying? "Was William ever abusive?"

Marla's head popped up.

That was it. She couldn't think of another question to make the woman talk so she turned on the D.A. stare, known to make the most dishonest criminal babble. Eyes to eyes she pushed her will on Marla. To her credit Marla pushed back, before finally giving in.

"You'll never find those records. Randolph took care of them," Marla said as if Claire already knew what she was talking about.

Think fast. Abuse. Records. "William hit you? You had him arrested?"

"I signed on to be a Cobb, nothing else." She put her empty glass back on the tray. "When things got rough, I left."

"But you told Randolph?"

"Didn't have to. People talk."

Marla's gentility had a bite to it now, but Claire couldn't figure out whether the anger was directed at William or Randolph. Her next question was laced with dynamite, but she had to ask. "Do you know if William roughed up anyone else?"

"Whatever are you asking?"

"Did he have any girlfriends he might have roughed up?"

"William? Unfaithful? That was never a problem."

"How can you be so sure?"

"Well, a wife just knows, that's all." A vengeful smile tweaked her lips.

Chapter 12

Sunday June 19, 2005
Larose, LA

Notre Dame de Grâce was back from the road; its red brick façade surrounded by a manicured lawn and picture-perfect hawthorn hedges. High-arching, stained glass windows adorned both sides of the church, which despite the full parking lot, looked deserted. Claire checked her watch. Fifteen more minutes.

As she left her car, a flock of sparrows, plucking at the too green lawn, flew off only to light several yards from the sidewalk. She imagined the congregation kneeling at the altar, chomping their communion wafers with self-serving grins. Once again they'd managed to wake up early, make it to church, and sit through the service without falling asleep. For most of them, she knew that was the holiest thing they'd done all week.

She followed the sidewalk around the west side of the church. It led to a private cemetery where everything—walkways, tombstones, mausoleums, grave markers, flowerpots—was white as if covered with freshly fallen snow. If it hadn't been created white, it had been painted white.

Because of the water table, all the graves were above ground.

Her mother's raised gravesite looked like a long white bench where one could rest one's tired legs. The simple white concrete slab was decorated with a white concrete cross. Someone had laid a bouquet of pink dahlias beside the cross. The blooms were fresh.

Claire bent on one knee. "Hi, Ma."

This was the first time she'd been back since the funeral and a few words seemed appropriate, but she had no illusions about death, or an afterlife. She'd been against a cemetery burial. She'd wanted Ma buried on her land, her own place, but as usual, Philippe had prevailed.

"Who's Mamma Anna?"

The scent of gardenia, lilac, and rose laced the humid air and stretched like soothing arms around her.

"The woman wants something and I bet you know what."

She leaned back on her heel. She didn't believe in spirits and knew that the answers in her head were of her own making, but it sure felt good to talk to Ma again.

"Well, I best go see to this woman—your friend."

She stood and started to step away. A fresh breeze grazed her cheek, carrying smells from her childhood—cut flowers, fruits cooked into jam, and lemon oil. In an instant, they were gone.

Goosebumps rose on her flesh. *Chair de poule*, she heard, carried on the wind. "Ma?" Her gaze drifted over the tombs.

At the front of the church, the priest's deep voice boomed through the stained glass windows. Claire gritted her teeth. What was she doing here? She'd been tripped up, sucked in, and by what—a sleight of hand, a disappearing act.

She hated being manipulated, but she couldn't fight her curiosity.

An hour out of her Sunday morning. *Get over it.*

What was an hour if she gained information about Billy Ray? With both the post office and library closed for the weekend, Mamma Anna was all she had to work with. What had she said?

Isn't that the guy who's running for sheriff?

Probably meant nothing.

Claire leaned against the trunk of a pecan tree. Two days had passed since the incident at the post office and with each day that strange feeling grew—a feeling that the old woman knew something. But what? Had she worked for the Cobbs? Known someone who had? The last thing she'd said was about the church. Well, where was she?

Across the parking lot, Claire spotted a telephone pole where she might tack another flyer. Ol' Billy Ray should have seen one by now. She smiled.

Yesterday, she'd posted a good number in Cobb's New Orleans neighborhood, and also in Houma, and all over Raceland where he'd grown up. Tomorrow, she'd drive to Tulane and hang the last few. She had to try and get a meeting with the dean. And while she was in New Orleans, maybe she'd pass by the Elections Office to see if anything had been added to Cobb's bio.

The church organ hit a crescendo passage, the music rising as the double walnut doors swung open. Two altar boys in white smocks stood at either side of the doors. A priest, wearing a white billowing robe, stepped outside and turned at the top of the stairs to await the congregation. Two other altar boys carried the totem cross down the stairs and cut around the side of the church. She stepped closer, wondering if she would recognize Mamma Anna in her Sunday best. Folks down here didn't have much, but what they had came out on Sunday morning.

Couples, children, families filed past. A few faces looked familiar, but no one she could name.

"Claire?" She heard a voice behind her.

She swung around and caught sight of Philippe and Suzanne looking at her like she'd just touched down from Neptune.

"What are you doing here?" Philippe snapped.

She was wondering something close to the same thing. She'd been watching the front door and hadn't seen Philippe leave the church. Then it dawned on her that there was a side door.

"Business," she said from habit. "I'm waiting for someone. Suzanne, how are you?" She hugged her sister-in-law.

"Sheriff business?" Philippe snapped.

"Philippe," Suzanne said, her look admonishing. "Ah, let him go," she said, watching her husband stomp off toward his truck. "He doesn't understand and he never will so don't even bother."

Claire sighed, "It's my problem, not—"

"You don't have to convince me. For that matter, you don't have to convince Philippe. It's your battle."

Surprised by her sister-in-law's friendliness, she felt awkward and wished she knew Suzanne better. "The house looks real nice. Thanks for cleaning up."

"Wanted to make it a little more comfortable for you. Listen, why don't you come have Sunday dinner with us? Suppose I could round up that other no-good brother of yours."

Claire glanced out at the parking lot. "I don't think Philippe would appreciate that."

"Nonsense, you're his sister. We just won't mention William Cobb."

"I'd sure like to see Chet."

"He's at a sleepover, we're on our way to pick him up. He wants to see you, too. Say around noon? We're still over in Green Acres. You remember how to get there?"

Claire nodded. Suzanne glanced back at the church. "Who you meeting anyway?"

"Woman named Mamma Anna. Do you know her?"

Color drained from Suzanne's face. She took a step backward. "You're into that stuff?"

"What stuff? She says she knew Ma."

An arm slipped into Claire's and she felt herself pulled off balance. "Chérie, you looking for me?"

Mamma Anna's black eyes glinted. Sweat sparkled on her forehead. Instead of the turban, stiff dark curls threaded with gray strands covered her head. Her striped dress was gathered with a belt at the waist and hung down below her knees. Her white patent-leather pumps reflected the sun.

"Wasn't that the plan?"

Mamma Anna laughed, but didn't reply.

"Mamma Anna, this is…," but Suzanne was gone. Claire turned in time to catch her sister-in-law climbing into Philippe's truck.

Strange. She turned her attention to Mamma Anna, who was speaking with another woman, a congregation member.

They spoke Creole, then a few words in French. Claire noticed the Haitian accent more when Mamma Anna spoke French. Haitian French was more musical than the local Acadian French.

"You look different," Claire said once they were alone.

"A mask. Clothes mask our bodies, our bodies mask our personalities, and our personalities mask our souls." Mamma Anna extended her arm and waved to someone else. "I'm glad you're here. Would you like to speak with Father Murphy? He replaced Father David, the priest who buried your dear mamma."

"I told you, I'm not a believer. And I'm not a hypocrite either. I'm here for one reason, and that's to speak with you."

"I'm flattered."

Coy, cute. Mamma Anna smiled and Claire had to force herself not to walk away. The sun burned hot on her neck and shoulders. The humidity was weighing her both physically and mentally. She didn't have time for some old woman's games. But she couldn't afford to overlook a source. "I want to know, do you know something about William Cobb?"

"I know about religion." Mamma Anna leaned against Claire's car. "Why don't you believe anymore?"

Anymore? She looked Mamma Anna in the eyes. What was the old woman playing? The intense black eyes held her gaze.

"Oh, I don't know. I'm an assistant D.A.. With the things I see it's hard to pretend there's a god orchestrating the whole mess."

"That's not why."

"Then why don't you tell me?" The woman was pushing it. If this stunt was about religion, the woman was going to be sorely disappointed.

"Religion is personal," Mamma Anna said. "All the *things* you see in Baton Rouge aren't personal."

Claire exhaled long and slow. "Okay, fine. Let's see, my Pa died when I was five. I started having doubts then. Personal enough?" Had she'd been wrong? Maybe the woman didn't know anything. "I do believe in the Law. Right. Wrong. If you know anything about Mr. Cobb, you should share it with me. It's very important."

"Who hurt you?"

"Lady—"

"I saw it in your palm. I have the gift. Who attacked you?"

Claire looked down into her hand and remembered the woman stroking her palm at the post office. "If you have the *gift*, you should've seen that too."

"The wound's too old, too deep. I saw the pain left behind. The incidents I see are more recent ones—like a broken heart."

Whoa. Claire cleared her throat as if it could help her win back her composure. "I see that I've made a mistake. I thought you could help me, but—"

"I can help you, chérie, but you have to forget about your laws. They're manmade and as fickle as man. I belong to a higher power and that power can be yours."

Oh, brother. She opened the car door. "Sorry, I'm not looking for salvation."

"I'm offering you a solution."

Mamma Anna walked around the car and opened the passenger door. "Would you give me a lift? I want to show you something."

A lift? Was she nuts? But Ma would be livid if she dare refuse such a request from an older woman. Even so, she wanted to be free of Mamma Anna and her unsolicited convictions. Why did religious fanatics always feel responsible for nonbelievers? How many times had she argued religion with Vincent?

Vincent. Had Mamma Anna really seen their breakup in her palm? Nonsense.

Mamma Anna climbed in and fastened her seatbelt without waiting for Claire's reply.

Claire looked the frail woman over and knew she couldn't kick her out. "Which way?" She pulled out of the parking lot.

"That way." Mamma Anna pointed left. "You need to turn off the road after Valentine. Oh look, the meadow lilies are already blooming. Usually they don't flower until after Saint Jean's. Summer'll be short this year."

"Is that still celebrated down here?"

"Sure is, coming up on Friday. The feast is Thursday." Mamma Anna's leathery finger rose. "Turn right, here."

Claire turned onto a gravel road not much wider than her car. As she drove, the flatlands gave way to three-foot-high swamp grasses with a few willow trees spread about. The grasses gave off a bitter smell and foretold a water source. They passed more willows, then baby cottonwoods, then bigger, stronger ash, red oak, and sweet gum trees. The woods blocked out the scorching sun, cooling the air inside the car.

"Pull over, there by the 'V' tree."

Claire did as directed, stopping beside a split V-shaped tree trunk. Her car blocked more than three-quarters of the road. What did the woman want to show her out here?

"This is it. You remember how we got here?"

Claire glanced at the V-shaped trunk and nodded. Didn't look like anything special.

"Remember it well," Mamma Anna said, stepping from the car. Her face winced as she put weight on her left foot.

Claire felt a pang of guilt. She should have been nicer. "I can take you as far as you need to go."

Mamma Anna slammed the door shut. "I'm where I need to be." She bent and propped her elbows inside the open window. "We're having a little party Thursday evening, 'round midnight." She paused. "Come back, you'll find what you seek." She stood, turned slowly, and limped into the woods.

Where did she think she was going in those patent-leather pumps? Claire watched the woman make her way through the trees. But before Mamma Anna disappeared from view, she heard the old woman's voice.

"Together, you and I can give back to Billy Ray. We'll right his wrongs."

Claire leaped from the car, bumping her elbow on the door frame. "What did you say?" She ran into the woods, using the same path as the old woman, but found herself alone among towering pines.

"Mamma Anna?

"Mamma Anna!"

Chapter 13

Sunday June 19, 2005
Green Acres, LA

Philippe's neighborhood wasn't much more than tract housing—identical ranch-style homes set side by side, pitched roofs, aluminum carports, juniper hedges. Claire stopped at the first intersection. A lawnmower whined nearby.

Philippe could afford better. He and Joe had worked construction since she was in high school. By the time she'd begun college, they'd started their own company and were hiring day laborers. They'd helped her and Brian with college expenses. Philippe had money. So why did he choose to live in a place where the houses bore no distinction and the yards no trees? The place was barely a step up from Villette. Ten more miles north and he could live in a nicer home in a cozy neighborhood or in one of those golf club communities with the ninth hole right off his backyard.

She pulled into the driveway, parking behind Suzanne's station wagon and next to a row of rhubarb plants. Philippe's truck was missing, but before she could wonder why, Chet, her four-year-old nephew, burst out the side door, the aluminum screen slamming behind him. She threw open the car door as he dashed toward her, his tennis shoes slapping the concrete.

He'd grown so tall since his visit to Baton Rouge. She wrapped her arms around him and scooped him into her lap. He craned to look over her shoulder at the two wrapped packages on the passenger seat. "Whoa, big guy, give Auntie a kiss."

She planted her lips on his cheek, his plump skin soft and smooth. "What sweetie, you think those are for you?" she teased.

Chet reddened. "Yes ma'am."

"Now why would you think that?"

"'Cause you always give me presents." Chet's grin grew wider and he giggled. She kissed the top of his head.

"Cher, give Aunt Claire some space," Suzanne called, coming through the doorway.

"Wait, I want another kiss."

Chet's wet lips met her cheek.

"What do you say?" Suzanne said as Claire handed him the packages.

"Thank you." He clutched the two packages to his chest and ran for the house.

Claire closed the car door. "He's changed so much since your trip to Baton Rouge."

"That was two years ago. Kids change fast during these years."

"Looks like I chased Philippe."

"Course not, come on inside." Suzanne brushed her hands over her apron. "He went to ask Joe to join us. It'd be nice to have the family together. We don't see much of Joe since Brian died. Well, Philippe sees him at work and all, but he's kind of a loner, I guess."

"He always was."

Natural light from south-facing windows warmed the kitchen. The aroma of slow roasting beef and vegetables thickened the air. *Pot au Feu*. Her favorite. She'd once told Suzanne she made it as good as Ma. Suzanne had remembered.

As the soothing smells led her to the stove, Claire thought of her other older brother, Joe. Two years younger than

Philippe, Joe had distanced himself from the family early on. He gave up trying to be as smart as the younger Brian, but competed with Philippe in sports and hard work. When the two started a business together, she'd never thought it would work, but that was fourteen years ago.

She lifted the lid on the unhinged pressure cooker and breathed in the rising steam. "Umm, Joe have a girlfriend?"

"Always. They come and they go."

"You talking about me?" Philippe asked, the screen door slamming.

"No, *ton frère*. Where is he?" Suzanne leaned left as if she expected Joe to be hiding behind his brother.

"Finishing a job in Paradis. Says he wants to keep at it."

"But it's Sunday."

He threw his hands in the air. "Joe lives by his own time clock. Said he'd stop by the house to see Claire."

Claire felt invisible and noticed Philippe avoiding her gaze. She settled the lid back on the pot. "Is that the only reason Joe can't make it?"

"Yeah, the only reason." His jaw tensed, but he didn't look in her direction.

Suzanne slipped her arm in his and led him to the oak slab table. "Philippe, you promised."

"Hell's bells. First, she comes down here stirring up family business. Now, she's hanging around that voodoo woman."

"What's he talking about?" Claire asked Suzanne.

"Like you don't know," Philippe said.

Suzanne puckered her lips and made a face. "Mamma Anna."

"Mamma Anna's a voodoo woman?" Claire pulled a chair out and sat across the table from Philippe. She leaned forward on her elbows, looking him in the eyes. If he had something to say, he could say it to her face.

"The real thing, I've been told, not like those tourist shows up in New Orleans," Suzanne said. "She's the top, the Queen Bee. They call her a Mambo. I don't know what that means."

"If you didn't know, what're you doing with her?" Philippe's hands were clenched together on the tabletop.

"I ran into her at the post office. Said she was a friend of Ma's, but, I don't know, there's something weird about her. She's been hinting she knows things that might help me."

"She ain't no friend of Ma's," Philippe said, standing. He walked to the refrigerator. "She's trouble. Best stay away from that one."

Suzanne looked to be ignoring them as she dropped into the chair that Philippe had vacated.

Philippe held up a Budweiser can. "You want one?" he asked Claire.

She shook her head. "On second thought." She stretched out a hand. "The old woman invited me to some gathering Thursday evening. You think it's a voodoo thing?"

Philippe popped the top and handed her the beer. "They're gonna cut you up and feed you to the gods. I'm telling you, you best stay away."

Suzanne nodded, but still looked as if her thoughts were elsewhere. "Thursday's Saint Jean's Eve," she said. "It's a big voodoo night. Up in New Orleans, there's a party out by Lake Pontchartrain." She slid around to face Claire. "You'd be safer heading up to the lake. I hear it gets a little wild, some stripping, some naked bodies maybe, but no one gets fed to the gods."

Philippe sat and Suzanne brushed hair from his face.

"The gods feed on me, they're likely to get indigestion." Claire reached into her handbag and pulled out the small gray sack tied with red yarn. "I found this my first morning at the house. Found it wedged under the doorframe." She handed the gris-gris to Philippe. "You think she knew Ma?"

"Ma was friendly with everyone. Maybe she knew the woman from church, but Ma didn't cotton with this stuff, thought it was creepy."

"Mamma Anna told me she was at Ma's funeral."

"Another lie." Philippe handed back the gris-gris without looking inside.

"No. She was," Suzanne said. "I remember. I saw her and wondered what she was doing there. She stood in the back with the others from church. Claire, I also remember she was watching you. It spooked me at the time, but then after the funeral, we were all together talking, and I completely forgot to mention it."

"I don't think Ma would get involved with Voodoo," Claire said. "I'm with Philippe on this one. It must have something to do with Billy Ray."

"Ah, here we go again." Philippe threw his head back.

Claire put down her beer. "She said as much. Said something about giving back to Billy Ray. Then, something about righting his wrongs."

Philippe leaned forward. "I'm telling you, Claire, the woman's trouble. She's manipulating you. She knows the buttons to push. Anybody says anything about William Cobb—you go running."

"That's the thing. She didn't say William. See, even you call him William. No, she said Billy Ray, which means she knows him from his past. No one calls him Billy Ray anymore, not even his ex-wife."

"That's as lame as your gold tooth theory."

"Okay." Suzanne raised her hands in the air. "No more about Cobb or Mamma Anna. I don't want any fighting today."

Philippe stood, reached for his beer, and kicked the chair away. It crashed to the floor behind him. "Yeah, no more about *Billy Ray*." He headed out the door. "Or that damn company of his."

His company? What did that mean? Claire turned to Suzanne for clarification, but saw something in her sister-in-law's face that told her to leave it alone. Suzanne's gaze, with a wrenching sadness, followed Philippe out of the room.

Blue Belt was Cobb's construction company. Had Philippe worked with him? Were they or had they been friends? Would that explain his anger every time she mentioned the man?

Chapter 14

Sunday June 19, 2005
Paradis, LA

Paradis was northeast of Green Acres, a series of
interconnecting neighborhoods off Highway 90. A flashing
red arrow to Joe's worksite would be helpful, but town was
small enough that Claire expected to see her brother nailing a
roof or carting wallboard at any moment. She turned into the
first residential neighborhood.

If there was a connection between Philippe and Billy Ray,
Joe would tell her. Philippe's comment about Blue Belt had
been torturing her all afternoon and she found herself
imagining all sorts of crazy scenarios. Only Suzanne's
moratorium on Billy Ray had kept her silent through lunch.

Suzanne came from good Cajun stock and when she said
no more, she meant no more. Claire wasn't about to
challenge her and knew Philippe felt the same. Growing up,
Philippe had been the man of the house, but he always
minded Ma. In their marriage, she'd noticed that Philippe
was strong, but Suzanne ruled.

In the next neighborhood, a group of boys were playing
kickball in the street. They groaned and slinked to the side of
the road, letting her pass. After snaking through two more
streets, she pulled out onto the Old Spanish Trail, which
paralleled 90. How many more neighborhoods could there
be?

She continued south toward Bayou Gauche Road, but
hadn't so much as seen a house under repair, let alone full
construction. She pulled to the side of the road, killed the air-

conditioner, and rolled down the windows to listen. No pounding hammers. No electric drills.

This was turning into one huge waste of her time. One more pass. Then she'd give up. But she had way too many questions and going home without talking to Joe would be hard.

She pulled back onto the empty road. A quarter of a mile down she caught sight of a new road angled off to the left. Thick large-cut gravel covered a red clay foundation. There wasn't a road sign.

She eased onto the gravel, accelerating slowly, the rocks crunching under her tires. Through a stand of trees, she saw what looked like the wooden frame of a new home. She drove another half of a mile before finding the entrance to the development.

The corner house was a finished colonial. A sign planted in the unseeded yard designated it as the "Model Home." A Mercedes and a Range Rover were parked there; neither looked like it belonged to a workman. She passed the house, driving until the gravel gave way to a wide red clay path with unpaved drainage ditches on each side.

Two pickups were parked between two newly framed houses. A small broad Mexican man with thick arms was carrying a stack of boards on his shoulder.

She turned her car around and watched. Joe would be easy to spot with his reddish-brown hair the same color as Ma's. Bright light made his head look like a fire cactus. Something he'd hated as a boy.

The small man glanced her way and then disappeared into one of the framed houses. A little later another man stepped out of the same house and looked toward her car. He was lean, stringy, his hair wild even beneath the baseball cap. She cut the engine and stepped out.

"Joe."

He walked stiffly, reserved. He didn't seem to recognize her, but he hopped off the foundation. Probably thought she was one of his ex-girlfriends. She chuckled. He'd almost reached her car when recognition lit his face.

"Sis. I told Philippe I'd come by the house."

"I know, but I thought I'd stop by, say hi, see how you're doing." They embraced with a quick, awkward hug.

"Come up here, out of the sun." He led her across woodchips and Styrofoam pieces back toward the house's cinderblock foundation.

"Where're you living now?" she asked.

"Got me a trailer down past Villette."

"A trailer? I thought business was good."

"It's okay. You know me, I don't need much."

He had inherited Ma's good looks, but also Pa's need to simplify life. Having six mouths to feed must have driven Pa crazy.

"Do you know how Pa died?"

"You came all the way out here to ask me that?"

"No. Just something Philippe brought up the other day."

"Well, let's see." He leaned his butt against the cinderblocks. "Ma used to say he was attacked by an alligator out on the bayou."

"Until now, I thought that was true."

He grinned. "Think Ma was giving him a hero's sendoff. As I got older, I heard other stories from men who'd known him. Seems there was a rifle involved. Some say it was an accident, others say, well, it weren't. Guess it comes down to us never really knowing for sure."

"But he's dead?"

"That he is."

She thought about what little she knew of Pa. She envied Joe for knowing more. She imagined Joe sitting in a dark bar somewhere next to someone who'd known Pa well. But wait, who'd known him better than Ma?

He scooted up onto the house's floorboards then patted a spot next to him, gesturing for her to do the same. "How you been?"

"Okay."

"Married?"

"No. You?"

"No."

He slapped his thigh and they laughed. She wasn't sure why, but neither was considered marriage material. Growing up in Villette, not much was expected of them, but the Rivets had broken the stereotype. Philippe and Joe had a successful business. Brian had gone to college, and she'd earned her law degree. Still, their childhoods had marked them. Brian, the gentlest of the four, hanged himself. Joe was living in a trailer, and she lived for one thing and one thing only—to put her rapist behind bars.

A sadness swept through her. Living just shouldn't be that hard. At least Philippe had escaped the Rivet curse and found happiness, although he hadn't been too happy since she'd come to town. "What do you know about Blue Belt Construction?"

Joe's gaze traveled over the lumber and equipment scattered before him. "Blue Belt's been around for about ten years now. Built their reputation on underbidding everyone else. Took about five years before their buildings started falling apart. They'd cut cost using inferior materials, labor, and cutting code, stuff like that. By the time the lawsuits started, they had a solid reputation with some solid contracts.

The lawyers convinced the public that Blue Belt had been cuckolded not the clients."

"Does Philippe have a problem with the company?"

"Don't know if you can call it a problem. He don't like them much."

"Because they do shoddy work?" She'd seen more than dislike in Suzanne's face. "You and Philippe ever have a problem with them?"

Joe removed his cap. "Guess you could say that." He combed his hair with dirty fingers, and put the cap back on. "We've been hired a few times to fix their crap. Had to replace the stud walls in one building. Not an easy job, let me tell you."

If they were getting paid for the replacement work why would Philippe get angry? "So that's it?" There had to be more to the story.

"Well, there's that other thing, you know."

"I don't know."

"Must have been five years ago, no, let's see, Chet's what, four?"

She nodded, wondering what this had to do with Chet.

"If Chet's four, it must have been between five and six years ago that we won a bid for a strip mall over in Raceland. We went up against some bigger companies like Blue Belt. First time too, mostly we stuck to houses. Anyway we underbid everyone. We underbid Blue Belt and won the contract. Suzanne was pregnant at the time. But something happened. She had some kind of accident, fell or something. She lost the baby and Philippe was just tore up about it. Next thing I know, we'd lost the contract."

"How could you afford to underbid Blue Belt?"

"This was about the time they had some cash flow and were stepping up the quality of their work. Also we cut out the middleman. Philippe and I aren't just foremen. We do a lot of the work, which cuts down on employees."

"Who got the contract?"

"Blue Belt, of course."

"I didn't know Suzanne lost a child."

"Like I said, it happened before Chet was born. Don't guess Philippe wanted folks to know. He and Suzanne stayed to themselves for the longest time."

"Wasn't Blue Belt's fault, why would he be angry at them?"

He shrugged. "Maybe angry with himself. I know I was. I figure we lost the contract because he was so caught up in his pain. He didn't take care of business. I tried to talk with him once. That's when he told me to forget it, we'd lost the contract. He could have passed the work over to me, but you know how he is—Mr. Big Man."

"You ever bid against Blue Belt again?"

"Nope. We went back to building houses. Been doing it ever since."

She tried to remember Philippe's exact words, but something didn't fit. The anger. The way he'd stomped off. The pain in Suzanne's eyes. That wasn't lost business. The rest of lunch had felt strained, and not because of Billy Ray. Something else was going on between them. Something private. The baby?

"I must have misunderstood Philippe's anger," she said, looking up into Joe's face. His skin bore the sun, scorched rather than tanned like Philippe's.

"Easy enough to do. Sometimes I think he's the most conflicted man I know. Nothing is ever simple with him, know what I mean?"

"Yeah."

"He's competitive, too. I always had the feeling we were going into the strip mall business to compete with Blue Belt. Philippe had already taken a dislike to them."

Joe slapped his thigh and stood. "I got to get on back to work, but I'll stop by the house one of these evenings, take you out for some crawfish."

"I'll hold you to it."

* * *

On the way home, Claire thought about what Joe had said. He didn't seem to know about Ma's deathbed revelation to Philippe. Most likely, Philippe took it upon himself to bid against Billy Ray, to use his business as an act of aggression against the man. But personal tragedy struck. Knowing Philippe, he probably thought God was paying him back for having acted badly toward someone else.

Claire turned in at Hal's, a country store that had served Villette, Gheens, and parts of Clotilda for as long as she could remember. This was where Ma sent Philippe to get milk, butter, and occasionally lemons. Lemons were Ma's vice, that's what she used to say. She hated to eat fish, even a meaty catfish, without dousing it in lemon juice, and, try as she might, she never managed to grow them. She once grew a lemon tree about three feet tall before it dried up and died on her. After that, she gave up, said some things just had to be accepted and she had to accept that she couldn't grow a lemon tree.

Claire parked next to the old style gasoline pump. The store hadn't changed much. Lucky and Camel cigarette stickers still graced the front window where Anheuser Busch was written out in yellow neon. To the left of the building were three rotting car shells that looked like the same three she remembered from childhood.

Another relic was the old Creole, Ory, who sat near the entrance in a red metal lawn chair. Back when she was young, other old folks would sit out there too, listening to his stories or just watching the world go by. Today Ory was alone, lounged back with his head propped against the building, eyes wide yet unmoving. If he wasn't dead, he sure was old enough to be. Who knows, he could be dead. Maybe Hal had him stuffed as a memento.

She walked toward the entrance, but when she reached the door, Ory sprang to his feet. She took a step back.

Pointing at her shirt, baring yellowed teeth, he yelled, "Bai! Bai…tadja… pupa…bai… Bai…bonbu…dios." His crimped, arthritic fingers jabbed at her chest as she backed away.

He'd yelled loud enough to be heard in the next parish, but his words were so thick with dialect, she couldn't understand what he was saying.

Hal rushed outside, his heavy round belly wobbling, the exertion showing in his red veined face. "What's up, old man?" He turned to her. "What did you do?"

"Tadja!" Ory yelled.

She threw her hands up, but her movement frightened the Creole. He whipped around and scurried across the parking lot as fast as his ancient stick legs would move. He kept yelling at her over his shoulder. "Bai…tadja."

"What's he saying?" she asked Hal.

"Bai means go, but the rest, pss, I have no idea. You really upset him, though. Never seen ole Ory like that. Hey, I know you."

He stepped back and looked her from head to toe. "Rivet, right? You're Catherine's girl, Catherine Rivet. Damn girl, you look just like your mamma. Last time I saw you, you were nothing but arms and legs."

She turned to watch the Creole disappear into a grove of pecan trees.

Chapter 15

Sunday June 19, 2005
New Orleans, LA

Billy Ray unlocked the door. The reception office was dark and too cold. Worst of all, it smelled like Tammy Lee. Gardenia. Made him want to puke. He should fire her ass, but he'd gone through six secretaries before her and she was damn good at keeping folks off his back, assholes like his father. But that attitude of hers needed some adjusting.

He shoved his keys back in his pants pocket and headed down the corridor to his office. Wonder if sheriffs had obedient little mushroom secretaries that didn't argue with their superiors. If Tammy Lee opened her mouth one more time, he was going to dropkick her to Ohio.

"Sheriff William Cobb," he said aloud.

That cheered him right up.

In a few short months, he'd be Criminal Sheriff of the most populated parish in Louisiana. Like the others before him, he'd have his picture taken, with the Louisiana flag and the US flag draped behind him. A noble image for a noble man.

He flipped a switch by his office door and an electronic motor clicked on. The blinds inched up the windows allowing daylight to creep into the somber room. He raised the thermostat and, as the air conditioning hum shut off, he walked to the glass and looked out over the city. Sundays were pretty quiet except over in the French Quarter, but his office didn't face that direction. Instead, he looked out over empty streets, a few pedestrians—lost tourists most likely, looking for the Garden District.

Behind him the door clicked open. Smelling like a smokestack, Darryl ambled in. His stink always arrived a few seconds before he did.

Billy Ray strutted to his desk, his chest puffed. "Where you been?" He dropped into the plush leather chair as Darryl slinked toward him with his "fuck you" gait.

"Been out hunting these down. You seen 'em?" He tossed a handful of colored flyers across the desk.

Billy Ray picked one up and looked at his likeness printed in black ink. "What's this? Where'd you find them?"

"All over town. Went down to that post office yesterday." Darryl nodded at the flyers. "Larose. Bitch wouldn't tell me who owns the post box. Thinking I might go back around midnight one night, take a look for myself."

For such a small guy Darryl was a tough cuss. Biceps, the man was made of steel. Didn't come cheap either. Keeping Darryl close cost him almost thirty thousand a year. For that kind of muscle one's got to pay, and Darryl was worth it, every penny.

"You done good. I got me another problem I'd like you to look into." He leaned back and intertwined his fingers. "Sit down. Take a load off. The ex called this morning. Seems someone from Baton Rouge came around asking after me."

"She say anything?"

"Marla? No, well, I don't know for sure. She says no, but she's about as trustworthy as a sinking boat."

"Bet I can get the truth out of her."

"Marla's not to be strong-armed. Ever." But he'd sure like to drive over there and knock some sense into her. He'd heard her highfalutin laugh trickle over the line, taunting him, letting him know she'd indeed said something she shouldn't. Bitch.

"You worried?" Darryl asked.

"Me? Nope. She wouldn't risk angering the old man. That much I can always count on. She worships the money he walks on. Woman's name was Claire Rivet. Rings a bell. Sound familiar to you?"

Darryl pulled a pack of Marlboros from his shirt pocket and took a cigarette. He offered the pack to Billy Ray.

"No, thanks."

"Rivet, Rivet, does sound familiar." Darryl lit the cigarette and drew in a breath, dropping his head back to enjoy it. "Wait." A cloud of smoke rolled from his lips. "A few years back, there was a contractor, wasn't he a Rivet?"

Billy Ray rubbed his forehead. "Refresh my memory." The telephone rang and a green light flashed on the console. "Hold that thought." He grabbed the receiver.

"Thought I'd catch you in the office," Hank said. "Man, you work too hard."

"You son of a gun, thought you'd be out fishing by now."

"Car's packed, heading out, but I wanted to give you a call before I left. Outside church this morning I saw one of these flyers, had your picture and a bunch of questions. Wanted to know if you'd seen one yet?"

Billy Ray reached across his desk and picked up one of the flyers. He looked into his own face. "Got one in front of me now. Don't look too interesting, though."

"Political bullshit, I reckon. Okay then, wanted to make sure you'd seen it, that's all."

"Thanks, Hank, and if you catch too much today, you know where to find me."

He replaced the receiver. "These here flyers are upsetting my constituents. I'd like to know who's responsible. If it's that old sheriff, someone's got to know. Maybe the press."

Darryl nodded.

Billy Ray congratulated himself again on finding Darryl. The man was a professional. Didn't need someone to spell out every little detail; had a mind of his own. "What were you starting to say before the call?"

Darryl reached across the table and stubbed his cigarette out in the ashtray.

"'Bout five years back, a small outfit won a bid out from under us. He underbid and we had to rough up the wife before he'd withdraw from the contract."

"I remember." It had been awhile since he'd come up against opposition on a bid. "Rivet Brothers Construction, something like that. They mostly do home building." He flicked the leather blotter, caused it to rise. A check was stuffed underneath. "You think it's the wife?" But Marla had said the woman was from Baton Rouge. "Or a relative looking to tie me to the beating?"

Darryl shrugged.

A long time ago, but Billy Ray didn't like loose ends. "Is there anything to tie me to the beating?"

"Naw. Clean job. His word against yours."

"Said she's a DA. I don't need trouble just now. Damn, I wish I knew what Marla said to her."

Maybe he should go by, see the boys. Marla would probably take great pleasure in giving him a blow-by-blow of the conversation, the sick bitch. What was that other thing she'd said? *Your past is coming back to haunt you.* What did that mean? Marrying *her* was coming back to haunt him, that's for sure. Biggest regret of his life, that was. Why'd he ever let the old man talk him into it? He hadn't had a day of peace since.

He drummed his fingers on the flyers. "You think that Rivet woman could be putting these around?"

"You'll know soon enough."

"Good. You keep an eye on her for me. Let me know what she's up to. But keep your distance. Like I said, don't need no trouble right now."

Chapter 16

Monday June 20, 2005
New Orleans, LA

Claire hadn't seen Percy since law school although they often shared information or strategies by phone. She'd forgotten how handsome he was until she spotted him strutting the length of the restaurant. Tall, broad shouldered, coffee-colored skin. He wore his hair in a short dread style that irritated his boss and the other DAs, but no matter how much they complained no one was going to fire Percy. He was too good a lawyer and no one wanted to meet him on the other side of the courtroom.

"You're as beautiful as ever," he said, sliding into the booth beside her rather than across the table. "Word has it, you and that lawyer are over."

"His name is Vincent and yes, we've had a parting of the ways."

"It's been awhile, I thought this one was a keeper, but you've never been big into keeping them."

"Look who's talking." Back in school Percy had dated one woman after another with long periods in between. Various rumors about him circulated. She didn't listen to gossip; she understood better than most that people could have many reasons for not getting attached.

"Hey, I'm almost engaged. Call the press."

"Almost?"

"I've asked, she hasn't answered."

Claire picked up the plastic menu. "That in itself is worth the congratulations." The air simmered with the smell of oysters and crayfish, green onions and garlic. "What's decent in this dive?"

"All the homegrown stuff. Think I'm getting the catfish po-boy."

"Homegrown. Are you kidding? This place is a chain. Those fishing nets on the wall have tourist written all over them. We even have one in Baton Rouge."

"Oh, excuse me. I grew up in New Orleans so it's homegrown to me. I forget you're from bumfuck."

"Hey, you razzing on my crib," Claire teased with a low, deep voice reminiscent of Leroy Milson, her last convict.

Percy laughed. "Hey, I got one for you. A nigger walks into a bar—"

Claire held up a hand. "Stop now." Percy liked to tell black jokes that left his white co-workers unsure of how to respond to the punch lines. It didn't work so well with his boss, who was the first African-American District Attorney of Orleans.

"Okay. A Polack walks into a bar—"

"I mean it, cut it out. How's the étouffée here?"

"One day, you need to lighten up. Etouffée's good. They make it with shellfish. The oyster's Louisiana isn't bad either if you like oysters."

"I'll stick with the étouffée."

Percy gave their order to the waitress. He leaned back and crossed his arms. "So why are you in Orleans and why the interest in William Cobb?"

Claire spread her napkin across her thighs. "Surprised by Cobb's run for sheriff. Never struck me as the law-abiding type. Now, I hear the mayor's backing him. Is that true?"

"Mayor's looking for a Senate seat and needs Randolph Cobb's Washington contacts. Last I heard, the mayor's heading some wetlands restoration project to get environmental backing from folks like the EPA. After the logging lawsuit last year, the mayor's ready to do anything to improve his image from save a few egrets to hug a few trees. If you want my opinion, somebody better do something about reinforcing the levees around the city. One good hurricane season and this town will be a new lake and the fishing won't be good."

"What does that have to do with William Cobb? I don't see him hugging anything."

"Randolph Cobb's participation is hinged on the son's nomination for sheriff."

Claire flicked at the corner of her napkin. "Really? You think William is only running because his father wants him to?"

"Quite possible. If you haven't noticed, Randolph has a serious God complex."

As the waitress delivered their ice teas, Claire thought about what Percy had said. Could it be that William's run for sheriff wasn't a power issue?

Percy picked up his glass. "I never forgot what you told me in law school," he said, "you know, about the Cobbs."

Claire felt her face heat up. She wasn't the kind to talk about personal problems, in confidence or otherwise. That was part of why going against Cobb now was so difficult. Soon everyone, including friends like Percy, would know her story, but she was certain she'd never told him anything about Billy Ray.

"Not sure I remember, what did I say?"

He set his glass down and leaned close enough to whisper. "One night when we were studying for an exam, you said always keep my ear to the ground about the Cobbs. You said it could make my career. Remember?"

Claire nodded, although she had no recollection of the conversation.

"Without Randolph and William, the civil courts in this city would be empty," he said. "But I've never seen anything come into the criminal courts."

That didn't surprise her, not after what Marla had said. "Let's say William knocked his wife around, but the charges disappeared. Is there any way to find the original warrant?"

Percy leaned back into his seat. "You can always check the sheriff's records for the incident report. Warrants disappear, but for some reason incident reports get overlooked, maybe because they remain in the sheriff's office instead of the courthouse. Was it in Orleans?"

"Probably not."

"Just to show off, I did dig up an incident report on William. Battery. Got into it with one of his foremen. The case was dropped before he was charged. My bet is the foreman got paid off. The report, though, shows low tolerance or lack of emotional control. Could be a wife beater. Who told you he knocked the wife around?"

"She did. Was catty about it, though, so I'm not sure it's true. She might be trying to get her ex and his nomination in trouble. Something tells me I'll never find any evidence either way. Oh, but she did mention a daughter. Have you ever heard of Randolph having a daughter?"

Percy shook his head. "Far as I know, William's an only child."

"She said the daughter died young. I would really like to know the cause."

Percy took out his phone and punched in a number. "Do you have a name and a parish?" he asked Claire.

"Probably Lafourche Parish and they called her Bunny. Don't have a clue what that's short for."

He spoke into the phone. "Can you search the state's death records for a female, last name Cobb, died say before age 25, and in my lifetime. Don't get smart. Try Lafourche Parish first, then Orleans. Thanks." He put the phone back in his jacket. "Anything else I can do for you?"

Claire watched the waitress set the steaming étouffée before her. Smelling of shrimp and herbs, it overflowed the large bowl. Some buttery roux splashed over the side and onto the table. The waitress wiped it away before leaving.

Claire turned to Percy, who was busy stuffing mayonnaise-covered pickles back into his po-boy.

"Thanks for the help," she said. She hoped she wouldn't lose his friendship when he learned why she wanted the information. Would he look at her differently, treat her differently when he learned she, too, was a victim?

"I'm still hoping to make my career," he said, licking mayo from his finger. "If you get something on Cobb, you'll turn it over to me. This is my district."

Chapter 17

Monday June 20, 2005
New Orleans, LA

Charlie Dill was short and thick with a belly that hung
down over his belt. Male-pattern baldness hadn't been kind,
leaving him with a crescent of short dark spikes stretching
across the back of his head from ear to ear and a lonely set of
three strands that he combed over the top like dried creeks on
a desert bed.

"You're from the government," he said, ushering Claire to
a seat by his desk.

The smell of stale cigar smoke was masked only by the
humidity of a poorly functioning air-conditioner.

"I'm with the Baton Rouge District Attorney's Office,"
Claire said, looking at the various stuffed fish mounted
around the room. She recognized a few species and knew
they came from the Gulf. The largest was a three-foot long
barracuda and that was from the ocean.

"Not the Feds, then."

"No, not the Feds," she repeated, wondering why he'd
assumed she was.

Charlie relaxed into a chair next to her. "Feds confiscated
my fishing boat," he said. "They make me a little nervous."

Smuggling or drug running? She made a mental note to
have Erwin check the file.

"What can I do for you, then? Somebody in trouble?"

"We investigate everyone running for public office and I
understand you're a childhood friend of William Cobb."

"Billy Ray. Sure. He's going to make a great sheriff.
Can't think of anyone better for the job. Known him since I

was five. We played football together in high school and college." He slapped his belly. "Played until the wife's cooking got me. Not Billy Ray, though, he's still in great shape. He could still play, but hell, we're all too old now."

"What can you tell me about his childhood? What type of boy was he? Mischievous? Well-behaved? Did he have lots of friends? Was he popular?"

"Popular? Not really, average, I guess. But the place is a little more developed today. Back then, we didn't live in neighborhoods like folks today. I lived down the road from Billy Ray, I mean William. A good bike ride away."

"What about at school? Did he have friends?"

"Course he had friends. He could be rough, though, kids tend to shy away from that. But he was a good kid. Had to be with that father of his."

"Was Randolph strict?"

"Shew! Man's meaner than the devil on Sunday. He'd knock Bil—I mean William around if he stepped an inch out of line. I've seen him knock him right upside the head. I can tell you, William learned real early not to mess up."

Abused. And devious—what kid doesn't mess up? Fit the profile. "Ever seen William hit anyone?"

"Hit? Like punch? No." Charlie stood and walked around the chair. Shook his head and brought his hand up to his mouth as if to hold his lips closed.

"You ever get in a fight with him?"

Charlie shook his head, but he was looking at the barracuda.

"Not even kid stuff? You said he was rough."

"Well, yeah, kids mess around, but we never fist fought or anything." Charlie looked uncomfortable as he moved about the small space between his chair, desk, and the wall. He wandered back to the chair and propped his hands on the back. "When I said he was rough, I meant football. He mowed me down in football once, broke my nose." One finger moved to the bridge of his nose, massaging the length as if it still hurt. "He didn't mean to. Just football."

Charlie nodded several times as if pleased with himself. Marla was right; this man wouldn't say anything against his buddy, but the father stuff was good. "I understand he had a sister."

"Bunny. Sweet girl. Nice as could be." He nodded again.

"Randolph knock her around?"

He slipped back into the chair. "No way. She was the apple of his eye. Spoiled the girl rotten."

"Was she older or younger than her brother?"

"A few years older. A nice kid. Terrible what happened to her."

"What happened?"

"You don't know? Story was in all the papers. She was raped by the gardener, a black fellow. Beat her to death when she wouldn't stop screaming."

The spicy étouffée rose in the back of her throat. Beaten to death. "Do you remember what year that was?"

"Let's see, I was eighteen so must have been, ah, oh, round nineteen-eighty-five or so. Think that's what got William thinking about law enforcement. I mean, he was always interested. As kids, whenever we played cowboys and Indians, he always had to be the sheriff. Funny. But I think what happened to Bunny cemented the thought in his brain. He'll make a good sheriff and it's about time someone like William cleans the place up. New Orleans has gone to hell."

Claire pulled out her notebook and wrote the date next to Bunny's name. She fought every muscle in her body not to react to Charlie's revelation. Billy Ray had been eighteen also. The year was branded on her heart. "Did they catch the perpetrator?"

"Gardener, you mean? Oh sure, but he tried to escape when they were bringing him in and someone shot him. Never made it to trial."

"Convenient."

"What's that?"

Claire shook her head. She wrote the word "gardener" on her pad to help clear her head. This was big, she wasn't sure how yet, but it was big. "When Bunny died, what was the evidence against the gardener?"

"You mean like DNA. They didn't do that stuff back then. I was a kid. You know how self-centered teenagers are. Don't remember much, but I know someone who saw it."

Claire lowered her notepad. "Someone who came forward?"

"No, not then. He told me he didn't tell no one at the time it happened. Told me years later. Said I was the only one he ever told. We were out on a boat, baking in the sun, getting drunk. I thought he was making it up until he told me the details. Couldn't make that shit up. 'Cuse my French."

The room was closing in on her. Claire found it hard to swallow. She thought she knew, but had to ask without leading the witness. "Who told you this?"

"Billy Ray. He saw the whole thing."

Chapter 18

Monday June 20, 2005
New Orleans, LA

Claire rushed along the sidewalk, weaving through people like traffic cones. She held her cell phone clutched to her chest. Her head spun with questions. Had Billy Ray really seen his sister's rape? Had that been the inciting incident that sent him on his own rampage? But the death of the gardener, that gave her pause. Too neat. And if Billy Ray had witnessed the rape, why hadn't he tried to help his sister? He was eighteen, a footballer. Why didn't he do something?

Or maybe the rapist was someone he couldn't stop?

His father?

She released a long, slow breath.

Or—dare she even think it—had Billy Ray raped his own sister? Charlie wouldn't repeat everything that Billy Ray had said in confidence, but he'd told her enough that, like him, she felt sure that Billy Ray had been there.

She pulled the phone away and punched in the number she knew by heart. "Erwin, I need you to look into a case file for me." She gave him the year and the name. Charlie Dill had said Bunny had been short for Barbara. "Find out everything you can about the gardener. Supposedly, it made the newspapers. The gardener was killed as they were bringing him in."

"This have to do with that rape over in Raceland?"

One way or another. "I need everything you can find. Oh, and do you ever work with any investigators in New Orleans?"

"I'll have to look. What about your lawyer friend? Can't he give you a few names?"

Claire thought of Percy. He could give her a few names, but his investigators would surely share everything they found with him. She couldn't take the chance. "I want to leave him out of this for the moment, when I find something, I'll bring him in."

"Okay then, I'll find a couple of contacts and email their addresses to you."

"Oh, but send them to my temporary email address." She spelled out the address and dropped the phone in her bag.

The stroll through Billy Ray's family had been beneficial, but the only way she was going to convict him was to find evidence against him. She needed to turn her focus to finding victims. She needed to learn more about the Tanya Bonaventure case and try to link the beating and rape to Bunny's assault. They didn't collect DNA in eighty-five, but they did collect other evidence, enzyme blood testing or maybe even a rape kit. Hopefully, Erwin would find something.

Percy had mentioned incident reports. She checked her watch. Records would close at five. She'd never make it to Lockport before then. What else had Percy said? A fight with a foreman. Probably not worth pursuing since it would be hard to link to an assault on a woman.

Interesting, how Marla's glowing description of Randolph conflicted with Percy's and Charlie's description. She obviously admired the man while Charlie seemed to fear him. Percy admitted he'd never met him, but Randolph's reputation was one of an immoveable stone. No one wanted to go up against him.

Chapter 19

Tuesday June 21, 2005
Jefferson County, TX

That squirrelly feeling was crawling up Rena's back again. She'd hitched lots of times and never been scared, but something about this guy, the way he talked, like he was someone important, rubbed her wrong.

Headlights hit the driver's face. He was dressed okay. Suit, tie. Maybe doing business 'round here. The car was decent. Clean. Quiet. She ran her hand over the smooth leather seats. The air felt good, too, after pounding the asphalt all day. Someday she and Eddie should get a car like this.

The guy was probably all right. Eddie said she had a big imagination. The last exit sign for Beaumont floated past her window. The state line wasn't far now. Soon she'd be out of Texas and that much closer to South Carolina.

"How far you going?" she asked the driver.

"Not sure. You?"

He had Louisiana plates, most likely not going any farther than that. "My boyfriend's stationed at Fort Jackson," she said. "I'm going to see him. I'm Rena, by the way."

He tilted his head toward her and grinned. Not bad, not too old, she thought. He'll want a blowjob, they always do. That was okay. Nothing came free. That's what her daddy always said.

A blowjob was a small price to pay for getting her out of this Godforsaken shithole. "You work in Texas?" she asked.

She saw the exit coming up, but was surprised when he took it. Only thing that way was farms and some bayous. "You need gas?" she asked.

"Need to relieve myself. Hope you don't mind."

Yeah, right. Like she hadn't heard that one before.

Darkness filled the car as the highway lights fell behind. Every now and then they passed a farmhouse, but very few other cars. The guy showed no sign of slowing. Did he have a specific spot in mind?

Right about the time she opened her mouth to ask, he turned onto a rural road. A sign pointed the direction to Sabine Lake.

Oh, that feeling again. Maybe it was the isolation. Except for the full moon, there were no other lights at all, not even the occasional headlights. "Don't you think this is far enough?" she said.

He didn't answer, but slowed the car. At the right, after the guardrail ended, three large mountains of what looked like woodchips loomed in the headlights. He pulled the car over and parked beside the first mountain.

Finally, Rena thought. Time to get the hell out of here. But it'd take her a couple of hours to get back to the highway. Nobody would pick her up this far out. Almost one a.m.. Better she find a quiet spot for the night and start again tomorrow. Maybe she could catch a truck in the morning.

Keeping an eye on the driver, she reached for the door handle. Without a word, the driver slid out and pranced around the car. He was taller than she'd thought. She waited to make her move. When he disappeared behind the woodchips without so much as a glance in her direction, she released the handle. He did have to piss. Man's got some privacy issues, she thought, relaxing into the soft leather. She closed her eyes. Quiet was all she heard as the weight of sleep bore down.

The car door popped open so fast she almost screamed. The man grabbed her by the arm and yanked her out. She stumbled and fell, catching the car rim with her free hand. "Hey, slow down."

She tried to stand, but he was dragging her toward the woodchips. *Jerk.* "Wait a minute, would you?"

The fist flew out of nowhere, striking her breastbone and sucking the air out of her chest. "Shit," she said, catching her breath. This was not how she liked to do things, but she stopped resisting, went with it. He responded. He let her walk, leading her, but she was on her feet.

They passed all three woodchip piles and kept going through the scrub and into the woods. She tripped over a fallen branch and he jerked her straight, but with less force than before. "We don't have to do this rough," she said. "I don't mind paying for the ride, if you know what I mean."

The next punch sent her flying through the air. Landing hard, her skull cracked against something solid. He was on her, straddled, his knees digging into the soft of her underarms. He fumbled with her shorts, yanking the zipper apart. He pressed down on her chest and jerked her pelvis up, tugging down her underpants and shorts with one hand. She gulped for air. A warning alarm was ringing in her head, but she didn't take notice until she heard the crackling of her tee shirt ripping up her chest. Now, the alarm was ringing so loud she couldn't tune it out.

He held something out to her. "Put this on," he said.

She reached up and took the smooth, wide ribbon from his hand. In the moonlight, she wasn't sure of the color, lavender maybe.

"Put it on," he ordered.

Oh, God, she was going to die. He was going to strangle her. She didn't want to die. *Oh, God.* "Listen—"

"Not around your neck, in your hair," he said.

His toneless voice sent a chill down her spine.

What? Her fingers wouldn't move. "How?"

He snatched a chunk of hair, lifting her from the ground. "Tie it."

She wrapped the ribbon around the hair he held and knotted it. He released her and she thunked to the ground.

"In a bow."

Her hands trembled so much she had to loop the ribbon several times before she had a bow. Slowly, she lowered her hands. The ribbon thing was freaky. The alarm kept ringing. This wasn't just some guy out to get himself off.

He punched her in her ribcage, moaned, and then shook out his hand.

She sucked in another breath, realizing he'd hurt himself. She remembered his hands on the steering wheel, a couple of cuts and bruises around the knuckles. That was what had bugged her. She'd thought his hands didn't match the fancy suit and car, sure didn't match his "I'm so important" speech. He'd hit someone else. He liked to hit.

Why hadn't she left the car?

A strange sense of calm settled over her. Maybe she wasn't going to die. She just had to take it. Weren't like he had a knife or a gun. And with any luck that last punch hurt him as much as it hurt her. She wiggled down, flattening her back against the uneven ground.

He climbed back over her, spreading her legs apart. He unzipped his pants and rubbed against her, and then again with more force. He growled.

He wasn't hard, not even close. That worried her. He might hit her again as if it were her fault he couldn't be a man. She moaned, hoping the sound would turn him on. It turned Eddie on.

"I need you to scream."

"What?"

"Do it. Scream," he said.

Sure. How loud, asshole? With his weight crushing her, only a squeak passed through her lips. He rolled off and she gathered air for the muther of all screams when something hard slammed into her skull. Bone cracked. The ground started to spin.

"Scream!"

She drew in another breath, her body trembling with the effort, and let lose a scream so loud it burned her throat.

He was back on top of her. He pinched her breast and she arched in pain. She cried out. His finger jabbed into her, tearing at the dry skin. Then he was in her. Pumping. He grew urgent, moving fast. He pushed her legs farther apart and she felt she might split in two. He shoved deeper, each thrust pounding her into the rough earth.

"Again," he said.

Her head throbbed. She might puke. She gathered her force and yelled. She knew he wanted it loud. Maybe he wanted to get caught. But who would hear them out here? A fireman, maybe. A fireman? Why was she thinking about firemen? Her daddy was a fireman. When she was little he'd let her ring the firehouse bell.

Her eyes flew open when the man reared up above her. The way his teeth flashed beneath the full moon, he sort of looked like a werewolf. Then she saw the rock as he lifted it with two hands over her head. She tried to turn away, but it caught the side of her face hard. A rushing sound filled her ears. Little green dots danced before her eyes and faded to black.

Chapter 20

Tuesday June 21, 2005
Villette, LA

Next to her tea and toast, Claire spread the contents of
Billy Ray's file across the dining table. She sorted the
information she'd been collecting since law school by date,
sliding her notes from Marla and Charlie's interview into the
proper sequence.

She looked over what she had: a copy of Billy Ray's high
school diploma, his university entrance exams (lower fortieth
percentile), his marriage certificate, his sons' birth
certificates, a separation agreement, two real estate deeds (a
town house in New Orleans and a plantation in Houma), a
newspaper article stating his political aspirations.

She checked her watch. Cell phone reception at the house
was spotty; she'd have to walk to the road to make an
appointment with Tulane's dean. It would be interesting to
get his take on Billy Ray's expulsion, especially if, as Marla
said, everyone "went ballistic." What else?

She jotted *City Elections Office* on the first line of her
legal pad. There, she hoped to find any personal information
she didn't already have. Because of his candidacy, Cobb's
personal records were public domain.

Victims, she wrote on the second line in large type. Where
would she find them? They existed. She'd spent enough time
around rape counselors to know that what Billy Ray had done
to her was not an isolated incident. She'd been ten and he'd
been eighteen. One counselor she'd worked with on another
case had explained the difference between a rapist of
opportunity and a pedophile.

Where was that interview? It was important; it mentioned an inciting incident. A trigger.

Had Bunny's death turned Billy Ray into a rapist? Ah, here. The interview listed possible characteristics of a serial rapist: abused as a child, not intelligent, shallow emotions, lying, ego-centric, low tolerance.

His father physically abused him or does abused as a child mean sexually? She'd have to look that one up. Not intelligent—he got kicked out of school for bad grades. Emotions. She had no idea of his emotional state. Same with lying. Ego-centric—wants to be sheriff, but that could go more toward wanting power, although Charlie said as kids Billy Ray always had to be the sheriff. Percy found the incident report that shows low tolerance. Even if charges weren't filed there is evidence the fight took place.

She leafed through other pages of notes, those she'd collected over the last five years. Billy Ray had left her for dead. Maybe thought she was. Who was she to him but some low-rent kid from the bayou?

She thought again of Tanya Bonaventure and the similarities to what had happened to her. She'd have a better idea if she spoke to the coroner, but if Billy Ray was responsible, and she knew he was, it proved he wasn't a pedophile.

With any luck, there were other survivors. Or bodies.

But where to look? She jotted Tanya's name below *Victims*.

Further down she wrote, *University?* A local paper or university press would list any rapes or violent crimes in the area. Next she scribbled *Priest/Minister*. Would Billy Ray have confessed to someone?

Neighbors. Day after day, neighbors picked up information. She would interview people who'd known him growing up, who'd known him at the university, who'd socialized with him during his marriage.

Arresting Officer? Summer of '96. If Marla had filed a complaint, Randolph's lawyer might have paid to keep Billy's record clean. She'd need to check the sheriff's archives for an incident report. And what about an officer, someone with a conscience might want to set the record straight? A long shot. Randolph Cobb could afford the price of silence.

What was she forgetting? What other trails needed exploring?

Laughter, high-pitched and childlike, drifted through the screen door. She glanced up from her work. The nearest neighbor was old man Yardey and he lived three miles to the south, that was, if he wasn't already wearing a gravestone.

She looked back over what she'd written. She wasn't a detective, but compiling a comprehensive account of Billy Ray's life was the first step to leading her to his victims. He'd made a mistake when he didn't kill her. He'd made other mistakes. Serials always did.

Again the childish laughter, then a deeper voice like Ma's.

She turned toward the bedroom. Was she hearing shades of her past buried within these thin walls? She shivered despite the heat. That icy sensation spread through her, the one Ma used to say meant someone had walked across her grave.

The voices continued.

She crept to the screen door and peered out.

On the path that led to the street, a tall light-haired woman dressed in a sleeveless yellow housedress and plastic green flip-flops was walking toward the house. A tow-headed child with short curly hair was balanced on her ample hip. At her feet, a little girl with blond pigtails backed up and wrapped her arms around the woman's legs, causing the woman to stop.

"CeeCee," the woman called as Claire pushed open the screen.

Claire blocked the sunlight with a raised hand. "Jessie?"

"Don't tell me I've changed, 'cause I ain't. I'm still the purtiest girl in Lafourche."

"Well I don't know, looks like you have some competition wrapped around them legs there." Her grammar had slipped again, but with Jessie it felt natural.

Jessie tried to step forward, but the little girl blocked her movements. Claire walked down the steps and around her car.

"Luc dropped us off, hope you can drive us back. We're sporting one car these days. Oh, this here's Hanna, she's three and a half." Jessie tried to break the child's clasp around her legs.

She bent before the child. "Hello, Hanna. I'm Claire."

The girl curled backwards into her mother, her brown eyes shining. "Hanna, stop being so shy. Say hello." The girl turned away and buried her head between her mother's legs.

Claire straightened. "How are you, Jess?"

"Except for these two, I'm a woman of leisure. This here's Wyatt, more energy than a nuclear power plant." Upon hearing his name, Wyatt bounced up and down on his mother's hip and giggled. Jessie leaned over to place him on the ground, but he let out a warning yell and gripped her arm so tightly that she reeled him back onto her hip.

"You didn't have kids the last time I saw you."

"Been eight years, CeeCee. Your mom's funeral. I ran into Philippe over at the Piggly Wiggly, said you were here for a visit. Surprised me a bit, you coming back now that you got a good life up in Baton Rouge. Sorta surprised him too."

Jessie's girlhood gaiety peeked through the layers of maternal authority and Claire had the urge to wrap her in a tight hug.

"Come on, let's get outta the sun," she said instead.

Inside the door, Jessie handed Wyatt to Claire. "Hold on to this for a minute." She didn't wait for a response, just plopped Wyatt into Claire's arms. Then, knowing the house as she did, she walked to the kitchen cabinet and withdrew a saucepan and a wire whisk. "Toys."

Wyatt smelled like a bundle of baby powder and sour milk and felt like a curious cat. The more he squirmed the tenser Claire grew. She cooed in his ear, but he pulled away. She rocked him side to side as Suzanne had done with a younger Chet. As he tried to crawl from her grasp, she tried to find him a more comfortable position. Unable to free himself, his eyebrows drew together and his cheeks grew red. "Shhhhh," she tried again, but a cry burst from his lips and tears filled his little blue eyes.

"Jessie!"

Jessie grabbed him and put him on the floor with the kitchen utensils. She knelt and played with him long enough to get him interested. Wyatt's tears dried up as fast as they'd appeared.

"Sorry, Jess." Claire stooped next to Wyatt. "I've never been good with kids."

"They're not as breakable as you might think." Jessie shook the eggbeater like a silent rattle.

Claire watched her friend. This Jessie was a stranger. True, they'd been together at the funeral, but it had been a difficult time. She'd resented that Jessie had cared for Ma during her final days when she'd been told only that Ma wasn't feeling well. She'd tried not to hold that against

Jessie. The decision had been Ma's. She hadn't wanted to disrupt Claire's studies.

She stood, backed away a step.

Jessie stood also, smoothing her dress down the way Ma used to. The gesture so familiar yet so disturbing coming from Jessie.

"Philippe did a good job on the house, didn't he?" Claire blurted out.

"Like she never left, ain't it?"

Jessie's eyes dropped to the papers spread across table. She walked over and picked up a newspaper clipping of William Cobb. "This why you come back?"

Claire rushed over and scooped the pages together into the folder. Claire reached for the clipping in Jessie's hand, but she pulled it away.

"Jessie, please. Hand it here. I was working. I'll put it away so you can fill me in on these beautiful children of yours."

Jessie glanced again at the clipping before handing it over. Then she walked to the sofa and sat beside Hanna, who was busy plucking the cotton sheet from the cracks where it had been tucked as a sofa cover.

"Hanna, stop that."

"Why is there a bed sheet on the sofa, mamma?"

Still shaken, Claire stuffed the file into a kitchen drawer. Jessie's question had mirrored Philippe's almost to the word, but it didn't make sense; Jessie didn't know anything about Billy Ray. How could she?

"The sofa's old, Hanna. My brothers and I weren't very nice to it when we were kids so it has lots of holes and stains. We cover it with a sheet so it looks pretty again."

"Your ma told me to keep you away from him." Jessie tightened Hanna's pigtails by pulling apart two clumps of hair. The child winced. "Told me on her death bed, 'Keep my baby away from that Billy Ray. He'll destroy my girl,' is what she said."

A wave of vertigo washed over Claire. Wasn't that what Philippe had said?

"In your words, CeeCee, why'd you come back?"

Claire looked up. As the youngest she'd always caved to Jessie's will in the past, but now she felt the power of the courtroom, the desire to win. This was her secret and she'd share it when she was ready.

The saucepan clinked on the wooden floor. The metal whisk scraped its surface. Wyatt gave a gleeful cry.

"Why would Ma say something like that?"

"That Winn-Dixie's a car dealership now."

Golden rays cut through the screen splitting the room in two. Claire felt the rays on her back, felt the room heating up. Jessie was always difficult to follow, but first Billy Ray, now Winn-Dixie. "Jess, I want to know what Ma knew about Billy Ray or how she knew. It's important to me." Was it possible Ma'd known from the beginning? No, she'd have done something. Surely.

Wyatt cried out. Jessie's gaze flew to the child. He'd lost his grip on the pan and couldn't turn it over.

"I don't have no diploma like you, but I promised your ma. I loved that woman. I might be dead if she hadn't fed me all those evenings. If it wasn't for her, I'd have been sent off to one of them foster homes, or girls' schools where they beat you or worse. So if she tells me to keep you away from that guy, you better believe I'm gonna do it even if I have to tie you to a chair."

"Jessie, you're talking crazy."

Wyatt's piercing scream stopped the conversation. Jessie shoved Hanna off the sofa and then flipped the pot over for

Wyatt. "Remember, I was there that day in the Winn-Dixie and what happened to you was no female problem."

Claire started to speak, but stopped. Sweat beaded on her forehead.

"You don't remember, do you?"

Claire shook her head, but her shoulders had tensed and her throat felt like someone had lit a match and thrown it in her mouth. Her insides—her stomach, her bowels—were being sucked down into the earth.

Jessie took no notice of her discomfort. "I was sixteen, just gotten my driver's permit, so you were…what…fifteen about? Your ma forced Philippe to lend me his broken-down excuse for a car. Remember that orange thing that made all the racket? You and I, we drove over to the new Winn-Dixie in Raceland. They were having a big ole Grand Opening with free hotdogs and stuff. They had a marching band and games. Remember that?"

The smell of Philippe's ratty car filled Claire's memory. She remembered the band playing one of those songs that marching bands always play, but the memories were separate, not strung together. Jessie had worn pink jeans. Why were these incidents locked up so tight? But several years of her childhood were also in that dark, hidden compartment along with the morning that the Dean had called her into his office and told her they had found Brian, hanging in the boy's locker room. Since Ma was deceased by then, she'd had to identify the body.

She knew these events had happened because Philippe spoke of them, as Jessie was doing now, but she had no recollection of them. And each retelling brought on a visceral effect inside her, dredging up emotions she didn't know she had.

"Remember me driving so slow 'cause I was afraid of messing up that hunk of junk car? Jessie asked.

For Claire the scene unfolded as if she were watching herself onstage, a remote actor in a play. A spring afternoon. Excited to ride with Jessie in Philippe's car. During the drive, Jessie had gone on and on about some guy that worked at the new Winn-Dixie. That was why Jessie was wearing her nice pink jeans. Claire'd been more interested in the free hot dogs.

"We was in line," Jessie said. "You were buying some corn for your ma. Billy Ray was the cashier. All the girls in two parishes had a crush on him. He broke some hearts, too. Oh, sorry, guess I shouldn't say something like that."

She remembered Jessie's hands pressed to her back, pushing her forward in line. "Can you see him?" Jessie had whispered in her ear. "Cute, ain't he?"

She'd risen up on her tiptoes, but was too far away. "No, I can't."

Jessie shoved her farther to the left.

"Now?"

The woman in line in front of her wore large, round, plastic hair curlers. The curlers blocked her view. She giggled and leaned past the woman's broad shoulders. He hadn't changed at all. His jaw protruded, his chin, a feral point, and the dull blue eyes.

Then, the world drew in around her as if she and Billy Ray existed inside a bubble. Silence encircled her. The bag of corn dropped to the floor, as did her change purse. The sound of pulsing blood roared in her ears. He looked up, his eyes moving in slow motion until they met hers.

She became aware of people moving away from her and of those eyes, those horrid blue eyes, sliding down her body. His face contorted into a sort of sneer.

Jessie had cried out, staring down at the ground. Everyone was looking down.

Claire's gaze had traveled toward the warm liquid pooling between her tennis shoes.

Claire yelped as if she'd burned herself on a hot burner. Looking up, she noticed Jessie and Hanna watching her with strange expressions on their faces.

"Yo, Claire? You all right?" Jessie asked.

She drew in a deep breath and nodded, but she wasn't all right. "How old did you say I was?"

"'Bout fifteen, maybe a little younger. You don't look so good. Your skin's lost some color. Come over here and sit." Jessie patted the sofa beside her.

Claire didn't feel too good. She crept to the sofa, sliding down next to Hanna, who handed her a Time magazine off the side table. "What else do you remember?" she asked Jessie.

"When we got home and I told your ma, she said that you hadn't gotten your monthly yet and your body was messing with you. But female problems don't make you wet yourself. Hanna, honey, let mommy talk to CeeCee. That a girl."

"Is that how Ma learned his name?"

"Billy Ray's? I guess. I mentioned how good looking he was as I was telling her what you done. The rest of the evening you wouldn't eat, wouldn't talk, just sat here on the sofa staring into space. Your ma left with Philippe later on, and I sat with you. Well, I played cards with Brian. You were pretty much out of it."

"That was the day it became real. Before that, it was…a child's nightmare."

"What became real? Tell me the rest of it."

She watched Jessie hug Hanna, the way a mamma did when she sensed danger. She wondered how Ma must have felt that day. Where she had gone that evening?

"Billy Ray raped me." Her voice betrayed none of the emotion that was knotted inside her.

Jessie sucked in a breath. Her lips drew together in a thin line. "He was so popular," she said. "I suspected something awful bad must have happened...a broken heart...but that?"

"It happened before, back when I was ten. At first I didn't understand. I remember being in the hospital, drugged, in a confused state. Then, because we never talked about it, I grew to believe the rest of it...well, I thought it hadn't really happened. When I saw him that day, I knew it had."

"Mommy, when are we going home?" Hanna asked, snuggling against Jessie's knees. Jessie kissed the top of the blond head.

"Soon, sweetie, soon." She looked up. "You sure it was him? That was like what...four no five years later? What if it was just someone that looked like him?"

Claire remained silent. Jessie would believe what she wanted. For that matter, so would everyone else. Until she found evidence.

"Tell me about that night when Ma left with Philippe. Do you know where she went? Did she confront him?"

"Philippe drove, guess you should ask him."

So Philippe had known all along. Like Jessie, had he promised Ma? Was that why he was acting the way he was?

"Mommy," Hanna cried.

"Yes, sweetie." Jessie turned back to her. "We better hit the road, the natives are getting restless."

"Okay. I need to talk to Philippe, too."

Chapter 21

Tuesday June 21, 2005
Green Acres, LA

The car wheels lost traction when they hit the graveled shoulder. Claire lifted her foot from the accelerator and allowed the car to slow on its own. When she regained control she steered back onto the asphalt. She swung through the next curve at the posted speed.

Ma hadn't told Philippe about Billy Ray on her deathbed. Philippe had known since the night Ma had made him drive her...where? The Winn-Dixie? It didn't matter where. He'd lied.

The car accelerated. Worse than lying, he'd made her doubt herself, her memories. He'd better have a darn good reason. As it stood, she'd never forgive him. She slammed her foot down on the brake, sliding into the intersection and running the stop sign. Not another car in sight. She slapped the steering wheel. She'd never forgive him.

"Philippe!" She knocked so hard on the aluminum frame that the screen door bounced each time her knuckles made contact.

Had he promised Ma? Was that why he had tried to dissuade her? That was no excuse. Why else would he have lied?

"Philippe!"

The door opened and little Chet stood looking up at her, his blue eyes radiant and a glowing smile stretched his lips. "Hey, Auntie Claire, what you doing here?"

She took a step back, clasped her shaking hands. "Hey, sweetheart, I'm looking for your daddy."

"Claire?" Suzanne scooted up behind Chet. She pushed the screen wider. "Come on in. Chet, mon chéri, let Claire in."

She hadn't planned on Chet. She could hardly tear into Philippe in front of his son. She stroked her throat. "I need to speak to Philippe. It's rather urgent."

Chet wrapped his arms around her legs. "Are you staying for dinner?"

Peering into his sparkling blue eyes, she rubbed his fluffy hair. *The innocence of children.* "I have things I have to do. I can't stay today."

His cherub face fell. She knelt, wrapped her arms around him, and kissed his forehead. "You're so sweet. Don't ever change."

"You want to watch cartoons with me? It's Superman."

"Mon chéri, run on back to the tele," Suzanne said. "Claire and mommy need to talk."

"You'll come?" he asked, his eyes wide with the question.

Claire winked. Giggling, Chet ran from the room, his tennis shoes flapping the hardwood flooring.

"Philippe rarely comes home for lunch any more. What's up?" Suzanne asked. "You look like you're ready to do battle. Has he done something?"

"You could say that." She wasn't ready to discuss this with Suzanne, not before she had a go at Philippe. She looked away, knowing she needed to change the subject. She needed to calm herself. "I saw Joe Sunday."

"How's he doing?"

Suzanne led her to the table. They both sat. "Would you like some tea or coffee?" Suzanne asked.

"No. I have to get back. I need to make a few important calls."

"Are you going to tell me why you're looking for Philippe in such a fury?"

"I'm in a rush, that's all. I thought he'd still be here. Do you know where he is?"

"No. They're working on several houses, could be at any one of them. You want me to give him a message?"

She stood. "I better go." Then she remembered why she'd thought of Joe. "Joe told me about your miscarriage. I'm so sorry. Philippe never said a word."

"No. He wouldn't. He blames himself, you see."

"He tends to do that a lot. Who knows, maybe he is to blame."

Rather than angry, Suzanne looked disappointed. "Why would you say that?"

"Meanness. Sorry. Like I said, I should go. I might say a few other things." She started for the door, but turned back. "I just found out he lied about something important. Why does he do that?"

"Is this about Cobb?"

"Partly, but it makes me doubt everything else he's said. I can't trust him, Suzanne."

"He's trying to protect you. He takes that role very seriously."

"I'm not a kid anymore. I'm trying to do something important for this community. I need his support, not his lies." She pushed open the screen. "I better go."

She slammed her car door with the force of her frustration. She turned the key and hit the button to lower the windows.

"Wait up, Claire."

Suzanne was standing beside the car. She bent and stuck her head inside the open window. "There're things you don't know, things we don't talk about."

"There's a shocker. We don't talk about anything in this family."

"Claire, please. Come inside, this isn't easy for me."

Easy for her? But her sister-in-law's expression spoke louder than her words. She couldn't just drive away. Suzanne needed to talk. "Okay," Claire said, turning off the engine.

Back at the table, Claire accepted the coffee mug. Suzanne poured a second mug and sat across the table. She aligned the salt and pepper shakers with her coffee mug as if securing a border between them.

Claire brought the hot coffee to her lips as she watched Suzanne fidget.

Suzanne turned and glanced over her shoulder and out into the living room. She turned back without looking up.

Claire set the mug between her hands. "In my line of work I hear a lot of horrible stories," she said. "You can tell me anything, very little surprises me." That wasn't exactly true. She was always amazed at man's inhumanity. But listening to victims gave her a certain distance. Sitting here with Suzanne, it felt different. If Philippe had—

"It's just that it's hard for me. That was a difficult time. Philippe would kill me if he knew I'd told you."

She leaned forward. "Told me what?"

Suzanne propped her forearms on the table and slouched into them.

Claire saw her reserve and waited. She took another sip of coffee enjoying the slight hickory flavor.

Suzanne pulled herself back up. "I'm not sure what your ma said to Philippe about Cobb. He never talked about it, but it bothered him, bothered him for a long time. Looking back, I think he wanted to talk to you after the funeral. He was in real bad shape back then. I thought he was just upset over your ma's passing, but I noticed his behavior toward you when you got so fired up that no one had told you how sick your ma was. I asked him about it and that's when he said your ma had said something."

Suzanne fiddled with the salt and pepper some more. "To make a long story short, I think it ate at him. A few years back, Philippe and Joe decided they wanted to grow the company. They bid on a piece of business property in Larose."

"I know about this, Joe told me."

"Did Joe tell you that after they won the bid, Cobb threatened Philippe?"

She froze. Something lined up in her mind, just a little out of reach. "Go on."

"When Philippe didn't back down, Cobb sent a couple of guys to rough me up. Thing was, I was four months pregnant. I lost the baby and Philippe has never forgiven himself."

Claire turned away. She couldn't look at her sister-in-law. Instead, she picked at a place on the table. "All the more reason to want Billy Ray behind bars."

"First off, Philippe's guilt doesn't just sit with what happened to me. What I didn't know before but have figured out over the years is that Philippe had been looking for a reason to go up against Cobb for a long time, maybe because of what your ma said to him before she died. This real estate deal was his big chance and not only did he lose, I got hurt in the process.

"Second off, I'm not saying Philippe's afraid of Cobb, but I think he's afraid he can't keep us safe if he went up against the man again. Now that you're determined to confront him, Philippe's worried about you. He's afraid he can't keep *you* safe."

"He's not responsible for me."

"Course he is. Has been since you were little." Suzanne nodded. "Look, us Cajuns are born with determination, and I want that man in jail almost as bad as you do, but I'm afraid. I got Chet to worry about. Man's already killed one of my babies. I have no reason to think he wouldn't do it again. And although he's more stubborn than an ink stain, I love that brother of yours. I don't want to lose him. Cobb's evil. He's a man without a conscience."

"That's why he can't wear a badge. Do you know what kind of power that badge will give him? He has to be stopped. I have to find some of his victims, if any are still alive, that is. It's going to be tough, Suzanne. I won't lie. Do you think Philippe would testify if I could find evidence of what happened with Blue Belt?"

"There's no evidence. You think those bullies are going to admit Cobb sent them?"

"How do you know it was Cobb?"

Suzanne looked heavenward, rolled her top lip and bit down on it. Several minutes passed in silence.

Claire waited. The question was important. Did Suzanne know for sure Cobb sent them or was she supposing? Had Philippe told her it was Cobb?

Suzanne dropped her head. "Who else? They were bidding against Blue Belt and as soon as Philippe dropped the contract, Blue Belt took over."

Not proof. "If Blue Belt profited I can understand why you think Cobb had a hand in it. If you could identify the thugs, I could test how loyal they are. I could deal with them, offer them immunity, they might talk. A pregnant woman was beaten, surely—"

"The men who did it knew I was pregnant. I told them. Did it make them hit higher, or softer. No. They didn't care then, they don't care now. They had a job to do. It's as simple as that." She looked across the table with hooded eyes. "Don't think you'll find any of Cobb's victims down here. In this parish, his father owns practically all of the refineries and most of the businesses. Work is hard to come by. Don't look for any locals to upset the status quo."

The coffee lay like lead on her stomach. Now, Cobb had a death grip on her family. "Then I'll stick with the rape angle. I know down to my toes that Billy Ray killed that woman last week. I have to find the proof. Don't look so doubtful. It's what I do—prosecute rapists. And I've been told, I'm rather good at it."

"Tread softly down here. Cobb has more friends than a porcupine has spikes. For a time I was afraid Philippe might go after Cobb himself. Then I got pregnant again and Philippe backed down. He didn't back down because of Cobb, he backed down because of the man's friends. They're the ones that'll get to you when you aren't looking."

Chapter 22

Wednesday June 22, 2005
Bayou, LA

Not long past midnight, Mamma Anna heard the footsteps before she saw the bushes part. Ory's dark shape drew closer and firelight bounced over the contours of his stern face. Like her and Bernadette, he was clothed all in black, but unlike them, he wasn't dressed for a ceremony.

She stood, the pain in her hip arguing with her, and stretched to kiss Ory on each cheek. Man needed a wash. "Comme je suis content de te voir, mon ami." Ah, yes, very happy to see him.

Ory reached deep into a sack slung over one shoulder and drew out something wrapped in a linen cloth. He handed it to Mamma Anna.

"Merci," she said, receiving the bundle with both hands. "Bernadette, get Ory something to drink." She sank back down on the log and cradled the package in her lap. She pulled free the string wrapped around it and then folded back the linen flaps.

The fingerlike petals of the hibiscus asper leaves were already dried and crumbled at her touch. She lowered her head and drew in a heady whiff. "Whoa! Très bien, très bien."

Bernadette handed Ory a corked bottle of rum and then sat down beside Mamma Anna. "That them?"

"Straight from Haiti," she said, folding the linen flaps back over the leaves to protect them. "We can start. Do you have everything I asked for, the yew, the yarrow—"

"Blood from a black pig, osmunda fronds for the dreaming. Course I gots 'em. Wait here." Bernadette stood.

Mamma Anna ran down the list of ingredients. The spell was a strong one, had to be. It was one thing to draw the girl home, back to a place of love and family; completely another to lure her out into the bayou, a place of hidden dangers. She would have to connect the lure to memories of safety. That was where the hibiscus asper came in. They'd cost a pretty penny, but if the spell worked, it would be worth all the money she had. It had to work.

Bernadette returned carrying a wooden crate. She placed it on the ground near the fire and unloaded the contents. She turned the crate over to use as a table and set a shiny black bowl on top. "You need something personal, you have time to get that?"

Mamma Anna bent to reach into a cloth bag at her feet. She lifted out a pinecone angel. As soon as she'd seen it in the tiny house, she recognized the delicate aluminum wings, the gold sparkles, and the pipe cleaner halo as the work of a meticulous child. One touch told her the story of how that eight-year-old child had worked in secret, fashioning the angel with love. Christmas morning, the child had wrapped it in red paper and presented it to her devoted mother. Abandoned, it collected dust on a handmade bookshelf until she had chosen it for the important work ahead.

"Ory, ma cher, tu dois partir maintenant." Yes, he had to leave because they would be summoning Marinette Bwa Cheche and she could be cruel to the men folk.

Ory stood, gripping the rum bottle by its neck. He didn't wait for an explanation. Maybe he recognized the deep red candles in contrast to the black robes she and Bernadette wore. Most men knew to steer clear of Marinette.

He kissed both her and Bernadette before slipping into the darkness beyond the fire. Bernadette moved the circle of candles closer to the fire, her skin slippery with sweat.

Mamma Anna slid over on the log, pulling the crate table between her legs. Marinette was too aggressive a loa for her old bones. She'd let Bernadette be the vessel tonight. "You ready?"

The red-brown screech owl whinnied like a horse as Bernadette removed it from the cage. It warbled a different call and found a perch on Bernadette's arm.

"You remember the order?" Mamma Anna asked. "Once you join with Marinette I'll ask her help with the spell. When it's done we'll send it to the girl in a dream. Marinette's feisty. Haitians' loas often are. She'll take a lot out of you so be prepared."

"Been waiting to meet Marinette Bwa Cheche a long time. I'm young, I can handle her."

Mamma Anna hoped she could. "You're a good hunsi. I can't afford to lose you. Be careful, but most of all, don't lose yourself." If the spell wasn't so important, she'd never invoke Marinette. Ten years ago, the last time she'd called on the loa, it almost killed her.

Chapter 23

Wednesday June 22, 2005
Villette, LA

Claire was seated next to Brian as Pa rowed through the sallow water. A shiny slime covered the surface reflecting the moon. Nearby, a red-brown owl perched on a cypress root. As they passed, she felt sure the owl was looking right at her.

"Keep your hands in the boat," Pa said. "Don't want to give 'em to a gator." He rowed with one oar, sometimes using it as a pole to push through the tall grasses.

Brian kept pretending to dip his hand in the water. She knew he only did it to frighten her, and it did. "Papa," she said, but as soon as Pa looked up Brian stopped.

"What are we looking for?" Claire asked.

Pa nodded to the left. "Know a good place for crayfish."

She looked over her shoulder, but as she did she realized she was a grown woman, not the four-year-old. She turned back to Brian and he looked just as he had the last time she'd seen him in college. His lips parted and he smiled sweetly, filling her with the warmth of his love.

And she was awake. The room was dark, but she felt safe. This was home. Her home, she thought as she was falling, falling, back into the arms of sleep.

She was back in the bayou, but this time alone. An alligator glided through the water at the bottom of the rise where she stood. It took no notice of her and she realized she wasn't afraid. Why would she be? As a child, the bayou had been her playground. A constant adventure she shared with Pa and her brothers. She'd learned to swim here, learned to fish, and to track animals.

The waterways had been the roads that had gotten her to church and school. And as a teen, she'd come to sit within the massive cypress trees, her place of solace where she could hide after that horrible day at the Winn-Dixie.

She turned to walk up the rise, but the scenery had changed. The rise had given way to a flat forest of pine trees, their branches high over head. She'd never been here before. She shifted and glanced around.

"Pa? Pa, are you there?" Her voice was high and she realized she was a little girl again with little hands. She wanted to run, but her legs wouldn't move. She wimpered. "Pa?"

A figure moved out of the shadows. It inched toward her until she recognized the voodoo woman from the post office. She was dressed all in black.

"What do you want?" Claire asked, her voice shaky.

The woman didn't say a word, but pointed off to the left. Claire turned and gasped. Billy Ray was strung up to a tree branch. His head tilted lifelessly toward his chest.

Claire bolted up, sweat clinging to her skin. Every detail of the dream played again in her mind. Two dreams in one night. But for the life of her she couldn't remember the first one. She checked her watch. 3:33.

She lay back against the pillow. Was it worth going to sleep again? She thought about the dream. What had frightened her? Billy Ray dead? Wasn't that what she wanted?

* * *

Claire checked the battery of her cell phone. Low and she still hadn't heard from Erwin. She slipped outside and held the phone up. She checked the reception. Still nothing. She'd have to walk to the road again. As she started down the tire-lined path, she wondered why she thought one day she'd check the reception and it would magically work. Wasn't there a saying about doing something over and over and hoping for a different outcome? Wasn't it said to be the definition of insanity?

A yellow jacket buzzed around her head and she swatted it away. She should have driven out, then she could have blasted the air-conditioning and charged the phone at the same time. When was the parish going to get electricity out here, anyway? It'd been at least ten years since it was first talked about. Ma hadn't wanted it. Another expense, she'd said.

Heat wafted off the asphalt in waves. Claire checked her phone. Three bars. She found a thick elm offering shade and punched Erwin's number.

He answered on the third ring. "I was going to call you. I emailed two investigators' names to you this morning."

She'd have to go by the library to read her email. "Have you found anything on the Cobb girl's murder?"

"Not as much as I expected. You said the story was in all the newspapers. I found a two-paragraph mention of it in a local Lafourche paper and nothing else."

"That's strange. The murder of a prominent man's daughter should have garnered more than a few paragraphs."

"Tell me. I did get a copy of the death certificate. It's also in the email I sent you. The Records clerk told me someone else had ordered a copy the same day."

A beetle landed on her shoulder and she flicked it off. "Probably Percy. I started to look into it before I had all the details. What about the gardener?"

"Man named Churchill Whitaker. No priors. I tried to get a copy of the investigation file, but it's gone missing. This doesn't smell good."

"Par for the course down here." With the back of her hand, she wiped the rolling sweat from her forehead. "How did the newspaper articles disappear? Charlie Dill said the story was in *all* the papers."

"You said he was a kid at the time, did he even read the papers?"

"Thanks Erwin, I owe you. I'll check out the investigators you sent and give you a break."

"Don't owe me a thing. Long as you get the guy who killed that poor girl, reckon I'll be happy enough."

Claire closed the phone. Maybe she should give Percy a call, make sure he was the one who'd ordered the death certificate.

"Hello, child."

Claire swung around to find Mamma Anna standing in the trees behind her.

"What are you doing here?"

"Came to remind you of the Feast of Saint Jean's tomorrow night."

"You're the one who left the gris-gris."

"To protect you. Bring it with you tomorrow."

An alarm sounded in Claire's mind. Mamma Anna had known she was staying at Ma's before their meeting at the post office. She remembered her dream from the previous night. The one where Mamma Anna had Billy Ray hanging from a tree. "What do you know about Billy Ray?"

"I gots lots to tell ya, but not before tomorrow night."

Claire's phone rang. Percy's name appeared in the screen. "Excuse me, I should—" She looked around, but the old woman was gone. She spun a complete circle, no trace of her. The phone rang again.

* * *

Claire drove to the Larose Post Office. Only two full business days had passed, and she knew better than to expect anything from her flyers so soon, but a daily trip to the Post Office needed to be added to her planning. The sooner the better.

After being promoted to Assistant DA, her prosecutions had come easily enough, but the voice in her head kept telling her this case was different. This was the one that mattered.

Was she competent enough to go after Billy Ray? Could she face him in a courtroom and maintain her composure? Not only would she need more evidence than she now had, she'd have to open the doors to her damaged soul, the ones she'd long ago nailed shut. That terrified her.

She parked next to a police car and caught sight of two officers heading around the rear of the building. She walked in the front door and headed straight for her post box. Empty. Hopefully, she'd have better luck with her email or her visit with Tulane's dean.

She started for the door, but noticed her flyer was gone. The "Pickup for Sale" flyer and the one for the missing child were there, but Billy Ray's picture had been torn off. A scrap of yellow paper was left attached to the pushpin.

She strutted to the counter. "Excuse me."

One postal clerk stood at the back door, speaking with the police officers. The other clerk slouched on a stool, sorting envelopes. She looked up and shot Claire an icy glare. "Yeah?"

"Is there a problem?" Claire nodded toward the officers.

"Had a break-in last night. Nothing big, probably some kids having a few kicks."

"Vandals?"

The clerk didn't answer.

"I posted a flyer on the local bulletin board last Friday and it's been removed. I'd like to know why."

"Wouldn't we all." The clerk sighed, put down her envelopes, and sashayed over to the counter, her hips swaying side-to-side like coneflowers in a breeze. She propped an elbow on the counter and leaned left to look over Claire's shoulder at the bulletin board. She leaned back. "You the one with box two-ten?"

"I am," Claire said. "Do you have something for me?"

"Naw. Some guy was in Saturday morning wantin' to know who had box two-ten. He tore off your flyer. None to happy 'bout it either. See if it ain't in the trash can over there."

"Did you tell him who had the box?"

"Naw. Ain't legal."

"Thanks." Claire knew what passed for legal in this part of the world was up to one's discretion.

The yellow flyer lay inside the black metal can, balled tightly. She reached in and pulled it out, flattening the paper against the bulletin board. Cobb had political backing. She had to expect that not everyone hated him the way she did. Then a strange thought came to mind. She held the flyer up to the clerk.

"Excuse me, but was this the man that asked about my box?"

"Naw. He was older, but a white guy. Skinny little runt, rough looking."

"Thanks again."

She stuck the pushpin into the good corner. No doubt others had been removed too, but she would replace them and continue replacing them until she had what she wanted. Billy Ray would never be sheriff. Not while she was still breathing.

Chapter 24

Thursday June 23, 2005
New Orleans, LA

"Do you have any other questions, Ms. Rivet?" The way
the dean spoke her name, she would have thought it had three
syllables. He slid from behind his polished desk and stood.

She stood also. The short, round man with his uppity
attitude was as phony as the antiques decorating his office.
When he'd launched into his diatribe of personal privacy, she
knew he was on the Cobb payroll. Indeed, he had boasted
about annual donations made to the school by Mr. and Mrs.
Cobb and how support from alumni was the foundation on
which Tulane created new programs. She'd tried not to yawn.

If she asked anything else, she'd be showing her hand to
the opposition. For it would certainly reach Billy Ray. If she
only had a hand to show. But she had learned that two Tulane
women were raped while Cobb was a student. Not from the
dean, but from the school newspaper. Before the meeting,
she'd slipped into the library and read through the headlines
of back issues.

"Call me if I can help you with anything else." With a
self-serving grin, the dean closed his office door in her face.

Two women, Marsha Louise Baker and Zeta Mary White.
Claire headed down the stairwell. Baker had been raped
during December of Cobb's second year, the year he was
expelled from Tulane. White had been raped in May of the
year he graduated. But Billy Ray was at Nicholls that year,
but what if he came back to Tulane to visit friends, or his
girlfriend Marla, or football buddy Charlie?

Stress, final exams, a perfect fuse.

She pushed open the glass door and stepped into the afternoon heat. Her gaze locked onto a man across the quad. Was he watching her? He tossed his cigarette, ground it with the toe of his boot, and turned in the opposite direction, heading toward the parking lot.

Her mistake. A little too early in the process to get paranoid, but she hadn't forgotten that a man had asked for her box number at the post office.

With cell phone in hand, she headed toward her car. She punched in her assistant's direct line.

"Vilma. I need you to research something for me. You'll find everything I need in the state database."

"Hold on. Okay, I have a pen. Go."

"Could you check on any rape cases filed in Orleans Parish involving a Marsha Louise Baker or a Zeta Mary White?"

"I thought you were on vacation."

"I need all information on these two cases ASAP. Also, I need a current address for each woman. All I can tell you is that they were freshmen at Tulane University between 1975 and 1980. They could be married by now."

"Makes it tougher for a current address."

"I know. Erwin can help if you get stuck, but I don't want to bother him unless it's necessary. Get the social security numbers and check with DMV. Email me everything." She fished through her bag for the paper with her new email address.

"I have some messages fr..." The last words fuzzed out.

"Vilma? Hello?" She slapped the base of the phone, then took a few steps toward the building.

"Hello?" She hit the phone again.

"You want your messages?" Vilma asked.

"Sorry, I'm losing reception."

"First, Vincent called a couple of times, very vague. Doesn't he know you're on vacation? This one's marked important. Mr...I can't read the name, oh, he's the super of your apartment."

She ignored Vilma's question about Vincent. "I'm using an outside email CCrivet@hotmail. Use it instead of the office one."

Next she punched in Vincent's work number. But after the first ring, she disconnected. What was she going to say? Why would he call her? Did he want to come for the rest of his things? The apartment was empty. He could come by when he wanted, ah, but he didn't have keys. The super had keys. That must have been why he'd called. She checked the phone's battery level, then punched Vincent's number in a second time. What if he wanted to reconcile? What if he wanted to know where she was? She disconnected before it rang. She looked at the faceplate before giving up and throwing the phone in her bag.

Chapter 25

Thursday June 23, 2005
Villette, LA

Claire kicked off the bed sheet. A cooling breeze blew through the house, but it was still too hot for a cover. Her hand groped for the light button at the side of her watch— 11:45. She rolled to her stomach, her fist so tight that her fingernails cut into her palms. Three punches—forceful and angry—slammed into the pillow. Rolling back onto her side, she closed her eyes and tried not to think of Mamma Anna, sacrifices, or gris-gris, but last night's dream with Billy Ray hanging from a branch stuck in her mind.

A few minutes later she lit the watch again—midnight. Officially, Saint Jean's Eve was over and Saint Jean's feast had begun. According to legend and her big brother, she was safe. She hadn't been sacrificed to the devils of the night nor had her blood sprinkled across the crops.

"Hallelujah."

She swung her bare legs across the mattress to the floor.

Moonlight split the main room in chiaroscuro patterns. No books to read, no television to watch—what else cured insomnia? Vincent. She winced. The distance between Baton Rouge and Villette hadn't made the difference she'd hoped for. He had opened her heart and taught her trust; he had defined love. Her fingers found his gift, the gold cross, at her neck.

Where was the comfort of his memory? She wanted to remember his laugh, his touch, his taste without this pain, this hollowed emptiness. But she couldn't, not yet. Maybe later. After Billy Ray.

Billy Ray. What would happen *after Billy Ray?* She'd
never imagined that far into the future. Would she go back to
Baton Rouge, to an empty apartment and a job that was no
longer necessary? Or would she stay in Ma's house and
search for the peace Ma had found living here on the edge of
civilization?

Billy Ray. She had survived his hatred, but it still ran like
acid through her blood, burning every aspect of her life. On
her best days she couldn't imagine that changing, even when
Billy Ray was in prison. Evil always left its residue.

She walked back to the bedroom, looked down into the
jumbled sheet. No, she was not going to the bayou. Not
tonight. The old woman was manipulating her. Philippe saw
it, too. Sacrifices indeed.

But Saint Jean's Eve ended at midnight. The danger was
past.

One detail tickled the back of her mind. Mamma Anna
had called him Billy Ray, not William Cobb. It meant she
knew more about the man than his public persona. But was
Philippe right? Was her calling him by Billy Ray a red flag to
avoid?

Could be.

But she wouldn't sleep until she knew.

* * *

Her car engine broke the solitary silence, its lights sliced
the darkness.

After dropping the old woman off, she'd gone to the end
of the road and learned it dead-ended at a high dirt levee.
Night made the search for the turnoff difficult. She struggled
to find the exact spot where she'd left Mamma Anna. She
half-expected to see other cars, but there were none. Was she
too late? Had everyone gone?

Then, she caught sight of the tree trunk split into a "V." She pulled off the road and parked, but it would be impossible for another car to get past on the narrow lane.

She walked into the woods, following the same path the old woman had taken. The white bark of the birch trees now shone neon against the moonlight. A patch of Southern pines loomed overhead. She glanced up and around, surprised by the cloaking power of the huge trees.

"Mamma Anna," she called, half-expecting the old woman to reappear as mysteriously as she had disappeared the day before.

Codling moths flew past her face as she paused, waiting for her eyes to adjust. Male crickets, looking for mates, chirped in the underbrush. Toward the levee, tree frogs quonk-quonked. And overhead, leaves rustled, jostled by unseen birds. What she didn't hear were party sounds—no music, voices, or dancing—or ritual sounds—chanting, humming, or prayers. Her watch showed 12:25.

Switching on her flashlight, she crept deeper into the woods. Something stung her left arm and when she slapped at a second sting, her hand came away dotted with blood. Buzzing filled her ears, and bugs filled her nose and mouth. She dropped the flashlight. The swarming mosquitoes stayed with the light, covering the handle.

Backing away, she untied the sweatshirt from her waist and pulled it on to protect her exposed skin. With the tip of her foot, she tried to switch off the light, but the angle was wrong and the flashlight, still lit, rolled into a mound of dry leaves. The full moon would have to be enough light, but the heavy flashlight was her only weapon.

Maybe she should grab the flashlight and just go home. That made more sense than stumbling around in the dark, looking for a voodoo queen.

The light flickered as insects flew in and out of the beam. She bent and switched it off. The buzzing at her ears died down. The swarm dispersed. She brushed her clothes free of the remaining bugs and wiped her face with her sleeve.

Then, she heard a noise.

A snap.

She crept backwards, her hand clenching the flashlight's handle.

"Mamma Anna?"

She turned a full circle, scanning the shadowy terrain. A high-pitched whinny sound and the branches above shook with a powerful sway. She threw her head back to look as something took flight. Red-brown against the blue-black sky. She caught her breath. A screech owl. Only a screech owl.

Electricity tinged the air, prickling her skin. At first she thought the mosquitoes had returned. Then, a soothing wind blew across her, she felt the protection of her Pa and of the nature she'd befriended so long ago. The woodsy smell of ground cover and dead leaves brought forth a memory. Pa'd brought her into the bayou to hunt nutria, those ugly little rats. So young, she barely remembered Pa, but she hadn't forgotten the smells of loam and the drying blood of hunted animals.

She took a step, then another, listening. Her unexplained fear of the voodoo woman seemed absurd here in nature. Nature, these woods, were comfort. Voodoo. Superstition.

She stopped and sniffed the air. She smelled it now, the sour odor of fresh blood, fresh kill. A prickly sensation, like a thousand tiny ants, crawled up her spine. Sacrifices!

Nonsense. Men hunted; animals hunted; animals died. She raised her nose and sniffed again trying to get a direction, but the smell had blended to the point that she'd lost its distinction.

Two golden eyes watched her from beside a rotten log. She approached with caution, wondering if the animal might be injured. But then it rustled off through the underbrush.

"At least you're alive."

She watched the rustlings left in the animal's wake. Again she questioned her sanity, but she felt safe as if the tree trunks were her personal bodyguards. What was she looking for—party hats or slaughtered lambs?

A natural trail led through the brush. As long as she stuck to the trail, she'd find her way back. But just in case, she laid a twig diagonally across her path every hundred feet or so, another trick she'd been taught as a child. People got lost in the bayou, she'd always been told. Now, she wondered if such stories weren't created just to scare children into behaving. Either way, she laid her sticks.

The ground squished beneath her tennis shoes. In the bayou, the earth waged an endless battle against water, both struggling for domain. The change in terrain might mean a body of water was near, or it might mean nothing. She looked back from where she'd come, hoping to use her car as a marker. But she'd walked too far.

The larger trees had fallen behind. Here were younger pines with thinner trunks. Tall bamboo sprouted in bunches. The levee was in the opposite direction, but the lighter foliage could mean that a bayou curved around. Anything was possible out here.

After walking a few more minutes, her tennis shoes were soaked and the wet canvas rubbed against her bare skin, promising blisters. She longed for boots. A patch of high reeds stood before her. Maybe Philippe didn't believe in alligator attacks, but she figured an alligator would much rather eat her smooth leg than stinky nutria. She gripped the flashlight like a weapon, swinging it side to side across her body to clear her way through reeds.

Alligators. Were they her biggest risk? What madness had brought her out here in the middle of the night? Billy Ray. Always Billy Ray. Chasing the demon. Was the old woman laying a trap? If so, she was walking right into it.

Claire smelled the water before she saw it, not the fresh, rejuvenating smell of a rolling river, but the putrid, stagnating smell of water rotting away tree roots, marshland, and animal carcasses. The reeds opened. A mass of water hyacinths stretched before her.

The shoreline abutted their wide leaves, and what looked like a pond lay behind the plants, but the night was too dark to know for sure. Its source might snake off under the cover of the massive cypress trees on the opposite side. But the smell and the hyacinths suggested a bayou.

Silhouetted against the sky, the branches of huge cypress trees hung down over a vaporous haze, which hovered above the water. Spanish moss draped branch-to-branch, creating a lace collar on the foggy curtain. Moonlight raked the southern edge where she stood.

If this was a pond, she could walk around it, but how long would that take? Was there even another side? Most likely, she was standing at the edge of a waterway. With this light, it was impossible to tell.

She might be stubborn, but she wasn't stupid. Except for the no-see-ums she kept coughing up, she was alone. Wandering around the edge of a pond or waterway, not a good idea. She'd get lost, hurt, or eaten by alligators. If a party was going on, even a voodoo ritual, she should have heard something by now. No, this was it—the end of the trail.

Then a drumbeat vibrated across the water's surface. Or was it her imagination? Water splashed over the bank at her feet. She jumped back and shot the flashlight beam at the sound.

Another splash, this one out on the water. Using the light, she looked for the glint of red. Alligator eyes shone red at night. How did she know that? But she remembered sitting in the boat with her father and the red marbles rolling across the water's surface. "Alligators," he'd said. "Keep your hands in the boat."

On the opposite shore, the scaly cypress leaves wavered as if blown by a breeze, but the air was still. Everything that moved in the bayou moved as slowly as the transformation of earth to water or water to earth. Rapid movement, like the water splashing at her feet, signaled danger. She stepped back again and passed the beam along the water's edge.

Out of the darkness, a deep roaring laugh swelled over the water. She recognized the laugh and wondered how such a small woman could create such a racket? It must be a trick—microphones maybe—but trick or not, the old woman had found her.

Mamma Anna's face burst through the fog, her smile sinister. Claire's breath caught in her chest. She backed farther from the shoreline. Alligators were the least of her worries.

"Mawu-Lisa nous protège," Mamma Anna called, lifting her arms skyward in the fog. Claire understood "protect us."

Streamers of cloth—red, yellow, and orange—whipped around Mamma Anna through the cloudy mist, enlarging and empowering her small frame. As she drew nearer, hovering above the water, she appeared magical and larger than life.

Claire switched off the flashlight. Without the glare refracted against the fog, she saw the raft on which Mamma Anna stood. A simple wooden platform built on four oil drums. It bobbed just above water level. The wooden bench that stretched across two-thirds of the platform served to enhance the illusion of Mamma Anna's mythical height. She stood in the center as someone at the rear guided the raft with a pole.

The raft hit the shore and bounced off. Mamma Anna didn't falter. The floating cloth, which had engulfed her, was nothing more than pieces of colorful chiffon sewn to the woman's gown. They fell motionless around her.

"Come aboard child, I'll show you how to deal with that demon, Billy Ray." Mamma Anna stepped down from the bench and stretched her arms to Claire.

Chapter 26

Friday June 24, 2005
Bayou, LA

Mamma Anna noticed, as she hoisted Claire aboard the raft, that the young one didn't hesitate. The magic words, Billy Ray, were all she needed to steer this one to the end of the earth. Claire was strong though, both in body and mind. The spirits would fight for her. And that single-mindedness.

She was perfect.

The raft rocked for a moment, then steadied. Mamma Anna felt the surge of youth as she held onto Claire's arm. She lowered herself to the bench and motioned Claire to do the same.

"Ask your questions, I know you have a few," she said, as fog settling in around them. Oh yes, the young one wanted answers. Her intensity was almost overpowering, but too much, too soon would frighten her away. Her spiritual side, now that was a closed-off attic, dark and dusty and full of cobwebs.

Mamma Anna clasped Claire's hands. She would take her time with this one.

Behind them, their guide pushed the raft through the bayou, water melodically trickling off the pole as it rose and fell, directing their course.

The young one pulled her shoulders up. "Who did you ask to protect us?"

"Back there? I'm glad you were listening. Mawu-Lisa, creators of heaven and earth."

"Thought that job belonged to God."

"God gave the command."

The young woman started to smile, but stopped. "You're serious."

"I am. Mawu is the moon. She guides us in the dark. Lisa is the sun. He protects us in the day."

Ah, she was having none of it. Youth. Mamma Anna thought about the young ones within her own congregation. They'd much rather watch television than practice the religion of their ancestors. With minds like theirs so few remained to pass on the old ways. But this one. She was book smart, oui, but a blackness covered her soul and kept her from truly knowing herself.

Hocus-pocus—that's what this one was thinking. She could read the girl like a flashing neon billboard. So, how could she prove that what she had to offer was more than nonsense? Maybe with the right mix of truth and illusion.

"You think my deities are just voodoo hocus-pocus?"

Claire leaned away. Something close to fear shone in her eyes.

"Don't mean to frighten you, child. I figured that if I threw your doubts back at you, you'd take me more seriously."

"How did you know what I was thinking?"

"You wear your thoughts on your face. You're far too honest for your own good. I only wanted to prove my friendship."

"Then put away your games and tell me what you know about Billy Ray."

Mamma Anna sighed; she had to love the eagerness. "I know what he did to you." She glanced away from Claire's wounded face. It was too hard to watch. "And about the others."

"Others?"

Claire leaped off the seat. "You know of others?" The raft jerked. She lost her balance and stumbled, but Mamma Anna was there with arms raised. She clamped Claire's forearms, allowing her to steady herself.

"Sit down, child. I don't know them by face, but I know they exist."

"I knew it." Claire sat. "Is Tanya Bonaventure one of his victims?"

"Who?"

"The woman raped and murdered near Raceland Junction. Did Billy Ray kill her?"

The weight of her years settled deep inside Mamma Anna. She hadn't expected another one. "I don't know of this woman."

"It's all over the papers. Haven't you read about it?"

"I read palms. I read expressions. I read the spirits. Newspaper stories are at least twice, if not more, removed from their source. They're no good to me."

"Then how do you know about me?"

"Your mamma. We volunteered together at a hospital over in Houma. She was worried about you. Wouldn't say much, only that you were going to law school. Most mothers would be proud, boastful. Not yours." She paused, remembering the gentle Rivet woman with the aching heart and the tender smile that she offered to all.

"I don't believe you. She wouldn't have told you, she never spoke about it."

"Don't remember exactly how it happened, seem to think she handed me some magazines. I took her hand, just an instant, but long enough to see…"

"You saw Billy Ray?"

"No, child. I saw the violence. I put the rest together later…with you."

"I doubt that."

Claire turned away. Probably trying to hide her thoughts, Mamma Anna sensed with a chuckle. Silly girl. It wouldn't be easy to gain this one's trust. She trusted no one.

The raft wove through the massive cypress roots that buckled and knotted above the water's surface. When it hit solid ground, Claire was jolted forward, but stayed seated.

Strength but no balance. Mamma Anna took in the girl's hesitation. "One more minute," she said. "Jezwa will tie up." Once she felt the raft secured, she stood. "Stay close. We'll see better once we're away from this fog."

Claire trailed behind, mud sucking and slurping as she pulled her tennis shoes free of the soft earth.

She'll never make the hill with those shoes, Mamma Anna thought, but her young soles are probably too tender to remove them. "Here child, watch me, then do what I do."

From a nearby weeping willow, Mamma Anna grabbed a handful of stringy branches and used their strength to hoist herself up the slight rise of the bank. As she reached the top, a groan escaped her throat. That had taken more effort than she'd expected. "Here." She released the branches, letting them float back down into place.

The young one tugged, slipped, and then tried again. Muscles bulged in her slender arms. Her left foot started up the rise, but her right foot slid off in the opposite direction. If not for her grip on the branches, she would have collapsed face down in the mud.

"Wet tennis shoes," Claire said, grabbing the branches tighter.

"Come on child, how hard can it be? If an old woman like me can get up the rise, so can you." She chuckled.

Claire placed both feet on the rise, determination set in her features. Biting her lower lip, she climbed the branches, hand over hand, until her feet found traction. She reached the top with sweat glistened on her brow.

She gasped for breath. "Isn't Saint Jean's Eve over?"

"Oui. Now's the Feast. The longest day of the year and the beginning of seven days of voodoo ceremonies. Come. We sacrificed a rabbit and a goat earlier—now we must eat."

Chapter 27

Friday June 24, 2005
Bayou, LA

Claire trailed the old woman through the thick growth of cypress trees, half-worried that she was to be the next sacrifice. They stepped into a flat, grassy glade. Clouding the air with wood smoke, three fires burned: one to the south, where a dark-skinned man turned an animal carcass stretched across the flame on a spit, and another sixty yards away, where several dark women sat on logs beneath an old oak dripping Spanish moss. The last fire was directly in front, abandoned but warming the opening of a three-sided wooden shack.

Through the veil of darkness, a nutria screamed. The high-pitched sound sent a quiver up Claire's spine.

She glanced again at the goat, rotating over the fire. Sacrifices.

"Our humfo." Mamma Anna gestured to the shack behind the fire. "Where we hold our ceremonies."

The building was supported by four skinned pine trunks, staked into the earth at each corner and covered by a corrugated aluminum roof. The north side was walled closed with two-by-fours. The other two sides were half walled up and the front—the south side—completely open. In the center of the shack, a red pole grew from the ground, reaching up through a hole in the roof. At the base of each pine trunk were three red candles and one white. Shiny gold Christmas garland wound one bare trunk, rings of colorful beads wound another.

Behind the humfo, two silk flags fluttered, but there wasn't a spot of wind. Claire was unable to make out their elaborate emblems or inscriptions with only the firelight.

She walked with Mamma Anna around the fire and to the far side of the humfo where a black cross, crowned with a black bowler, jutted from the earth. Nearby, a red bougainvillea grew from a large earthen pot up along a simple wooden trellis. A few feet from the plant, a bright colored tablecloth covered a long, narrow table.

Mamma Anna pointed to the table. "Here's our altar."

On top were wooden framed pictures of printed images propped at different angles: a man on horseback, his sword drawn and pointing heavenward; a woman dressed in red, a gold cross at her neck; a man in long robes with snakes intertwined at his feet. Other odd items lay among the frames: a deck of playing cards, three unopened rum bottles, Christmas tinsel, a red silk scarf, sunglasses, beaded necklaces, a brush and comb set, lipstick, several hats of different styles, and a perfume bottle with a gold atomizer.

Claire pointed to the images. "Are these departed spirits? Do you pray to them?"

"Look closer." Mamma Anna's hand caressed one of the frames. "Here's Saint Ulrich. Here, the Virgin Mary. And this, Saint Patrick. We call the Saints 'Loa.'" She pointed back to the framed image of the man on horseback. "You know him as Saint Ulrich, but for us this is Agwé, protector of navigation and fishing."

Mamma Anna caressed the frame of the Virgin. "This one's Ezili Freda. You might meet her tonight. She's quite active during Saint Jean's."

A strange sensation washed over Claire, not quite fear but discomfort. She glanced down toward the group seated under the oak. "Why are they watching me?" The man roasting the goat was looking, too, been since she arrived.

Mamma Anna raised her hand in the air and gestured. Everyone turned away. "They're wondering if you're friend or foe. We get a few whites here, not many."

Claire's attention drifted back to the group of women. Some were peeling vegetables; others stirred pots that they held for a time over the flames. At the oak's far side, several children slept curled on mats. At least, she hoped they were sleeping. She sucked in a breath.

She, too, wondered whether they were friends or foes. If she were to die this night, out here in the web of bayous, who would know? She would simply disappear.

Vincent. How she wished she'd told him all the things she'd hid from him. How she wished she'd told him how much he meant to her and the hole his leaving had left in her heart.

What about her family, her brothers, Philippe and Joe? It would look as if she'd been taken from her bed. She'd left it unmade, her clothes strewn across the floor. A mystery never to be solved.

And Billy Ray. He would go on raping and killing whomever he pleased protected by a sheriff's shield.

Off in the distance, several men stood together. Cigarette smoke and the red glow of burning tips moved between them. She couldn't see what else they were doing, but one of the men looked to be the old Creole, Ory, whom she'd seen out front of Hal's. She remembered their encounter—how he'd gone wild at the sight of her, and then run off. Had he tried to warn her? Was that what his strange words had meant?

She didn't belong here. "I need to go." The fear that she'd somehow outwitted now blew through her flesh. Hairs rose on her arms. She glanced around the glade, searching an escape, but water was everywhere. The only way back was by the raft she'd come in on. She was trapped, an animal in a cage.

"What are you so afraid of?" Mamma Anna's tone was as challenging as her stance.

"Nothing." Fear had a smell, she wondered if Mamma Anna could smell hers.

"Good. I have a few other things to share with you before you leave."

Could the old woman really read thoughts? Nonsense. But then she'd gotten her here, hadn't she? Had she used some type of mind control? "My sister-in-law says you're the Queen."

"I'm a mambo, the priestess of ceremonies. Each ceremony has either a priest or priestess, sometimes both."

"How do you resolve this with the church?"

"All these folks..." The old woman stretched her hand toward the others. "...are Catholics."

"Voodoo is sacrifices, dolls stuck with pins, and gris-gris. Catholicism is prayer, devotion, good works."

"Ah yes, and you would know."

Claire didn't like the woman's smug expression. "I've seen the ceremonies up in New Orleans."

"Ahhh." Mamma Anna flicked her wrist as though to slough off her words. "Take Christianity—you have your Catholics, Baptists, Methodists, Episcopalians—the same religious concepts. Voodoo, too, has different disciplines."

"You mean that New Orleans's Voodoo is different from your Voodoo?"

Mamma Anna picked up a rosary of colored wooden beads from off the altar table. "The purest Voodoo came from Africa, the Dahomey and Yoruba regions of Nigeria.

You can read this in any library. But when our brothers sold us to the French and Spanish, the changes began."

Her accent deepened as she told the history. "The Europeans, afraid of our dark skin and strong bodies, hoped to control us by forcing us to believe in their merciful God."

She fingered the wooden beads. Firelight played over her dark features. Sweat ran down her chest. "In public, we prayed to their God, but in secret, we practiced our Voodoo. As years flowed into generations, the two religions grew together. For example, our loa, Dambala, takes the form of a snake."

Mamma Anna pointed to a screened crate under the altar table. The flickering firelight reflected on the thick black tubes of reptilian skin, curled and folded together.

Claire stepped back. "Is it alive?"

Mamma Anna nodded. "St. Patrick, a snake charmer. See the connection? Not exact, yet similar. When slaves were sent to America, other changes came to the religion."

"How do you know all this?"

Mamma Anna bowed her head. "Ma mère. She was a great mambo in Haiti. So feared by the French, she was set free. She became a medicine woman. I practice what I learned at her side."

"You apprenticed?"

"No." She clucked her tongue. "Mambos are born with great powers. I inherited mine."

Claire remembered Mamma Anna's revelation about Vincent. "Palm reading?"

"I read palms, change people into animals, oh, and I can stay under water for several days." The old woman chuckled. "Between you and me, forty minutes underwater is about all I can stand." She laughed again. "Let's go meet the others."

Chapter 28

Friday June 24, 2005
New Orleans, LA

Billy Ray leaned back in the leather chair, his elbows out, chest extended. The den's overhead light made him squint. "Awwwwwwooo."

Charlie chuckled and reached for the glass sweating a stain on the coffee table. "You gonna wake the dead, hollering like that." He shook the ice cubes, then held it to his ear and shook them again. He set the glass back on the water ring. "Damn, we done finished another bottle."

"Hold on." Billy Ray pushed down on the armrest, but as he stood dizziness caught hold, sloshing his vision around the room's crown molding. "Damn!" He sank back into the chair.

Charlie slapped his knee and slouched to one side. "Don't think we need another. As is, I'm gonna have to ask you for the room downstairs. Don't think I can make it out to the country tonight."

"Room's yours anytime, you know that. Phone's by the stereo if you want to call the wife."

"Hell, it's after one. She's long since gone to bed and forgotten about me."

"Well, you're pretty forgettable, Charlie boy." Billy Ray rubbed his eyes and forehead. The bruise beneath his right knuckle smarted. He massaged the deep purple spot with his index finger. His left hand was pretty well healed, a little yellowing, but the right... "Man, a bottle and a half. We're getting old."

"Don't drink like we used to. That's a fact."

"We don't get together like we used to neither," Billy Ray said. "Yep, everybody's got their shit, family, responsibilities. Got to tell you, I miss the old days sometimes."

Charlie lifted his cigar from the ashtray. "You ready for all the shit that's gonna rain down on you when you're sheriff?"

"Ready and waiting. Someone's got to clean up this town. Sheriff we got now's a pussy, pure and simple."

"Ah, come on, he ain't that bad."

"No? Violent crime is up even in the Quarter. Our perfumed little tourists are afraid of getting beat up, getting robbed. Tourism's been dropping steady for the last three years."

Billy Ray tipped his glass back and let an ice cube slide into his mouth. He pictured the plump little tourist bitches who came to town ready to party. As sheriff, he'd have his pick and nobody could say a word.

He rolled his glass between his palms. "Yeah, hardworking folks are losing income, losing business because of the addicts, the dealers, the gangs." "Let me tell you, first day on the job, you'll find me cracking some heads. We don't need these vermin in our city. Nope, no more."

Charlie exhaled a smoke ring. "You better take it slow—a white sheriff in a mostly black city."

"Don't spout that po-lit-tic cor-rect bullshit at me. Hell, I don't care how dark they be, they break the law in my city, I'll knock 'em this side of Sunday."

Charlie waved him off with a floppy slap at the air. "City's definitely not like it use to be."

"With me sheriff, folks like you won't be afraid to walk the streets. I'll put the fear of God into those lowlifes. I'll start with a good thrashing and if that don't move 'em out

I'll—" Billy Ray caught himself. Didn't matter how good a friend Charlie was, some things you kept to yourself. One of dear daddy's cardinal rules.

He chuckled and patted his rock-solid gut. He'd learned something from the old man, after all. Yep, sure did: keep your business to yourself.

Charlie puffed on his cigar. Billy Ray thought about his daddy. When his bruised knuckles began to ache, he realized he'd been clenching his hands into fists.

He shook them out and leaned back, the chair creaking with his weight.

"You think that Robert's a sissy boy?"

Charlie put down the cigar. "Sierra Club Robert?" Imitating Robert's voice, Charlie added, "Delta Chapter."

Both men laughed.

"'Thank you so much, Mr. Cobb, for your help with the shoreline erosion issue.'" Billy Ray said imitating the man's nasally speech and pinched face. "'You can't know what this will mean to the egrets that live in the wetlands.' Egrets, my ass. I'd like to blow his egrets out of the water."

Charlie rocked back and forth on the sofa as if he were listening to music. After a long silence he said, "Know what we oughta do? We oughta go huntin'. We ain't been huntin' since…since you blew George's foot off." He pointed to the fireplace. "That's what that fire reminds me of, the huntin' lodge. Never saw so much blood. Had to hire a couple of boys to clean it up."

Billy Ray shook his head. "I told him not to touch my damn gun. Man never could listen. And I don't want to shake you up, ole buddy, but there ain't no fire. It's summer."

Charlie threw back his head and laughed. "I know that. I was just remembering is all." He rose to his feet and stumbled. He bent to pet Shep, Billy Ray's hunting dog, but the dog's head popped up, its teeth bared as a warning growl vibrated in its throat.

Snatching his hand away, Charlie straightened and lumbered over to Billy Ray's gun cabinet. "Damn, boy. How many rifles you got in there? Shame you never use 'em anymore."

Billy Ray joined his friend, pulling a gold key ring from his pants pocket. A dozen keys jingled. He flipped through the ring twice before spotting the short key. "Got it. Move aside."

The cabinet clicked open, revealing more rifles than were visible through the glass window. Charlie removed one of the shorter ones. "This a Marlin?"

"Yep. Eighteen-ninety-four P. G. Takes a forty-four magnum. Cool thing with this is, you can share cartridges with your revolver."

"You got revolvers, too?" Charlie placed the Marlin back on the wooden pegs.

"A couple. They're in the safe. Look at this one. Just bought her." He pulled out a longer rifle, dark and contoured. He handed it to Charlie. "Takes a three-hundred W.S.M.."

Charlie turned it over in his hands, admiring the workmanship. "Damn. You could kill an elephant with that."

Billy Ray puffed his chest out. "She's my baby."

"You going to Africa or something?"

"What would I do in Africa? Once I'm sheriff, there'll be plenty of hunting for me to do right here."

"Don't know what you'll use this thing for, a three-hundred pound serial killer, maybe." Charlie handed the rifle back. "She sure is pretty."

Billy Ray locked the cabinet. He paused a moment, looking through the glass at his Winchester. She sure was beautiful.

Charlie shuffled across the room, but Billy Ray missed what he'd said. "Come again."

"Said, I remember the first time I went huntin'. Me, my daddy, I think Randolph was with us too, but you weren't. Don't remember why. You remember your first kill?"

Billy Ray walked back to his chair. He massaged his knuckles.

Charlie slumped down on the sofa. "Ah hell, I'm sorry. I know you don't like to talk about killing. But I gotta ask. Is it because of what happened to your sister? That government woman I talked to was asking about her. I told you, didn't I?"

"Yep, you told me. Don't matter anyhow. Bunny's my daddy's business, not mine."

Chapter 29

Friday June 24, 2005
Bayou, LA

The rada drums began with quick static pops. Mamma Anna said they were always played in groups of three, that the different sizes and shapes created different rhythms and different rhythms evoked different loas.

"I know you were feeling skittish earlier, but I hope you'll stay for the ceremony," Mamma Anna said, lowering herself next to Claire on a log outside the humfo.

Claire looked at the gold painted skull tied to one of the humfo's supports. "Do you ever sacrifice humans?"

Mamma Anna closed her eyes and shook her head. "Where do such ideas come from, child? If you stay, you must promise not to speak of this to anyone. The ceremony's private, for initiates and their invitees. That's why we're hidden out here so far from civilization, same as those slaves in Haiti that I told you about."

Despite her doubts, Claire nodded.

Mamma Anna flicked two fingers at a tall buxom woman dressed in a white peasant blouse and full, white cotton skirt. "This here's Bernadette, my hunsi. She's going to brush your lips with this liquid. It symbolizes that your lips are sealed, that you'd rather have your organs ripped from your body than reveal what you've seen here."

"Nice image."

Bernadette dipped her fingers into the clay bowl and then brushed them across Claire's lips.

Claire shot up off the log. She spit as the excess liquid seeped into her mouth. "That's blood! I can smell it." She spit again.

"Goat's." Mamma Anna offered her a rum bottle. "Here, drink."

Claire took the bottle and threw back a swig. She gagged. The goat must have been the one that they'd just eaten.

She sat back down beside Mamma Anna and handed back the rum. She watched men and women crowd into the humfo. Bernadette carried the snake crate and placed it next to the red pole at the center.

"We begin with a prayer to Legba," Mamma Anna said. "He guards the portal to the spirit world. After that I perform the opening, Bernadette will take over the ceremony and I'll be free to answer your questions."

Mamma Anna rose but for a moment didn't move. "You stay here, outside." She took another sip from the rum bottle and then followed the others into the humfo.

No problem, Claire thought, watching as everyone squeezed together inside the small shack. She stood to get a better view of what was happening.

The men and women swayed, rocking to the drumbeats. Some hummed, others chanted. Then the crowd pulled back, opening the area around the center pole. Mamma Anna, holding on to the pole, danced around to the right, then switched hands and danced to the left. She stopped and clapped her hands twice.

Someone threw her a sword, which she caught horizontally. After whipping the sword from its sheath, she tossed the leather to Bernadette. With both hands, Mamma Anna clasped the carved handle and circled the blade high over her head, chanting something in French.

Firelight bounced off the blade and across the expectant faces of the crowd. The night grew warmer as heat rose from the bodies moving inside the humfo.

The blade spiraled down, circling until the tip faced the earth. Then, with great force, Mamma Anna slammed the point into the ground. For an instant the drums stopped. The sword wavered from the impact. As it stilled, the drumbeats began again.

Mamma Anna's head rolled around on her neck. She opened her mouth and spoke in a voice Claire didn't recognize. With the drums and the chanting, Claire couldn't be sure, but she thought it might have been a man's voice.

A woman in the crowd began to twitch. Her arms flapped one direction as her body jerked in another. The others drew away, giving room to her spasms. Then, the woman dropped to her knees, her body in constant motion.

Claire wondered whether this was theater to impress her or if the woman had actually worked herself into a hysterical state. She'd heard of such things with the Holy Rollers and some of the Baptists groups, but they called the rolling around "receiving the spirit" and the blubbering "talking in tongues."

"Bienvenue au gardien," Mamma Anna called heavenward, her voice normal again.

The drum rhythms changed, becoming more harmonious, and everyone, including Mamma Anna, sang in French. A man handed Mamma Anna a rattle draped in beads. As the old woman shook it, the rhythmic sound was mesmerizing.

Feeling more relaxed, Claire let herself sway with the rhythm. The rum was causing her to lower her guard. Her hand gripped the gris-gris in her pocket. Before she'd met the woman, Mamma Anna had left it at the house. She stopped rocking. She'd vowed not to come looking for Mamma Anna tonight, and yet here she was. She set the rum bottle down on the log. She had to stay alert.

Inside the humfo, the possessed woman writhed on the ground, moving closer to the priestess's feet. The song ended on a high note and as it did, the possessed woman's body snapped to a stiffened position.

Two men bent and lifted the rigid woman to her feet. Her head fell back, her chin arched in the air. Her head began to rock side-to-side, stopped, then rocked again.

The two men who had lifted her linked arms with the possessed woman and led her to one of the humfo's front supporting beams. Too close for comfort, Claire stepped over to the far end of the log as Bernadette brought the woman a black cross, a red bandana tied across the center. The woman wrenched the cross from Bernadette's hands. All the while, her head tilted backwards and rocking.

Mamma Anna kissed the rattle. She bent on one knee before the possessed woman. From her vantage point, Claire couldn't be sure, but it looked as if Mamma Anna passed the rattle over the possessed woman's body.

Mamma Anna stood. She walked back inside the humfo to the center pole and Bernadette joined her. Both women had their arms arched open at their sides as if squaring off for battle. Bernadette turned a circle to the right and then curtsied before Mamma Anna. Bernadette repeated the turn to the left, her movements in sync with the drum beats. She curtsied, then one last time to the right. Both women lowered their arms.

Bernadette knelt before the priestess, bending to kiss the ground three times. Mamma Anna took Bernadette's plump hand and helped her stand. Then, Bernadette spun three pirouettes.

Claire's legs grew heavy. Unimpressed by the drama, she sat on the edge of the log. Why had she been so frightened? How was this different from the priest of Ma's church blessing the bread and wine and offering it to the parishioners? It was all ceremony.

Mamma Anna and Bernadette continued their ritual in the background as each congregation member took a turn kneeling before the possessed woman. The woman clasped hands or shook the clothing of the person before her. Her head was still tilted back on her shoulders, her eyes closed.

Claire found the woman's blind precision amazing. A good trick so how was she doing it? There must be something reflective beneath the roof. Claire leaned low to look beneath the humfo's roof. No mirrors. And the corrugated roof wasn't the least bit reflective.

Mamma Anna, her dark skin glossy with sweat, walked toward Claire, carrying yet another rum bottle. Her limp was worse and she favored her left side as she moved.

"What are they doing?" Claire asked her, pointing to the center pole of the humfo.

A man and woman, both dressed in white, were sprinkling white powder between their fingers. The powder fell to the ground, creating a circular design with symmetrical patterns woven inside. Mamma Anna sank down on the log and drank a long, slow swallow from the bottle. She passed the rum.

"No thanks," Claire said, waving away the bottle. Rum bottles were everywhere—at dinner, with the dancers, on the altar—and a bottle was always near Mamma Anna.

"They're preparing a *vévé*, drawings which symbolize different loa," Mamma Anna said before pulling a long swig on the rum. She wiped her mouth with the back of her hand. "They're using white flour because Dambala's color's white. Afterwards, anyone with sacrifices for Dambala will place them on the vévé and then Bernadette will summon the great loa."

"Is that why she's dressed in white?"

"Oui."

Mamma Anna's voice was weak. Claire sensed fragility in the old woman that made her think Mamma Anna's time was drawing to an end.

Back in the humfo, Bernadette opened the snake's crate.

Claire gasped. "What's she doing?"

"She's preparing for the snake dance."

"It's huge!"

Bernadette pulled the serpent from the crate and draped it around her shoulders like a shawl. She held its pear-sized head cradled in her right hand as the snake wrapped her shoulders. Its tail curled beneath her left arm and around her back.

Claire realized that she wasn't as afraid of the snake as she should be. It must be the rum. She turned toward Mamma Anna's voice.

"When Legba opened the gates to the spirits, Dambala attached himself to the snake. Now sacrifices can be made and Bernadette will dance with the snake to see if the loa would like to ride her instead."

"Ride? You mean like a horse?"

Mamma Anna laughed. "Sort of. Think of the difference between your physical body and your spirit. The loa mounts your spirit like a rider to a horse and the two—your spirit and the loa's spirit—take control of your physical being. The rider has the most control because the horse gives it up to him. Does that make sense?"

Claire accepted the rum bottle and lifted it to her lips. "What's the point?"

"For the loa, it has a human body with which it can enjoy the pleasures of the flesh like food, drink, and sex, but since the loa might not have had a body recently, it may have forgotten how to drive one. That's where the human spirit is helpful."

"What does the horse get out of this? Guiltless pleasures?"

"It's a great honor to be ridden by a loa. There's a crossing of energy—spiritual energy."

Claire turned her attention back to Bernadette, the coils of the black serpent lifted over her head as she danced. Why had the old woman wanted her to see this? Why had she brought her here?

"What does all this have to do with Billy Ray?"

"There're different types of loa. Tonight we dance for the Rada, tomorrow the Petro, who're a bit more aggressive. Then there's a third type." Mamma Anna paused as if she was about to reveal a great secret, but knew better.

"Oh, I get it," Claire said. "I'll get a spirit to take care of Billy Ray." She couldn't even laugh at how ridiculous that sounded. "And what exactly would this spirit do—tickle his feet, soggy his cornflakes, turn his teeth green?"

Mamma Anna didn't blink, but squared up her shoulder. She fixed her gaze on Claire and whispered, "Kill him."

The force of the words hit Claire hard. She felt the old woman's hatred and was taken aback. "Oh…ah…I thought you said Voodoo wasn't evil."

"Evil's relative."

"No, evil's evil."

"Was what Billy Ray did to you evil?"

"Without a doubt."

"And you want to right that wrong. Does that make you evil?"

"I want justice, not revenge."

"Ah, what's justice, but due reward? What's revenge, but due reward? Psss." She flicked at the air. "Billy Ray's hurt too many people. He needs to be stopped."

"So do a Voodoo to give me the power to stop him."

Mamma Anna looked back at the dancers. "That must be your choice."

Claire felt the rada drums' rhythms pulsing through her heart. Each distinctive beat wove its magic. The rum had left her lightheaded. She wanted to join the congregation, to dance, to move with the music. Was this what those Holy Rollers mistook for possession?

Chapter 30

Friday June 24, 2005
New Orleans, LA

A dry, woodsy smell filled the tiny bedroom. Claire batted her eyelids open. She pushed herself up. The odor of last night's fires tinged her hair and skin. She rubbed her throbbing temples, unable to believe she'd gone out to the bayou, but the mud tracked to the edge of her bed left little doubt. She burped.

Her stomach felt as if stinky swamp grass was growing inside.

Her canvas tennis shoes lay crumpled under the weight of dried earth, and balled into a mound at the foot of the bed were her jeans, caked with mud and what looked like blood. She gagged, remembering the goat's blood on her lips. Where was her toothbrush?

On the coffee table in the main room was another souvenir of her evening. She picked up the sealed rum bottle and turned it over in her hands. Mamma Anna had sent a loa home to protect her. The rum was for when the loa was thirsty. Well, the loa must have done the driving too because she sure didn't remember getting home.

She carried the bottle to the bookshelf. Was she supposed to drink it and then pretend that the loa drank it? Was that how they perpetuated their beliefs? It didn't matter. She wasn't ever drinking rum again and she sure wasn't going back for anymore voodoo mumbo-jumbo. No matter what Mamma Anna thought, Voodoo wasn't going to bring Billy Ray to justice.

192

* * *

After brushing her teeth twice and a quick sponge bath,
Claire drove to New Orleans for her meeting with the great
Randolph Cobb.

Cobb International was located in the Central Business
District and housed in the top two floors of New Orleans'
tallest building. Before stepping into the elevator, she read
the directory and noted that the Shell Oil Company occupied
several floors. Cobb owned refineries. Was this cohabitation
healthy competition or a symbiotic relationship?

The elevator doors opened onto an opulent waiting area
with high ceilings, beige leather sofas, and a twenty-four-foot
curved reception desk of polished cedar topped with a marble
counter. Glass walls and doors to both the right and left
blocked off the offices and their noise, leaving the reception
area weirdly silent.

Claire gave her name and was told to take a seat. Just how
long would the mighty Randolph keep her waiting? she
wondered. To get the appointment, she'd used her standard
line about interviewing the candidates' friends and families,
but was truly surprised that she hadn't had to argue more.
Percy had warned her that an open door to Randolph Cobb
wasn't easy to come by. He must really want his son to be
sheriff.

Several minutes later, Marla sashayed into the room from
the door at the left. She was dressed in a fitted skirt suit with
a Givenchy handbag hanging from her shoulder. She smiled
with that cat-that-ate-the-mouse smile of hers as her gaze fell
on Claire.

"Fancy meeting you here," Marla said. She ran her hands
down her skirt as if to straighten it. "Randolph is ready to see
you."

Claire stood. "Will you be joining us?"

Marla pressed a finger into her chest. "Moi? I wouldn't think of it. Good luck."

Wondering what she was walking into, Claire watched Marla leave. When she turned back, one of the two receptionists was holding the left glass door open for her.

"At the end of the corridor," the woman said, stepping aside for Claire to pass.

Randolph Cobb was busy signing papers as she stepped into the office. He remained seated, not bothering to look up, as he gestured with the tip of his gold pen for her to sit.

The office was decorated in a contemporary style. Hard-edged furniture and very little color. There were no family photos on Cobb's desk or knickknacks to warm up the space. On one wall was a framed photo of President Bush like the kind found in government offices. Below that photo were several others. Randolph Cobb with Senator Breaux. Cobb with Governor Blanco. Cobb with President George H. W. Bush. Cobb with Percy's boss, the District Attorney of New Orleans. Cobb, in hunting clothes, with Vice President Cheney.

"You have twenty minutes," Cobb said, shoving the papers aside. "I expect we'll be done in ten. What do you want?"

"I understand you're busy and I want to thank you for seeing me. As I told your secretary, I'm interviewing—"

Cobb held up a hand. "I know what you told my secretary. My friend, Governor Blanco, has confirmed that a committee does indeed interview family members of those running for office. She also confirmed that you aren't on such a committee so I'll ask again. What do you want?"

Hardball. She should have known that eventually someone would check her story, someone like Randolph Cobb. She looked across the desk, her mouth as dry as a dust mote. Cobb's face was stern; a meanness in his eyes. She wasn't a good enough liar to bluff her way out.

Randolph didn't wait for her to try.

"What is the purpose of the flyers you're putting up?" he said, clasping his hands and leaning toward her.

He couldn't know the flyers were from her. Could he?

Again, he didn't give her time to answer.

"Cobb International provides services around the world in the exploration, development, and production of oil. We have 200 field camps in 72 countries. I don't know what you're hoping to find out about me through my son, but I have enough lawyers to keep you busy for a very long, long time." He released his hands and leaned away. "I'll also point out the obvious—smarter lawyers than you have tried. That's all I have to say. You may leave."

She didn't move. Randolph Cobb was so used to the world revolving around him that he couldn't even conceive that she was truly interested in his son. What would he think if she told him what she really wanted? He'd hide every piece of evidence before she could find it. He'd done it before and he was good at it. No, she couldn't tell him the truth, but she still might learn something if she hit him hard.

Cobb reached for the papers he'd previously discarded and started to read.

"Sir, if you had researched me thoroughly, you would know that I prosecute crimes against persons, crimes like assault, rape, and murder. I don't care about your company, or how many employees or stockholders you are ripping off. What does interest me is the death of your daughter."

That got a reaction, however slight. "My daughter? That was a lifetime ago. And the man was caught, the crime paid in full."

Interesting expression. "I understand William was a witness to the crime."

"You understand wrong."

"Was there a witness?"

"Not that I know of."

"Then how do you know the right man paid for the crime?"

"The evidence. Go find the police report and read it. Isn't that your job? Why are you wasting my time on ancient history?"

Was that a bluff? If the file was missing surely he knew about it. "A little over a week ago another woman died in a similar manner. I can't help but wonder if there's a connection."

"I'm in the oil business. You're in the police business. We have nothing more to discuss." He leaned back in his chair as if waiting for a challenge. As he did, a sarcastic grin spread his thin lips and a gold tooth glinted.

* * *

Claire tried not to run back to her car. The voices of her doubters turned in her head. Philippe: everyone has a gold tooth, even me. Jessie: Billy Ray? Are you sure, it was a long time ago? Percy: Randolph Cobb has a god complex.

And who knew better than a D.A. the fallibility of eye witnesses? Documented evidence proved that memory starts to fade the minute an incident is over. That was why witnesses had to be interviewed as soon as possible. Also proven was the fact that a memory diminishes every time you revisit it. She'd been fifteen when she saw Billy Ray again. How much could she trust her memory?

And Bunny. Who raped Bunny? Charlie said Randolph spoiled her. Could that have been a perversion? Was it possible? Was Randolph guilty and Billy Ray innocent?

No. He couldn't be. Sometimes your body knew things your brain couldn't process. That day in the Winn Dixie proved that. But hadn't she blocked out that particular memory for almost half her life? How could she be sure now? How many witnesses had she interrogated, who swore they'd seen one thing when overwhelming evidence proved otherwise?

No. She knew what she knew. She'd been taken by surprise. First by Marla's presence then by...

Had she really seen a gold tooth? She'd caught the bounce of light. Maybe he'd been chewing on a paperclip and it wasn't a tooth at all.

Stop.

Whether Randolph had a gold tooth wasn't the question. If this was any other case, she'd trust herself. These other voices would have long ago been snuffed out, and yet, the doubts kept coming back like a bad case of indigestion.

Chapter 31

Friday June 24, 2005
New Orleans, LA

The Elections Office was a whitewashed storefront in the Central Business District. The air-conditioning unit, stuck through a window on the rear wall, banged and rattled and clanged. Claire tried to ignore the noise as she filled out the request form to obtain a list of Cobb's financial supporters.

"What about press releases?" Claire asked the clerk, a young woman wearing a skirt two sizes too small and with a mouth full of chewing gum.

"On microfiche. Want to see 'em, too?"

Claire nodded and the clerk disappeared into a back room, leaving a trail of drugstore perfume.

She felt uneasy in the temporary office space. The two-foot poster of Cobb's sneering face didn't help. A horrible photo. She looked away.

During the drive over she'd noticed that many of her flyers had been torn down. While she was in town, she'd reprint another hundred. But flyers weren't enough.

Her nails tapped the Battle Hymn of the Republic on the counter. She needed a private investigator. November was creeping closer every day. If she couldn't find any victims, at least she had to find something, anything that would keep Cobb off the ballot.

Where was that clerk? She checked her watch. She crossed the room and stood before the plate glass windows lining the front of the building. The street was filling with traffic, the beginning of rush hour. The caustic exhaust fumes were filtering in through the flimsy aluminum door joints.

Her gaze followed the cars and she caught sight of the man she'd seen at Tulane. Scruffy beard, tight tee shirt, cigarette stuck between his lips.

What was it the postal worker had said? Skinny and rough looking. He fit the description. This was no coincidence. He was leaning against a silver van, focused on something farther down the street, but if he turned his head a little left he'd see her.

She rushed back to the whitewashed counter. She didn't like being alone.

"Hello. Excuse me," she called. She glanced back over her shoulder. The man had moved out of sight. "Hello!"

The clerk peeked around the corner then stepped into full view. She held a coffee mug in one hand. "Oh, um, I'm still looking. I must have misplaced the microfiche, but don't worry. It has to be here somewheres." And she disappeared.

Claire checked her watch again. She didn't like this. Cobb's records should be readily available for journalists. Oh! Maybe she could start an investigation by putting in a call to the Times-Picayune and letting someone over there know how difficult it was to get information on the candidate for sheriff. It might raise a few questions about his past.

The door behind her opened. She stiffened. The glass pane behind the counter caught the visitor's reflection. The man was tall and stocky, dressed in pale blue linen suit. His footsteps were heavy on the linoleum.

"You want info on William Cobb?" The voice was gruff.

She turned her head and looked up in to the blue-gray eyes she hadn't seen in over nineteen years. A cold sweat broke out on her skin. Her eyes darted to the window, to the door, searching for an escape route.

He smiled and the gold canine tooth caught the fluorescent light.

He looked more like his father than she'd expected. He stepped closer, towering over her. Her mind spiraled back to the field where the black-eyed Susans grew. The smell of dried grass filled her nostrils. Her hair pressed the dry earth.

"Why are you looking into my business? You want to ask me something you ask me, you hear? Leave my family and my contributors alone."

She lay in the field, her left side aching. The beast, the monster climbed over her, blocking out the sun. She couldn't breathe. Her chest hurt, her legs hurt, her insides hurt. She gasped. The lack of oxygen brought her back to the office.

Billy Ray studied her, the feral point of his chin tightening. He reached into his jacket and shoved something yellow into her face. "What are these about?" He stepped even nearer.

The page was too close to read, but she recognized her flyer. The puzzle pieces were snapping into place. The skinny guy had followed her to the post office. He'd told Billy Ray or Randolph or both about the flyers. He'd led Billy Ray here.

The heat of Billy Ray's skin caressed her. Bile rose in her throat. She knew that she should double over or she'd lose it, but she held her stance, the muscles in her thighs twitching from the effort.

"I don't know what you're up to, Lady Lawyer, but give it up. You're out of your league around here. This ain't fancy Baton Rouge. Down here, we take care of our own."

As if on cue, the clerk ambled back in the office with a roll of microfiche.

"Clotilde, hon, could you give us another moment, please?"

"Oh, Mr. Cobb," the young woman said, sounding relieved.

Claire reached for the countertop. "No! Please stay. I want a witness."

The young woman shot Claire a tight-lipped smile. "Sure Mr. Cobb, I'll be in the back if you need me." And she left.

Claire was trapped. She gripped the countertop, her nails piercing the soft wood. What was Cobb saying?

" ...upstanding community..., ...law abiding...."

His voice sounded far away as if traveling through a tunnel.

"You got that!" he shouted.

She jumped and balanced herself against the counter. She was fighting, struggling with the darkness that was creeping in like kudzu. She forced air into her lungs, steadied herself. The aluminum door clicked shut. She glanced up to find that she was alone. She stumbled to the plastic trashcan, dropped to her knees, and vomited.

Chapter 32

Friday June 24, 2005
Lockport, LA

"Left! here!" Billy Ray shouted. They'd almost missed the turn. It was that damn Rivet woman. "That bitch look familiar to you?"

"Don't think so," Darryl said, his eyes never leaving the road.

"Got your cell phone?"

Darryl reached into the cubbyhole beside his seat and pulled out the phone.

Billy Ray back-dragged the pages in his little black phonebook until he found Aaron Butler's phone number. "Aaron works at the state capital. Let's see what he knows."

He tapped in the number and raised the phone to his ear. "Aaron, Billy Ray here. How you been?" He winked at Darryl.

"Well sir, I can't believe you took time away from your campaigning to give me a call. What can I do for you?"

"What can you tell me about a DA named Claire Rivet?"

"Assistant DA. She hasn't made the big league yet, but I hear it's only a matter of time. She's pretty good at what she does. Why you asking?"

"Met her today. She's down here asking questions. I was wondering what she's up to. That's all."

"Getting to know the players, are you? Good idea. Rivet's sort of made a name for herself prosecuting rapists. Seems someone told me that she's never lost a case. Sounds hard to believe, but yeah, that's right, I read it last week after the Leroy Milson trial."

"Rape cases, huh?" Billy Ray turned to look at the passing scenery.

"Heard you had a bad one down there recently. A young waitress. Rivet must be working it."

"That was way over in Raceland. Why would a Baton Rouge prosecutor be involved?"

"Maybe she's consulting? Now, with the computers, we're always sharing some kind of information. Why you so curious?"

"Just keeping an eye out. Made me wonder."

"You ought to spend time with her. After you're sheriff, you're going to want friends like her."

"You're probably right. She's a looker, too."

"Cobb, you'll never change."

"You either, Aaron, that's why we're friends. Thanks for the info and you'll be receiving an invitation to my inaugural party real soon. Look forward to seeing you."

Gazing out the passenger window, he passed the phone back to Darryl. He knew now why she'd looked familiar. He'd seen her picture in the paper last week. If she's looking for a rapist, why was she putting his picture up all over town?

"What did he say?" Darryl asked.

"Take a right here. Let's head down to Lafourche. He said she was probably down here investigating that rape last week. You heard about it? I'd like to talk to the officers in charge. That would be the Criminal Operations Center over in Lockport. Get on Ninety South."

"Why's she putting up those papers about you?"

"You sure it's her?"

"Saw it. The name listed for the box in the postal log was Claire Rivet." Darryl chuckled. "Maybe she thinks you're a rapist."

"Funny. Keep laughing. I'm running for sheriff. Rumors like that could do me in. Wouldn't the old sheriff love that? 'Billy Ray Cobb—rapist.' I can hear him now."

Billy Ray massaged his knuckles. This day was getting longer by the minute. "Listen," he said. "What about the wife, the one you and your friend knocked around. After I left, you boys didn't rape her, did you?"

Darryl slapped the steering wheel. "Hell no! Come on," he said. "Teaching someone a lesson is one thing, raping's another. That makes it personal. And that ain't right."

Billy Ray crossed his arms over his chest. A bad feeling stirred in his gut. The Rivet woman showing up meant trouble. Her interest in him was suspicious. He'd better find out what was going on and find out fast.

* * *

Darryl parked in front of the Operations Center. "You don't mind if I don't go in," he said, smirking.

"Wait here then. No, go across the way there and get a coffee. I won't be long."

Billy Ray pushed open the glass door and stepped into the icy reception area. The desk to his left was empty which he figured was normal for the hour. Most civilian workers were already headed home. As he walked to the open corridor, he was struck by a disturbing thought. What if the Rivet woman was here? If she was investigating the Bonaventure rape, she might have an office, or cubbyhole, or something right in this very building.

A young deputy stepped out of a side office and showed surprise to see him. The kid stood straight enough, but the shoulders of his uniform sagged like they were a size too big.

"Mr. Cobb." The young deputy extended his hand. "Padgett. We met at a Law Commission's breakfast, a couple of weeks back."

Billy Ray caught sight of the name badge pinned over the left pocket. "Sure, sure. How you doing, deputy?" He remembered the deputy well, but he'd always had a mind for weak faces.

The kid kept shaking his hand until he thought it'd fall off. "Can I help you with something?"

Billy Ray let his glance travel through the room. "Hope so." Maybe he should make a quick excuse and get out. Oh, what the hell. Rivet was pretty shaken up when he'd left her at the Elections Office. She couldn't have gotten over here faster than him. "I'm looking for the officer investigating that rape over in Raceland Junction last week."

The deputy's eyes stretched open. "You got information?"

"Afraid not, I'd just like to talk with the officer, deputy."

"That would be Major Argrais. He's head of the investigation, but he's on the phone. Hold on, let me see when he'll be free." The deputy rushed up the corridor and disappeared into an end office.

A Major. Billy Ray scratched his head. He had to be careful what he said. Make sure he wasn't too anxious. Could always play the "Cobb money" card, but the sheriff angle was probably better. Common foes and all that.

A strong looking man with salt and pepper hair approached. His compact build spoke of discipline and confidence. "I'm Major Argrais, how can I help you?"

Age, fifty, Billy Ray guessed. Might be younger, but not much. "I'm William Cobb. I'm running for Criminal Sheriff up in Orleans Parish." He watched the man's face for any telltale sign of loyalty to the current sheriff. He saw nothing in the earnest greeting, but then the Major's gaze dropped to his bruised hand.

"Nice to meet you. Hope you won."

Billy Ray glanced down. One bad spot left, but two other knuckles were light purple. "Not a fight, I'm happy to say. Smashed it over at a site. I also own Blue Belt Construction."

"Padgett says you might have some information on the Bonaventure case, that right?"

He didn't like standing out in the open where the Rivet woman could see him if she happened in. "Is there someplace we could talk?"

The Major tilted his head as if to gesture down the hall. "My office."

Walking down the corridor, Billy Ray peeked through the glass partitions into the other offices. No Rivet.

He took the seat offered and waited for the Major to close the door.

"I'm afraid your deputy misunderstood. I don't have anything to offer you. I ran into an assistant DA in New Orleans. She was asking a bunch of questions, making some folks uncomfortable, so I was wondering if she was working on your case?"

"You must mean Ms. Rivet. She's not working on the case per se. Though she mentioned that my case was similar to one she is working on. An older case I believe she said."

Older? *The Rivet Brothers?* "Did she say how old?"

The Major shook his head. "She did come around here, oh, last Friday I think it was."

What was that bitch up to? Little late for the brother to file an assault charge. She'd know that too. "You have any credible leads?"

The Major's expression changed. Had he asked too many questions? The way the man was looking at him, Billy Ray felt like a math problem that the Major was trying to solve. Simple curiosity? Could be. He'd seen it before. Folks always wanted to size him up, trying to decide if he deserved his daddy's money.

Billy Ray shifted in the metal chair. "Here I am asking about the case and I'm not even sheriff yet. Hope you don't mind, but that DA got me curious."

The Major leaned forward. "I don't mind. She has me *real* curious, too, but I don't have anything to tell you."

"I guess there wasn't any evidence. Witnesses or anything?"

The Major said nothing. Not the chatty type. Billy Ray figured he'd better shut up, too, but he wasn't leaving half-cocked. He wanted to know what that woman knew, if anything. "Otherwise, you would have made an arrest already and I don't remember reading anything about that."

The Major's gaze never shifted. Bet the man was great in an interrogation, Billy Ray thought, crossing his hands. He shifted again. "And those reporters have a way of getting information. Lord knows how they manage."

Major Argrais appeared to relax, leaning back in his chair, his arms moving to the rests. "That's true isn't it? Once everything is publicized it's hard to tell the witnesses from the suspects. Always find it odd…"

"What's that?" Billy Ray asked.

"Which folks are interested in my cases."

Oh. "Guess I'll have to deal with all that soon enough," Billy Ray said. "And don't you worry, this conversation is strictly confidential. I was just wondering if I could help that DA in any way. She is a looker, don't you think?" There. That got a real smile. Sex was a motivation any man could relate to.

The Major clasped his hands, interlacing his fingers. "You should talk to her. If she's asking questions up in Orleans, you two can help each other out. She's very professional."

Billy Ray stood. "I'll do that. I thank you for your time. And please, don't hesitate to ask, if there's something I can do to help with your case. Because of my daddy, I have plenty of influential contacts."

"I'm sure you do," the Major said and cocked his head.

Chapter 33

Friday June 24, 2005
Bayou, LA

Claire drove. She'd been driving for hours, her mind
numb. Leaving New Orleans, she'd headed north planning to
escape the state. After reaching the Mississippi border, she'd
been overcome with the urge to say good-bye to Vincent so
she cut west, back toward Baton Rouge. As dusk crept over
the Baton Rouge skyline, she traveled the familiar streets to
Robert's apartment where Vincent was staying, but she
couldn't get out of the car. For almost an hour, she sat parked
in front of the building. Did she really want to run? Was that
the answer?

She'd known it would be difficult to face Billy Ray again
after all these years. She'd planned for it, but freezing up,
complete paralysis. Her body had betrayed her mind. And
why? She wasn't afraid of Billy Ray. She'd prosecuted men
like him for years.

In the dark, she turned the car around and drove to
Villette. What if the skinny guy had followed her home?
What if he knew where she was staying? She passed the
turnoff to Ma's house and then passed the turnoff to Green
Acres. She couldn't go to Philippe's either. He'd take one
look at her and know something was wrong. That would
provoke another fight. All evening, she'd been fighting her
thoughts. She didn't have much fight left, but she wasn't
ready to be alone.

For a few more days, Mamma Anna and her band of
sun/moon, whatever, worshipers were celebrating Saint
Jean's. At this point, a little rum might be medicinal. With

midnight a few minutes away, Claire found the narrow lane and parked in the same spot.

The air was as tight as a vacuum, the humidity claustrophobic, and the earth, hot from the day's sun. Thunderstorm weather. So familiar, she could almost taste it, and although she didn't feel the slightest symptom yet, she knew she was in for one hell of a migraine.

She stomped through the reeds, drawing closer to the water's edge. Her tennis shoes absorbed the blossoming moisture like a dried sponge. If she'd thought for one second she'd be back out here, she would have bought wading boots in the city. Why had she come?

Billy Ray.

He'd caught her off-guard once, it wouldn't happen again. She stumbled through the underbrush.

Being out here with others would be more comforting than being home alone, analyzing every sound. Besides, Mamma Anna, with her rituals and pagan beliefs, intrigued her.

When she reached the shore, the raft was waiting. Jezwa, with his captain's hat askew, stood at the rear. Last night she'd noticed his odd appearance, but hadn't understood what was off until now. His massive hands were thick and strong like those of a man thirty, but his thin, narrow shoulders curled forward like those of a ninety year old. He was crooked and askew, yet strong and capable. And he was white.

Mamma Anna had said some whites joined the ceremonies, but Claire didn't remember seeing Jezwa except on the raft. And there was something else too...something that reminded her of Pa. Was it the tilt of his head? Or the easy stance?

"Where's Mamma Anna?" she asked him.

Jezwa stared into the darkness.

As she planted one foot and then the other aboard the raft, he nodded slightly. What had the old woman said about a loa taking a human body? If such things were possible, which they weren't, Jezwa fit the bill. He was put together like a handmade doll of sticks and building blocks.

He lifted the guiding pole in his powerful hands and Claire wobbled toward the bench, her wet shoes slipping on the deck. Had he been waiting for her? Was Mamma Anna that sure she'd return? Had the old woman read the future and known that she'd run into Billy Ray today? No. The old woman couldn't read the future. Jezwa probably transported people back and forth all evening. The glade, as far as she'd seen, was accessible only by boat.

With the flurried sounds of buzzing insects, she settled on the bench. She reached into her pocket for the gris-gris, but realized she'd left it on the kitchen table. She'd forgotten the rum bottle, too, but if her guardian spirit was thirsty, surely there'd be enough at the ceremony.

* * *

Fire blazed before the humfo. It burned higher and hotter than the previous night. The smell of wood smoke and fried onions filled the glade. Claire walked over to the crowd, standing near the woodpile.

Mamma Anna danced—quick, static jerks—her purple robe billowing beneath a belted red sash. A dark blue turban, wrapped around her head, bobbed back and forth from shoulder to shoulder. In one hand, she held a calabash, in the other a rum bottle, open and splashing about.

But the ceremony was different from the previous night. The drumming was wilder, the beats more urgent. The air sizzled with electricity.

Three women crawled across the ground, their backs arched and feline, as others slithered like snakes closer to the earth. A white woman sat perched on a log, her knees drawn up into her chest. Her head jerked side-to-side as she hooted like an owl. Two men and a dog walked on all fours, the men imitating the dog, and the real dog barking at the game. Both men and women gyrated around the center pole, twitching about. Mamma Anna danced in and out of the craziness. When she passed a person dancing or crawling, she sprinkled them with the contents of the calabash—a fine brown powder—then a few drops from the rum.

The vacant stares of the dancers stopped Claire cold. Their erratic movements looked inhuman. She rubbed the back of her neck, glanced around for something familiar. Coming here had been a mistake.

She looked back at Mamma Anna. The woman's dancing had a violent edge to it. Claire turned and started to walk away, but a tall, thin man in a long white toga stretched out his hand, offering her an opened rum bottle.

The sweet burn made the hairs on her arm stand on end. After a second sip, she walked back to the woodpile and the other spectators. She offered the bottle to the woman at her left. A claw of a hand reached for the rum and Claire looked down into a face that looked older than Europe. With a toothless grin the woman brought the bottle to her lips and chugged.

A loud pop rang out. Several dancers dropped to the ground. Claire, recognizing the smell of gunpowder, hit the dirt, too. But Mamma Anna bobbed in and out of the congregation with her calabash and rum. Claire scanned the dancers for a weapon.

A second pop shot from the fire. Claire jerked toward the sound. A gray-haired man stood near the fire throwing back rum and tossing firecrackers from his pockets into the flame. She stood and brushed her jeans. The toothless woman standing next to her crinkled her nose and grinned and then offered her the half empty rum bottle.

The music died. Bernadette ran to Mamma Anna with a bright colored beach towel. Trading the calabash and rum, Mamma Anna accepted the towel and dabbed her soaking face and chest. Bernadette tore the cork from another bottle with her teeth and handed it to the drummers who were huddled together lighting cigarettes. A few of the earth crawlers began to stir. Others lay flat, unmoving, as men and women stepped over them to place offerings, or talk with friends.

"Pas pareil," Mamma Anna said, walking toward her. "I told you tonight would be livelier."

When the priestess drew closer, Claire noticed that the rich hues of her dress were due in part to the sweat of her body. It had drenched the upper portions of the light cloth, turning it a vibrant purple. The bright blue turban was also soaked.

"What's with the firecrackers?"

Mamma Anna laughed, but without her usual gusto. The dance had visibly taken its toll. Her face looked drawn and frail, her movements were stiff and pained, and again, she favored her left leg.

"Tonight we sacrifice to the loas known as Petro. They like gunpowder and loud noises. Come, let's sit." Mamma Anna limped to a log bench on the other side of the humfo near the altar. Before sitting, she grabbed a rum bottle from the altar.

"They also like this. Here, taste."

Claire took the unopened bottle and sat beside Mamma Anna on the log. She pulled the cork and brought the bottle to her mouth. The taste was less sweet than last night's rum, and brimming with exotic spices. "That's good. What is it?"

"It's called Kimanga, a rum of Caribbean spices. That's the way the Petro drink it. Will you join the dancing tonight?"

The drummers were already warming up near the humfo. Claire was warming up with the Kimanga. It had almost made her forget about Billy Ray. She handed the bottle back to Mamma Anna.

"Sure." She watched two women who'd been lying on the ground crawl to their knees. "I don't believe I just said that."

Mamma Anna linked her arm in Claire's and gave her a little pat. "Let's go."

They walked toward the humfo where the others were gathering in a circle. Mamma Anna dropped Claire's arm and limped on into the center. A woman handed Claire a rum bottle. She passed it on to the person at her left, two seconds before another bottle arrived from the right.

The drums began, each beat linked to the next. The crowd chanted and swayed. Claire, carried by the rhythms, realized she'd already drank too much. The crowd shoved into the humfo. A skinny reed of a woman stepped forward, into the center, gripping a live chicken by the neck. When she held it in the air, the chanting grew louder. A crack of gunpowder flew from the fire, then another snap, not so loud.

Claire glanced over her shoulder. Behind the group she was in, a man cracked a leather whip. He sent the tail sailing through the air and then snapped it back. She laughed. It was a circus.

As the music continued, she swayed with those around her, floating and forgetting the events of the day. More rum appeared in her hand. She took a sip and passed it on.

Mamma Anna had regained her force. She stomped around the center pole, tapping to the drumbeats.

Where had she come from? Claire had lost track. Hadn't Mamma Anna been at her side? She turned to see a man she didn't recognize. He handed her a bottle.

The whip snapped again and the woman lowered the chicken almost to the ground. Reaching behind her, the woman drew a wide-bladed knife from the earth. She yelled a few words in French. The crowd repeated them.

The whip snapped. Claire jumped.

In one large arc, the woman swung the knife, slicing off the chicken's head. Blood spewed from the neck and Bernadette rushed to catch it in an earthen bowl. When all the blood had drained, the man with the firecrackers stepped forward and wrapped the limp chicken in newspaper and carried it off.

The chicken woman lifted the bowl of warm blood to her lips and drank. Claire gagged. Rum rose at the back of her throat, but she couldn't turn away. The bowl was passed from mouth to mouth, each person sipping the liquid.

Mamma Anna carried the bowl over to her. "Drink, child."

She brought the bowl to her lips, but as the odor reached her nose she couldn't. She passed the bowl to the man at her left and looked back into Mamma Anna's angry eyes.

"You should drink the blood. You will anger the loas."

How could she anger something she didn't believe in? What would they do? Cut off her credit? She swayed to the rhythms. "It's good," she said. "I'm good."

The chicken woman prayed, her palms pressed together, her head tilted back, her words directed toward heaven. In one unified movement, the crowd swayed right then left. As if tethered to an imaginary cord, Claire allowed herself to be carried with the others. It was a powerful feeling. Not only was she one with those around her, a profound feeling of peace encompassed her. She couldn't imagine ever leaving.

A white flame burned across the sky and moments later, a crack of thunder.

"That's not possible," Claire said to Mamma Anna.

"Petro ceremonies sometimes upset the atmosphere. It's nothing to worry about. We may see Sogbo tonight. He's the loa of lightning."

"You don't understand. I get headaches, blinding migraines when it storms."

"Does your head hurt?"

"Not at all."

"Rejoice. The curse has been lifted. Remember the spirit I sent home with you—looks like he's earned his rum."

Another trick. And a pretty good one. Claire tilted her head back and watched as another white arrow shot across the dark sky. So beautiful. She tried to remember a time when she hadn't cowered at the rumble of thunder, when a flash of lightning hadn't crippled her with pain. Had to be the rum. What else—a loa?

A woman near Claire fell to the ground and spun around on her back like a break-dancer. As she stood, she spoke in a man's deep voice. The words were nasally as if spoken through her nose, which made it difficult to tell whether she was speaking French, or English. Several women gathered around her, laughing. The woman sounded ridiculous.

Bernadette drew up behind the woman and placed a top hat on her head. The woman then shuffled around the circle of people, giving her comical discourse to whomever would listen.

A second woman dropped to the ground. Her twitching body rolled to the edge of the humfo, then back in again. She

stood and she began to dance, her legs kicking, her skirt
spinning with a fiery passion. She clapped her hands above
her head and stomped her feet.

"Spanish?" Claire asked the priestess.

"Guédé-Loraye, she likes storms."

Before long everyone was dancing like Guédé-Loraye
with bold movements, clapping hands, and stomping feet.
The drumbeats thumped inside Claire's heart, the music
pulsed through her blood. She spun and stomped, carried
around the humfo by a sense of freedom she'd never known.
She spun faster. Hands reached for hers and she danced with
the old, toothless woman until the rhythms broke them apart
and carried them on to other partners.

A man in a black bowler rose up before her. Except for his
rolling shoulders, he stood static. Claire thought of a broken
robot. She laughed and danced circles around him, tempting
him to move with a push here and a tug there. A woman,
with a blue scarf tied over her head, scooted up behind her
and elbowed Claire away.

Claire stopped dancing. "Hey."

"Heeeeey," the woman imitated without looking at her.
The woman tore off the scarf and tossed it into the wind.
Next, she pulled her cotton blouse over her head and her
naked breasts danced in the firelight. She shoved her frilly
skirt down her legs, stepped out of it, and then twirled it over
her head. Stark naked, she rubbed her body up and down the
man in the black bowler. The man kept rolling his shoulders
as if the woman wasn't there.

Fat raindrops fell. Thunder exploded above them.
Droplets clinked on the corrugated roof, harmonizing with
the drums. The dancing circle widened, spreading outside the
humfo. Men and women slipped and bobbed beneath the
heavenly spray. Claire turned back to the naked woman.

She'd removed the man's clothing and their naked bodies sparkled with rainwater.

"Baron-Samedi and his wife Madame Bridgette," Mamma Anna whispered in her ear. "It's not polite to stare."

"Are they going to…?"

"Who knows? Does it bother you?"

Did it bother her? Wasn't it illegal? Did possession constitute a lewd public display? She was struck by how sheltered she'd been. The only people she'd ever seen naked had been her few lovers. She'd never even seen a porno film. But any outrage she tried to muster about the naked couple floated away in the drum rhythms. Her logic was being derailed by the music. The drums commanded her.

She rocked with the beat, lifted her head as fresh drops burst upon her face. Clothing floated around her as men and women ripped off their shirts and skirts. Dark thighs shimmered in the firelight. She hardly noticed. The warm glow was growing inside her, the music and the peace.

Time stretched out before her. She was rolling over the ground, rolling in the mud, rolling through puddles full of rainwater. Someone held her, rolled with her. She clung to his strong shoulders. Vincent with his broad chest, his strong arms. His cologne filled her senses. They flipped over. He kissed her neck. Vincent. Oh, she would hold him forever. This time she wouldn't let go.

She opened her eyes, reached for his lips, but the face wasn't Vincent's. She recoiled. His sneer—the golden incisor—his breath, hot against her face. Billy Ray. He tore at her jeans, trying to find an opening.

She screamed. She scratched at his eyes, but he didn't stop, his hands digging at the waistband. She screamed louder, fighting him away with her elbows, but she was pinned flat against the ground.

A bright blue turban appeared above her. The priestess grabbed Billy Ray by the hair and yanked him off, but not before Claire noticed something odd, something terribly wrong. Billy Ray's skin was dark…as dark as Mamma Anna's.

Claire scrambled across the glade on all fours, screaming, crying, shaking all over. She rose to her feet and ran toward the water. Behind her, Mamma Anna's voice boomed, but she was too frightened to stop. Billy Ray's sneer flashed before her. She switched directions, reaching the cypress patch, but the raft was gone. Billy Ray's words echoed on the water: *"Down here we take care of our own."*

She leaped from the bank to a thick growth of cypress roots. She crawled from one to the next, the wood wet and too slippery to grasp. She had to get around the inlet.

"Claire, stop! It's all right. Stop!"

But she couldn't stop. She had to escape. Before her, a small piece of land lay wedged between two trees. She leaped for it. Her hand reached for the next branch, her foot balanced on a broad root. And then, her wet tennis shoes lost traction. Her grip faltered. She slipped, flailed to catch hold. But the murky waters of the bayou closed in around her.

Chapter 34

Saturday June 25, 2005
Luling, LA

Direct heat warmed Claire's face. She cracked her eyes open, but the light stung and bleached her vision. She closed her eyelids. So, this was death.

"Claire?"

Again she tried to open her eyes and focus on a blurred silhouette. Vincent? Oh, no, Vincent was dead, too. She'd seen him. Where? In her arms. In the darkness. Rapid images blazed through her mind: Vincent, lightning bolts, frenzied dancers, gunpowder blast, barking dogs, dripping blood, chickens, and...and...Billy Ray.

"What have I done?" Her voice sounded guttural, her words indistinguishable. A strange sound like curtain hooks sliding along a rod and then the brightness faded.

She tried to move, but a sharp pain ripped through her shoulders. A groan escaped her throat. With each breath, her ribs ached, her head throbbed. Billy Ray had killed Vincent.

"No!" She propelled herself forward, pain and all. Strong arms caught her across the chest.

"It's okay. You're safe. Lie back. Easy. That's good."

"Vincent?"

"It's Philippe. You're in a hospital. A fisherman found you floating on a pirogue in the bayou. What were you doing in the bayou?" He didn't wait for an answer. "Does this have to do with Cobb?"

Hospital? His voice sounded shaky. Was he afraid?

The door near the foot of her bed swooshed and a dark haired man in a white lab coat walked in. It came together at once: the bed, the smell of cleaning fluids, the smell of urine.

"Ms. Rivet, I'm Dr. Beaubien. I'm glad to see you're doing better. Do you have any questions since this morning?"

Her mouth felt stuffed with cotton. "This morning?"

"Our examination?"

She looked to Philippe for clarification, but his attention was focused on the doctor. "I don't...remember."

"Okay. That's to be expected with a head injury. You were pretty much out of it when I saw you earlier. The good news is that, except for a few abrasions and a broken collarbone, you're doing fine. You were admitted unconscious, which indicates trauma to the head, perhaps a slight concussion, but the tests we ran earlier don't show anything serious, such as swelling. We'll keep you here another twenty-four hours or so for observation, but if nothing develops you can probably leave tomorrow."

"That's great," Philippe said. Again the shaky voice.

"I'll pass back by before I leave. Until then, get some rest." Soft footsteps receded, the door bumped shut, and a cushiony silence again filled the warm room.

Strange images spiraled behind her eyelids like water through a drain. She opened her eyes and searched Philippe's face for some clue of what was going on.

He bent closer and her gaze traced the deep worn grooves between his brows. "What can I get for you?" he asked.

"I just need to rest a bit...if you don't mind."

His lips parted, then he nodded. "Of course. I'll be close by if you need anything. I'll step out..." He pointed over his shoulder. "And grab some coffee."

Later, she awoke to his touch. "Sorry to wake you, but I need to run a few errands. Suzanne's coming by after work, which will be in about two more hours. I was wondering if you wanted me to call Vincent?"

Vincent? Soon, she'd have to tell him she and Vincent broke up. She started to sit, but pain jabbed her left shoulder. "Ouch."

"Don't. You heard the doc. Relax."

She sank back onto the mattress feeling the ache in her ribs. "Don't call Vincent. I'll call him later."

"Okay. Well, is there anything I can get you before I leave?"

She glanced past him. She hadn't heard the door open, but Mamma Anna stood behind him, smiling.

"What?" Philippe half-turned, following her gaze. He stiffened.

"Claire, child, I hears you's here. I come to see how you doing." Mamma Anna stepped forward, ignoring Philippe as she removed Claire's hand from his. "Hears you's taken a fall."

A new dialect. Accents, dialects, the old woman could step into them at will. Then it struck her: Mamma Anna wore accents like most people wore clothes—whatever best fit the situation. That was why she'd tried several accents that first day at the post office. She'd been searching for the one that would make Claire relax. A trust factor, or more, a manipulation of trust.

"Fine. I'm fine." Claire flashed on Billy Ray's face bent close to hers. She sucked in a breath and a bolt of spine-tingling pain ripped through her ribs. Then she remembered Mamma Anna's powerful hand pulling him off. He wasn't Billy Ray, he was... Confused, she drifted.

"Listen, Claire needs to rest now," Philippe said, forcefully. "You should come back another time."

222

Claire rubbed her forehead. "It's okay. You can go. I'll visit with Mamma Anna until Suzanne arrives. I'll be fine."

Philippe looked unsure. She knew that he didn't want to leave her with Mamma Anna. "She's an old friend of Ma's. It's okay."

He shot Mamma Anna a threatening look. "I'll be back soon."

An eternity passed before she heard the door catch. "What happened? Why was Billy Ray there?" Another wave of pain shot through her chest.

"He weren't dare."

"Oh, talk normally. I'm on to you and Philippe probably is too."

Mamma Anna chuckled. "I told you to drink from the bowl. We don't do the sacraments for fun. They're handed down to us, generation after generation. They all have their purpose."

"Because I didn't drink some dead chicken's blood, Billy Ray showed up? You're going to have to do better than that."

"Billy Ray wasn't there. You showed all the signs of being ridden by a loa, but something went wrong. I don't know why…I think it's because you didn't drink the blood. If the loa had truly taken over your body, you would have enjoyed her pleasures. Instead, you saw your fear."

"Are you saying no one was on top of me? I saw you push him away." But she remembered something else, a detail that made no sense.

"Ernest. But he, too, thought you had the loa with you. Like I said, you showed the signs. He was coupling with the loa—not you. I told you, when the loa share a body, they share the pleasures of the body also."

She closed her eyes trying to sort what she'd seen, but the images were too disjointed. "Does Ernest look like Billy Ray?"

"That's what I'm telling you, child. You weren't seeing through the loa's love, you saw through your fear. You scared poor Ernest half to death. I don't think he'll ever recover." Mamma Anna paused, raised her ear as if listening for something out in the hall. "As soon as I realized what was happening, I shoved Ernest away, but you were frantic. You took off, running like a crazy person. I think the spirit was still connected with you, but she couldn't join you completely so everything was confused for you both."

"I remember falling."

Mamma Anna sat in the chair next to the bed. "Oh, you fell all right. The loa had had enough. She left your body quite fast, I'm afraid. During a normal possession, there's a vacuum sort of feeling as the spirit departs, but for you, I think the loa left with such speed it upset your body's balance. Next time, drink the blood."

Claire closed her eyes. Like there would ever be a next time. Mamma Anna was an enigma. She knew about Billy Ray, but rather than saying what she knew, she'd led Claire on a wild goose chase across the bayou. And for what? Claire was no closer to catching Billy Ray than before.

"What's the matter, child?"

"You tell me." Claire opened her good hand and held the open palm toward the old woman.

"You're discouraged because you don't think you'll catch Billy Ray Cobb. I don't need your sweet palm to tell me that."

"What do you *need* to tell me what you know?" More images were returning. The Elections Office. Claire rubbed her forehead. "Stop teasing me."

"I told you, I don't know anything that will convict the man, but I do know ways to terminate a reign of terror."

"Look at me. This is where your games have brought me." Reign of terror—she knew more. Had to. "You claim to be clairvoyant, have you seen something, anything that could help? Tell me!"

Mamma Anna heaved a sigh. "I can help, child, but not with the sight."

"Despite what you think, I don't believe in Voodoo." The magical events of the previous evening skipped about her. Could the rum explain them all away? "Granted, you have your tricks, but how can they work if I don't believe in them?"

"Maybe you're a non-believer, or maybe you believe more than you know." Mamma Anna laughed, her shoulders bobbing. "Remember the storm? Where was your migraine?"

Claire swallowed, searching for an argument, but she didn't want to argue. She was tired of fighting. She wanted answers. "I'm plain out… desperate."

"And so you should be. What else do you have besides me? You are up against a great evil. You need my help. Come Thursday night. Meet me at the raft with a black cat. Thursday."

"A cat? Where am I going to find a cat?"

"You must find one, black ones hold the most power."

"I don't…understand."

"You don't need to. Together we will destroy the devil that goes by the name of Billy Ray Cobb."

The old woman squeezed her left hand and a soothing stream of warmth traveled up into her sore shoulder.

Mamma Anna reached into a bag, hanging at her waist. She pulled out a silk scarf and unfolded it. "Here are some herbs I prepared for you. Chew a pinch every four or five hours. You'll heal faster and feel better. The stuff they give you here just dulls the senses." She placed the scarf on the bedside table and left without another word.

Claire remembered the raindrops on her face, the warm moisture running over her skin. Mamma Anna had cured her migraines. She reached for the herbs. She pinched off a few and put them on her tongue.

Chapter 35

Sunday June 26, 2005
Green Acres, LA

Philippe cursed then marched out of the den. He didn't want to fight, but if Suzanne kept it up that's where they were headed. Sure, she knew about a lot of stuff, like how to deal with Chet's asthma attacks, or how to negotiate the best fish prices. She knew about religious stuff and social stuff, but, by golly, she didn't know about this. She hadn't lived with Claire, hadn't seen her single-mindedness conquer just about everything she set out to do.

Hell, once when Claire'd dropped one of Ma's dinner plates and broken it into pieces, she'd glued the pieces back together minus one that was too damaged. The next day at school she'd fashioned the lost piece out of plaster of Paris and brought it home. With a kitchen knife, she'd whittled that plaster for more than an hour until it fit perfectly into place. Perfection—that was Claire.

"What if it's time someone took Cobb on?" Suzanne's voice trailed him into the kitchen. Then, there she was, waving a finger. "Once he's sheriff, he'll be able to do whatever he likes and no one's going to question him."

"He can do whatever he likes now."

"All I'm saying is—"

"I know what you're saying, and I'm telling you Claire doesn't know what she's biting off. She wants Cobb's hide."

And someone's got to stop her. Someone's got to keep her out of trouble because that's where she's headed. Sure as eggs was eggs, she was.

"Even so," Suzanne continued. "Maybe you should let her be. The newspapers say—"

"The newspapers praise her up and down, yeah, I know how to read, thank you very much. But what the newspapers don't say is why she's such a great prosecutor. They don't say that every time she brings down a rapist, she's bringing down William Cobb. She's had enough blood, now she's moving in for the kill."

"If he's the monster she says he is then he should be stopped. Did you ever think of that?"

"Yeah, sure, but by Claire? How you gonna feel when some woman steps up to you in the market and says that your sister-in-law's a boldface liar 'cause she's known William all her life and he's a fine citizen? Or how you gonna feel when you ain't chosen for one of those church committees you like so much because there's too much gossip circulating?"

"If Claire wins, Cobb goes to jail. Gossip dies, even the worst of it."

"How long you think it'll take to get Cobb behind bars? It's been more 'an twenty-five years. She ain't gonna find any proof after twenty-five years. It takes proof to make folks believe you. Look at that O.J. case. Hell, they had all kinds of proof and he got off, and you know why, 'cause he's rich. Rich folks get off and guess who else is rich—that's right! Cobb's daddy's been in the oil business since there was an oil business down here. He's got libraries, streets, even a hospital named after him. Ma knew better than to tangle with him. Claire's just stupid."

Philippe reached for a toothpick from the shiny metal dispenser. He placed it between his back teeth and bit down hard.

Suzanne, with her hands on her hips and her mouth set, was ready to give him hell. But hell, he had nothing left to say. He turned and left the kitchen by the side door. He'd said his piece.

Across the carport, he opened the garage door and stepped into his atelier—a real atelier, not some boards Ma set up across two sawhorses where he had to bring his tools inside every night so they wouldn't rust. No, sir, here he left his tools wherever, and he had shelves to store his wood, and hooks to hang his screwdrivers and wrenches. He had a table saw and a band saw, a router table and a lathe, a drill press and bench grinder.

His kingdom. Here, he alone made the decisions, and he had decisions to make. What was he going to do about Claire and her obsession? He'd promised Ma, after all, but even if he hadn't, as the oldest, the responsibility fell to him. If only he'd done what he was told that day, nothing would have happened to his baby sister and she wouldn't be hunting down a monster now.

What if she was right? What if Cobb had killed that Bonaventure woman? He gnawed the toothpick, spinning it between his thumb and forefinger. He shouldn't think like that. Claire was obsessed; look what she did for a living. But he had to admit, he didn't like the idea of the man wearing a badge.

Cobb had been what—eighteen? Nineteen? He'd gone on to get an education, played football. Folks change. Nowadays, Cobb hired men to do his dirty work. Leaves less traces. The image of Suzanne's battered face and bandaged head floated through his head. The toothpick splintered between his teeth and he spit it on the concrete floor. He'd let her down. His own wife. Same as he'd let Claire down all those years ago.

He walked to his workbench and hung the loose tools on the pegboard. He vacuumed the sawdust from the floor. But the image of Suzanne followed him, punished him. It echoed his neglect.

Outside, evening hung like a dusty curtain. In the close-cropped lawn, crickets chirped. Suzanne was probably putting Chet to bed. Suzanne. She worked in Orleans Parish. What if Sheriff Cobb went by her office? Why would he do that? What if her car broke down on the way home and Sheriff Cobb happened by? Oh, he didn't like that picture, not one bit. His wife.

"Damn you Claire—look what you done dug up."

On a shelf above the table saw, he reached for a long wooden box. He carried the box to his workbench and dialed the combination into the lock mounted on the front. The lock clicked open. A dark green canvas bag lay inside. He pulled the bag out and turned it over in his hands. His Remington 700. A gift to himself after he'd won the parish shooting contest three years in a row.

He laid the bag on the workbench and unzipped the canvas. A Remington's accuracy was what he'd needed to enter the statewide contest and he'd won that last year. Maybe this year he'd give someone else a chance. Then again, maybe he wouldn't. He removed the rifle and wiped down the metal with an oiled cloth.

Claire was right, someone had to take care of William Cobb, but her way was stupid. Twenty-five years later you can't accuse someone of rape, not a Cobb anyway. Big Daddy's lawyers would tear her to shreds and leave nothing for the buzzards to pick over. And if that weren't enough, there would always be Cobb's men, the ones who'd turned Suzanne into a bunching bag.

Yeah, he owed Cobb. He peered through the scope. Sometimes the old ways were the best ways.

Chapter 36

Monday June 27, 2005
Luling, LA

A male nurse rolled Claire's wheelchair toward the
hospital exit. The rancid bayou had been washed out of her
clothes and they smelled flowery like a fabric softener.
Wearing the tee shirt she'd arrived in, the air-conditioning
was chilling; goosebumps covered both arms despite the stiff
gauze sling holding her left arm in a bent position. Her head
throbbed just enough to be annoying and to make matters
worse, Philippe stood next to the revolving doors.

"This isn't necessary. I said I would call a cab. Don't you
need to work?"

Philippe took control of the chair, pushing it out into the
warm summer morning. After the chemical hospital odors,
the smell of gardenia and the more sour smell of fresh cut
grass were oddly comforting. She drew in a deep breath and
closed her eyes, but a pinch in the ribs brought her back to
the moment.

"What am I going to do about my car?" she asked.

Philippe locked the chair's wheels and helped her to her
feet. "Police found it. Joe and I drove it to the house last
night." Philippe opened the truck door and helped her in.
"Why you worried about the car? Doc said you need to rest
for a few days."

"I need to go by the Larose Post Office."

He started the truck, the heavy engine rumbled with
authority. "A broken collarbone and you aren't fixing to slow
down, are you? Reckon I could hide your keys."

"Don't you dare." She had a lot to do and now, only one arm to do it with. A list began streaming in her mind: post office, private investigator…

"You still haven't told me what you were doing out in the bayou."

"Want the truth or a lie?"

His eyebrows pinched together and he looked as if he wanted to hit her.

He'd probably split a kidney if she told him that she'd been practicing Voodoo. "Think about it before you answer," she said.

"Forget it. Getting a straight answer out of a lawyer is about as likely as squeezing wine from a lemon."

"Now with the lawyer jokes. As if I haven't heard them all." Didn't matter though, she'd never tell him the truth. The darkened glade drifted into her thoughts, the burning fires, the flickering candles. It had been a strange couple of days what with coming face-to-face with Billy Ray and Suzanne's confession. Suzanne.

Ignoring the pain, Claire swiveled around in the seat. "You knew Billy Ray was the man who raped me. Ma didn't tell you on her deathbed. You've known since I saw him at the Winn Dixie."

His face flushed.

She didn't wait for him to deny it. "Don't worry, I guess I understand why you lied. I don't think it's right, but I understand. I also know what he did to Suzanne."

Philippe's head whipped so fast in her direction that he lost control of the steering wheel.

She clutched the shoulder strap to keep it from pressing her ribs. "The road!"

He swerved back into the lane and cursed.

"I went to your house to confront you with what I learned from Jessie. That's when Suzanne told me about the miscarriage. By the way, she knows Billy Ray ordered it if you have any doubt."

"She can't be sure."

"Give the woman some credit. She knew you were in a bidding war. Once you gave up the bid to Blue Belt, it wasn't hard to figure out. Philippe, this is one secretive family, we have to break the cycle. You're a father, you have to break it."

Silence filled the next mile.

Then Philippe spoke. "It was my fault." His features looked strained.

Lately, she had a knack for hurting people. "Why was it your fault? Did you send those men to beat her up?"

His voice was a whisper. "I should have been there."

"Nonsense. They made sure you weren't." She rubbed her shoulder as if it would stop the ache. "Get rid of that self pity. Put your anger where it belongs—on Billy Ray."

"You'd like that wouldn't you! You'd like me to forget about my responsibilities and run headlong into your crusade against Cobb." He brushed his eyes with his thumb. "You're wrong about me knowing. I didn't know nothing until Ma told me before she died."

He didn't say anything else and Claire debated whether an argument was worth it. Then all of a sudden, he spoke.

"I remember the day, the Winn-Dixie opening, you acting weird, Jessie rattling on about something that had happened, but to tell you the truth, by then, I was working long hours and I paid little attention to what went on at the house. Ma asked me to drive her to the Winn-Dixie. I thought she wanted to see it, but then she told me to stay in the car. Thought that was weird, but I never asked Ma."

He became silent again. She wondered if he was reliving the day or thinking about how much to hide from her.

"Ma told me." He glanced at her. "When she was dying, she said that she'd asked the manager for the clerk's name and learned that he was the son of the refinery king, Randolph Cobb. He was working there to pay off some debt to his father."

"A debt?"

"You want to hear this or not?"

"Yes, I do, I'm just brainstorming. The Winn-Dixie job was something I couldn't figure. I knew he wasn't very bright, but why work in a grocery when your father was Randolph Cobb? He got into Tulane because of football and later flunked out, but Randolph financed his son's mistakes at every turn. But sorry to interrupt, go on."

"Don't know about all that. Maybe his daddy owned the store. Ma said that she went straight to the police station and told her story to the chief. Ma insisted she spoke to the chief. He had listened, then politely told her that he'd look up the case file and reopen the investigation."

"Then what happened?"

"According to Ma, she didn't hear anything more. A few days later she went back. Chief told her that no such case was opened on your rape. Ma said he must be mistaken. She remembered an officer at the hospital writing down everything. She insisted there was a file. But he said without a case, without evidence that a rape took place, he wasn't fixing to disturb Randolph Cobb. He informed Ma that there were laws that could put her behind bars if she persisted on calling Billy Ray a rapist without evidence."

"Randolph paid him off. Maybe the whole police force. Must have. In the state of Louisiana, there's no statute of limitation on rape of a minor. If a file wasn't opened at the hospital that night, she could have opened one at any time."

"Five years had gone by. And Ma was afraid, afraid for you. You'd put it behind you until that day at the Winn-Dixie. She thought if she left it alone, you'd get back to normal again, but you never did. That was the day you changed."

Philippe missed the turnoff to Gheens, but she was too upset to point it out. Poor Ma. Torn between doing what was right for the community or what was best for her child. Ma had no way of knowing that if Billy Ray went to prison maybe her daughter wouldn't have had to face the fears and demons that each new morning brought.

The day she'd changed. She finally understood that. Although she'd heard it before, from all her siblings, she'd never grasped it until now. She'd lost her joy the day she'd learned that monsters did exist. How could someone go through that and not change?

They stopped in front of the Post Office. "Go check your box," Philippe said.

She found herself speechless.

"I'm not waiting all day."

Slowly, she held onto the truck frame and climbed out. It was too late for her to ever be the woman Ma had hoped she'd be, but she would stop Billy Ray. That would be her gift to Philippe and Suzanne.

When she came back, Philippe was standing beside the truck staring down at his work boots.

"Counting the scuffmarks?" she asked, opening the door. She set the stack of envelopes on the seat and climbed in.

As Philippe climbed in, she held up the stack for him to see. "Hopefully, something in one of these will help me." She dropped them into her lap.

"Good luck." His tone was sour.

He was still in a mood. How could she find neutral territory? "How far would you be willing to go to stop someone you knew to be truly evil?" she asked.

"He does business like a lot of men down here, that doesn't make him truly evil."

"Okay, forget Cobb. This is a philosophical question."

"My philosophy holds with God."

"Okay. What if you prayed to your God that he do something to rid the earth of a certain person and then, that person has a heart attack? Is it your fault that your prayers were answered?"

"Would I be praying for justice or revenge?"

She sighed. With him everything had to be an argument.

"All right," he said. "If I was praying for justice, I'd be open to the decision of a higher power. *If* I was praying for revenge, I'd be praying for what I thought I was owed. Much less holy—revenge."

She wondered about her own motives, tangled somewhere between honorable and vindictive.

"Let me put it another way," he said. "Vengeance is mine... saith the Lord."

"Right, so we let these criminals run loose and let God deal with them in the afterlife. Next, you'll be telling me capital punishment is murder."

"*You* said it."

"I tell you what, if the only way to rid the Billy Rays of this world is to kill them, then I say, prepare the slaughter." Anger rose in her voice and why shouldn't it? She was angry. Twenty-five years ago a teenaged boy raped and brutalized a ten-year-old girl. He'd left her for the buzzards to pick over. Honestly, was it justice she wanted?

When she crawled inside the skin of that little girl, when she remembered the terror, the fear. He'd taken part of her life; he'd stolen her children. Was justice enough? Or was Mamma Anna right?

Chapter 37

Tuesday June 28, 2005
Villette, LA

Claire awoke after twenty hours of a drug-induced sleep feeling clearheaded enough to know she'd worked the medication through her system. Mamma Anna was right about it dulling her senses. Despite the gnawing ache in her left shoulder, she vowed to stick with the herbs.

She shuffled to the sofa. The letters she'd picked up from the post office the day before were stacked in a pile on the coffee table. Before falling asleep, she'd read through a few and found two from unhappy customers, one of those sounded downright incensed at Blue Belt's building practices. According to Mr. J. C. Blunt, his warehouse, which was built by Blue Belt, had to be completely torn down and rebuilt by another builder after failing several city codes. Blue Belt sued him for wages on the bad construction and won their case. Mr. Blunt was still paying off the rebuild because of the judge's decision. She'd counted two threats against Billy Ray and one libel against the judge in the two-page letter.

She sat, picked up the remaining twenty-some letters, and started opening them. One letter called Cobb a "communist pig," another called him a "capitalist pig" and another just called him a "pig." All but five were filled with venom, but not the right venom. No one had called him a "rapist pig."

Refolding the last one, she was overcome by the futility of it all. How many letters would she have to read? Hundreds? Thousands? Some were obviously written by people who had a bone to pick, not necessarily about William Cobb. Was it even possible to gather the type of information she needed this way? If these letters were an indication, then the answer was a big fat no. What else? A classified ad? A website?

Placing an elastic band around the stack, she stuffed the letters into the kitchen drawer on top of Cobb's folder. At the stove she turned on the gas and lit a match. She tilted her head back and forth, side to side with a twinge to the left. She walked to the panty and stared at the half-empty shelves. She'd already lost three days to her injury. She snatched up the bread loaf.

Back at the stove, she laid two slices of bread down on the griddle. Later, she would call Major Argrais. Perhaps he'd received the Bonaventure autopsy and tox screening. But could she drive? She squeezed her left bicep and then her left hand without the slightest sensation of pain. The ache was higher. Did she need that part to drive? The only discomfort was if she turned her head left too fast or too far. If she drove slowly and was careful, she could handle the steering wheel.

Her gaze fell on the rum bottle. It looked half empty. Was the light playing tricks with her vision? She squinted. She strolled to the bookcase, trying to figure out what she was seeing. Picking it up, she examined the seal. Unbroken. Yet a good portion of rum was missing. The last time she'd seen it, it had been full.

Had Mamma Anna switched the bottles while she was in the hospital? Did the old woman really believe that she was gullible enough to believe a spirit drank it? She rolled the bottle between her fingers, trying to see if it was a trick. Could the liquid be hidden in the cap, or in a second glass lining? What game was the priestess playing? Putting it back on the bookshelf, she waited to see if it would refill. It didn't.

The smell of burnt bread filtered across the room. Forgetting the rum, she rushed to the stove and flipped the toast over. Too late. Both pieces were grilled black. She didn't like the idea that Mamma Anna had been in the house. But...hadn't the house been locked when Philippe had dropped her off? Tossing two fresh slices on the griddle, she glanced around.

Spirits? No way.

She flashed back on the transformation of Vincent's face into Billy Ray's. She gasped. She'd been drunk, she reminded herself. No loas or possession just an intoxicated brain resolving the two most important men in her life.

* * *

After breakfast, Claire found her cell phone in the car's glove compartment. The battery was dead. She'd have to drive around for a while to recharge it. She could drive to Lockport and talk to Argrais in person. But then she had another idea.

In the passenger door pocket along with the cable she needed to connect the cell phone, she found Erwin's email with the names of two investigators in New Orleans. She should start there. Get someone out doing legwork while she interviewed.

Folded into Erwin's email was Vilma's email. She hadn't found a trace of the second rape victim, Zeta Mary White, but the first one, Marsha Louise Baker, had died of breast cancer a year ago. More disappointment.

Claire plugged in the phone and started the car. She pulled her arm from the sling and felt a moment of hesitation before hitting the accelerator. Only physical pain, she reminded herself. She could handle it.

The first investigator's office was located in the French Quarter a few blocks from Jackson Square on Ursuline. With the tourist season in full swing, parking was impossible. She drove several times around the block before giving up and heading down Decatur Street to a parking garage.

The address belonged to one of the older buildings with laced ironwork bordering three balconies. The office, painted in pastels and decorated with large green scheffleras, smelled fresh and lemony, the scent of fine furniture polish. A large wood-bladed fan rotated overhead, solely for ambience of a bygone era since the office was well air-conditioned. A woman in a blue seersucker dress, belted neatly at the waist, sat poised behind a reception desk. All very civilized in classic southern fashion.

She had expected something different: a dark, dingy office smelling of foul cigarettes and whisky, a secretary with beehive hair and violet eyes. She didn't know why she thought of private investigators like lurid, secretive creatures. Erwin, one of the two investigators her office employed, was nothing like that. Maybe because this was New Orleans, a city with an unsavory history full of pirates, drug runners, and corrupt politicians.

Investigators were known as grunt men and that's what she needed now—a grunt man—someone to track down every person Billy Ray knew, or came in contact with. What was his link to Tanya Bonaventure? She couldn't do it all and build a case before November.

"You may go in now," the woman said, her head turning toward the rosewood door as if she were expecting someone to come out.

When Claire walked in, Pete Nesbit stood. "Miss Rivet, I'm so pleased to meet you." He reached across the desk to shake her hand. "I've recently read about one of your cases in the newspapers. Here, have a seat." He motioned to a leather wingback chair in front of the desk. "What can I do for you? Does it have anything to do with that injury?"

She touched the sling, still unsure how much to disclose. "I'm down here collecting evidence on a rapist." She left off "suspected." "I'm looking for an investigator who can help with the leg work—track down victims, collect evidence that may be several years old."

"Sounds like I'm your man. See this?" He laid his hand on a thin screen computer monitor at his right. "I have a database you wouldn't believe. If your rapist is from Louisiana, I can tell you the last time he clipped his toenails. Also I have me several guys out on the street, and I hire only the best."

"The man I'm investigating was born in Raceland. I should tell you this is a high profile case. This person is running for office in the November elections."

"The higher the better." He rubbed his palms together. "Nothing I like better than nailing some scumbag who thinks he's too good to get caught. Who we after?"

Full disclosure? What's it going to be? "I need some guarantee this conversation goes no farther than this room, even if you decide not to take on the case."

"I'm licensed. It would be unethical for me to talk about anything we discuss. I've made my reputation on being ethical, Miss. Rivet. I assume you checked me out before coming here today."

"My office did." His computer looked impressive and the office screamed successful, although discreet. She had to give up the name. Without the name, he couldn't look into Cobb's history. "It's William Cobb."

Pete Nesbit's friendly demeanor crashed to the floor and shattered. His shoulders rose, his back straightened, but the smile stayed in place. "William Cobb is no rapist." His declaration was made slowly, deliberately.

Dare she try to persuade him? "I have information that says he is."

"William Cobb is a church-going man. He has kids, two sharp boys. He's a fine member in this community and you aren't going to find anyone down here who says different."

"Mr. Nesbit—"

"Good day, Miss Rivet. I'm sure even you make mistakes."

She stood. "I'm sorry to have wasted your time."

"And a waste it was."

Outside, she found comfort in the stream of summer tourist. The anonymity of wandering among the unknown faces kept her anxiety from rising. She'd put Billy Ray's name out there with the worst possible results. Was she that naive? After the dean at Tulane, she should have been prepared, but never in her wildest imagination had she suspected so many people knew Billy Ray.

Or did they know him? Maybe they were just worshipers on the golden altar of Randolph Cobb.

Walking down Royal Street, she thought back on Nesbit's icy behavior. She'd expected argument, disbelief even, but not his cold, contained aggression. Well, one thing was for certain—if Billy Ray didn't know what she was after, he soon would. Ethics or not. Nesbit had made himself clear. She removed the email from her handbag and read the second address. A block from the courthouse.

Did she dare try again? What did she have to lose? Nesbit was probably on the phone to Billy Ray this very minute. She'd either find an impartial investigator or she wouldn't, but she had to try.

She reached St. Ann Street and turned left heading for Jackson Square. The crowds were heaviest here and more aggressive. She should have turned off sooner. Protecting her shoulder with her good hand, she dodged the unending trail of men and women.

Then she spotted him. Across the road leaning against a brick wall. The same man she'd seen outside the Elections Office. Her step faltered. She stopped and as she did, a map-reading woman in a straw hat and sunglasses slammed into her. She bit her lower lip to fight the pain shooting from her shoulder down her back.

"I'm terribly sorry, so sorry. Are you okay?" the woman said.

Claire nodded, but as she did her eyes moved back across the street. The man was gone. Her gaze threaded the pedestrians. No sign of him.

Billy Ray's friends were popping up like lice. She thought about her options. She could dart into a store and hide out, but for how long? Was the man's presence a signal that Billy Ray was near?

Her stomach tightened. She tried to swallow.

"Miss Rivet?"

She froze. He was beside her, close enough that she smelled cigarette smoke wafting off his clothes. He looked one-fourth merchant marine and three-fourths criminal liability. He wore a jean jacket on one of the hottest days of the year. What was he hiding beneath it?

"Who…are you?"

"Your guardian angel. I'm here to tell you, you've been warned. The next time we meet won't be so pleasant."

"I'm an agent of the courts. Do you really want to threaten me?"

He smirked and was gone, swallowed up by a group of tourist, college kids swaying while trying not to slosh the beer out of their plastic cups.

244

Chapter 38

Wednesday June 29, 2005
Des Allemands, LA

The office trailer rumbled with the low, off-kilter knocking of the air-conditioner's compressor. Philippe reached into his desk drawer and pulled out the Smith & Wesson he kept there for protection.

"I'm going to shoot the damn thing."

Across the trailer at the drafting table, Joe chuckled. "You do that, we're going to roast alive. Manard said he'd be by tomorrow. Give it another day."

"Another day of that pounding and I'll shoot myself." Philippe slid the pistol back into the drawer. The noise was driving him batty, he couldn't think, couldn't concentrate.

"I've been meaning to talk to you about this weather," Joe said. "It's hotter than a two-dollar whore on the Fourth of July. Humidity this thick, this early means—"

"Hurricane weather, I know. One already hit Florida. If you can believe it, they're saying this season is fixing to be double last season. We need to finish up the houses we got going. Make sure we get them closed up before August."

"We got the one done, it's waiting for the kitchen. The two over in Paradis ought to be closed by August first."

"That'll work," Philippe said. "We'll get the supplies locked up for the month of August like usual. You going anywhere?"

"Fishing. You?"

"We wanted to take Chet to Disneyworld, but we'll have to keep an eye on the weather. Don't want to get caught down there in a storm." He looked over at Joe's desk. Clean enough to lay tracks. Hell. He returned to the stack of files littering his desk. Earlier, several had spilled onto the floor. He glanced back down to make sure he'd gotten everything. Best get Suzanne over here again to do some filing. This was ridiculous. He pulled a stack toward him.

The flimsy door rattled as someone tried to open it. "Pull hard," Philippe called, and the door tore open. As his visitor stepped into view, Philippe wondered if his nerves weren't playing tricks on him.

"What the hell are you doing here?"

Joe looked up from his drafting.

"Afternoon, gentlemen, my name's William Cobb." The man reached his hand toward Philippe, but Philippe ignored it.

"I know who you are. I asked, what are you doing here?" The last time Cobb had wanted something, he'd sent his message with musclemen. Something big must be in the air for the man to come himself.

Joe stood and walked toward Cobb, but Cobb didn't offer his hand a second time. Philippe remained seated behind his desk. Cobb didn't deserve his respect and he sure wasn't fixing on giving him any.

"I'd like to talk with Mr. Rivet about some business," Cobb said to Joe. His manner was professional, his intent, direct.

"I'm Mr. Rivet," Joe said.

Philippe bit back a smile. Joe wasn't put off by anyone, not even a Cobb.

Cobb glanced at Philippe. They'd never officially met. "Yes, of course. I meant Mr. Philippe Rivet."

Philippe gave Joe a half nod.

"I was just heading out anyway." Joe paused as if to convey a message, but Philippe wasn't quite sure what. Then, Joe stepped toward the door.

"Hold up." Philippe opened his desk drawer and pulled out the Smith & Wesson. He leaned over the desk and offered it to his brother. "Take this or I might find an occasion to use it. This way, if anything goes down, you'll know I didn't start it."

Cobb held up his hands. "Now, now. I'm just here on a little business matter. No need for artillery."

"Yeah, I've done business with you before. Here Joe, take it."

Joe grabbed the pistol by the barrel, but didn't move to leave. Philippe gestured him out.

Cobb pulled a folding chair over to the desk. "Mind if I sit?"

"You fixing to be here that long?"

Cobb sat, his frame large and solid. Philippe figured he couldn't take him out with his fist alone. Cobb wasn't one of those football players that had let themselves go to fat after the winning season, but then Cobb never had a winning season, had he? He'd disappeared from football almost as fast as he'd appeared.

"Make it quick. I got things to do and wasting time with the likes of you ain't one of 'em."

"Then I'll get right to the point. I believe you have a sister named Claire Rivet."

He should have known. Hell, he had known, only he hadn't expected a public appearance. Wasn't really Cobb's style.

Cobb kept talking, a feigned seriousness etched into his face like he was trying to sell a used car. "That sister of yours is going around saying some unsavory things about me. I understand she tried to hire a private investigator to investigate me."

"Claire's a damn good prosecutor. If she's investigating you, I'm sure she has her reasons. Reckon I should tell her what I know?"

Cobb leaned back in his chair and crossed his hands in his lap. Philippe noticed the fading bruising around the man's knuckles. He'd been fighting with someone.

Cobb took a deep breath and expanded his chest like a rooster. "You and I both know that wouldn't be a good idea," he said.

Didn't matter, Philippe thought, she'd found out everything on her own, but Cobb didn't need to know that. He looked back at the bruises. "Guess you beat up the wrong person this time." It pleased him to see Cobb rattled.

"You still live over in Green Acres?"

"If you found my office, you certainly know where I live." Watching Cobb, Philippe realized he could be watching himself. They were both in the construction business; both had built their companies from the ground up, even though he didn't benefit from his daddy's money; and they both had crews that depended on them to feed their families. They used the same suppliers, the same day laborers. So what had made Cobb go so wrong?

Despite everything else Cobb had done, Philippe had a hard time believing this was the man who'd done those horrible things to his sister. He looked normal enough, not like some pervert. Okay, the man was unscrupulous, most rich men were, but leaving a girl like that, naw, that was something else altogether.

Then, he thought of another beating and about his unborn child. The doctors hadn't even said if it had been a girl, or a boy. "I think you best go now."

"Not till I say what I came to say."

"I don't really care what you have to say."

"I don't like what that sister of yours is insinuating to my friends. I want her stopped and if you can't stop her, I will. You know I can." His voice had changed from friendly to forceful. "So what do you say?"

Like Claire would listen to him. "You mess with my sister, you're messing with the law. It's got nothing to do with me."

Cobb made a nasally noise. "Don't be so naive. You get a grip on her or I'll find someone who can."

Blind rage burst from his heart. He was on his feet, but fighting for control. "Get out!" He grabbed onto the side of the desk, tightening his grip until it hurt. He ought to rip the man apart here and now.

No, not now. The rage receded a notch and he could see clearly again. He had another plan, a better one. He pointed to the door. "Go."

With his hand on the doorknob, Cobb turned back, "You know better than to ignore me." And he left.

Philippe slammed both fists down and a pile of folders slid off the desk and crashed to the floor. The trailer door popped opened and Joe stepped in. He placed Philippe's pistol on the desk. "Thought you might need this."

Philippe grabbed the gun, squeezing the grip with all his might. "That son of a ..." He lowered his head and closed his eyes. Not yet, his time will come. He released his grip and shoved the pistol back inside his desk drawer. "Thought you were headed home."

"You got me curious, seemed a better idea to hang around a bit in case you needed some brotherly advice. What did he want?"

"Wanted to talk to me about Claire."

"That all?"

"Go on home."

Philippe looked down at the fallen stack of files. "Hold on, I'll go with you."

Chapter 39

Wednesday June 29, 2005
Lockport, LA

Major Argrais closed his office door and gestured for Claire to sit. He looked over her sling. "I expected to hear from you before now, but I see you've been occupied," he said. He sat behind his desk and leaned forward. "You want to file a complaint?"

Claire massaged the arm under the sling. "This was an accident and it did slow me down for a while. You said on the phone that you have the toxicology reports."

He slid a manila folder across his desk. "There's a copy for you. Autopsy and tox reports. Not much to go on except the hair did turn out to be dog, but it could have been a stray that came across the body. Her folks are pressing us to release the body. I don't see any reason not to."

"I'd like to go by the coroner if it's okay."

"Do it soon. Body's supposed to be released by Friday." He dropped the ballpoint pen he was holding, almost threw it, and leaned back. "You ready to tell me about this other case you're working on because I need some direction to go on here?"

The private investigator's aggression was still fresh. So was that hired thug's threat.

"No?" he said, answering himself. "Let me tell you a story then. Last Friday I get a visit from one William Cobb. Ah, I see you know the name. Nice guy, friendly. Says he knows about your investigation into the Bonaventure case and as a candidate for sheriff he feels we, he and I, should do all we can to assist you because of your famous reputation. Odd thing is," Argrais paused, shook his head. "He isn't sheriff, yet, so what can he actually do?"

Claire held still, trying not to react, but her thoughts were shooting off in several directions.

The major continued. "Next thing I notice are the man's hands. Some old bruising on the left, yellow edges. I'd say a little more than a week old, but two knuckles on the right hand were deep purple and sore looking. He told me he'd had an accident at a worksite. Guess it's possible. Then, over the weekend my boy and I go to buy him some new cleats. Football season's coming up. Anyhow, I spot this flyer taped to a light pole. You seen these?" He drops one of her flyers on top of the manila folder.

She pretended to read it because from the corner of her eye she saw Argrais studying her. He was a smart man and he had put it together. She wanted to fill in the rest, but he was her last hope. If she told him now and he turned against her…well, she couldn't let that happen. If she offered him evidence, he'd have to listen. If he didn't, she'd go up the food chain until someone did and that could mean his job.

He continued. "At first glance it looks like one of Cobb's dissenters is looking for information to use against the man. But then the more I read it, I wondered, what if someone had another agenda?" He leaned forward. "Then I had the oddest thought. I remembered you telling me your suspect was, now how did you put it, 'an important man in the region.' Go ahead, read over that again. You can see how it might just be someone looking for information on William Cobb for any reason."

She looked up expecting Argais's gaze. He'd try to stare her down. She knew the maneuver, used it herself. If anyone had the power to stop her investigation, he did. "My brother tells me Cobb cuts corners with some of his buildings to finish them at a lower price than his competitors. I imagine that causes problems for the owners of those buildings. Then there's the father. He's also an important man. There must be hundreds of people looking to take one or both Cobbs down."

Argrais shook his head. "That's the way you're going to go? I expected more from you." He pulled another manila folder from his desk drawer, opened it and pulled out a photograph.

He dropped the photo in front of her. "Heard about this earlier today. Girl found in Texas, beaten, alive, but just barely. Frontal lobe damage, which may or may not inhibit her memory. She's not talking yet. Evidence of sexual assault. She wasn't hit with a fist, though, she was hit with something harder. Forensics is testing a rock found at the site."

In the photo, the girl's face was splotchy and buried beneath bulbous mounds of blue skin. Her jaw looked strange, flattened, probably broken. Blood streaked her long brown hair.

"The rock-beating makes me think it's a copy-cat," Argrais said.

Claire kept her gaze on the photo. "Unless the perp's fists were still damaged from the Bonaventure killing." The attacks were escalating. Something was bothering Billy Ray.

Chapter 40

Thursday June 30, 2005
Villette, LA

The morning air was as still as death. There were no birds flitting around the garden or insects buzzing from blossom to blossom. The only sound, a low-level drone, probably from a distant refinery, felt ominous.

Claire skipped breakfast. The sleep had done her good and except for a little pain, she was starting to feel like herself again. Although her heart wasn't in it, she made her daily drive to the post office. Two weeks and not a single lead.

All she had to do to keep Billy Ray out of office was to prove he was involved with Suzanne's beating. But Philippe would never go for it. He was too afraid for Suzanne and Chet. In truth, after yesterday, she was too. Billy Ray's friendship force reached far and wide.

She tossed the new stack of letters on the passenger seat and lowered herself into the car. Her chest was tight, her shoulders tense from the ache of her collarbone. The herbs could help, but now more than ever, she needed a clear head.

She pulled out of the post office parking lot, her hands clammy on the steering wheel, and headed for the New Orleans library. Around the first curve, she stopped on the turnout and waited to see if anyone was following. To find Ma's house would take a surveyor's map. She felt sure that Billy Ray's man didn't know where she lived. But he had to be picking up her trail somewhere, most likely, at the post office. After two minutes an oil truck barreled past, but no cars. She waited another minute before pulling back onto the road.

Around the next curve, the letters, bound with an elastic band, rolled off the seat and onto the floor. She couldn't reach them without considerable pain so she left them where they fell. She thought about the electronic message boards. Tulane's had been a complete waste of time. Ninety-five percent of the posts had nothing to do with Cobb. After today, she wasn't sure she'd bother with it again. The flyers and post box had generated letters. Lots. People liked to rant and Billy Ray's unsavory building methods gave them lots of fodder. She'd learned of several civil cases that had gone his way and shouldn't have. But nothing in the letters could be used in a criminal case unless she could prove he was bribing judges and that would be more difficult to prove than his rapes. No. It came down to legwork, face to face interviews and she couldn't do it all.

Tonight was the night of Mamma Anna's special Voodoo. For the life of her, she couldn't remember what the old woman had called it. But she wished Mamma Anna had been more specific. The dream with Billy Ray hanging from a tree came back to her.

She wasn't about to do anything illegal.

And what was that nonsense about a cat? She had to find a black cat. Insane. No amount of dancing, chanting, or swigging rum would bring Billy Ray down. So why was the possibility taking up space in her head when she had so much more to do?

She was ready to admit that the glade held a mystery. Although she'd never said it aloud, she'd felt its weight, its power, and she'd seen...well, there was...

The strange images rolled through her mind like they'd been doing for days. She flinched at her thoughts.

Traffic slowed. She inched along to the turnoff for the library. She parked in the same parking garage and sat a good ten minutes, studying the cars coming in and going out. After a moment of silence, courage surged through her. This was it. She grabbed the stack of letters and slipped from the car.

All the computers were taken and a signup sheet for those waiting had two names listed. She added hers and went to the information desk.

"Do you have any books on Voodoo," she asked the female clerk.

The clerk didn't so much as raise an eyebrow. "Look around two ninety," she said.

Claire followed the stacks to the two hundreds. Voodoo Music. Voodoo Priestess—Mambo. Voodooism.

She grabbed a book about Marie Laveau, the most notorious mambo in Louisiana's history. As a child, she'd listened to stories of Marie.

Carrying the book back to the computer bays, she read that in 1830, Marie Laveau practically ruled New Orleans. Everyone—the mayor right on down to the mulattos who worked for her—was afraid of her "powers."

Marie had been a hairdresser to the city's rich women. She used what she overheard about impotence, mistresses, and lovers to influence the men of New Orleans by convincing them that she could read their minds.

Fascinating, but Claire doubted Marie had any real power beyond a cunning sense of manipulation, which she passed on to a daughter who kept her image alive for another sixty years. Mamma Anna was also a study in cunning: her deep laughter, her disappearing acts, her claims of clairvoyance. All could be explained away like a magician's illusions.

The one thing Claire couldn't explain was the woman's focus on Billy Ray. Was she only trying to help? Why? Because of Ma? Didn't feel right. What did she owe Ma?

That aside, was there really a way Voodoo could stop Billy Ray? Her mind scoured the possibilities. She wanted it to be true. She ached for a solution. A fast solution. But another part of her was petrified that Billy Ray would find her again. Remembering their last encounter, she doubled forward in the plastic chair, rocking and hugging the book to her chest.

She took a deep breath. If she didn't find a way to stop him, he'd remain free to rape, brutalize, and kill. She squeezed her eyes closed and exhaled. Most of all, she was terrified that she would never get him out of her head. He'd haunted her for too long.

Two computers freed up at the same time and then a third. She logged onto her email. Next, she logged onto the message board at Tulane and read through the responses to her last message. Fewer replies, but all political slurs and angry students eager to be heard.

This wasn't working.

Where could she find a black cat? Did she really need one?

Anything was better than reading the message board. The letters. She grabbed the new stack and went looking for an empty chair.

Most were the same type she'd already read, nothing more original than the message board, but about a third of the way through, she came across a plain white envelope containing a single white page. The note was short, typed, and cryptic enough to make her curious.

> William Cobb is an example
> of all that is wrong with this
> world. I've known him all my life
> and I do NOT believe he should be
> elected sheriff.

> *If I can do anything to keep*
> *this from happening please feel*
> *free to contact me at 822-7424.*
> *Becky*

Claire set it aside and finished the others. Nothing. She picked up the white sheet and read it a second time. Vague. She'd known Billy Ray all her life. So? Claire had known Philippe all her life and what did she really know?

Becky might know if anyone around Billy Ray went missing or if there were any scandals that Marla had edited out. A female. That was something, wasn't it?

She had to face facts. She was grasping. Oh, she'd talk to Becky. She'd continue with her investigation, but she was going to the bayou tonight. She'd do the Voodoo. She'd sell her soul if that's what it would take to rid the world of Billy Ray.

Insane. She'd lost all objectivity. Billy Ray had finally driven her insane. She'd chewed on her hatred for so long, it had eaten a hole through her brain.

Chapter 41

Thursday June 30, 2005
New Orleans, LA

Claire counted five rings before Becky answered. She introduced herself and thanked Becky for her letter. The girl's voice was dry and muted. She wouldn't give a reason as to why she'd written the letter.

Would she be more forthcoming in person? "Could we meet someplace where we can talk about William Cobb?"

"That's not possible. I shouldn't have written."

"But you said you wanted to help keep him from being elected. Have you changed your mind?"

"No."

It was like pulling the words out of the girl's mouth. "You said that you've known him all your life. I'm sure you could help me with my investigation." Even if the woman knew a neighbor, some friends—anything that might lead somewhere else.

"You're investigating him?"

Had she said too much? She scanned the letter. Her gut told her that this was a waste of precious time—she had to prepare for the Voodoo—but her brain said never overlook a source.

"I'm an Assistant District Attorney." She left off the jurisdiction; the girl probably wouldn't pick up on it anyway. "Our conversation will be kept completely confidential." She hoped. "What do you think about giving me an hour of your time?"

"I don't know. I don't know you."

"I'm easy to spot. I broke my collarbone so I have a big white sling across my chest." Maybe flaunting her weakness would make her more appealing.

The girl didn't reply.

"Becky, just an hour. You name the place."

After more cajoling, the girl caved. Claire scribbled the address of a coffee shop on the outside of the envelope.

The coffee shop was near Tulane and not far from where Claire had first seen Billy Ray's thug. Was Becky another of Billy Ray's friends? Was this another trap like the Elections Office?

Claire stayed locked in the car until the heat started to melt her mascara. If someone was following her, she hadn't seen him. But if this meeting was a trap, he already had her destination. She stepped out and looked around. She scanned the faces for the thin guy, but no doubt Billy Ray had others on his payroll. She clutched her handbag like a weapon and headed up the sidewalk.

The café's bohemian interior sported walls with peeling hand-painted murals, tables and chairs that looked as if they'd been made in a first-year design class, and a clientele that didn't believe in personal hygiene. She sat at a table near the back. Secrets were more easily extracted in hidden places.

She turned down coffee and ordered an iced tea with a fancy name. Be casual, professional, she reminded herself as she tried not to stare at the door. She read the menu. She read the titles of the murals. She read the menu again. She checked her watch. After tasting her tea, she pulled a photocopy from her handbag and started to list questions on the back. She checked her watch again. She still needed to get by the coroner's office. Tomorrow Argrais would release the body to the family.

At ten minutes after the hour, she understood that she'd been stood up. Or was it set-upped? She glanced outside, studying what she saw: a man in work coveralls, a woman pushing a stroller, shoppers with carry bags, and students, lots of students with old tattered knapsacks and shoulder bags. A busy corner, city buses, lots of traffic—easy to get lost in traffic. Another ten minutes. Perhaps the girl had been detained.

As she signaled for the check, a slim boy who'd been seated by the door stood up and walked toward her. With one eye on the approaching stranger, she dug through her handbag for her wallet.

At least, she should call Becky before leaving. "Are there public phones?" she asked the waitress.

"Next to the toilets. Don't know if they work, though."

"Are you Claire?" the boy asked, stopping beside the waitress.

Claire handed the waitress a five-dollar bill. The boy looked about twenty, twenty-one, most likely a student. He wore baggy tan slacks with an oversized maroon tee shirt that reached half way down his thighs. His blond hair was cut short and even shorter on the left side. He wore a pierced loop in his left ear. His face was dirty and bubbling with blackheads. His body odor smelled sour and much too old.

He pulled out a chair and sat opposite her. "I'm Becky."

Oh, female. Claire covered her surprise with a wide smile. The androgynous student look. "Nice to meet you, Becky." She offered her hand and noticed that under the ton of filth, Becky's face was thin-boned and fine featured. Her hand was small and timid. "Would you like something to drink?"

"No. I've been watching you, trying to decide if I should come over. I'm a student at Newcomb." Becky's hands twisted together as she talked. "I saw the message you put on the Tulane message board. Well...I assumed you put it up."

Interesting. She'd never put her P.O. number in the message board. She'd planned to or maybe send it privately if any responses looked promising.

"I also saw the papers posted around," Becky added. "There's one at the bus stop I use for summer school."

Claire nodded, hoping to draw the girl out with silence, but Becky pulled into herself, offering no further information.

"I don't believe William Cobb should be sheriff, do you?"

Becky looked as promising as a migraine.

"Sheriff?" Becky paused. "No, I don't either."

Her voice was shy, her eyes cast downward. Claire's disappointment grew—a total waste. The coroner's office was at least a thirty-minute drive. She didn't know what she hoped to learn there that wasn't in the autopsy report, but once or twice in the past she'd picked up information that way.

"How do you know Cobb?" She persisted since Becky wasn't offering her anything.

"I used to live up the street from him and Marla—that's his first wife. They're divorced now."

"I know Marla. I've spoken with her already."

That looked to surprise the girl. "My parents were their friends. I use to babysit Marc and Mathieu, their kids."

Marc was nineteen and Mathieu, what, seventeen or eighteen? "You can't be much older."

"I'm almost twenty-six. I've got one more year at Newcomb because I dropped out for a while."

Dropped out? Wasn't that a marker for trauma? "What are you studying?"

"Social sciences. I want to help people, to make a difference."

Her last hope shot down. Becky's motive had to be political. She'd wasted enough time here. "How can you help me, Becky?"

"From the tone of your flyers, hmm, it seems like, hmm, you're looking for damaging stuff against Billy Ray. That's what we call him—Billy Ray." Becky twisted her hands inside her crossed arms.

Claire checked her watch. "What information do you have?"

Becky looked away and Claire sensed she was missing an important detail. What could it be? Babysitter, Newcomb student, neighbor? "I don't pay for information, if that's what you're after."

To Becky's credit, she looked insulted. Hurt.

Claire backed up. "Anything you tell me is confidential. I'm a lawyer and you'll be treated like a client—client/lawyer privilege."

The girl looked down into her clutched hands. Claire sat straighter. She leaned in and forced on her business smile. It seemed vital now to put Becky at ease. "I realize it's difficult, Billy Ray being friends with your parents, but this is important. I hate to use the cliché, but it could mean life or death to someone."

Becky's face lost its color. "It's nothing concrete, just rumors."

"Rumors are good. I'm checking every lead. It's very important Becky." Claire tried to meet her eyes, but couldn't; they were still downcast.

Becky placed her elbow on the table and leaned forward. "I heard about this girl."

Claire's pulse sped up. She'd thought, hoped, that Becky had been a victim, but underneath the dirt, she looked too healthy. Billy Ray didn't leave his victims healthy.

"I heard he did something terrible to her," Becky said, her fingers twisting together, her torso rocking.

A strong reaction for a rumor. "Are you all right?"

"The girl's in a hospital now." Becky glanced around the coffee shop as if to reassure herself. "That's what I heard anyway."

"Do you know which hospital?"

Becky shook her head.

"Where did you hear this?"

"I just heard it. Around. It frightened me because I lived so close and all."

"During the time you kept his kids, did he ever frighten you?"

"No." She shook her head. "Never." She shook her head again.

Too emphatic. She had to go out on a limb. "Becky, it's probably true. I know for a fact that Billy Ray's a dangerous man. If you know more, you need to tell me. I can help. Is this girl a friend of yours?"

Becky stood up. "I don't know more. I've got to run or I'll be late for my last class." She grabbed her sack from the floor and rushed out, her stench lingering.

"Becky!"

Claire grabbed her handbag and ran out into the humid afternoon. "Becky!" But the girl had disappeared. A bus pulled away from the curb. Through black exhaust smoke, Claire scanned the windows.

Was it true? A girl. A hospital. It fit with what she knew about Billy Ray, but it would take forever to search every hospital in the area for a nameless girl, one who may or may not exist.

That wasn't really the problem, was it? Mamma Anna had promised her a solution. A solution today. Billy Ray's violence was escalating if she counted the girl in Texas. And she did. From the site where the girl was found, it was a straight shot down I-10 into New Orleans. But finding evidence against Billy Ray required time and manpower— none of which she had.

Chapter 42

Thursday June 30, 2005
Raceland, LA

The deputy coroner opened the refrigerated locker. The tray with Tanya Bonaventure's body rattled out over the rollers. "We moved her here from the cooler earlier this week," he said.

The deputy coroner was tall with long brown hair that touched his shoulders. His glasses were dark rimmed and made him look older than he probably was. The name tag on his white jacket had Mark written on it, but he made no move to introduce himself after Claire had introduced herself and handed over Argrais' personal letter.

"Do you need much time?"

Claire shook her head. The chance that she'd find something on the body was slim, but in cases like this she felt the need to pay her respects to the victim before digging into every aspect of her life.

The chilled room was a hodgepodge of smells: formaldehyde, cleaning solvents, decay. She looked at Tanya. What did this broken body have to say about her murderer? Tanya was five years older than the girl in Texas. Different coloring. Different body type. Claire noted the Y incision of the autopsy now stitched roughly closed. The deep purple pooling on Tanya's skin surprised her. "She was found face down?"

"Yes, and as you see here," he pointed to an area on her face, "already some autolysis before the body was found."

She looked over the area around Tanya's left eye. "She took it here pretty bad. If the perp were facing her as he would if he was on top of her, he'd be punching here with his right fist."

"Correct. But he did punch her on the right side hard enough to break a rib and that's what ultimately killed her. I wouldn't jump to conclusions on right handed or left, but I think we can say he's pretty strong."

She pulled Argrais's folder from her bag and removed a photo of what looked like a ridged area of a bruise. "What's this?"

Mark took the photo and flipped it top to bottom. "In this direction, it's the imprint the fist made in the contusion on her cheek. See here."

Claire looked at the cheek, then took the photo and studied it. "I'm done, thank you," she said, stuffing the folder back in her bag.

The refrigerated locker snap shut as she walked to an empty gurney a few feet away. "This way," Mark said as he opened the door for her.

"Do you still have her personal effects?"

"I think the crime lab returned them. You want me to check?"

"Please."

She followed him up the stairs and through a set of carpeted office cubicles. Somewhere above the muffled sound of a radio and Kenny Chesney's voice sang a familiar song. Mark led her to a small room with a round table and four chairs.

"Wait here. I'll see what I can find."

The room was painted a soothing yellow. A cross with a crucified Jesus hung in the center of the wall with the door while the other three walls were decorated with paintings of large flowers in yellow, pink, and white. She figured this was the room where families got the news that no one wants to get.

Not all death was violent, she reminded herself. It only seemed like it because she'd made a living dealing with the one-point-seven percent of the population who were victims of violent crimes.

Mark returned, a burgundy cardboard box in his hands. He set the box on the table and pulled out two plastic bags filled with clothing. He handed her a pair of latex gloves that matched his own.

She put them on as he spread the contents of the bags on the table. She picked up each item. Two leather sandals. A cotton gauze shift, ripped up the side. A green thong, torn. A charm bracelet that looked like real silver although the four charms that hung from it looked like a cheaper metal. A lilac hairclip in the shape of a bow, hard, painted metal of some type with intricate lacelike detailing around the edge.

She turned the hairclip over. It had a double latch that snapped it to the hair. She hated hairclips, couldn't understand why people wore them. Ma'd once punished her for tearing one from her hair and throwing it across the room. But she'd never stuck another one in her hair. Claire turned it back over and fingered the bow. Something about the color bugged her. It didn't match the dress. The shift was bold with reds and oranges. And Tanya had been a blond. The pastel color would have been lost against her hair.

She put the clip down. So Tanya wasn't a style maven. What did that matter? She picked up the dress, smelled it, but her eyes moved back to the hairclip. Hadn't the girl in Texas had something that color in her hair? A lilac ribbon.

That sure is a pretty hairclip you got there.

Claire's head shot up. "What did you say?"

Mark dropped his chin to look at her over the top of his glasses. "Me? I didn't say anything."

She put the dress down and glanced around at all of Tanya's effects. Looked once more at the hairclip.

That sure is a pretty hairclip you got there.

Icy cold tendrils crawled up her spine as the walls melted away and she was on her knees gathering snapdragons into a bouquet for Ma. She'd looked up. Across the field a boy ran down the road. He looked up too, but kept running. She didn't know him. She went back to picking her flowers. Ma was going to like this one.

She heard a noise and the boy was beside her, his head blocking the sun.

"That sure is a pretty hairclip you got there," he said.

Chapter 43

Thursday June 30, 2005
Green Acres, LA

Philippe dropped the Times-Picayune to the table. The newspaper's corner dipped into his coffee cup, drinking in the last drops of brown liquid. William Cobb's black-and-white photograph stared up at him. Broad smile, relaxed stance—he photographed well. Sure didn't look like the rich asshole he was.

Claire was gonna get herself killed. She'd already pulled one stunt and ended up in the hospital. She wasn't up to Cobb's caliber. Men like that were so power drunk they swayed as they walked.

Philippe remembered the way he'd looked in his office. Smug. But was he really the one who'd attacked Claire? Hard to believe despite what she thought. He'd have to have been a kid, a teenager. Course, everyone knew teenagers did some crazy shit.

The man sure didn't look like a serial rapist, though. For all his posing and his snide smile, the jerk looked like a normal jerk.

But in the trailer, Cobb had been scared. He'd smelled like a wild buck, facing a gun. Philippe looked up. Thought he'd heard Claire's voice in the room with him: *and why would he be afraid unless he was guilty?*

She was right. Why else would he want Claire silenced unless he had something to hide? Claire might be wrong about the other girls. It could've been an isolated incident. Isolated or not, what he done was wrong. Philippe didn't need a fancy doctor to tell him that if he'd found her ten minutes later she might not be alive today. Yep, alive and on the warpath.

How had he let it happen? He'd been good with the little ones after Pa's disappearance. Ma had enough on her just feeding the family. He always knew where to find Brian or Claire, knew their favorite play spots. How had she slipped past him that day?

He hadn't asked that question for a long time, but it wasn't like he'd get an answer now. If he didn't do something this time, she'd end up dead. He owed her. Besides, he had plenty of other reasons to hate Cobb. He didn't need Claire's battle to spark his flame.

He looked back at the newspaper. The article said that Cobb would be speaking to the Knights of Columbus. He recognized the address—a rec hall not far from the Garden District. He knew the neighborhood. Three speakers starting at eight p.m.. Three speakers at thirty minutes each would push the time to…what…nine-thirty. Add another thirty minutes for chit-chat, questions and that made it ten p.m.. It'd be dark by then.

An idea had been rumbling around in his head ever since he read the article. He hadn't planned for it to happen so soon, but he hadn't expected Cobb waltzing into his trailer, either. Truth be told, he'd been thinking about it for years, every since Suzanne lost their baby. Yesterday, Cobb had given him another reason. If he got caught, but he sure wasn't planning on it, Claire'd be able to plead him down. What was it they called it? Temporary insanity due to mental stress. Something like that.

He walked into the family room and removed his Remington from its perch over the chimney. He kept it there during hunting season. Heat from the fire kept it dry. Little early for hunting, but he'd cleaned the gun the other night. He'd wanted it ready for action.

At the kitchen table, he laid the rifle across the open newspaper. What if someone saw him, a witness? He had responsibilities. What about Suzanne and Chet? What about Claire? If he'd done his job all those years ago, she'd have been safe instead of facing danger now.

He wouldn't be seen, that's all. He'd get off one good shot and get the hell out of there. One good shot—between the eyes. That was the surest and fastest too. What if he... No what ifs. He would aim for the head—one good shot.

* * *

Philippe checked his image in the bathroom mirror and grinned. He'd darkened his gray eyebrows and beard with coal dust he'd ground himself. The shoe polish on his face made him look like a black fellow. Well, not quite. He should put some on his hands too. His hair disappeared easy enough under his Saints cap. With a little soap and shampoo, he'd be a different person, unrecognizable.

"What're you doing?" Suzanne asked.

He whipped around so fast that his Saints cap flew off and into the bathtub. He thought he'd heard a car door, but she wasn't due home for another hour and a half.

"What's your rifle doing on the kitchen table?"

"Thought you were going to your sister's?" He retrieved the cap and tucked his hair up under it.

"Good thing I didn't from the looks of you. What's going on?"

"Where's Chet?"

"In his room, getting ready for bed. He's not feeling well, that's why we're home. Now, are you fixing to tell me why you're dressed like that?"

"Got some business, is all." Philippe pushed past her and headed toward the kitchen. Wouldn't be good for Chet to see him with his face painted.

"You're not leaving this house until you tell me what's going on."

Philippe picked up the rifle then turned to Suzanne. Her gaze was locked on the newsprint, her face frozen.

"Forget you saw me," he said and walked to the backdoor.

"You're going after him, aren't you? Oh Lord, I knew this day would come. Philippe you can't do this. Philippe? Look at me."

"Lower your voice. I don't want Chet to hear."

"You don't have to do this. Claire will find what she needs to put him away and we'll all be safe. Please. Let her do her job, she's good at it."

"You seen Claire lately? You seen that sling around her arm? Next time, there won't be time for a hospital. Cobb'll make sure of that."

"You can't do this. God is the only judge. You know that. With or without Claire, Billy Ray will have his judgment day. And you'll have yours."

"I got to go. I don't expect you to understand, but I gotta."

"No you don't. Do you think Claire wants this? Do you think I do? If you go to jail what will happen to me and Chet? I lost a child to that man. I don't want to lose a husband too. Please, I'm begging you, don't do this."

"What he done to you was my fault for going up against him. I've had to live with that. But what he done to Claire was sick, perverted. He got away with it twenty-five years ago. He ain't getting away with it now. I have to do this."

"Philippe Jean Rivet!" Suzanne hands flew to her hips. She stomped her foot. "If you do this, I'm divorcing you. I can't live with a murderer. I can't live with that on my conscience. You make your choice, but I mean every word I'm saying. I love you, but I will leave you. I don't want my son raised by a man who believes killing is the only way."

Her voice was the one he hated, the one that made him recoil. She meant business, but there was no other way. Claire was right. Cobb could not become sheriff.

He stepped out into the carport. The screen slammed behind him. Why'd she come home early? He unlocked the truck and zipped the rifle in its canvas case then shoved it beneath the seat. He glanced back at the door expecting Suzanne to be there. She wasn't. He climbed into the truck.

Chapter 44

Thursday June 30, 2005
New Orleans, LA

Philippe drove around the block twice, surveying the rec
hall's layout. The rectangular parking lot was full with
several cars parked along the back curb. No matter, he didn't
intend to park. The exit might get too congested when he'd
need to make his getaway. He was curious though, as to how
many folks were in attendance. He also wanted to scout a
good shooting position. The lot was one possibility, but not
much cover. A hedge at the front looked more promising.

There, a hemlock hedge. Hemlocks made for good cover,
airy enough to fit inside yet the dense green needles would
hide almost everything. The hedge wrapped the southwestern
corner of the red, brick building. He could come up from the
rear, but what kind of angle would he have on the front door?

He drove back to the road and circled the block once more
before finding the perfect parking space, one that allowed a
quick entrance into traffic and was also located behind the
rec building. He wouldn't have to run far. Well, it was a
perfect spot if the hedge allowed him a good shot. Or else
he'd have to park toward the front of the building and take
the shot from the parking lot—much harder to pull off, easier
to be seen.

Another option was not to fire from here at all, but to
follow Cobb home, and hope he could get off a good shot in
private. But he didn't know where Cobb lived and that posed
too many variables like remote controlled garages. No, this
was the place. He felt it—one good shot.

What should he do with the rifle? He couldn't carry it around, on the other hand, he wasn't too comfortable leaving it in the truck to get stolen either. It was early. The sun was hooked to the horizon like a child that didn't want to go to bed. Judging the time on the dashboard clock, the speakers were probably getting started. He'd wait till it got a little darker and then check out the hedge for the best shooting angle.

Sounded like a plan. He shut off the engine, slouched back against the seat, and closed his eyes. Suzanne's angry expression filled his mind, her words filled his ears.

A car horn jarred his thoughts and when he opened his eyes, headlights blinded him. "Oh no. No!"

He turned the key in the ignition to check the time. Nine-thirty. Hell's bells—what had he done? He leaped from the truck, grabbed the rifle case, and slung the strap over his shoulder. Don't rush. Don't draw attention. Nothing more natural than a hunter returning home. Only it wasn't hunting season.

He rounded the corner of the rec building. A guy at the front door was taking a smoke, but he was looking off toward the parking lot. Philippe glanced that way too. All clear. He slipped behind the hemlocks.

The hedge was planted about a foot from the building, leaving him enough room to maneuver. He removed the rifle and rolled the canvas case down to the size of a hotdog bun and stuffed it in his back pocket. As the door swung open, the smoker stepped away. The two steps leading down to the sidewalk began filling with men and women.

Philippe raised the rifle, focused through the sight. How could he have fallen asleep? Wasn't like he killed a man every damn day. Heat swelled in his chest. He hated rushing. He scanned the crowd. Cobb, oh, Billy boy.

The angle was all wrong. From here, the best he could do was a shot to the back of the head as Cobb was leaving. No man deserved to be shot from behind—not even Cobb. Between the eyes. That's what he wanted, a clean shot. But it was too late to move his truck and find a place at the front of the building. He'd have to do what he could.

He inched deeper into the bushes, closer to the front of the building. The risk would be in getting away fast. His Saints cap snagged on a branch. He wedged in as far forward as possible. The angle wasn't much better, but if he saw Cobb coming out the door and the shot was clear, he figured he could make it.

More folks left the rec center. Too many milled around. Through the rifle sight, the bodies ceased to be human and became obstacles to a goal. Why didn't they leave? Didn't they have families waiting? His thighs were burning. He adjusted his position to accommodate the pain.

Something was moving beneath his shirt, crawling along his arm. He dropped his aim, reached inside his hunting shirt, and grabbed the pest. A wood spider. He flicked it over his shoulder, and steadied his aim.

He set up again. The waning moon wasn't much help. Luckily, the front of the building was lit by a lamp. The crowd had drifted toward the parking lot and several car engines roared to life. Good. The less, the better. But no sign of Cobb. What if he'd missed him?

Then it was God's will.

God's will! He was camped out in the bushes about to shoot a man and he had the balls to evoke the Lord's name? Had he no shame? This wasn't the way Ma had raised him. The Sixth Commandment: thou shalt not kill. Suzanne was right. How could he profess to be one of God's children, sitting here with a rifle in his hands?

He'd been lax and Claire'd suffered for it. He'd been arrogant and Suzanne had suffered. Now, he had to repair the damage before either suffered again. He owed them that.

If he didn't get Cobb out of the picture, who would? Claire? One week and she'd already ended up in the hospital. Naw, he owed her. But who was he to pass judgment on Cobb? Who was he to order his execution?

He pulled away from the sight. The wood spider was back, resting on the branch above the gun barrel. "Ah great, a witness."

What did a spider know of killing? Most weren't even harmful. But then there were those others that planned their attack, spinning a complicated web to snare their prey.

He glanced back at the door. The crowd was finally thinning, but still no Cobb.

This wasn't right and no amount of chewing it over would make it right. Suzanne knew better. She always knew better. Would she really divorce him? Course she would and he couldn't blame her. Did he want Chet to have a murderer for a daddy?

"Oh Claire, forgive me. I can't do it." He wiped away a tear.

If he ended up in jail what would become of Suzanne and Chet? Who'd protect them from Cobb's friends? He loved his sister, but he loved his wife and son more.

"Mr. Cobb," someone called.

Philippe stiffened. He raised the rifle and looked through the sight. Cobb stood in the doorway, speaking with a group of men, all official in their business suits. One man broke away and started down the steps. A clear shot if he wanted it.

His finger stroked the trigger. If he wanted... No. It would be so easy... No. Claire's bloody body flashed before him. Tears blurred his vision.

"Thou shalt not avenge," he whispered, raising his head.

The wood spider leaped from the branch onto the rifle barrel. All of a sudden, the gun fired.

The sound carried across the clearing.

Chapter 45

Thursday June 30, 2005
Bayou, LA

The reeds glistened. Ahead, in the wavering shadows, Mamma Anna appeared. No flowing chiffon or bright colors tonight. She looked muted in a simple dark dress and brown turban. Behind her, Jezwa stood immobile, his captain's hat tilted to the left, blocking his face.

The old woman had known she'd come. Again, the uneasy feeling. Since she'd left Becky, it had been gnawing at the back of her neck like an insect starved for blood. She was missing something. A detail she'd not paid attention to. But what or who? Becky? Mamma Anna?

All of a sudden a bolt of light flashed from the raft. She stopped in the middle of the path. Jezwa glowed. She squinted for a better view. No, Jezwa was just Jezwa.

It happened again. The glow formed bones, a skeleton. She stared at the skeleton in the captain's cap. Then, the brilliance faded and Jezwa changed back into the awkward image of a man. Mamma Anna didn't appear to notice the light or Jezwa's transformation.

The old woman was messing with her again. Why now? She was here, ready to do the old woman's bidding.

"What are you waiting for?" Mamma Anna stood. "Where's the cat?" She stepped off the raft and marched down the path like a woman with a mission.

"I had a busy day."

Mamma Anna looked like she was going to scold her, but made a tsk sound instead. "Come then." She turned and headed back to the raft.

As Claire climbed aboard, her gaze wandered back to the boatman. "Is Jezwa all right?"

"Sit here. Why you asking?"

"He seems different tonight."

Mamma Anna chuckled. "What's different about him?"

"He...sort of...glows."

Mamma Anna chuckled again.

Claire leaned into the priestess, shielding her words. "He's just strange, that's all."

The old woman laughed harder.

"Stop! Stop laughing."

"You're funny, child. What do you see when you look at Jezwa?"

"Jezwa. What do you see?"

A sly smile spread Mamma Anna's lips. She glanced back. "Hum, I see a strong, muscular, African, serious yet with glint of mischief in his eyes, the son of a great warrior."

"African? The man's as white as his cap."

"What cap?"

Another game. Claire glanced out across the dead water. Fireflies danced in and out of the cypress roots. Jezwa's pole swished. "Why are you giving me a hard time?" she asked.

Mamma Anna's face lost its humor. "Jezwa's a spirit. My eyes see him differently from yours. Everyone sees him their own way. He's here to serve you."

"You're saying a puff of smoke is lifting that pole and pushing this raft closer to the island?"

Mamma Anna tsked again. "I never said he was smoke. He's a spirit, and the way he reveals himself to you is important only to you."

Ridiculous. Jezwa was no more a spirit than she was. What was she doing here? An educated woman. An atheist. Voodoo was...well, whatever it was, it wasn't for her. A quick, sharp pinch in her collarbone reminded her of her last visit. What else did she have to break before she let go of the fantasy?

"I'll be with you the whole evening, child. Someone else presides over the ceremony tonight. Magie Noire ceremonies require a special kind of priest."

Huh, this *magie noire* better be worth it because this was the last time she was coming out here. "What about the cat?"

"Always strays out here. I caught one yesterday."

Jezwa secured the raft, as Mamma Anna scampered up the bank. Claire turned to look one last time at the boatman. Right. A spirit?

She struggled with the weeping willow branches, twisting them around her good hand, using the shortened length to pull her up the rise. By the top, she was gasping for breath.

Beneath the massive cypress trees, the glade lay in darkness. Only one fire burned, the one before the humfo. The silk flags and the bougainvillea tree were gone, as were many of the humfo's bright decorations. The altar table had been moved nearer to the fire. Colorful jars, more rum bottles, and several gris-gris bags were scattered on top, replacing the saints' pictures and other shiny items that been there the last time. No lit candles to light the way only the firelight. The effect was more sinister, more of what she expected from Voodoo—dark colors, skulls, crosses, and gris-gris. The gloom hinted at ghosts and demons.

She glanced around the humfo. "Where's everyone?"

"We'll just be a few this evening. Most can't afford the price of magie noire. Come meet the boko. That's the ceremonial priest."

Price? What price? No one had said anything about money.

Four men and three women huddled near the priest. Two of the women and one of the men were white. Including her that made four whites, more than she'd seen at the other ceremonies. The tallest of the group was the priest. Well over six feet, he wore a multicolored turban with beaded bands that dangled down his back like glittery dreadlocks. His white cotton shirt, which he wore unbuttoned to the waist, had puffed sleeves and a ruffled collar, and made him look like a swashbuckler. A bright gold medallion hung on a thick gold chain around his neck, decorating the dark, oily sheen of his chest.

As she drew nearer, he stopped speaking with the others and fixed his marble black eyes on her.

Her gaze dropped to the medallion. Carved into the gold was a vicious scene of carnage. Contorted faces and writhing bodies. Floating above the pained figures were two ghostlike apparitions, looking pleased with all they saw.

"The War of Independence," the priest said, his voice lyrically mocking.

Claire stepped back, putting space between them.

The priest's lips curled into a smile. "Good idea, ma belle." His gaze bore down on her.

He was rotten. She sensed it with every pore of her being. There was little difference between this priest and Billy Ray. They were both less than men, and more like a dark disease feeding off the flesh of others.

"Ma petite, tu a fais ton choix?"

She turned to Mamma Anna. "What does he mean 'have I made my choice'?"

"Give us a minute," Mamma Anna said to the priest. She led Claire away from the others and lowered her voice. "You must understand, once you call on the dark spirits to do your bidding, they can demand payment at any time."

"You didn't tell me about any payment."

"Are you willing to give up everything to get Billy Ray?"

Claire didn't have to think about the question—no sacrifice was too great to put Billy Ray where he belonged. She nodded.

"I knew that, but it's better I ask. There are many who love you. In your palm I saw a handsome young man. Remember? Can you afford to forfeit that love?"

Hating herself, she nodded. For more than half her life she'd lived, studied, worked for one goal—getting Billy Ray. "Will anything happen to the people I care about?" To Vincent?

"No physical harm if that's what you mean. As I said, you might lose their love. You must be prepared to give up everything for the spirits because the black spirits are a jealous lot. If they feel that your love for someone or something exceeds your allegiance to them, they will cause the object of your affection to become the object of your affliction."

Mamma Anna appeared to be waiting for something. Finally she asked, "Are you ready?"

"I don't like that man."

"You shouldn't. A boko is a priest of evil. The black spirits are his only friends." Mamma Anna took her hand and led her back to the fold.

"Ma petite, tu a fais ton choix?" The tone of the priest's voice was as before.

"Yes." She nodded. *Crazy* popped into her mind, but as it did so did the image of Tanya Bonaventure's battered body. She clenched her teeth.

The priest bowed. Everyone grew silent. The priest began to pray, slow rhythmic phrases, not in French but Spanish. When he raised his head he focused on her. She cowered.

She had a strong desire to run, to escape, but she kept her gaze locked to his. She had to try. "Ma, forgive me."

"Bien. Circle around the fire." The boko released his visual grip. The group fanned out, creating a wide circle. Mamma Anna stood to Claire's left. Behind them, one drum—larger and wider than the rada drums and with a darker, denser tone—kept a sad, steady beat. Another woman shook a rattle, the metal pellets hissing.

The priest stepped forward, his strong arms outstretched, his hands heavenward. He sang in Latin, at least it sounded Latin, but Claire couldn't be sure.

A woman wearing a black lace dress and shawl stepped forward and tossed a handful of salt into the fire. Next, she lifted a cup of liquid from the altar and threw it into the fire. The flame roared and flared higher. The air filled with the smell of gasoline.

A white man with thick, stumpy legs opened a wire crate at his feet and withdrew a squawking chicken. He plucked a handful of feathers from the bird's back and passed the chicken to the next person in the circle. One after the other, each person took turns ripping feathers free. Claire, with one working hand, found the task impossible. She handed the bird off to Mamma Anna.

"No you don't. Here, I'll hold it. Pull."

She did as she was told, flinching as the bird squawked its displeasure. After the bird had made one full rotation, the priest took hold of its body in one hand and its head in the other. He bit into the chicken's neck, ripping open the throat. Blood sprayed across the salt woman's chest as she rushed forward to gather the liquid in an earthen cup.

Claire closed her eyes against the violence. She reminded herself that they ate their sacrifices. Knowing that the chicken was about to be eaten eased the disgust of the ceremony. Thank goodness no one ate cat.

The cup was passed around. Mamma Anna handed it to Claire. "Don't even think about not drinking tonight, remember what happened the last time."

Claire placed her lips on the rim. The smell turned her stomach and she gagged as the warmth ran over her tongue. Barbaric. She forced the liquid down her throat.

"Viens ma petite." The priest motioned to her with his raised hand. "Come."

All eyes were on her. She glanced at Mamma Anna who nodded. Stepping forward, she stopped before the priest. His hands were warm on her shoulders, his palm like a heating pad, soothing her broken collarbone. Then, he turned her in three circles. She finished the rotations facing the fire. Behind her the priest recited a prayer.

The others repeated part of the prayer.

The tingling, which had started in her legs, crawled up her spine. She felt a bloating, no it felt more like—

"Pass your hand over the flame," the priest said.

She swiped her right hand across the flame.

"What do you feel?"

"Heat."

"Step closer."

She inched closer, fearful of the cloth sling. What if salt lady threw in more gasoline?

"Closer!"

He repeated the prayer. The others repeated theirs.

"Pass your hand," he ordered a second time.

She reached out, but this time felt nothing. It frightened her.

"What do you feel?"

"Nothing."

"What do you feel?" he asked louder.

"I don't feel the heat anymore."

"What else?" Still louder.

"My legs...I don't have sensation in my legs." Her legs felt weighted and welded in place. She was paralyzed and too close to the fire.

"Bien."

"Bonjour," the group said in unison.

"Bonjour, Ezili-coeur-noir," the priest said.

"Bonjour, Ezili-coeur-noir," everyone repeated.

"Donne-moi le chat." The French flowed from Claire's lips as if it were English. What had she said? What was going on? She felt divided, like someone else was stuffed inside her skin, someone who spoke fluent French.

The priest stepped into view and the stumpy-legged man handed him a black and white cat. Black is more powerful, echoed through her head.

The priest held the cat by the scruff of the neck. He lifted it into the air above his head. Claire's heart seized. What was the cat for? She'd remembered Bernadette, dancing with the snake over her head, a vehicle for the loa to join with. She'd sort of thought... But now, after the chicken. If he bit into the cat, she was leaving.

She tried to speak, but a hollow airy sound escaped her throat.

The priest pulled a hunting knife from a sheath belted at his waist. One glint of the metal and she understood. Sacrifice. Of course, black is more powerful. She tried again to speak, tried to scream, but her words jumbled into gibberish. The pins-and-needles started in her hands. The spirit was taking more control. She had to act fast. For the cat.

She focused all her force into the center of her chest. She had to break free.

The priest raised the knife.

Her whole being locked onto one word. "No!"

Startled, the priest paused. He craned his head, looking her over from head to toe, then he continued. The blade's forward thrust caught the cat in the throat. The priest drove the knife downward, slicing through the dull dark fur. Intestines spilled to the ground. Blood matted the fur and dripped from the white hind paws.

Claire screamed again, but her lips stayed silent as the sound bounced around inside her head. Shards of images cut her consciousness: headless chickens, zipped body bags, black-eyed Susans, bloodless corpses, a shiny gold tooth, red police tape, William Cobb for Sheriff posters, Tanya, Becky, the cat.

The priest threw the cat's carcass to the ground. He raised his slick red hands heavenward.

"No!" Claire managed a second time, still frozen in place. The sheer might of concentration left her weak, her heart pounding. She breathed deeply, drew her force inward, and concentrated on breaking one leg free. When that didn't work, she launched herself sideways, falling at the priest's feet.

Then blackness.

Was she dead? The drums had stopped. The night silent. Not a sound. Not a single sight. But she was moving. Slowly. Crawling. The sour smell of sweat was everywhere. Was it hers?

She was flying. The air flew over her as she tumbled. Something broke her fall. Where was she? A light. She turned toward it. Branches hung down partially blocking her view, but she saw people, lots of people.

There were men and women, well dressed couples walking away from the light. Where was she? How did she get here? A steel rod rose beneath her and stopped. A rifle barrel. How did she know that? It looked so big. She looked back at the light and froze. Billy Ray. Was this another trick of Voodoo? No. The rifle was aimed at him. Was she holding the rifle?

How could she? Not at this angle. *Shoot him*, she wanted to yell, but as before, she was paralyzed. Billy Ray turned toward her as if he were looking right through her. He grinned and she saw the tooth, the one that haunted her dreams.

The rifle started to move away. *No!* she cried, but her voice was silent. With every ounce of hatred she had for Billy Ray, she reached out and grabbed the rifle barrel.

The report vibrated through her, fading back into the sound of the voodoo drums. A mirage. What she'd seen was nothing more than a fantasy. She was on the ground, her body stiff as a corpse. The priest's leather sandals moved in and out of view.

She reached for the dead cat. Rolled to her back away from the fire's heat. Air. She could breathe again. The spirit was weaker, but present.

"Bil...ly...Ray!"

Her broken scream startled the others. They circled around and peered down at her.

Too many dead. Too much blood. Too much. A ten-year-old girl. Tanya. The girl from Texas. Death. And others— Mamma Anna said others. Violence. Too much. Bloodshed. Too much blood drawn for Billy Ray.

Tears washed down her face. She tried to wipe them away. She understood now. She had to stop Billy Ray, but without spilling more blood. She would fight him, but not like this, not with more death.

"No, you don't." Mamma Anna rose over her. The old woman yanked her to her feet. She tore the cat from Claire's arms and flung the carcass across the glade. "You're not running again! You've started something here and you're going to finish it."

Claire faltered on numb legs, but Mamma Anna jerked her straight.

The priestess's eyes were wild. "You came here to do something, *et mon dieu*, if you don't do it, I will kill you myself." She threw Claire to the ground.

She struggled to her knees. "You don't understand. I know what I have to do."

Mamma Anna grabbed her sore arm and jerked her up a second time. Pain shot across her chest and she fell against the old woman. Sensation tingled her legs. She was regaining strength, but Mamma Anna wouldn't let her go.

"You get over there and finish the ceremony—you owe it to your mother, you owe it to your brother, *and you owe me*." Fury contorted the old woman's face to where Claire barely recognized her.

With every inch of her body, she felt the old woman's threats, but she no longer had the stomach for the violence or bloodshed. She glanced at the altar. How could she keep going? What more did they expect of her?

As if reading her thoughts, Mamma Anna's hand arched back to strike her. The priest jumped between them, grabbing Mamma Anna's arm.

"You can't force the magie noire. You know that better than anyone." Then he said something harsher in French.

Mamma Anna struggled around him, lashing out at Claire with her free hand. The stumpy-legged man joined the priest in trying to restrain the priestess.

Mamma Anna's voice carried over the heads of the men holding her. "If you don't finish off Billy Ray, I'll kill you. I'll hunt you like a muskrat, no matter where you go, and I'll kill you."

The tingling stopped. The spirit's presence was gone. Despite Mamma Anna's fury, a peaceful sensation settled over Claire. She turned away.

The cat lay lifeless, a dark lump. Nothing more Claire could do for it. She looked at its blood, covering the front of her shirt and sling. She turned back one last time. Mamma Anna flailed between the hands of two stronger men, a weak old woman, struggling, fighting for control.

The raft was waiting, Jezwa at the back with his pole. From the moonlit sky, a huge black shape dove toward Claire's head, spreading massive wings. Her right arm flew up to protect her face and the bird let loose an eerie cry.

Then, the bird was gone, vanished in the night.

Chapter 46

Friday July 1, 2005
Villette, LA

Claire dreamed of the hidden glade, her skin warm from the heat of the three burning fires. Mamma Anna swirled beneath sparkling stars, the beads of her turban clinking and clanking. Smoke swelled from the flames, filling the glen with a thick gray mist. As Claire moved through the mist, she coughed. She coughed again and the glade disappeared. Her nose stung from the acrid smoke, but she could no longer see the fires.

Coughing hard, she rolled away from the heat, forcing her eyes open.

A thick haze choked the tiny bedroom. Bright orange flames leaped across the main room, inching nearer to the doorway.

What? How?

Dry cypress burned fast. The floorboards scorched her bare feet as she ran through the doorway. The flames roared stopping her. The path to the front door was blocked. The heat from the fire pushed her back into the bedroom.

The small window above the bed was the only way out. Jumping to the mattress, she looked out the window. The fire hadn't reached the back clearing. She punched the mosquito screen free and sucked in a breath of clean air.

How was this going to work? Without the strength of her left arm she'd never pull herself up high enough to make it through the opening. She leaped off the bed and landed on her jeans, still wet from the bayou.

She snatched them up and then reached for her handbag on the dresser. She launched both through the window. Where were her shoes? No time to look, the flames were getting closer.

She looked for something to step up on. The handmade drawers didn't look strong enough to hold her weight, but they were all she had. She yanked out the top one and shook her clothes to the floor. She yanked out the second one and dumped Ma's linen's.

She stacked one on top of the other at perpendicular angles for more strength. She climbed on the mattress, testing her weight on the drawers. They wiggled beneath her.

Flames crackled and climbed the bedroom doorframe. Heat swelled above her. The fire had reached the roof. She had little time before it would collapse, but she needed more height. All at once the air shifted. Two red-orange bolts shot across the bedroom walls, snapping up the wood in their path.

The roar from the main room was deafening. A beam crashed to the floor sending a cloud of burning embers swirling into the bedroom. She ducked and covered her head. A sizzle, and the caustic odor of singed hair.

"Ah, ah, ah." She batted wildly at her head afraid her hair had caught. The fire was less than two feet away. The walls blazed.

She shoved her head outside, clamped the window sill with both hands, fighting the searing pain in her left shoulder. She used her bare feet to climb the scorching wall. She tumbled, head first through the window, the screen scraping skin from her back. She flipped before her back slammed the ground, knocking the wind out of her chest.

For a moment she lay still, overcome by the ache in her shoulder, the burning in her back, and the throbbing in her ribs. A familiar scent caught her nose and she yanked open her eyes.

"Mamma Anna?"

A thunderous sound jolted her to her knees. The house leaned into itself. She grabbed the jeans and handbag and pulled herself up, her left arm dangling painfully at her side.

Thick smoke and burning branches blocked the path around the house. Flames skipped through the treetops like malevolent elves illuminating the night sky. She had to get to the car.

She ran to the well, and pulling her tee shirt over her head, she primed the pump. Almost naked, she shoved her shirt under the running water.

The house exploded. The sky lit up like Mardi Gras. Embers ignited the dry underbrush. The gas. The car. She had to reach the car. She threw the wet shirt over her head, gripping it as she ran farther into the woods. She circled around toward the front. Flames leaped the drive. Tendrils burned across the dried path. The fire was spreading fast. A small tree crashed behind her.

She fumbled in her handbag for the key ring. A burning branch fell to the ground. *Forget the car.* But the woods. She had to call someone. But the flames were too close. How close did they need to be to explode a gas tank?

A second branch broke free. She ran for the passenger door, the handle burning her hand. Wrapping the wet tee shirt over the burn, she tugged the door open and threw her clothes across the interior. She crawled over them and rammed the key into the ignition. She hit the accelerator. The car jerked forward, then died.

"No. No!"

She turned the key again, pumping the gas. The engine caught. She cut the wheel left to avoid the burning drive and headed into the trees. The car bumped and scraped over the undergrowth. As she inched away from the flames, she pulled back onto the path.

Reaching the road, she slid to a stop, slammed the gear into park, her hands shaking, her legs and arms trembling from exertion. If the fire kept burning toward the rear, it would hit water on its own. The real risk was if it jumped the road, then it could burn on for a few more acres. Other homes might be lost.

She climbed out of the car. She shook out the wet shirt, now almost black from cinders, and pulled it on. Gravel cut at her bare feet, as she reached into the car and pulled out the jeans. A wet tee shirt and soggy jeans—all that remained.

Smoke was weaving a ghostly path through the trees. Ma's house was gone, the only remaining piece of her parents. Philippe had kept the place up. He'd be the hardest hit. Another thing for him to blame her for.

Billy Ray's file was gone too, everything she'd collected. Her vendetta—that was the word Philippe had used—had cost her everything. First, Vincent, the man she'd loved. Second, Ma's house and her history. And third, the rest of her family, once they learned how she'd hooked up with Mamma Anna and what had happened to the house.

Ah, but she still had her career. Despite trying, she hadn't done anything illegal tonight, hadn't shot or hung anyone. But she hadn't caught anyone either.

A lone figure stepped through the smoke. Mamma Anna.

"What have you done!" Claire screamed. "Why are you trying to kill me?"

Mamma Anna continued walking until she reached the car. "I'm not trying to kill you. Who do you think woke you up? Who do you think alerted the firemen?"

In the distance, sirens broke the silence.

"What do you want?"

"You know what I want. I want you to finish what you started. This," she gestured back toward the house, "is punishment. And believe me, I will keep punishing you until you do what needs to be done! Now go, but be back at the glade tomorrow night."

The sirens grew louder. They'd be here soon.

Mamma Anna was walking back into the smoke.

"Let me drive you back," Claire called, but the woman ignored her.

Claire started the car. Two fire trucks passed her on the road. She turned south on route 308. What was wrong with the old woman? Why had the priestess become so incensed when she refused to do the Voodoo?

The ceremony and the magie noire, the spirits and the blood, all swirled through her head like a bad dream. If only it had been a dream. She'd seen things that made her question her sanity. She'd felt things she couldn't explain away, but after the reality of the fire, the rest was more like a mirage. What wasn't a mirage was the old woman's wrath.

* * *

In Houma, Claire found the Ramada Inn where she and Vincent had stayed one weekend. The office light lit the otherwise dark motel, but when she tried the door it wouldn't budge. The reception desk was empty, but the Vacancy light was flashing like a beacon. She knocked several times before spotting the night bell. She rang.

An older woman with too much sun exposure and too little hair shuffled out a rear door and across the office. She made a face when she saw Claire's bare feet. She pressed an intercom button and leaned forward to speak.

"If you're looking for a room, we're full."

"Vacancy sign is flashing."

"We don't take in vagrants."

Claire wanted to laugh until she realized she was homeless, and looking as trustworthy as a three-dollar bill. No bra, filthy wet shirt, soggy jeans, and no shoes. Luckily, she'd had the presence of mind to grab her handbag. She had the means to pay, and, at two a.m., she wasn't leaving without a room. She knew the law so she could bully the woman, point out her legal rights, or—

She removed the credit card from her wallet. "Listen, I know how I look. My house just burned to the ground. I lost everything, even my shoes." As she'd hoped, the disdain melted from the woman's face and, whether moved by the credit card or by real concern, the woman unlocked the door.

"Hon, that's horrible. Don't you have any family?"

"It's late. I don't want to worry them. Tomorrow is soon enough."

She stepped aside and allowed Claire to come inside. "This is no time for you to be alone." She locked the door and hobbled to the reception desk. She picked up a phone and placed it on the desk in front of Claire. "Give them a call."

Family. Right. She could see Philippe's sour face reflected in the glossy desktop. "They have small children. I couldn't possible disturb them at this hour."

The clerk took the phone back. "How about I call. It will sound more professional like that."

She slid the credit card forward on the desk. "Tomorrow. Right now, I need a room and a shower."

The clerk reached under the desk and pulled out a registration form. "You do smell like a smokestack." She slid the form across to Claire. "I think we can find something, if you're not too picky."

Picky? She needed a room; she needed rest. Tomorrow, she'd figure things out. And she had a lot to think about—like keeping Mamma Anna away because she wasn't going back to the glade. Was the priestess crazy or just not used to being refused? Ironic, wasn't it? After everything, maybe prosecuting Billy Ray was the only way to save her life.

* * *

Room ten, on the front of the motel, smelled like a mixture of mildew and cleaning fluids. Claire switched on the air conditioning, hoping to cleanse the stench as she showered.

Half dry, she curled beneath the covers and thought about Vincent. Since the hospital, he'd been on her mind almost daily, although she hated to admit it. She rubbed her left shoulder. The original pain had returned with a vengeance.

Her thoughts turned to the fire. Nothing made sense. It was as if the old woman had her own vengeance to reap against Cobb. Was it possible that she too was a victim of Billy Ray's—maybe years ago, before she was so powerful? No, Mamma Anna wasn't a victim. The woman was way too scary.

But if she wanted a Voodoo against Cobb so badly, why didn't she do it herself? Claire closed her eyes and thought back to what she'd read about Marie Laveau. Too many questions remained unanswered.

One thing was sure, the old woman was after her now. She had to focus on that. Her best defense would be to find the girl that Becky had mentioned. She had to talk to Becky again. And soon.

A jolt, almost electric, shot through her. She bolted upright.

"That's it! The girl does exist." And she's connected to Mamma Anna. That was the only explanation that made sense.

She had to find the girl. She'd have to search every hospital from here to New Orleans? But how? If she could just talk with Mamma Anna. No, the priestess would never tell her where the girl was. Way too late for that conversation. But was there another way?

Chapter 47

Friday July 1, 2005
New Orleans, LA

Billy Ray ambled around the mayor's outer office, scanning a series of photos of past mayors. Pretty classy idea. He should get some photos like that for the sheriff's office. One of him with the mayor, one with the governor. Add one of those snazzy gilt frames. Jazz the place up like his daddy's office.

Felt good to be inside, away from the reporters. Damn leeches been hounding him ever since he'd left the hospital. Then, the summons from the mayor's office. Mayor probably wanted to have a press conference together. Show everybody that his candidate was doing just fine. Some poor shot was turning him into a celebrity. No way he'd lose the election now.

He stretched his back. The bandages around his chest and shoulder pulled.

The door swung opened and Charlie charged in. "Hey, there you are. I was looking for you downstairs. How's the arm?"

"Went clean through. Won't feel a thing until the injection they gave me wears off. Then I got these painkillers."

"You always were lucky. Paper says they haven't found the shooter."

"I'm thinking it was Blunt. The man's been sending me all kinds of threatening letters since I won the civil case. The police have already hauled him in."

"You don't seem real worried that somebody just used you for target practice."

"Worried? This has just guaran-damn-teed me the election win. I could go for the sympathy vote, but I figure when I find the person that fired that shot, everybody will know I'm the best man for the job. I got an investigator working with the police and my man, Darryl is working with him."

"You still need evidence."

"Hell Charlie, if nothing else I'll pay some fool to take the fall. Always somebody needs a little extra pocket money, if you know what I mean."

"You set this up yourself?"

Billy Ray laughed. "Wish I'd thought of it. I'm a shoo-in now." He took a step closer to Charlie. "Listen, I spent half the night at the hospital. What's going on that needs my attention so urgently. Doc says I need rest. I want to get back home."

Charlie looked around the office as if he didn't already know it was empty. He leaned into Billy Ray. "Can't make sense of it. I got the call around 2 a.m. but one thing I'll tell you is to keep cool. It doesn't sound good and if you fly off the handle, I think the environmental project, your nomination, all of it is going to hell."

"What you mean?"

"Everyone from the wetlands' project is going to be here. Sierra Club, Audubon…something's up with the mayor."

A stern looking woman wearing a navy pantsuit opened the double doors and walked across the office toward them. She held her fingertips pressed together forming a sort of pyramid with her hands. "You gentlemen may go inside now."

Charlie shot him a warning glance. Always the worrywart.

She led them through another office, where two women were working at computers, and then into a conference room. Robert, Barry, and a man he didn't recognize, were already seated at the table. The unknown man stood as they walked in.

"Edward Stinson." The man extended his hand. Billy Ray clasped it firmly.

He then turned to the others. "Hey guys. As you may have heard, I've had a rough night. I'm pretty medicated so if I speak out of turn, please be patient with me." That ought to cover his bases. "Where's the mayor?"

Edward Stinson stayed standing while gesturing to the empty chairs. "He won't be joining us today. I'm here on his behalf."

"Oh. Well, what about Glen?"

Robert and Barry exchanged a look. Something *was* up. Charlie wasn't exaggerating. "Is there something I'm missing here?"

"Glen won't be able to make it this morning," Charlie said and pulled out the empty chair beside his.

Billy Ray lowered himself into the seat, grunting as if he was in a world of pain when, actually, he didn't feel anything but put out. "Well, what's so urgent? Somebody have news from the coalition?"

Under the table, Charlie kicked him in the ankle. Billy Ray swung around, but Charlie's gaze remained fixed on Stinson. The others were waiting on Stinson, too.

Perspiration broke out under Billy Ray's arms. He started to tap his toe; something that calmed him around his father. The burner was lit under him and he wasn't quite sure why. He'd have thought with the attempt on his life, there would be a little more sympathy coming his way.

Edward Stinson placed his hands flat on the table and leaned forward in a confidential manner. "The coalition is still studying the various financial options available. There are some concerns that the Environmental Defense Fund may pull out of the project."

"Glen? Why's that?" He didn't like the little weasel anyway.

"There have been some rumors about your run for sheriff," Stinson said. "Questions are being raised about illegal activities. And then with last night's shooting."

Is that all? "Any political campaign has its rumors. So what's got your drawers in a twist?"

Charlie kicked him again.

Billy Ray grabbed Charlie's arm. "Charlie, you best stop before I knock you the other side of Sunday." He dropped his grip and glanced around the table. "Can we be more specific, fellas? I can hardly rebut innuendos."

The room fell silent. Somewhere behind him was the click, click, click of a clock with a second hand. Barry and Robert were looking at their laps, distaste stamped in their posture. The only one who would face him was his old football buddy.

"Don't get in a huff, Bill... I mean William. You know how these things get nasty," Charlie said.

"If something's being said, I want to know what. All this can't be over a bullet. For all I know, someone was shooting at ground hogs and a shot went stray."

"At this time, there's nothing specific to the rumors," Stinson said. "The mayor would like your guarantee that nothing will come to light that will, well, that might embarrass the people behind this effort."

"You mean embarrass the mayor, don't you?" So that was it. That was also why the mayor hadn't come himself. Pissant.

Everyone's attention was on him now, nervous and twitching. Robert looked like he might wet his pants. Good.

What would the great Randolph Cobb do? He would belittle them with indignation, but that wouldn't win them over, would it?

Nope, that tactic was better used one on one.

He stood. "Sorry to put you fine gentlemen in this awkward situation. It does seem we can't have an election these days without some kind of name calling. Personally, I find that type of politics disgraceful. If a candidate can't win on his own merit, he has no business running for office. If rumors are circulating about me, they are only that, rumors. I've wanted to be a sheriff since I was very young. I've led the kind of life I thought a sheriff should lead. Exemplary."

He drew in a pained breath for effect, wondering if they could see his bandages through his shirt. Around the table, heads nodded, chins softened. They were buying it. That damn Rivet woman and her flyers. Had to be what's gotten the mayor jumpy. He leaned back.

Charlie patted him on his good shoulder. "William Cobb's been a friend of mine for longer than I care to tell you. I can say, he's exactly the kind of man we want for Criminal Sheriff in Orleans Parish." Barry and Robert nodded. Stinson remained stone faced.

"I'm sorry if this meeting has made anyone uncomfortable, but I had to ask," Stinson said. He walked around the table to Billy Ray. "I'll get back to you about the coalition and we can set up another meeting."

"Sorry about this," Barry said, shaking his hand.

Then everyone except Charlie filed out.

Billy Ray rubbed his sore chest.

"You feeling anything yet?" Charlie asked. They walked out together.

"You mean besides pissed?"

"I tried to warn you. I got the call this morning about Glen being ready to jump ship on the restoration project."

"You had a heads up?"

"Not enough. That's what I'm trying to say. I think Barry and Robert and Glen have been meeting with the mayor behind our backs."

"All this posturing, it has nothing to do with the shooting?"

"Shootin' didn't help, let's put it that way. Now, they're convinced someone has a valid grievance against you. It's not looking good, the mayor sending that goon instead of facing you himself."

"Mayor's a pussy. Have you heard any rumors?"

"I've seen some flyers around town with your picture on them. There's some talk about an investigation, but no one can tell me anything specific. I think it's a smear campaign from the other camp. When you decided to run, you knew that every aspect of your life would be made public."

"I did, but it's hard to believe some folks, ain't it?"

"Listen, I'll give Robert a call and see if I can find out what's going on. I'll be in touch."

"Thanks Charlie, you're a good friend. Look, here's Darryl. Can we drop you someplace?"

"Thanks, but my car's out front. Go get some rest."

Billy Ray watched Charlie out the front door.

"Car's out back," Darryl said. "Something must be going on in the Quarter. All the reporters took off a few minutes ago."

"Good, the way I'm feeling I might just punch one of them."

"Problems?"

"Nothing. Just this environmental business."

He and Darryl left by the rear door. His shoulder was starting to throb. "Listen, plans have changed with this shooting. I won't be needing you today. You have an address on that Rivet woman yet?"

"She gives me the slip somewhere around Gheens. I've been staking out the 654/308 intersection and I usually catch sight of her there."

"Excuses are like assholes, everyone got one and they all stink. Get it to me, yesterday. I think it's time she and I had another little talk."

Chapter 48

Friday July 1, 2005
Houma, LA

After three washings with the motel shampoo, the tee shirt still smelled like she'd slept in a chimney, but finally dry, it would have to do. Clothes weren't her first priority. Fashioning a sling from a pillowcase, Claire slipped it over her head and gently slid her left arm inside. With any luck that would calm the pain that had been steady through the night.

She listened to three messages left on her cell phone. All from a frantic sounding Suzanne. She must have heard about the house. So much for telling Philippe.

Reception was flaky inside the motel room. She carried the cell to the door, and upon opening it, found a brown paper bag blocking her path. Inside was a clean, cotton housedress with snaps down the front and a pair of worn cloth tennis shoes about a size too small.

The desk clerk.

Claire changed out of the tee shirt and into the baggy housedress, which was three sizes too large. She checked her reflection and liked that the floral pattern camouflaged her braless breast much better than the damaged tee shirt. She slipped into the tennis shoes, folding the backs down so she could walk on them.

She stepped outside and punched in Suzanne's number. Suzanne answered on the first ring.

"Are you all right? The house. The fire chief called Philippe—"

"The house is gone, but I'm fine." What else could she say? She sure wasn't ready to tell Philippe about Mamma Anna. She heard a whimper. Was Suzanne crying? "I'm really sorry, I should have been the one to tell you, but it was late—"

"It's not the house. Have you seen the papers?"

She hated when someone asked that. It was never good news. "No. What's up?"

"Cobb's been shot. I need to talk to you. Now."

Claire fell back against the door frame. "Shot?" An image reared up before her eyes—Billy Ray standing in a doorway. The Voodoo. "Is he dead?"

Had she somehow killed Billy Ray? Maybe Mamma Anna finished the ceremony in her place? Wait, spirits don't shoot people. What was she thinking?

But why had she gone to the glade with blind ambition? Why hadn't she asked more questions about the magie noire? That was so unlike her. So illogical.

"Claire, you there?"

"Sorry, what did you say?"

"He's okay, Cobb. But there's more. I have to see you. It's urgent."

"I'm on my way to Notre Dame. I need to speak with the priest. I'll come by this afternoon after you get off work."

"I'm not going to work. This is urgent. I'll meet you at the church."

"Suzanne?"

"Yeah."

She glanced down at the housedress, the fabric billowing around her. "Do you have any clothes that would fit me? I lost everything except a pair of jeans and they stink something terrible."

"What do you need?"

308

"Underwear, shoes, anything you can spare."

"I'll see you at the church."

Billy Ray had survived. Was she disappointed or relieved? If she'd finished the ceremony, would he be on a slab now? Mamma Anna had promised as much. But maybe this had nothing to do with her. She knew nothing of the circumstances. Had he tried to rape the wrong person? Oh, how she hoped that was the case.

She'd love for a woman to blow his brains out. Too many men thought they had the right to defile any female they pleased. Leroy Milson came to mind and a few others she'd helped put behind bars.

But Billy Ray was personal. She'd be thankful if one of his victims took him out, but she wasn't going to. Last night she'd made her choice and now, she'd fight Billy Ray her way, with the law behind her and the whole world watching.

* * *

She reached Notre Dame de Grâce and found one other car in the parking lot.

Shaded by ancient oaks, she walked up the sidewalk, the tennis shoes dragging over the concrete. Inside, the church was empty and cool. Light filtered through the stained glass windows and frenzied dust particles rode the crisscrossing rays. She walked up the main aisle, the same aisle she'd walked so long ago, hand-in-hand with Ma. At a side altar, candles burned and behind the center altar, the vestry door was closed. She knocked.

A priest, about seventy years old with gentle rolls of white hair and a bulbous, porous nose, opened it.

"Hello, Father, my name is Claire Rivet." She offered her hand. "My mother was a member of this church until she died about eight years ago."

The priest took her hand and held it in a compassionate grip that made her want to pull away.

"How may I help you?" he asked.

"If you have a moment, I'd like to speak with you about a friend of my mother's."

He pulled the vestry door closed behind him. "Of course, let's go over here where we can talk." Still holding her hand, he led her to the first row of pews and they sat.

"I'm not the priest who was here when your dear mother was a member. That would have been Father David. I've only been here for the last five years."

She gently pulled her hand from his grip and clasped them together. "That's okay, I'm more worried about my mother's friend. She doesn't seem well." She thought of the old woman's limp—not a complete lie. "She's called Mamma Anna, do you know her?"

"Everybody knows Mamma Anna." The priest chuckled. "She's one of our more eccentric parishioners." He held up a finger to push home his message. "I don't mean any disrespect. She's done fine work for this church."

"The other stuff doesn't bother you?" Maybe she shouldn't bring up the Voodoo, but she found it curious that the church put up with it.

"The other stuff? Ah that, it's just superstition. Far as I know, it hasn't done any harm. If anything, it's helped draw more worshipers into the fold. Mamma Anna is always bringing us recruits." He chuckled again.

"I'm worried about her daughter." Was that a lie? Had she just lied to a priest? No. She was worried about her, if she existed. And what if she lied to a priest? He wasn't God. God! She didn't even believe in God. Why was she so nervous?

"Has there been a change?"

Claire released her breath. She did exist! "A change?"

A daughter explained so much: Mamma Anna's determination and the pure hatred in her eyes when she spoke of Billy Ray. But it didn't explain why the old woman didn't just do the ceremony herself.

"In her condition?"

"No I don't believe so. I'm sorry, it's just…well, if anything happens to Mamma Anna, who'll take care of her?"

"That's why the girl was moved up to New Orleans. The hospital's subsidized by the state. She'll be looked after."

"I've been living in Baton Rouge the last few years. I didn't realize she'd been moved."

"Hmm, some time ago, right about the time I came to the parish. I remember because we took up a collection to help with the fees. That hospital over in Thibodaux just about ate up Mamma Anna's insurance policy. Yes, she was moved to that trauma hospital in New Orleans—what's it called?"

Claire forced herself to remain seated. There weren't many state-subsidized hospitals around anymore. Most had gone private. Should be easy to find. "I'm not clear on her condition. Mamma Anna didn't want to talk about it."

"Poor girl never got any better. Such a shame."

"After the rape?"

The priest looked confused. "Rape? I don't know anything about that."

So much for that theory. "I'm sorry, I've been away so long. I hate to say, but I must have forgotten. Was it a car accident?"

"Story I heard was she was beaten within an inch of her life. Probably some racial thing. Folks still haven't learned to embrace the word of our Lord, 'Love thy neighbor.'"

She shifted on the bench.

"I wasn't here at the time," the priest said. "There's evil at every turn. We just have to pray and follow our savior to a better place."

"I'd like to visit her while I'm in the area. Could you remind me of her name?"

"Can't say that I recall it myself. Let's see—"

"It wouldn't be Zeta Mary Baker, would it?"

"No, Mamma Anna's name's LePage, and the girl is… Liz. Lize. Elize. That's it, Elize LePage. I remember now."

"That's it, I remember too." Another lie. So many lies. Lightning was surely waiting to strike her down. "I'm going to go visit her, see if I can reassure Mamma Anna."

"That'd be nice. That poor woman's been through so much with the girl."

Claire left the church, her mind surging, making lists of what needed to be done. She didn't see Suzanne standing next to her car until she reached the parking lot. "I can't believe it." The words burst forth. "I've found a victim. A victim. I have to get to New Orleans. How's Billy Ray? I still haven't seen a newspaper."

Tears streaked Suzanne's sunburned cheeks. Her puffy eyelids looked as if she'd been crying for a long time. Certainly not for Billy Ray.

"Philippe. He did it." Suzanne said, brushing a cheek with the back of her hand.

"What did he do?" Claire wrapped her good arm around Suzanne's shoulders.

"He shot Cobb!"

Shot… That didn't make sense. Suzanne was confused or lying. Claire dropped her embrace and took a step back. "What are you talking about?"

"It's true. He says he didn't fire the gun, it just went off. But he was there to kill him, I know that. It's his fault."

This wasn't happening. Suzanne was trying to trick her. Claire turned to look across the wide green expanse that spread past the church's sidewalk. Then she turned back. "Start from the beginning. Where is Philippe now?"

Suzanne shoved a stack of folded clothing at her. "Here are the clothes."

"I don't care about the clothes. Tell me what happened."

Suzanne placed the clothes on the hood of her station wagon and bent forward, weeping.

"Suzanne."

"Philippe's at home. You've got to talk to him. He's afraid to leave the house."

Claire squeezed her sister-in-law's arm. "Suzanne, focus. What happened?"

"Cobb went by the company trailer, threatened him, well, not him but...." She looked up, her eyes glassy. "He threatened you. Philippe wants to know if he's arrested will he get off because of Cobb's threats?"

"Backup. He went to kill Billy Ray because he threatened me? Ah, but Philippe knew Billy Ray meant business because of what happened to you."

Suzanne sniffed and nodded. "There's something I didn't tell you, something I've never told anyone, not even Philippe, but he must have found out. Billy Ray must have said something at the trailer."

"Calm down and tell me."

"Billy Ray was there that night. The night I lost the baby. He didn't hit me, but he was there. He told the others to hit me even after I said I was pregnant."

"He was there? Suzanne, you're lucky to be alive."

"But don't you see, that's why I don't think he's the man you're looking for. He's mean, but if he likes to hit women how come he didn't punch me himself?"

A good question, but Claire had too many questions running through her mind to focus on that one. "You could testify against him."

"That's not enough to have him put away. I got my family to think about."

A hard truth, but probably true. Claire nodded. "How's Billy Ray?"

"Paper says the hospital released him late last night. Can't be too bad. Philippe swears he didn't pull the trigger. He says the gun just went off."

"Guns don't just go off."

"That's why he's scared. He thinks there was a second shooter, someone who might have seen him. He could be right, you know. He's a really good shot. He wins all kinds of shooting contests. Hard to believe he'd miss."

"A second shooter that fired at the same time Philippe's gun when off? Listen to yourself." The voodoo drums thundered in her head. She remembered seeing a rifle barrel. Was the second shooter a spirit? Now, she was insane. "When did this happen?"

"Last night."

"What time!"

"The paper said about twenty after ten. Why?"

She released Suzanne and leaned against the hot car. "It can't be." Too many things needed sorting. Too much was happening at once. How much of this was her fault?

Suzanne pulled a tissue from her pocket and wiped her eyes. "Where did you get that hideous dress?"

"Okay, here's what we're going to do." Claire reached across the hood and removed a pair of blue jeans from the stack of clothing. She kicked off the tennis shoes and used her good hand to work the jeans up her leg. "Billy Ray is released so he's in no danger. Philippe hasn't been arrested

yet, so he probably wasn't seen." She pulled out the bra,
Suzanne had brought. Her sister-in-law was noticeably more
curvaceous. It wouldn't do at all. She searched the shirts,
choosing a navy tee. Turning her back to the church, she
slipped the pillowcase sling over her head and removed the
housedress. She put on the shirt. "Where's Chet?"

"Summer camp. Are my hips really that big?" Suzanne
tugged at the loose fitting jeans. "You need a belt."

"Do you have one?"

"No. Those are my skinny jeans, thought they'd fit. I
forgot shoes too."

Claire slipped back into the sling and then the worn tennis
shoes. "I need to go to a hospital in New Orleans. It's urgent.
Then, I'll go by and talk to Philippe. I assume he'll stay put."

Suzanne nodded. "I'll drive." She walked around her car
and opened the door.

"You should be home with Philippe."

"I can't look at him. I'm too darn angry. Let's go."

Claire reached for the car handle, but as she did a rifle
report rang out. She dropped to the ground, gravel pressed to
her face. She was looking through the hemlock branches at
the rifle barrel. And then she was back in the church parking
lot.

"Claire. Hon, are you all right?"

Suzanne was kneeling beside her.

"Did you hear that?"

"Hear what? I saw you faint. Bet you haven't had
breakfast. Come on, let's get you some food."

Claire nodded. She needed time to figure this out.

Chapter 49

Friday July 1, 2005
St. Tammany Parish, LA

Claire called the trauma hospital in New Orleans as
Suzanne sped past the New Orleans airport. They didn't have
an Elize LePage listed. The operator told her that the hospital
was a short term facility and if the patient required long-term
care, she may be at one of the three state-run mental health
hospitals. She gave Claire all three phone numbers.

The closest was located near the North Shore of Lake
Pontchartrain. Elize was listed on the adult ward. But the
reception desk wouldn't give her any information.

"We need to catch the causeway north," Claire said. An
old case came to her mind: a young mother of two small
children who had broken down after a local housepainter
raped her. Institutionalized to this day, the woman had never
managed to testify against her attacker. As far as Claire
knew, the man was still out there, looking for his next victim.

She shouldn't get her hopes up. Even if Elize was able to
file the complaint against Billy Ray, she might not want to.
Claire's own testimony would hold more weight if someone
else filed the original complaint. The important thing was to
get an indictment as soon as possible, to start putting doubts
in voters' minds. Keeping him out of office was almost as
important as getting him behind bars. Almost.

"I hate to make you drive so far," Claire said as the New
Orleans skyline dropped behind them.

"I can't face Philippe. It's good I keep busy."

"Did you know Mamma Anna had a daughter?"

The tires rumbled on the bridge. Suzanne remained silent.

"Her name's Elize."

"You know, I think I do remember hearing something. It's been awhile, it might have been about the time I lost the baby that's why I'm not sure. That's who you're going to see?"

"If I can. I can't seem to get much information by phone."

"Mamma Anna gives me the creeps."

Wait until she learned about Ma's house. "Me too. She's dangerous. Stay away from her."

The hospital was isolated behind woods that opened into a grassy expanse. Modern in design, the main building fronted a series of linked one-story buildings of beige brick.

Suzanne pulled into the circular drive that led to the entrance. "I'll drop you and park."

"I shouldn't be long."

Claire tripped on her loose tennis shoe as she stepped up to the reception desk. "I'm looking for a patient named Elize LaPage."

The woman typed on the computer's keyboard, paused, and looked up. "Le Page?"

"Yes. I'm sorry, LePage." La, Le, French was so difficult.

"I'm sorry, but the visitor's list is limited."

"I'm her lawyer. I should be on the list."

"Just a minute. Let me call my supervisor."

The pause gave Claire time to think. She could hardly say she was family; the skin color might come into debate, but it wasn't impossible. Lawyer was probably the best choice. She could confuse the supervisor with the legal ramifications of forbidding a lawyer access to a client.

A harried looking woman drew up behind the reception clerk. "What's the problem?" She looked straight at Claire.

The clerk pointed to the screen and explained the notation on the patient file.

The supervisor glanced down and then back up. "And you are?"

"I'm Elize's lawyer. I need to have access to my client."

"You aren't on the list."

"Her case is still open and I've been hired by Miss LePage's mother." She would need to have Elize sign a consent form before Mamma Anna heard about this.

The supervisor looked like she wanted to argue, but in the end, shrugged. "Come with me."

They walked through corridor after corridor, Claire slapping the Linoleum flooring with the badly fitting shoes.

"Within the last few years we've been switching over to more short-term care projects. The only long-term patients we deal with are adolescents with both mental and physical issues. With state budget cuts most of our long-term adult patients have been moved to larger hospitals, but because that posed a hardship to Elize's mother, she's been kept here. There are only three other adults left on the floor, all schizophrenics."

"What can you tell me of her condition?"

"Unchanged. From time to time there's some recognition, but because it's so rare it's hard to know if it's authentic."

The supervisor stopped before a pale green door.

Inside, six empty beds lined the walls, three to the right and three to the left. A dark green gris-gris hung from a hook over the last bed on the right.

Claire followed the supervisor toward the last bed where a person sat in a high backed chair, facing the window.

"Elize?"

Claire stepped around the chair to face Mamma Anna's daughter. Her breath caught.

Propped back against the chair sat a woman, almost ageless in appearance, her face, grotesquely deformed. Her right eyebrow curved downward the tip reaching almost parallel to the bottom of her nose. The inner corner of her right eye was barely visible under folds of extra skin. Flaps of dark bulbous skin hung where her right ear was missing. The swollen curve of her lips crinkled like cauliflower. Her left eye stared without seeing.

Claire looked away.

"It's not as bad as it looks." The supervisor stroked Elize's hair. "Her face is disfigured by keloids. When the skin contains a lot of melanin like in African-Americans, keloids often form where the skin is ruptured.

"Can they be removed?"

"Yes, but surgery pierces the skin and more keloids can result."

"Elize?" Claire said. The woman didn't move. "Can she hear me?"

The supervisor shrugged. "Elize's been with us for five years now. On a good day, she sits in this chair. On a bad day, she doesn't make it this far."

Five years. "How old is she?"

"Just turned twenty-seven, poor thing."

"She's been here since she was twenty-two? How long has she been like this?"

"Since she was eighteen, I think. The beating split her face and although she was sewn up, the keloids developed during the healing."

Eighteen years old. Ten years old. And Tanya—twenty-two. Claire's knees weakened and she backed against the wall to keep from falling. She'd misjudged. The monster was worse than she'd imagined. "I heard…ah, my file says…" Emotions were tearing her apart to where she couldn't even lie. She looked back at Elize. "Was she raped?"

The supervisor stroked Elize's hair again and gave a slight nod. "Scary, isn't it, that someone could do something like this."

And he may have just done it again. What was it Argrais had said, something about cracking an orbital bone?

She glanced at Elize's face. She thought she understood what Mamma Anna had seen in Ma's palm—not the attack, but a mother's shared pain. A vise squeezed her throat. Her eyes moistened. She should have killed Billy Ray when she'd had the chance.

"How does the visitors' list work?"

"Her mother must approve all visitors. Her mother comes and prays with her, but it's a long way for her by bus. Every now and then a few church members come with her. Oh, and there's a Newcomb student who reads to her once a week."

Elize shifted in the chair and started giggling. Then she grew still.

"She does that sometimes. It makes you wonder what is going through her mind."

Claire didn't want to know what was in Elize's head. If it was anything like the torment that drove her, they were all better off not knowing. Watching the young woman, she felt guilty for being alive, for being able to walk and talk, for being free to go after Billy Ray while Elize was sentenced to hell.

If she'd seen Elize before, would she have taken the Voodoo more seriously? Understanding Mamma Anna's pain, could she have killed Billy Ray? Probably.

"Wait. You said something about a student?"

"Such a nice girl. She's been coming for the last couple of years."

"Is her name Becky by any chance?"

"Yeah, Becky Warton. She was here this morning."

Claire felt flattened as if someone had just driven over her with a steamroller. Becky. She knew Elize and exactly where to find her. The girl's story had sounded weak and contrived. Why hadn't Claire noticed before?

She flashed back on their conversation in the coffee shop. She'd missed a lot. How did Becky know Elize? But more importantly, how did she know that Billy Ray was the attacker? For the first time since Claire'd entered the room, she could see the noose tightening around Billy Ray's neck.

She bent to Elize's head. "I'll get him Elize. If it's the last thing I do, I'll get Billy Ray."

* * *

Claire stopped on the steps outside of the hospital. She found her wallet and flipped through it for Argrais' business card. She punched in his number.

"Major Argrais, I may have found a second case that matches the Bonaventure case. I'm looking into the rape of a young woman, Elize LePage. The attack took place about nine years ago. After you've read the file, I'd appreciate it if I could have a look at it."

The Major cleared his throat. "Nine years ago, I was working upstate. Was it solved?"

"No. What's important is to see if any DNA evidence was found. If it hasn't been tested, I'll pay for any testing myself." She knew that thousands upon thousands of unsolved cases sat on shelves around the country with enough DNA evidence to convict, but until a suspect was found, the DNA went untested because of budgetary concerns.

"Tell me about the case."

"I'm afraid I don't have many details yet except the woman's name. Her age at the time of the attack was eighteen. She was raped and beaten and I have conformation on the attacker. But I need evidence, before I give you the attacker's name. That, I'm hoping you have."

"I haven't come across anything in our files that fits the Bonaventure M.O., but nine years ago, I'll check the cold cases and get back to you."

Tears filled her eyes. Could be the lack of sleep. But the thought of Elize, of what that monster had done to that poor girl, she'd like to tear him apart with her bare hands.

Chapter 50

Friday July 1, 2005
Green Acres, LA

Philippe paced the family room, shaking his head like he was trying to shake off a fly. "I don't deny it. I went there to shoot him. But I couldn't, Claire. I wanted to, but I didn't. I swear. You've got to believe me."

She'd never seen her brother so desperate. His hands flew as he spoke. He couldn't stop moving, couldn't stay focused.

"I dropped my aim. I was pulling the rifle away, then I felt someone. God this is going to sound stupid. Something, I felt some kind of a force. I swear, Claire, I swear. Then the gun fired. The damnedest thing. Just like that. It went off. I've never had a gun misfire before. Never."

She prepared her professional voice, the one she used to interrogate witnesses, hoping it wouldn't betray her fear. "Then what happened?"

Philippe's hands clamped his head. "It was like someone else was there."

"Was someone else there?"

"Naw, naw, I don't…think so. Been thinking about it all night. Reckon it's true what they say about the subconscious being a powerful force. Mine must be pretty damn strong."

His subconscious shot Cobb—what a defense. She'd heard them all: God told me to do it; a voice told me to do it; even, my dog told me to do it. But my subconscious? "As you were turning away, could a branch have caught the barrel? Could there be a problem with the firing pin?"

"I checked the firing pin a couple of days ago. I know how crazy I sound, so stop looking at me like that. A branch? Sure. Maybe."

Had she been the other person there? In what form? This was crazy. People don't dematerialize. But why couldn't she remember more? "Where did this take place?"

"In the city. The rec center. Cobb was giving some kind of talk."

The image she remembered was Cobb dressed in a suit, standing... "Were there men in suits standing around him?"

"I guess. It was a pretty fancy do."

She clearly remembered the gun barrel. If asked she could describe every detail. Had her spirit or her loa or some unbelievable thing pulled that trigger? Was Philippe taking the blame for her? "Let me just tell you what you are looking at. If the state charges attempted murder, or assault with a deadly weapon, you could get twenty-five years to life. Add use of a firearm and you have ten more years. Discharge of a firearm, another twenty."

"Fifty-five years! The guy's barely got a scratch."

"A bullet ripped clear through him. That's more than a scratch. You took that rifle out there for a specific reason. You're responsible for what happened next whether it was your subconscious, or the hand of God."

Or a loa?

Right. She was as nuts as he was. Mental illness must run in the family.

Philippe looked as if he might cry. "Then it was the hand of God, 'cause I can't think of nothing else."

"Grow up!"

"Sorry." His voice cracked. "It was just so weird." He sounded as if he was Chet's age. "I know it's crazy. Reckon I should be locked up."

Although breaking the law went against everything she believed in, she knew she was about to do it. Accessory. But she wasn't going to turn him in. How could she? She'd had the same thing in mind when she'd gone out into the bayou. Kill Billy Ray. However misguided his actions, Philippe had been trying to protect her. Billy Ray was the one who belonged in jail, not Philippe.

"Give me a dollar."

"Ah...I don't—"

"Break Chet's piggy bank if you have to, but give me a dollar."

He left the room and returned carrying his wallet. "Is a ten okay?" He held out the bill.

She snatched it away from him. "You've just hired me to be your lawyer. Now, we're bound by attorney/client privilege. Here's what you're going to do. When Suzanne gets back with Chet, you pack a bag and go away for awhile. If Cobb knows you fired on him, he might come looking for you rather than bring in the police. That's more his style. You take the family to South Carolina, or Texas. Get out of the state until I tell you it's safe to come back."

"Why would he think I shot him?"

"You said someone else might have been out there. Might have been one of his men. He's had one following me off and on. After he came to your trailer, he might have put someone on you."

"He has someone following you!"

"Step into your own life, Philippe. You're in a lot of trouble. Sit down, focus." She waited for him to settle down on the sofa. She stood before him. "I've found another one of his victims, but I'm waiting on more information. Something that'll hold up in court." She needed to talk to Becky, too.

Hopefully, the number was in her phone's memory because the letter burned with the house. "I need a few more days."

"If Cobb's gunning for you, you might not have a few days."

He's not the only one, but she wasn't going to tell him about Mamma Anna. Not now. Not ever. "Listen." She checked her watch. "There's one thing I need you to do before you leave. I want you to teach me how to shoot."

"I can't do that in an hour."

"You can get me started. I remember the basics of rifle shooting, but I want to learn to shoot a handgun. You got one?"

"Claire, you can't go after Cobb."

"I'm not stupid. It's for protection."

He paused, looked at her hard. "Come on out back."

Chapter 51

Saturday July 2, 2005
New Orleans, LA

Claire must have erased Becky's number in the phone's memory, but she had a last name and a neighborhood. Information gave her a possible number registered to what she hoped was Becky's parents. Becky answered on the fourth ring.

"This is Claire Rivet, we met—"

"Hey, I told you everything. I don't know anything else."

"You know Elize."

The line went dead. Claire hit the redial, and then had a better idea. She shoved the phone in her handbag and restarted the car.

Becky's parents lived in a middle class neighborhood west of New Orleans. Claire knew it from her list of Billy Ray's previous addresses. At one time, he'd lived there with Marla and their two boys. It might be interesting to interview some of the other neighbors. She checked the house numbers.

Becky's parents' house was a two-story, moss green colonial, a color that was popular with other homes in the neighborhood. Claire parked in front.

Becky opened the door before Claire reached the bell. "Omigod. How did you find me?"

"I have to speak with you."

Becky tried to shut the door, but Claire blocked it with her foot. "I could speak with your parents instead." Becky was twenty-six. There were no parental limitations. Claire could speak with whomever she wished.

Becky released the door and it fell open. "You wouldn't do that."

"Probably not. But I need you to tell me about Elize."

Becky stepped out on the stoop and looked around. She moved back up into the doorway and looked around again. "Let's go inside, but just for a minute. My folks will be back soon. I don't want them to know about this."

The living room was furnished with expensive furniture and classic fabrics. A bouquet of fresh cut flowers sat in the center of an ebony coffee table. Becky, in her grungy shirt and baggy pants, looked out of place. And she didn't smell any better than she had the day before.

Claire sat beside Becky on a lime velveteen sofa. "I have a few questions."

Becky's hands twisted in her lap, her gaze fixed on the oriental carpet.

"I found Elize this morning." Becky's hands stopped moving for an instant. "I'd like to know how you knew about her and how you know Billy Ray is responsible."

"I told you, I just heard it."

"Please, I know you visit Elize. You didn't just stumble across her while visiting your grandmother. It's not that kind of hospital. How did you know where to find her?"

Becky's hands rubbed her forehead, fished through her hair, and fell to a rest back in her lap, but she remained silent.

Claire didn't have time for this. "You know what I think? I think you witnessed what he did to her. You saw, but were unable to help her. And that's okay. You were young, Becky, only seventeen. How did you see? Did it happen at his house?"

A sniffle. Then nothing. Becky began to rock back and forth. Her hands trembled as she clasped her head between them.

Claire scooted closer, wishing she could see the girl's downturned face. "It's okay. I want to put Billy Ray behind bars so he'll never hurt girls like Elize again. But I need your help. You have to trust me."

Becky remained silent.

"I won't tell your parents. I won't tell anyone, but I need to know. That way, I'll know where to look for evidence that will put Billy Ray away." Becky's testimony was what she was truly after, but she'd worry about that later.

Becky's voice was a whisper. "I was twenty."

That wasn't right. "Nine years ago, you would—"

"I was on my way home from school." A tremor rolled through Becky's upper body. She paused. "He offered me a ride. He did things…it hurt. He said if I told anybody, I'd end up like Elize." Tears dropped from her chin as she sucked in a deep breath.

A victim? Her story didn't make sense. Why hadn't he brutalized her? That was his M.O.. Claire tried to imagine the scene, tried to figure a scenario in which Billy Ray wouldn't have beaten the girl.

She was a friend of the family. That worked. But why would he mention Elize? "Did he say Elize's name when he threatened you?"

Becky shook her head, but didn't look up. She rubbed her face with the palm of her hand. "He said…" She sniffed. "He'd do to me what he'd done to that 'nigger over in Thibodaux.'"

That sounded like Billy Ray. Claire pictured Mayor Moreau, an African-American, shaking Billy Ray's hand in one of the newspaper articles. She had to remember to send him a copy of the court transcripts. "How did you find Elize?"

"I didn't. Not right away, but I kept thinking about what he'd said until it was like all I could think about." Her voice grew softer. Claire strained to hear. "I remembered a rape happening a few years earlier. It had freaked my mother out. She was driving me back and forth to high school instead of letting me take the bus. I went to the library and looked it up in the old newspapers. By then I'd dropped out of Newcomb. I was afraid I'd run into him again. He came back once, looking for me at the bus stop, but I ran off." She paused, then started sobbing.

Claire waited. If she let go of her professional persona the pain would overwhelm her. This case was different.

Becky wiped her face. "I read about Elize and then I read about every rape case that followed until, well, until me. Hers was the only one that mentioned Thibodaux. She was hospitalized there. I thought it had to be her."

"Did the article say which hospital she was in?"

"No. I called around until I found which one she was in, then I drove over. When I saw her, I just knew. She was black, you see. It just fit what he'd said. I told her what he'd done to me. It felt good to talk to someone even if she couldn't understand. A couple of months later I went back, I just had too, but she'd been moved by then. When I learned she was up here, it felt like a sign. I started visiting her, reading to her, or sometimes just talking."

Becky looked up through red, puffy eyes. "The nurses say she's better when I visit. I know I feel better after seeing her. Thanks to her, I was able to go back to school. Sounds silly, but her strength sort of gives me strength."

Claire pictured the deformed young woman staring out the window. What Becky said didn't sound silly at all. She'd sensed Elize in that battered body, a strong presence unable to let go. Holding on to her silent world was her way of coping.

"Have you ever met Elize's mother?"

"Never, but I know she visits."

"Why haven't you told your parents?"

Becky shook her head.

"Are they still friends with him?"

"No! Thank God. After the divorce he sort of faded away."

"Do you think Marla knows about him?"

"Why would she?"

"Becky, you should tell your parents before you tell the police. They should hear it from you."

"Police? Forget it. No one's going to believe me. It happened a long time ago."

"And you've lived in fear since." Becky's gaze dropped back to the carpeting, but Claire continued. "I'm right, aren't I? Billy Ray is a dangerous man. It's probably a good thing you didn't tell anyone until now." Another tremor rocked through the girl. Should she stop pressing her? But Becky had to understand how important this was. "Billy Ray raped me when I was ten."

Becky raised her head, her eyes bulging with disbelief.

"That's right, ten, and I wasn't as lucky as you. He beat me up and left me to die, much like what he did to Elize. It's true. I also believe there are others, women who didn't make it like Tanya Bonaventure. Have you heard about her?" Becky nodded and Claire saw a flicker in her eyes. "You suspected Billy Ray, didn't you?"

"Do you have proof? What if he gets out on bail? He'll kill me."

"I have your testimony and mine. You knew him when he raped you. That's a strong eyewitness account. I'm waiting to see what's in Elize's case file. Whether or not there's remaining DNA evidence. Another thing to consider is that once the story hits the papers, more young women might come forward. It happens all the time. He let you live, there could be others. Also, attempted murderers rarely get out on bail."

"I'm too scared."

"I know, but you've been scared everyday since Billy Ray hurt you. You have to take back your power. Put him away. You can do that. Once he's behind bars, you'll stop feeling guilty every time you read about another Tanya."

Becky rose. "I know you're right, but I can't. I've thought about it a lot since I saw you. I'm too afraid, not just for myself, but for my parents. They're good people. This would kill my mother. I told you how freaked she got after she'd read about Elize, someone she didn't know."

"Think of all the women he'll have access to once he's sheriff. Your friends, your family."

Looking down at her feet, Becky nodded. "I'm sorry. I wish I were stronger like you, but I'm not."

Claire wanted to slap some sense into her, but there was still Elize's case file. If that didn't pan out, she might come back and tell Becky's parents herself. Unethical, yes, but Billy Ray had to be stopped.

"If you change your mind, I'm staying at the Ramada Inn in Houma."

Walking back to her car, Claire thought about how to make Becky change her mind. She'd done it before.

She removed the cell phone and punched in Major Argrais's number.

"I was wondering if you've found that file yet?"

"Ms. Rivet, I was just about to call you. My men have gone through every rape file within the last ten years and there is no Elize LePage. I'm sorry, but maybe you should try Orleans Parish. I couldn't authorize it myself because I don't have a solid link to the Bonaventure case."

"How can that be? If nothing else, wouldn't the hospital have sent you information on a beating?"

"Should have. I suppose it could be misfiled in a storage room somewhere. That happens with the older cases."

She thought about her own missing case file and wondered if Elize's was with it at the bottom of an incinerator. As she started her car, a silver Lexus pulled into the driveway. A middle-aged couple got out and glanced her way. Becky's parents. They looked nice enough, like the kind of parents that would want their daughter's rapist off the streets.

She watched them walk into the house. Maybe she should introduce herself. She got out and walked toward the house. Halfway up the walk, the front door swung open and Becky leaped out.

"What are you doing? My parents are here. Please leave!"

"One more question. Do you remember from your reading where Elize was found?"

Becky glanced over her shoulder. "It was a long time ago."

"Was it Lafourche? New Orleans?"

She glanced over her shoulder again. "Near Boutte—a field."

"Boutte. St. Charles Parish."

A field.

Chapter 52

Saturday July 2, 2005
New Orleans, LA

Billy Ray popped a pain pill into his mouth. Ah hell, he was a big guy. He popped a second one and washed it down with his bourbon. The sun had moved to the other side of the building. The den had grown dark while he'd spent most of the afternoon trying to get a handle on these so-called rumors. They were turning out to be as slippery as snot on a round doorknob. Even the old man had heard something. What though? No one knew what was being said or else they were afraid to tell him. He figured the latter.

He slid the chair closer to the computer. Typing one-handed was tricky, but his left side was killing him. He hit the enter key and up popped the phone number for the Criminal Operations Center in Lockport.

One piece of good news. Darryl had found that the Rivet woman was staying at a Ramada Inn over in Houma. Seems her house caught fire and burned to the ground. Darryl said the story was in the paper, but not in the *Times Picayune*, 'cause he'd checked.

Seems Mr. Blunt had an alibi for last night. Wonder if the Rivet woman was the one put the bullet through him? No way. She wouldn't have the balls. That stupid brother of hers would though. He'd have Darryl look into that later. This rumor stuff was more important.

He picked up the phone. "May I speak with Deputy Padgett?" He waited for the connection.

"Padgett here."

"Deputy, this here's William Cobb. I don't know if you remember me, but—"

" 'Course, I remember. Heard about the shooting. How you doing?"

Billy Ray switched the phone to his other ear. "I'm good, thanks for asking. When we spoke last week, you struck me as a right smart fella. I'm working on something here and thought of you right away." Boy, was that the truth. "Claire Rivet, have you met her?"

"Oh sure."

So eager. But that meant the Rivet woman wasn't bad mouthing him with the troops. "Ms. Rivet's working on a fascinating case and I understand she's been by your office looking for information."

"She hasn't been by for a few days, but we spent the whole day looking up a case for her."

"That's why I'm calling. I want to make sure she's getting all the assistance we can give her. She's doing research here in Orleans, too. Did you find what she needed?"

"No, sir. Never did, sorry to say."

"That's too bad. I wonder…" He paused for effect. "You think there's anything I can do?"

"The Major thinks the file must be in another parish. We don't have the resources here to request files from other parishes unless someone higher up gives us a green light. Hey, maybe with your connections, you could have someone check in Orleans."

"That's a wonderful idea. I knew you were the right man to call. Now, what file was it, wait let me get a pencil." He rattled his television guide to make him sound busy. "Okay, go ahead."

"It's a nine-year-old rape case, the name was Elize LePage."

Elize... He stopped writing.

"Mr. Cobb?"

"Got it. Thanks deputy. I'll see what I can do on my end. In the meantime, you folks assist Ms. Rivet anyway you can. She's a top prosecutor and we all have to help her get these criminals off the street. Good talking with you, again."

He picked up his glass and walked around the desk to the sofa. She was looking into the LePage rape. It'd been years. Years. How'd she learned about it? More importantly, what did she know? Whatever she thought she knew, she couldn't be certain, 'cause she hadn't seen the file yet. They'd never find it in Lafourche.

One thing in his favor.

The woman did like trouble. She'd kept up her investigation after his warning, after Darryl's warning. Stupidity must run in that family. And what about that brother of hers? He knew what a warning meant.

Damn, he hated when folks didn't take him seriously. He threw his bourbon across the room, smashing the glass against the brick fireplace. Shards tinkled to the hearth. Shep high-tailed it out of the room.

"Yeah, go on you." He rubbed his chin, the bristles of his beard just breaking the skin. Looked like the brother hadn't warned her. Unlikely. He'd been very specific.

The time for warnings, physical or otherwise, was done. That case file she was looking for just might have something in it. Something she could use. He'd been reckless, hadn't meant to do it. He'd promised himself that stuff was over.

He thought back to the promise. It hadn't been the first time he'd promised to stop. But something about the bitch's uppity attitude had pissed him off. Thought she was God's gift when all he'd done was offer her a lift. Well, he'd shown her.

He should have looked into that file years ago, but getting rid of it wasn't so easy. Sure, he could have paid someone to lose it, but back then the governor was cleaning house. Made it harder to know who to trust. Once he was sheriff, he'd take care of it himself, but he had to keep the Rivet woman away from it till then.

The conversation with Paul Nesbit was worrisome, but this was a whole other pot of beans. Rivet wasn't fishing. She knew what she was looking for. She was closing in. How had it gotten this far along? Time to call Darryl. Nope, something like this could come back and bite him in the ass.

Damn, if the only way to do something right wasn't to do it himself. It wouldn't look good if something happened to her now, not after her investigating him. But he couldn't wait. Where could he buy an alibi?

He picked up the phone, picturing pretty little Elize, all dressed up with that ribbon in her hair. He should have killed her. Thought he had till he read she'd been taken to Thibodaux for treatment. But she never recovered. A close call. Too close.

Thought it was all finished after that. He promised himself.

* * *

Okay. He had his alibi. Two men. A thousand a pop. Not cheap. They probably figured he was going after the son-of-a-gun who shot at him. Possibly he was, but he didn't think the Rivet woman did it. She worked the system, hid behind paperwork. She didn't know what it meant to get her hands dirty. So what was he going to do with her?

He looked at his yellowing knuckles. He needed something quick and that wouldn't leave a trace that could be tied back to him.

He opened his top desk drawer and ran his fingers over the Ruger forty-five automatic. Registered. He slid the drawer closed and walked across the room.

Kneeling before a teak end table, he slid open a secret door on the side and turned the dial. The safe clicked as the numbers fell into place. Tsk, tsk, tsk. Inside was a revolver, an unregistered thirty-eight. He reached into the cardboard box next to it and scooped a handful of bullets. He loaded the chambers and pocketed the extras.

He took the stairs down two at a time. The pain meds were doing their thing. He felt good, felt ready, felt sharp. Hell, yeah.

Reaching the garage, he considered his three cars. The black Mercedes would stand out at a Ramada Inn; the beige Cadillac was more the ticket, but it looked like a pimp mobile. If he had to get away quickly, a pimp mobile would draw too much attention. That left the Saturn. Dark green, discreet, but the damn thing was an automatic. Had no pickup. But how important was pickup? He needed to blend. He walked to the lockbox and removed the Saturn's keys.

Chapter 53

Saturday July 2, 2005
Houma, LA

A bolt of heat lightning danced across the night sky as Claire pulled into the Ramada's parking lot. She was beat. After leaving Becky's, she'd gone to see Major Argrais with the new information. She'd waited as long as she could to see if they would find Elize's file in St. Charles Parish, but left, when Argrais did, without news. Next, she'd passed by Philippe's one more time to make sure he'd left town. The house was dark and the station wagon was gone.

She killed the engine and massaged her sore shoulder. She watched the rearview mirror to see if anyone followed her into the lot. The spicy sauce of the po-boy she'd picked up for dinner smelled tempting. She should have bought two. She slipped her hand into the bag and pulled out a wad of fries.

A beat up pickup truck, a black tarp tied over the bed, drove past the entrance. Two more cars flew by, the headlights making it difficult to tell the makes. Her cell rang, muffled by the leather bag. She shoved the fries in her mouth and dug through her handbag, realizing she'd forgotten to charge the cell on the way back.

Argrais. "Good news. They've located the file and from what I'm told there are similarities to the Bonaventure case. The detective needs to do more research, but there's a chance some DNA evidence exists, too. I'll call you tomorrow."

Finally. Things were coming together. Once she had a copy of the file, she'd have to give Argrais Cobb's name. But by then, it would be too late for a cover up. Too many people would know about the file in case Argrais, or one of his men, had loyalties to the Cobb family.

She reached for another bunch of fries as she scanned the cars in the lot. She didn't like that Cobb had gone to Philippe's office. Sooner or later his threats were going to materialize. They had with Suzanne. They would with her.

She snatched up the bag with the po-boy and pulled the keys from the ignition. One last glance. With her hand on the door handle, she saw him. The red neon sign from the office cast a glow into the driver's seat of a car parked in front. From the shape of the head and the size of the shoulders, she figured the driver was a man. He looked wider and taller than Billy Ray's hired thug. She scanned the lot again. The other cars were clearly empty.

She released the door and put the keys back in the ignition. She picked at the few remaining fries, waiting for the driver to either get out or leave. He did neither. She sipped the iced tea.

Was he waiting for someone? Her? He hadn't followed her. Since leaving Becky's house, she'd been careful, pulling off the road several times to count cars and look around.

Maybe she should warn Becky. The cell phone battery was low as she hit Becky's number. Busy. She'd have to try later.

What now? Argrais. Should she bother him before she knew for sure? Saturday night. His officers were probably busy. She'd wait a little more. The phone went black.

"Great."

She restarted the car and plugged the cell phone into the cigarette lighter. It would take about ten minutes to charge for limited use. In the meantime, she'd keep an eye on the dark sedan. She took another sip of tea. The po-boy no longer tempted her. Her stomach was tight. She wished she knew what the man was waiting for.

She could back out of the lot and see if the car followed. Then, she'd have her answer. It beat sitting here, being paranoid half the evening.

The sedan's lights didn't come on until she reached the road. She caught sight of the white reverse lights as she turned left, heading back the way she'd come earlier. She wasn't paranoid. When she reached highway 24 a pair of headlights raced up behind her.

Lightning streaked the sky again and she got a good look at the car in her rearview. The same sedan. Her legs began to tremble, her knee bouncing as she tried to hold her foot on the accelerator. She continued east, wondering where to go. Philippe was the only one she knew with a gun and he'd left town. She didn't know where to begin to look for Joe's trailer. Hal's store would be closed by now.

The sedan stayed right behind her, not attempting to hide. Bold. She glanced at the gas tank readout. Enough to get her to New Orleans. If that was where she was headed. She looked around the interior for something to use as a weapon. Only the uneaten sandwich and her handbag.

At the intersection, she could turn north toward the city and hope to find a police station or some place safe to stop and call Argrais, or she could head south toward bayou country. Either way she had to make up her mind fast.

No one knew the bayou like she did. She'd practically been weaned in its ever-changing arms. From the time she could walk, Pa had taught her how to survive out there. Her brothers had continued her education. Plus, Mamma Anna was out there waiting for her. Or was she? Claire had ignored her warning and stayed away last night. Maybe there wouldn't be anyone tonight. The week of Saint Jean's was over. But the humfo didn't look temporary. The glade was well known to the worshipers.

She stopped at the sign. *Decide*. The sedan pulled up so close to her bumper, she could hear its motor idling. She knew the bayou country better than she knew the road to New Orleans, which, if she had to guess, was probably the opposite of the guy behind her. The road to the city was longer, too. She could make it to the raft in ten minutes. She turned south. Better to go with what was sure than risk the unknown.

She veered off at Galliano, figuring to lose him on the back roads. As she picked up speed in the turns, the headlights fell behind. She swerved onto a dirt road that led toward Catfish Lake. A thick cloud of dust filled her rearview.

This road didn't go all the way to where the raft was moored, but she could catch another road that did. Then, she'd have to take off on foot as fast as she could. Lots of trees for cover. No moon to speak of. And she knew the path. Shouldn't be hard to lose him.

If only Mamma Anna would be waiting. Blades of pain shot through her shoulder. Anxiety. She was cramping up. It hurt. The pain was making her light-headed. She needed to stop and free her arm, or she might pass out.

Since the last turn, the headlights had disappeared. He'd probably given up, but better not to take chances. One more left and she'd reach the road that would take her to the bayou. She could stop then just for a second.

At the asphalt road she turned, killed her lights, and pulled to the side of the road. She lifted her arm from the sling, letting the cloth hang loose around her neck. She massaged the back of her neck and shoulder, shaking out the hand.

She'd lost him. Easing back onto the road, she hit the lights and checked the door locks. She couldn't go back to the hotel. He'd be waiting. She thought of Elize. Hopefully, Argrais would have the file soon.

Claire reached for the cell phone and checked the bars. It had recharged enough to call Argrais for help.

The first impact threw her forward against the steering wheel. The passenger airbag inflated knocking the phone from her hand. Red hot pain sizzled from her shoulder down her arm. Her gaze flew to the rearview mirror. Moonlight flashed on metal as a second impact threw her sideways.

For an instant, she lost contact with the brake. The car slid forward. She used the steering wheel to pull herself back up. She slammed her foot down on the gas pedal. The car lurched as she straightened out. Behind, a car engine raced.

She swerved right. The passenger airbag blocked her view. Thank goodness she'd had the driver's airbag removed or she might have gotten trapped beneath. Headlights flashed on, filling her interior. He was close enough to ram her again. She swerved left, skidding onto a dirt road. The sedan missed her by inches.

She sped toward the bayou. A light fog draped the trees, hanging low but not enough to hamper her vision. The airbag was much more of a problem.

Metal crunched against metal. The car slid.

She yanked the steering wheel left, pulling onto the small gravel road that dead-ended at the levee. The sedan caught her right bumper, sending her skidding into the turn.

She stomped the gas pedal, throwing gravel up behind her. The rev of her engine was all she could hear. The fog grew denser. The road narrowed. She flashed her high beams, but was blinded by the reflection. She cut back to low.

All of a sudden, a bold light flashed, too intense for heat lightning. She squinted against its brightness. Silhouetted in the road ahead, a figure loomed. To avoid hitting it, she cut right too quickly. The car began to spin. The centrifugal force pressed her into the seat. She felt and heard the loud crash of contact. Then silence.

Jarring silence.

A tree trunk filled her passenger window, the airbag was deflated, and the passenger door was dented inward. She pressed her hand into the throbbing shoulder and took inventory of her other body parts. All there.

She was trapped. She popped the seatbelt and used the sling to brush off the broken glass. The driver's door was facing uphill. Her arm, ribs, and bad shoulder screamed as she tried to shove it open, but she had to get free, before the driver of the other car found her.

Her legs gave out as her feet hit the ground. She pulled herself up and leaned against the smoking hood.

On the other side of the road, headlights glowed at an odd angle in the fog. The stench of gasoline carried across to her. Should she try to help him out? He might be seriously hurt.

He'd tried to kill her.

Her legs were too shaky. She couldn't think. Give it a minute.

Across the road, the car door opened. The other driver fell into the road.

Billy Ray!

He hadn't yet seen her. A red stream ran down the side of his face as he struggled to break free of his shoulder strap.

She steadied herself against the car. Her breath coming fast.

He fumbled to stand, his icy glare locking on her.

He ducked back into the car. She didn't wait to find out why. Willing her legs to move, she pushed off from the car. Reaching the tree line, she felt safer. She ran as fast as her new sandals would allow.

The thick foliage offered cover and she ducked into the lush fronds. They would thin the closer she got to the water. But if she ran toward the water, she should find the raft. She turned. Her best hope was to find Jezwa and the raft. She kept running.

A shot rang out, echoing through the trees. The bullet passed far to her left, landing in a thick pine trunk. The vaporous fog was in her favor, but he was catching up.

Ahead, a patch of cypress loomed, their deformed roots ominous in the haze. Water. But not the inlet she was looking for. A blanket of Spanish moss cloaked the night. She'd have to turn west...unless the cypresses could offer shelter. She tripped over a branch and almost fell, but caught hold of the trunk. What if she could fold into a root cavern? She could hide, and then double back for the cell phone.

She ran in and out of the thick trees as near to the water as she dared, her bad shoulder a reminder of the slippery roots. A double trunk was rare, but not unheard of. If she could find one, the cavern beneath would be large enough to hide in. What about the cypresses with their knots low and flat to the ground? If she could slide under one...

The ground sucked at the sandals. Mud squished over the leather, slowing her down. The cypresses needed moisture. Alligators. She hesitated, but only a second. A dark underbelly, a deep recess, beneath a contorted root at the water's edge caught her attention. Above a loud, shrill caw carried through the trees. The fingerlike cypress leaves bristled at the sound.

He was drawing nearer. She could sense him the way one animal senses another. She dropped to her knees, tried to see beneath the roots, tried to judge if she could crawl in. Yes, an animal might bite her, but Billy Ray would do much worse.

The sucking sound of his footsteps grew louder.

Feet first, she started to slide in within the roots. Watery debris closed in around her. She was waist deep when something slid up against her. As Pa had taught her, she froze. Whatever the creature was, it had fur. She relaxed, but realized there wasn't room for them both. She crawled forward, the animal didn't follow.

Too late to run. He was close, too close. She'd have to hope he'd pass in another direction. She tensed, her ear to the ground as she tried to judge his location. Then, her gaze locked on something wedged within the massive root system. A fallen branch. Thick and round like a baseball bat. Her good hand closed around it. She jerked, but it didn't budge. She wrapped both hands and tugged. She pulled and pushed it back and forth trying to loosen whatever was holding it. Electric currents of pain ran up her neck and down her back as she struggled.

He wasn't going to touch her again. She'd die first. She yanked once more, twisting and snapping the tip, breaking half of the branch free.

The break was loud enough to have given away her position.

She crawled to her knees, dragging the branch. She stood. Inched around the outside of the trunk, careful not to step on a slippery root. Billy Ray's outline disappeared from view, but his steps sucked heavily on the wet earth.

Her toe stubbed a bent, empty beer can lodged within the roots. She reached down and snatched the can with her good hand. She pressed it against her thigh, collapsing it, making it more compact, ball-like. And she listened.

Not too soon.

Not too soon. She wasn't the best pitcher in the Rivet family.

A twig snapped. He'd heard her and was drawing near, only three, maybe four, feet from the tree. She stepped out and launched the can at his head. The pistol fired, but the bullet flew wide.

Lunging, she charged Billy Ray's face with the brittle point of the branch. It caught his cheek. He raised the gun and stepped back too quickly, his foot hit the wet roots and he fell. She flipped the branch over, grabbed a thicker portion, and swung.

He flailed. Using the gun, he tried to knock the branch away while trying to crawl to his knees. The branch cracked as it connected with his skull. He flew back and to the side. She swung it a second time, knocking him flat. His arm splashed into the water.

He didn't move, but she didn't care as rage strangled her. She raised the branch, swinging a third time. It split into two pieces as it smashed into his head.

Breathing heavily, she watched the blood blossom and then roll down his face. She couldn't drop the broken branch, despite the severe throbbing of her shoulder. She took a step closer, her grip so tight on the wood that her fingers cramped.

"Finish him."

She spun around. Mamma Anna stood poised behind her. The flash, the figure she'd seen in the road. In her dark hand, she held a pistol.

Claire glanced down at Billy Ray's empty hand. How had she taken the gun away?

"Here," Mamma Anna said, offering the gun to Claire. "He would have used it on you."

Claire knew to be afraid, but the adrenalin pumping through her wouldn't allow it. She looked into the old woman's angry face. True, he would have used it on her or worse. She shivered. She thought of her lost girlhood. She thought of Elize's. She could end it here. Now. Oh, how she wanted to. She reached for the gun with her sore arm, lightning pain ripped across her shoulders.

Judge and jury, no one would know.

She dropped the pistol back into Mamma Anna's hand. "I can't."

Mamma Anna appeared to grow larger before her eyes. "Kill him. Now." She shoved the gun at Claire's face.

Claire stumbled back, clutching the branch. What had the old woman said about owing the dark spirits? That was why she'd been recruited for the *magie noire*. Mamma Anna couldn't give up everything for the spirits. She had Elize.

"If I kill him, I'm no better than he is."

"That's sentimental crap. You'll never know the number of women he has destroyed."

"There's another way." Claire dropped to her knees, her body felt like lead. She reached across Billy Ray's prone body and ripped off his shirt pocket. Billy Ray didn't move. She swiped a corner of the torn rectangle across Billy Ray's bloody face. "With this we can put him away." She held up the bloody cloth. "Major Argrais has found Elize's case file. The officer he spoke with says there's DNA evidence just waiting for a match."

Mamma Anna gripped the revolver's handle. She didn't seem surprised that Claire knew about Elize. Billy Ray moaned. Claire scooted away. The old woman could blow them both away and no one would ever know.

"Billy Ray won't do well in prison," Claire said. "His kind never does. I can get the death penalty. I can tie him to Bonaventure. I'm begging you, let him suffer. Let him live each day facing death, facing his shame. A bullet is too good for him."

"No child, you're wrong." Mamma Anna lowered the gun. A sadness stretched into her face softening her features. "There's a storm brewing. Evil will rain down over this land, the likes of which you have never seen. Billy Ray will be a part of that evil. Mark my words. I speak the truth."

A prophecy. That was rich. How could anything be worse than what he did to Elize? "Put it in my hands. For Elize. I promise, he will not hurt another person."

Mamma Anna looked down at Billy Ray and then she looked at the gun in her hand. "Blood will be on your hands if you fail."

"I won't. I can't."

The old woman nodded.

Chapter 54

Friday August 26, 2005
New Orleans, LA

Claire glanced over her shoulder to the fuss at the back of the courtroom. A heavyset man was trying to squeeze into an already packed bench and those seated were having none of it. She couldn't believe the two posted guards were still allowing more people in, but by New Orleans standards, this was the "Trial of the Century." The media section was standing room only and had been for the last hour. She'd heard Dominic Dunne, a fancy crime reporter, had applied for a seat. Maybe that was the pasty-faced man with the round glasses. He looked like a mud worm in a pail of hungry trout.

Billy Ray was granted his speedy trial. The poor fool wanted to clear his name. He still planned to run for sheriff in November. After eight weeks of helping Percy prepare the case, she knew that wasn't going to happen.

She pushed her back against the wooden bench, Suzanne pressed next to her. The spectator's side of the rail wasn't anywhere near as comfortable as the prosecutor's.

Marla Cobb strutted in wearing an expensive looking linen dress and a fancy hat that draped down over one eye. She took a seat across the aisle in reserved seating. She crossed her hands in her lap and looked forward as if she expected all eyes to be on her.

More interesting than who was there, was who wasn't. Randolph Cobb obviously didn't think his son's trial was worth his time. That would disappoint the press. Billy Ray's hired thug, as far as she could tell, hadn't come to support his boss.

Mamma Anna hadn't shown up either. Claire hadn't seen her since that last night in the woods. She'd been busy with the trial preparation, but had expected the old woman to be there if only to see Claire keep her promise. Then, there was Becky. She still refused to testify. As information from the trial seeped into the media, Claire hoped she'd change her mind.

The case had become a divisional nightmare. The trial had been moved to New Orleans to better accommodate the out-of-town press and witnesses. Billy Ray's lawyer was pleased with the move. Perhaps he thought his client would benefit from a local jury. What was it Billy Ray had said at the Election Office?

Down here, we take care of our own.

Claire gave Suzanne's hand a gentle squeeze. That's right Billy Ray, and now, she was taking care of her own.

He was facing three charges in both her case and Elize's. Forcible rape, attempted murder, and assault with intent to commit great bodily injury. The D.A. felt Claire's testimony alone wasn't enough for a conviction despite her spotless reputation. At worst, it would sway the jury against Cobb. Elize's case was stronger. DNA evidence was always good, but the D.A. felt the photos of Elize—Mamma Anna wouldn't allow her daughter in court—would bring the jury to tears. He expected a conviction there.

The case she had worked the hardest on was Tanya Bonaventure. Two dog hairs found on Tanya matched Billy Ray's dog. Major Argrais and two other men were ready to testify to seeing bruises on Billy Ray's knuckles within days of Bonaventure's attack. And one eyewitness saw Tanya get in Billy Ray's Cadillac behind the diner where she worked.

Circumstantial, but an already sympathetic jury should be ready for a second degree murder conviction with the additional conviction of forcible rape and assault with intent to commit great bodily injury.

With luck, Mamma Anna would have his death. Until then, Claire was happy that he'd have to wake up every morning knowing he was going to be put down like a rabid dog.

She thought of Vincent. Lately, he was always there in the back of her mind. Once news of the trial had reached Baton Rouge, he'd called. They'd talked and she'd told him everything, all the secrets he'd never known. They'd be public knowledge soon enough. He wanted to drive down when she testified, wanted to offer support, but she'd warned him off. She wasn't sure she could say what needed to be said with his innocent heart taking it all in.

But for the first time that she could remember, she was planning a future. Too long, she'd lived life with a mission. Things were different now. She was different. She'd faced death and knew she wasn't ready to embrace it. In the woods, she'd faced Billy Ray, and won. This was the last battle.

And what about Elize? Claire'd wanted to see if something more could be done. She'd found a doctor in Atlanta, who'd given her hope. Mamma Anna would be the next hurdle.

Billy Ray was led in, his hands cuffed behind him. The chatter died down for an instant, then roared louder as insults were hurled across the rail. Seated next to the D.A., Percy turned to look at her. She wondered why. Next, the Honorable Renee Claiborne walked in. She didn't look happy, but judges rarely did.

The bailiff said, "All rise—"

But the judge stopped him. "The trial of William Cobb was set to start this afternoon," she said. "But Mother Nature has other plans. I've just received word that Governor Blanco has declared a state of emergency for Louisiana. A new path has been confirmed for Hurricane Katrina. It is believed that if Katrina does hit our coast, the storm surge may destroy the city's levees. This is exactly the type of storm that we have long feared. I can't impress upon you enough that should this happen, the consequences will be devastating. Therefore, I'm sending you all home, including the jury, so that you can prepare yourselves, your families, and your homes. This trial will resume at a later date. Mr. Cobb, your request for a speedy trial remains in effect. But it won't be today."

Say something! *Say something.* Claire wiggled, waiting for the D.A. or Percy to speak up. Sending the jury home now could result in having to start all over with jury selection. Put them up in a hotel at least until they were sure there would be a storm.

The judge stood and left the courtroom. Claire leaped forward and reached across the rail for Percy's sleeve. "What's with you? Why didn't you argue? Do you know what this could mean?"

"Are you kidding?" the D.A. interrupted. "That storm is growing and my brother says it's coming this way. He's never wrong. I'm going home and getting my wife, my kids, and we're getting the hell out of Dodge. I suggest you and Percy do the same." He snapped his briefcase closed.

"What will they do with Cobb?"

"Ask the bailiff. I'm out of here."

Claire glanced at Billy Ray. He was speaking with his lawyer. The overhead light glinted off his gold tooth. He was grinning.

Grinning. Big and bold.

A chill crawled up her spine.

He expected this. He was pleased, despite what this did to his speedy trial. Why? Where was his advantage?

There's a storm brewing.

She heard the words as if Mamma Anna was speaking next to her. She looked sideways, waiting for the old woman to appear. "He won't get away."

"What did you say?" Suzanne asked, standing at her side.

"Nothing." Did Billy Ray have a plan? Did he think he was going to get away? Was his hired man outside, waiting to make a move? They'd have to transfer the prisoners to higher ground. A breakout?

"Philippe says we should plan to leave town," Suzanne said. "We wanted to ask if we could stay in your apartment over in Baton Rouge."

"What? Oh, sure." Claire reached into her handbag and found her key ring. She removed her apartment key and handed it to Suzanne. "I thought the storm was headed out to sea."

"Changed direction again this morning," Suzanne said, looking at the key. "Aren't you coming?"

Sometimes Suzanne was more mother hen than Philippe. For now, she needed to be placated. "Yes, yes I am. But later. You get Chet and I'll meet you in Baton Rouge. I need to call about Elize, find out what the evacuation plans are."

Suzanne's raised eyebrow said she wasn't buying it, but Claire didn't have time to convince her. She had to talk to the bailiff, and not in front of Billy Ray.

She walked Suzanne out of the courtroom. "I have to talk with someone before I leave. Stop looking so worried. The storm isn't going to hit today. They do this every summer and most of these hurricanes are just thunderstorms by the time they reach us."

"You're the storm predictor in the family. I guess if you aren't worried, we shouldn't be."

Claire hesitated. She hadn't told anyone that Mamma Anna had cured her of that little affliction. "I haven't had a migraine in a few months."

They stepped outside. Sweat trickled beneath her blouse. The mugginess felt like 120 degrees, but at lunch, the thermometer had read a mere 91.

"Whew, feel that?" Suzanne said. "I think you should come with us. You're putting yourself in danger again. Philippe isn't going to like it."

"I have plenty of time to get back to your house and grab my things. You have to pack for three. Remember to take food and water for Chet. The roads might clog up if everyone heads out at once."

Last she'd heard the storm had lost strength. It had barely touched Florida. Afterwards, it had turned away from the Gulf Coast. She watched Suzanne go down the steps; then her gaze traveled over the heavy traffic on Tulane Avenue. It wouldn't be long before every artery leaving the city was blocked by people outrunning a hurricane that most likely wouldn't hit.

There's a storm brewing.

Mamma Anna wasn't always right, but the Cheshire smile on Billy Ray's face had been real enough. The old woman had predicted he would be free during a storm. Had the moment Claire feared arrived?

Inside the courthouse, the bailiff was talking with a man and woman and pointing up the corridor. When the couple walked away, he pulled out a key to unlock a side courtroom.

Claire called to him. "Sir, I need some information."

He blocked the door open with one foot and shoved the keys back in his pants. "What can I do for you?"

"I was wondering what's going to happen with the prisoners?"

He nodded, probably thinking she was related to one. "They'll be safely transported to some other facility."

"All prisoners?"

"Every one."

"Transported how?"

The friendliness faded from his face and he shifted a little straighter, taking on that seriousness she'd seen in the courtroom. "Ma'am, who are you?"

"I'm a witness, a frightened witness, in the William Cobb case. I'm afraid he's planning an escape."

An emotion crossed the bailiff's face, one she couldn't read.

"I have it on good authority," she said, as if a voodoo priestess could be an authority.

"I assure you, you have nothing to worry about. Now, I have to go."

"One more question."

He paused, his expression sullen.

"When will they be moved?"

He ducked behind the door and pulled it shut. She tried the handle, but it was locked. She rushed to the next door, another courtroom. Also locked.

The courthouse connected with Orleans Parish Prison, OPP, where Billy Ray had been moved to await his trial. To be transferred, the prisoners would have to leave from the rear. She pulled out her cell phone.

"Percy, will the prisoners be transferred today? It's not even raining."

"Who said they were going to be moved? OPP has over six-thousand prisoners. Do you honestly believe the state government is organized enough to move that many people this quickly?"

"Cobb is planning something, Percy. I saw him talking to his lawyer. The bailiff told me the prisoners were to be moved to other facilities."

"Hold on, let me make some calls."

Claire paced the corridor, the phone pressed to her ear. Percy came back on the line. "Bailiff's half right. There's no plan yet for the federal prisoners or the general population. Some lifers will be sent up to Angola."

"Cobb. Where's Cobb going?"

"Give me a sec, would you? I'm reading off the screen. Feds... No. High security... No. Ah, here it is. The twelve defendants whose cases are in play will be transferred to Pineville tomorrow morning at eight unless things change."

"Like what things?"

"As of the last report, Katrina hasn't turned back toward Florida. Word now is it's going to make landfall in Mississippi. Miss our coastline altogether."

"I knew it. What does that do for the trial?"

"Could resume Monday, but Claire, let's wait and see what happens tomorrow."

He was right. These storms changed hourly. Eight a.m.. After breakfast. That gave her time to check on Elize and collect her things from Philippe's house. She should probably try to get one of Philippe's guns, but that would open a whole new can of worms.

Chapter 55

Saturday August 27, 2005
New Orleans, LA

Saturday morning, Katrina again changed direction. A hurricane watch alert was issued for southeastern Louisiana. Seven a.m. beneath a graying sky, Claire drove to the prison and parked in the employees' parking lot. She had a clear view of the rear loading area.

At eight a.m. a short yellow bus pulled in and at nine a.m. the guards started loading. Claire chewed a granola bar as she watched. Two armed guards loaded two female prisoners onto the bus and left. Four more armed guards brought out a line of ten male prisoners. Each man was led onto the bus by two guards while the other two stood watch.

Claire's cell phone rang. Suzanne's name on the faceplate. She switched off the phone. Needed to save the battery. Opening the car door, she swung her legs out and sat on the edge of the seat. The day was heating up fast. Hopefully, the rain moving in would cool it down. She watched.

And then she spotted him. His swagger was unmistakable. Next to last in line. He was cuffed, arms behind his back. Two guards led him up the bus steps as they had done the others.

There's a storm brewing...

What could she do if he managed a breakout? She would follow him. Then, she'd call Argrais and have him rearrested. She could trust Argrais. He'd gone out of his way to get her what she needed to help Percy prepare the case. Argrais couldn't be bought.

A light drizzle began to fall. As the last prisoner was loaded, two long white buses pulled in behind the yellow bus. She closed the car door and watched all four guards talking together as the driver climbed the yellow bus's steps. One armed guard waved off the others and followed the driver into the bus. The door swung shut.

She started her car and watched the yellow bus pull out. As she drove to the exit of the parking lot, she noticed another car pull in behind the bus. A green Chevrolet, an older model. It had been parked in a neighboring lot.

The driver was of small build, but he wasn't the thug who'd threatened her. The hair was all wrong. Maybe it was a coincidence. Maybe the driver had pulled into the empty parking lot to make a call or get directions. Maybe he was a prison guard being reassigned.

She hung back almost a block for the first six blocks so as not to draw the Chevy driver's attention. Then they jammed up in traffic and she was forced to follow closer the rest of the way out of the city.

The I10 was packed with cars, but opened up west of Baton Rouge. Claire dropped back. Steady rain fell on her windshield, but the yellow bus was easy to see from a distance.

She was now sure that Mamma Anna had spoken the truth. She remembered the prophecy word for word, remembered the nights, too, that it had kept her awake.

There's a storm brewing. Evil will rain down over this land, the likes of which you have never seen. Billy Ray will be a part of that evil.

Outside Lafayette, the wind picked up and the rain slapped harder. Traffic slowed. The Chevy was still shadowing the bus. Claire sipped her cold coffee.

For the next hour, they inched up I49 North, the bus and Chevy in the right lane, she in the left. Then, ten miles south of Alexandria, the bus made an unexpected exit. Claire fought her way between cars and followed the Chevy off the highway. She'd mapped out the route, studied the alternatives, but this exit was way too soon. Her shoulders tensed as if snapping to attention.

As they passed an open gas station without stopping, she reached for her phone. Who could she call? Percy? The prison? Who could tell her why the bus hadn't stayed on the highway to Pineville?

The clouds were bulbous and streaked with black. She had yet to see lightning, but had twice heard the distant rumble of thunder. She fiddled with the radio. Katrina was at least a day out, but she didn't need a migraine to know this storm was a bad one.

The country roads were empty. They were making better time than on the highway. The bus driver must know what he was doing. She relaxed and switched off the phone. She slowed way down, stayed back from the Chevy. With her headlights on and the wrenching rain, she figured the driver couldn't tell that hers was the same car that had followed him out of New Orleans.

Ahead, she saw a farmhouse up on the right. She put on her blinker and when she reached the driveway turned in. She quickly spun a "U" and counted, four, five, six. If the Chevy driver was aware of her that should throw him off.

She pulled back onto the road and sped up. The bus was nowhere in sight. With the speed and the wind she felt the car's wheels leave the pavement. She slowed and cracked open her window to clear the foggy windshield.

No turnoffs so far. The bus had to be ahead, but she didn't like it out of sight for so long. She eased the gas pedal down.

The road rose slightly and curved. In some spots, mini rivers of mud and water ran across. She slowed into each curve to avoid sliding.

As she rounded right, she caught sight of the top edge of the bus rounding a left corner. After the next curve, a straight stretch let her see the lights on both the bus and Chevy. She exhaled. The wind was making it hard to stay on the road. Her hands were gripping the steering wheel so tightly that they'd begun to cramp. One at a time, she shook them out.

When the bus and Chevy reached the next left-hand curve, she noticed the Chevy's brake lights go off. The Chevy was speeding up. As soon as the thought entered her brain, the Chevy rammed the right rear corner of the bus.

A screech. The scream of brakes.

The impact sent the Chevy into a circular spin. The bus swerved sideways into the center of the road and made the curve on two wheels. The Chevy collided with a thud, head first into a live oak at the right-hand side of the road.

And then, Claire heard nothing but the rhythmic beat of her wiper blades.

She slowed the car, her heart racing. She pulled up behind the Chevy and killed her engine. She was wrong. The bus hadn't cleared the curve. It had nosedived off the other side of the road. The smashed rear corner was all she could see through a puff of smoke.

She switched on the phone. No reception. Not a single bar. She threw it on the seat and climbed out of the car. Hot rain beat down as she ran for the Chevy, the air thick with the smell of scorched brake pads. The tree had split the car's hood in half. She tugged on the driver's door, but it didn't budge. She wiped the window but couldn't see inside. She ran back to her car and pulled the tire iron from the trunk.

She smashed the Chevy driver's window. The man was slumped to the side, the windshield and dashboard bent inward. A river of bright red blood flowed from his crooked nose. From the swelling lump on his forehead, he must have hit his head on the steering wheel. She reached for his neck, felt for a pulse. He was alive.

A chorus of human cries rose over the drumming rain. She started to cross the road, but a huge gust of wind blew her backwards. She put her head down and trudged forward, struggling against the wind and rain. The bus had plunged down the side of a gully and the front part of the left side was submerged in the creek. Smoke rose from the rear, but no flames, no smell of gasoline. The damaged corner was streaked with the Chevy's green paint.

This was almost the same thing Cobb had done to her a few months ago. His name was written all over this accident. The Chevy driver probably hadn't been prepared for the wet and windy conditions. She ignored the cries radiating from the bus and reached out to touch the dent.

"Lady, help us."

She looked up into a dark face, his eyes above the half opened window.

Behind him other voices, some farther away: "Help! Help!"

Billy Ray. Where was he? Was he loose?

"Someone! Lord above, save us!"

"Lady, we's drownin' in here," said the man, calmly watching her.

"You see a big white guy, hair the color of wet sand?"

The man turned away and then turned back. "Yeah."

"He alive?"

"Yeah."

"He cuffed?"

"Yeah. We all is."

As others realized someone was there, the cries grew louder. Their words, their pleas tumbled together in a soulful whine.

She looked back at the Chevrolet. The driver hadn't moved. She couldn't just leave these people here. They could be hurt. She glanced up the road. The closest possible help would be the farmhouse she'd passed a few miles back. But the man said they were drowning.

Wind rolled up the gully, bending trees to their breaking point. As she reached the bus's door, lightning flashed overhead. One half of the double door was pinned open, rattling wildly against the storm. With the bus at a slant, she had to climb onto the first step to squeeze through the narrow opening. Once inside, she saw the driver's foot was tangled around the door handle, blocking it half open.

A strange high-pitched whining sound made her cover her ears. The dashboard lights were lit. She grabbed the keys and switched off the ignition. The lights died and the whining sound faded away.

"Help us!"

"Hey, bitch, over here!"

"My arm! My leg!"

The rising creek splashed against the driver's head. She lifted his foot off the handle. He moaned. She cradled his head, ignoring the echo of cries behind her. "Can you sit?" she asked.

"Think so."

He was disoriented, moving slowly. She lowered his leg while helping him to slide back into his seat. She opened the door all the way to let air in.

"Lady! Hey you, help us!"

"What about us!"

"Bitch, over here!"

The roar of the creek was deafening; the screaming, terrifying. She glanced down into the bus. Each prisoner was cuffed to a hook on the metal bar that arched over the top of the seat in front of them. The first seat on each side was empty. All the windows were half open and the first few seats on the left side were filling with water. One of the women prisoners was struggling to keep her head above the rushing water.

"Can you help me up?" the driver asked.

Thunder cracked against the sky. The sides of the bus shook from a heavy gust of wind. Everyone was silent for a second, and then started screaming louder.

Claire moved to the steps and shoved her shoulder beneath the driver's armpit. He used his hands to push up. "Be careful, the bus is tilted," she said.

"Shit!" he screamed.

"You twisted your foot on the door handle."

He shifted his weight to his good foot and steadied himself with his hands. Claire slipped back and the driver hopped to the lower step. The bus groaned and slid a few inches toward the creek. The driver shot through the open door. The bus slid again. Claire grabbed a rail and waited. The bus stopped.

The screams grew louder.

"Shut up!" she yelled. "We'll get to each of you." She reached her hand out the door to help the driver back inside. The driver misunderstood. He grabbed her hand and pulled her out. The bus groaned again but didn't move.

"We have to get them out," she said, landing beside the driver on the muddy bank.

"Fuck that," he said, his hair glued to his face. "They're scum."

"They haven't yet been convicted. We can't just leave them to drown."

"What have they ever done for me?" He started to crawl up the hill. "I ain't risking my neck to save the likes of them."

"You're serious?"

The driver kept crawling.

"At least give me the keys."

"Guard has 'em."

Claire whipped around. Where was the armed guard? If he was out of commission, there had to be a few prisoners trying to get to his gun. Billy Ray for sure.

The bus angle was now more extreme, making the steps harder to climb. The acrid smell of sweat and wet, dirty clothes rose to greet her. She reached the aisle, her lower foot standing on the joint where the lower seats were bolted to the floor. The woman struggling for air was using her cuffed hands to pull herself up.

"Help me!" she cried.

"No, Lady, over here!"

Most of the prisoners on the lower side were trying to keep away from the creek water rushing in the window. They were the ones screaming the loudest. The men on the upper side were watching in horror.

Urban rats. Most couldn't swim. Probably never learned. To some, water was deadlier than a bullet. She saw two white men, neither was Billy Ray.

Bet Billy Ray could swim.

The guard was almost at the rear, lying face down in the aisle. She hobbled forward, one foot on the lower seat joints, the other braced on the slanted aisle floor. Her soaked jeans made a sucking sound as she moved deeper into the bus.

"Who's hurt?" she asked, looking the prisoners over as she passed. They all said they were, but clearly, the biggest danger was the rising water.

Three seats from the guard, she saw a man on the upper side had managed to maneuver the rifle between his legs and was wiggling it up into his hands. She lurched forward, grabbed the barrel, and jerked it free. The bus teetered and groaned. Water splashed through the lower windows.

Screams rose over the roar of rushing water.

Then she saw him. Water running down his face.

"You!" Billy Ray said.

She backed up.

"Lady, don't go," said the man who'd spoken to her through the window. He was the only one still calm.

He was right. She needed to check on the guard. She had to get the keys. She fumbled with the rifle. It wasn't like Philippe's; she had no idea how to unload it. She glanced around. No place to stow it safely.

She slid into a vacant lower seat, her right foot pressed to the side of the bus. She maneuvered the rifle out the window, then tossed it as far as she could from the bus. The rushing current caught it and carried it downstream.

 Her wet jeans were heavier as she inched back toward the guard. Her hands trembled as she checked his wrist for a pulse. Nothing. He was facedown and not moving.

"He flipped. Hit hard," said the calm, deep voice.

Claire looked up at the man across the aisle from Billy Ray, the man who'd spoken to her through the window. She ignored him and grabbed the guard's boots. Maybe she could drag him to the front. He didn't budge.

Wind rattled through the bus, the sides shaking.

She rolled the guard's head to try for a pulse at his neck. Nothing. And his neck was not quite right. Broken?

She unhooked the key ring from his belt.

Another gust and the bus shifted, slid sideways into the water.

Everyone screamed. She grabbed a seat cushion and held on until the bus stopped. Three heads now bobbed in and out of the water.

The woman closest to the front, who'd been crying and calling for help, was silent, concentrating all her attention on getting air. Claire hobbled to the front, her heart beating wildly. She reached the sinking woman, grabbed her chin, and pulled her out of the water. The woman gasped. The key ring held thirty keys. Claire looked at it and at the cuffs. The woman's head sank beneath the water.

"Which one?" Claire yelled, holding the ring in the air.

"Look at the number. Find the number," called the deep voice from the rear.

She pulled the woman above water again and grabbed the cuffs, twisting them over. The number 121 was stamped in the metal. She fumbled the keys looking for a match. The ring slipped from her wet hands, but she caught it and started through them again. 110. 187. 146. 121! She shoved the key in the lock. It snapped and fell open. The woman's hands slid free and she lurched up and grabbed Claire around the neck. The bus shuddered.

"Okay, okay, you're safe. Crawl out of here. Slowly." The woman's dripping face was wild looking, the whites of her eyes blood red. Claire wasn't sure she was listening. She turned and placed the woman's hand on the edge of the seat. "Slowly," Claire said and shoved the woman forward.

Claire crawled to the next seat back. Another woman. Water had reached her chin and she was sobbing. Claire grabbed the cuffs. 148. She found the key and unlocked her.

The woman shot forward too fast sending the bus on another downward skid.

"Slow down!" Claire said as they both fell against the side of the seats. The woman froze. "Crawl to the front. Slowly."

The next seat back was empty. She unlocked four men, working her way to the rear on the lower side. As the last one stood, the bus moaned.

Everyone fell silent.

She held tight to the key ring and straightened. The last seat—Billy Ray. He'd probably asked for the rear, hoping to slip out the emergency door after the crash.

She climbed back one seat.

"You're going to leave me, let me drown?" Billy Ray asked, his eyes filled with fear.

"You'll have to wait for help to arrive." She lowered herself next to the guard. The guard's pallor had changed to a pale blue. She lifted his eyelid. The pupil was enlarged.

"What about innocent until convicted?" Billy Ray called. "My lawyer told me what you think I did. I didn't. I'm no pedophile."

She gripped the edge of the seat, scooted around. Her jeans struggled against her. "No. You're a rapist." She glanced across the aisle. Two men were watching her. One had hit his head and the swollen area was beginning to color.

A surge of wind lifted the bus. It crashed down hard vibrating every inch. Claire fell into an empty seat. She pulled herself up.

Billy Ray spit water. "I'm no rapist, either. You've got the wrong guy. I've got alibis." The gold tooth caught the flash of lightning.

She froze. He'd die if she didn't unlock him. The water was rising faster than help would get here. But how could she?

She didn't trust him. She was his enemy. He'd kill her first, then escape. She knew him.

"Lady, hey lady, over here."

She turned to see the nose of the bus sinking below the water line. Six more prisoners. She pulled herself, seat by seat, to the front and unlocked the first man on the upper side. Too eager, he jumped across the seat.

The bus made a collapsing sound and spun. Water gushed through the open doorway. The roaring grew louder. Claire stood thigh high in the warm current. The freed prisoner screamed. And screamed.

She grabbed his forearm and squeezed. "Stop! Stop screaming! Go to the back," she said, pointing. "There's an emergency exit. It might take two of you to open it." She reached for the next man's cuffs.

She unlocked three more men before they broke open the emergency exit at the rear. A current of wind sucked through the bus.

Breathing hard, she pulled herself into the next to the last seat. Her gaze fell across the aisle on Billy Ray. She couldn't do it.

She glanced at the man behind her. His calm was finally starting to crack.

"What's your name?" she asked, reaching for his cuffs.

"Tee."

Number 110. She searched the key ring. "Ti, like Petit?"

"Just Ti."

She nodded, too tired to care. "Think you can pull the guard out with you? He looks dead, but it doesn't seem right to leave him."

Ti nodded. She slid away to allow him more room.

Billy Ray coughed and spit water. "Stop," he said. "The guard. Reach in his top pocket. There's two thousand dollars in there. It's yours if you unlock me."

That explained the route change. The Cobb bargaining chip. The argument she'd never win against. He knew there would always be another alibi to buy, another guard, someone who'd take his money. She knew it, too.

Billy Ray yelled something that was lost in the roar of the current. Ti cocked his head.

"Go ahead," she said, nodding him out.

Ti dropped out of sight and then reached back in the bus and grabbed the guard's shoulders. The guard dropped over the edge.

The top of Billy Ray's head dropped down. A wave of water splashed across the aisle. Another gust of wind surged through the bus, lifting it. Claire lost her footing and started to fall. Downward.

Billy Ray's face burst through the water rising to meet her. A scream. Hers. She latched onto the seat in front of him, her nails digging in. She propelled herself backward into the aisle.

"Have mercy!" he yelled.

His head slid back under.

She scrambled, too fast, for the door. Leaping, she pushed away from the bus with her feet and landed in the mud on her hands and knees. A long sigh.

The squeal of metal. A loud swooshing sound.

She flipped around. The bus slid away, floated to the middle of the creek and began sinking fast. Water rushed around it.

And she watched.

Epilogue

Around 5:10 a.m. Monday August, 29, 2005 Hurricane Katrina made landfall three times in Plaquemines Parish, St. Bernard Parish, and St. Tammany Parish as a category three hurricane with winds at 125 mph. The storm surge compromised the levees around New Orleans and by the following day, almost 80% of the city was flooded. In Louisiana, more than 1,500 lives were lost. Hundreds more are still missing.

The End
© 2012

About the Author

Nicola Trwst has a gypsy heart. She currently resides in California, but has lived in Virginia, Georgia, France, and Canada. She loves languages and speaks several, including Pig Latin. Due to an overactive imagination, her stories thread many genres such as mystery, thriller, paranormal, and contemporary. Her short stories have appeared in several anthologies.

Other Books by Nicola Trwst
The Belvedere Club, A Briana Kaleigh Mystery

Coming in Spring 2013
Bolinas Bongo, A Briana Kaleigh Mystery

Discover more of Nicola's work at www.nicolatrwst.com